for Hilma

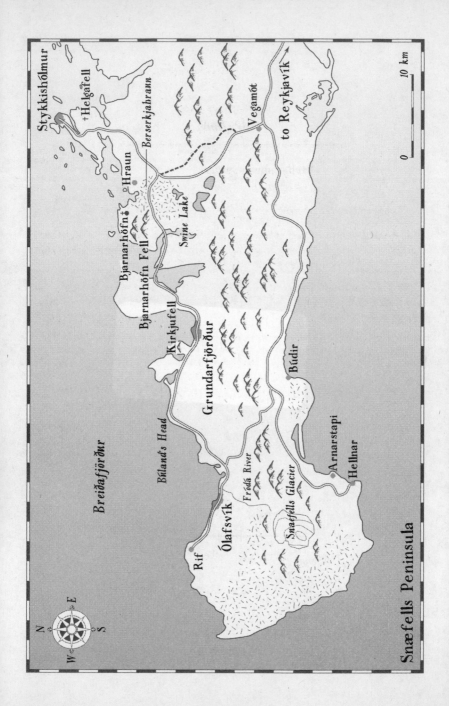

Snæfells Peninsula

SEA OF STONE

Michael Ridpath spent eight years as a bond trader in the City before giving up his job to write full-time. He lives in north London with his wife and three children. Visit his website at www.michaelridpath.com.

Also by Michael Ridpath

Where the Shadows Lie
66° North
Meltwater

MICHAEL RIDPATH
SEA OF STONE

CORVUS

First published in trade paperback in 2014 by Corvus,
an imprint of Atlantic Books Ltd.
This paperback edition published in 2015 by Corvus,
an imprint of Atlantic Books Ltd.

9 8 7 6 5 4 3 2 1

A CIP catalogue record for this book is available from the British Library.

Paperback ISBN: 978 1 78239 131 9
E-book ISBN: 978 1 78239 132 6

Printed and bound by Novoprint S.A. Barcelona

Corvus
An imprint of Atlantic Books Ltd
Ormond House
26–27 Boswell Street, London
WC1N 3JZ

www. corvus-books.co.uk

Gunnar of Bjarnarhöfn

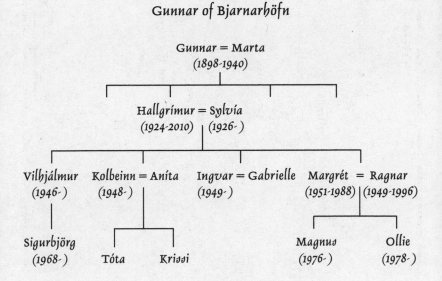

Gunnar = Marta
(1898-1940)

Hallgrímur = Sylvía
(1924-2010) | (1926-)

Vilhjálmur (1946-)
Kolbeinn = Anita (1948-)
Ingvar = Gabrielle (1949-)
Margrét (1951-1988) = Ragnar (1949-1996)

Sigurbjörg (1968-)
Tóta   Krissi
Magnus (1976-)   Ollie (1978-)

Jóhannes of Hraun

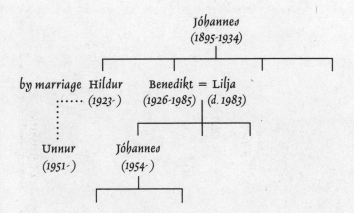

Jóhannes
(1895-1934)

by marriage ...... Hildur (1923-)
Benedikt = Lilja (1926-1985) | (d. 1983)

Unnur (1951-)
Jóhannes (1954-)

CHAPTER ONE

October 1988

B LESS.
   Much later, when Óli was an American with an American name, that was the one Icelandic word that he would remember. *Bless*. Goodbye.

Bless, Mamma.

He followed his mother out of the church by his grandparents' farm, trying desperately not to cry. Óli was ten and he was terrified. On one side of the tiny churchyard, right next to the turf wall that enclosed it, lurked an open hole. Óli had watched the men digging it two days before, struggling with the stone and the frost-hardened earth. The pallbearers carried his mother towards the hole.

The church was far too small to hold everyone who had come, but the priest's booming voice had easily carried out to the gathering of the sad, the respectful and the curious who stood outside. The priest had a big beard, a big ruff around his neck, a big belly and a big rich voice of authority. He told everyone what a wonderful, beautiful and good person Óli's mamma was. Óli knew all that to be true. But he was glad the priest didn't mention the shouting, the falling, the slurring, the throwing up.

The crowd formed around the hole in the ground, Óli right at the front. He wanted to cry; he wanted so desperately to cry. He also wanted to pee; why hadn't he gone to the toilet before? How had he been so stupid? He had wet his sheets for the

1

previous two nights, as he knew he would. He couldn't pee his pants at his own mother's funeral, could he?

He reached for his big brother's hand. Óli was too old to hold hands, but he didn't care and, if he did it stealthily, Afi wouldn't notice. Magnús gripped his brother's fingers in his own. Óli looked up at him. Magnús was two years older and fifteen centimetres taller than Óli. He was standing straight, chin out, mouth firm, eyes dry.

Afi had told them not to cry and snivel. And Óli always, *always*, did what Afi said. Magnús disobeyed him sometimes and got beaten for it. Óli seemed to get beaten anyway.

The pallbearers, including Óli's three uncles, were lining up his mother above the hole. A puffy black cloud rolled away from the sun, which shot pale beams onto the damp grass. A pair of eider sped low over the gathering, a duck and a drake, swerving and squawking in surprise at encountering so many humans in such an empty land. Óli glanced up at the farm, his home, his prison for the last four years, nestled against a steep snow-capped fell and a waterfall. The tiny wooden church lay between the farm and the sea, Breidafjördur – Broad Fjord – with its countless islands. And to the east lay the lava field, a kilometre wide. The fell, the fjord and the lava were the walls to Óli's prison.

His mother was steady now, above the hole. The priest intoned some words. Óli glanced across at his *afi*. To Óli his grandfather was old – he was over sixty, after all – and his hair was thin and white. But the farmer stood up straight; he was sturdy and strong, as was his face, etched by the gales flung at him over decades by the Atlantic. The corners of his mouth pointed down and his flinty blue eyes stared at Óli's mother.

Then Afi blinked, and Óli saw a tear, or half a tear, wriggle its way through the wrinkles on his grandfather's cheek, and slink beneath his white shirt collar.

That was it; the tears flooded from the little boy's eyes. But Óli stood straight. He sniffed, suppressed a sob, somehow managed to restrain himself from flinging his body on to the ground, or at his mother, or into the hole, from screaming, *No, no, no!*

Magnús squeezed Óli's hand. *His* cheeks were still dry.

They lowered the coffin. The family threw handfuls of cold damp earth on top of Óli's mother. Magnús stepped forward, but thankfully no one thought to force Óli to move. As Magnús returned to his position, Óli reached for his brother's hand again, damp and gritty with the soil.

Magnús stiffened. He was facing the far side of the churchyard. There a man stood alone: a tall man with a fair beard.

'It's Pabbi!' Magnús whispered.

Óli felt a surge of joy. He had noticed the man earlier, but he hadn't recognized his own father. Óli hadn't seen him for four years, since the age of six, when his father had disappeared to America, leaving his wife to the bottle and his sons to their grandparents. But in an instant the joy was replaced by fear. Afi would be cross. Afi would be furious.

'Come on,' Magnús said, tugging Óli's hand.

Óli let Magnús go. He wasn't that dumb.

Magnús walked over to the man, their father, and hugged him. The man's face, which had been sombre, broke into a wide grin. The man's glance turned up from his eldest son and searched out Óli. For a moment their eyes met, and Óli felt a warm feeling seep through him.

Then he turned away. The idiot! Didn't Pabbi know what he was doing? There was going to be big trouble. Big, big trouble.

Sure enough, there was. Afi noticed Óli's flinching. He spotted the stranger with his grandson. The lines by the side of Afi's mouth plunged even further downwards, and his face set into a glare of pure hatred as he strode over to man and boy.

Óli sought out his biggest uncle, Kolbeinn, and stood behind him, watching in dread.

Afi grabbed Magnús and tore him away. He then began haranguing his son-in-law. The crowd fell silent, straining to hear, but the breeze was blowing away from them and they could make out very little. Óli thought he heard the words 'killed my daughter'. That wasn't right, surely? His mother had driven herself into a rock while drunk. Then he heard his own name and that of Magnús.

The man, the stranger, his father, said little. He stood firm, listening, and then shrugged and turned, hopping over the turf wall to avoid pushing his way through the crowd by the white churchyard gate.

Óli watched his father walk away, wondering when, if ever, he would see him again.

As soon as he got back to the farm at Bjarnarhöfn from school the next afternoon, Óli went out to the chickens. They were allowed the run of the farmyard, but they sheltered in an old Eimskip shipping container, around the back of the farmhouse. He liked all the chickens, but his favourite was a small black hen called Indiana. Or at least Óli called her Indiana, after Indiana Jones whom Óli had watched agog on two occasions at the cinema in Stykkishólmur. Amma thought Indiana was a stupid name for a chicken, and called the hen something else, but Óli stuck with Indiana. Óli knew and the chicken knew it was her name.

He was worried about Indiana. She hadn't laid anything for several weeks now, and Amma had a strict rule: if a hen didn't lay, it wasn't worth feeding. Óli had started switching eggs around, but he knew that ploy wouldn't last for long. His grandmother was sharp-eyed when it came to chickens, even if she didn't seem to notice what happened to Óli and Magnús in her own house. And once she realized that Óli had been deceiving her, Indiana's days were over.

Óli had felt lousy at school all day. Not that there was anything wrong with school; he much preferred being there to being home. The other kids occasionally teased him, but Óli could usually deflect their taunts with submissive charm. It was the anti-climax after the funeral. The knowledge that he would never see his mother again. Nor, so he believed, his father.

4

Afi had kept his anger under control during the reception after the funeral at the farmhouse, but once everyone had left, he yelled at Óli and Magnús, ordering them to ignore their father if he ever made an attempt to contact them. Óli had quickly agreed, but Magnús had said nothing and received a couple of hard clips around the ear as a result.

That night, in their bedroom, Magnús and Óli had talked. Since the dreadful time when they had been moved up to Bjarnarhöfn from their little white house with its blue roof in Reykjavík, Magnús had been firm in his belief that their father would come and rescue them eventually. Óli had believed him for a year, and then another year, but then he gave up. Magnús was an optimist; Óli was a realist. You couldn't fight Afi and the life they were now living at the farm; you just had to learn to live it as painlessly as possible.

Their mother had been an intermittent visitor over those four years. They had been told that she couldn't look after them because she was ill. After a year or so, Magnús had figured out it was because she was drunk. Then, that summer, she had finally moved up to Bjarnarhöfn to join them. The boys had been overjoyed, and for moments they did seem to have their mother back. But only moments. When their grandfather had told them, with tears in his eyes, that she had had a terrible car accident, Óli was shocked, but not surprised. It was as if he had always known something dreadful was going to happen to her. He remembered her face when he had seen her lying serene in her coffin three days before. Calm, less puffy than usual. Sober in death.

Now Óli knew he and his brother were alone.

After seeing his father at the funeral, Magnús was full of hope. He believed he had been vindicated, that their father hadn't forgotten them after all. But Óli knew that Afi had scared him away. No one stood up to Afi. No one.

It was dusk. The sun dithered over the horizon beyond Cumberland Bay, its rays skimming off the surface of the grey fjord and throwing long shadows across the farm. Óli climbed into the shipping container and picked out an egg from one of the other hens to place under Indiana, who was sitting in her straw clucking gently to herself. He eased his hand underneath her body and, to his great surprise, his fingers touched something warm and round.

'Yes!' He grinned. 'Well done, Indiana, clever girl!' He risked a quick kiss on her crest, and dodged the resulting peck. Indiana squawked and settled herself proudly over her egg. Óli felt a surge of happiness run through him. Indiana could rely on him to look after her.

As Óli returned to the farmhouse with his basket of eggs, including the prize from Indiana, he heard the sound of a car. It was getting dark now, and he scanned the lava field in the evening gloom until he spotted two headlights and the shape of a vehicle. The approach to Bjarnarhöfn was across several kilometres of congealed lava that had been spewed over the landscape a few thousand years before. The nearest neighbouring farm, Hraun, lay on the other side of the field, and so if you saw a car, you knew it was coming to Bjarnarhöfn.

Óli waited. He didn't recognize the car. It was a large blue estate, a Ford probably, and it pulled up right outside the farmhouse. But he did recognize the man who climbed out.

'Hi, Óli, how are you?' his father called to him, with a smile.

Óli took a step back and didn't respond. But his heart was pounding with a mixture of joy and fear, and that warm feeling that had seeped through him at the funeral.

The farmhouse door flung open, and Afi stormed out. 'Ragnar! What the hell are you doing here? I told you never to come here again!'

'I've come to collect my sons,' said Óli's father calmly.

'And as I told you yesterday, I forbid it,' Afi said. 'Now get off my land, you murdering fucker!'

'I didn't kill her, Hallgrímur, you know that,' Óli's father replied quietly. He reached into the pocket of his jacket and pulled out a piece of paper. 'After you refused to let me speak to my children yesterday, I went to the magistrate in Stykkishólmur.

I have an injunction here compelling you to let me take them.' He handed over the paper.

Afi grabbed it and started to read, the paper dancing in his shaking hands. Óli knew he wouldn't be able to make out the words without his glasses.

'Svenni gave you this! I'll have a word with him. He'll soon change his mind.'

'He can't. The law is very clear, Hallgrímur. I am their sole surviving parent. I have a legal right to take them.'

'Bullshit! Anyway, where are you going to take them? To America?'

'That's right,' said Óli's father. 'They are coming to live with me in Boston. There are good schools there. They are ten and twelve; I can look after them.'

'But they are good Icelandic children. You would be making them Americans! That must be illegal.'

'It's not. It's what is going to happen, Hallgrímur. Now, can I see my sons?'

Óli ran into the farmhouse to find Magnús and tell him what he had heard. He couldn't believe it. He was going to leave Bjarnarhöfn, to live with his father.

And he was going to stop being an Icelander. He was going to become an American!

CHAPTER TWO

Sunday, 18 April 2010

'HE'S LATE, JOE.' Ollie looked at his watch. 'I said eleven-thirty and it's eleven-forty now.'

'Don't worry,' Ollie's companion said. 'Icelanders are always late.'

Ollie looked along the cliff path to the point where the road came to an end above the small natural harbour. They had picked a good spot. The path wound through black lava from the tiny village of Hellnar to Arnarstapi a couple of kilometres away, where he and Jóhannes had parked their car.

They were waiting behind a lava pinnacle, which reared up just above an undulation in the path. From there they had an excellent view of the approach, and could see without being seen. Except perhaps by the hundreds of sea birds that yelled and squawked all around them.

'I said *hálftólf*, right?' Ollie said. 'You heard me. *Tólf* means twelve. You told me that. And you're sure *hálftólf* is half past eleven, not half past twelve?'

The conversation had been difficult. Ollie had forgotten all his Icelandic, and his grandfather spoke hardly any English. But with the help of prompting from Jóhannes, Ollie had eventually made himself understood on the phone.

'It does,' said Jóhannes. 'I heard you. Eleven-thirty.'

'You figure it's an hour to here from Bjarnarhöfn?'

'About that,' said Jóhannes. 'He'll be here, Ólafur.'

Ollie was having second thoughts. Actually, they were more like third or fourth thoughts. His grandfather might be well into his eighties, but Ollie was still afraid of him. He hadn't seen him for over twenty years, and he couldn't rid from his mind the image of himself as a skinny ten-year-old, and his grandfather as a strong farmer. At thirty-two, Ollie was still skinny, but he must be stronger than his grandfather by now.

Ollie glanced at his companion. Jóhannes was probably in his fifties, but he was tall with a broad chest, and a powerful, determined jaw. Plus there was a tyre iron in the carrier bag he was carrying. And they would have the advantage of height and surprise from their hiding place above the cliff path.

He heard his phone beep in his pocket. An SMS. He checked it.

'Hallgrímur?' Jóhannes asked.

'No,' said Ollie, frowning. 'Just someone from back home.'

'You know Snaefellsjökull is up there in that cloud?' Jóhannes said, pointing to the north. 'Snow Fell Glacier. We could probably see it from here on a clear day.'

There was blue sky above them, and it was clear to the south over the gleaming sea. In the distance Ollie could make out the mountains they had passed on the drive up from Reykjavík, but to the north the ridge that formed the spine of the Snaefells Peninsula was shrouded in angry grey cloud.

'The first settler round here in Viking times was a half-man half-troll called Bárdur,' Jóhannes went on. 'They say when it was time to die he walked into the glacier at Snow Fell. No one found him. But since then he has guarded the glacier with his magical powers.'

Jóhannes was a schoolteacher, and although Ollie had only known him for a few days, it was long enough to realize that he never stopped lecturing. Which Ollie liked. The two men had slipped into a student–teacher relationship, which Ollie found comforting, encouraging even.

But Ollie wasn't sure he liked the sound of this Bárdur guy. 'Does that mean he's with us or against us, then?'

Jóhannes chuckled. 'Oh, he's with us. If there's one thing those Vikings understood, it was revenge.'

Constable Páll Gylfason grinned to himself as he climbed into his police car. This was the third time he had been called by Gunnhildur to complain about the young couple from Reykjavík who liked to have sex in the living room with the curtains open on a Sunday morning. The couple had pointed out that they were perfectly entitled to do whatever they liked in the privacy of their own home; it was Gunnhildur's problem if she insisted on spying on them. To Páll's suggestion that they pull the curtains closed, they replied that in the heat of the moment there wasn't time. Páll wasn't convinced by this. It seemed to him that their Sunday morning passion was becoming predictable. The real point he wanted to get across was that in a small town like Grundarfjördur, you didn't mess with women like Gunnhildur.

They were a nice couple, though. The woman, who was a new teacher at the school in town, had a foxy look about her, and had complimented Páll fulsomely on his bushy moustache, of which he was very proud.

He started the car and headed back home. The little police station near the harbour was left unoccupied on a Sunday. He turned on the car radio, looking for news on the Eyjafjallajökull volcano, which had erupted the previous week, chucking ash all over farms in the south and causing chaos to anyone trying to travel anywhere by air. Fortunately, because of the direction of the wind, most of Iceland had been spared. There was no sign of any ash on the Snaefells Peninsula.

But the wind direction could always change.

His police radio crackled into life. He recognized the voice of the dispatcher from Stykkishólmur.

'A body has been reported at Bjarnarhöfn. Suspected homicide. Sergeant Magnús Ragnarsson called it in.'

'I'm on my way.'

Páll whipped his Hyundai Santa Fe around and hit the accelerator, lights flashing, sirens blaring. A woman preparing to cross the main street, pushing a child in a buggy with another one holding her hand, stopped and stared. Bjarnarhöfn was about halfway between Grundarfjördur and regional headquarters at Stykkishólmur. Since Páll was already in his vehicle, he should get there first. If he hurried.

Páll remembered Magnus well. He was an American homicide detective who had been transferred to the Reykjavík Metropolitan Police, but he had been born in Iceland and spoke good Icelandic. They had worked together on a case involving a fisherman from Grundarfjördur the previous year, and Páll rated Magnus highly. He also knew that Magnus had family at Bjarnarhöfn.

Visibility was poor as mist pressed down on the road from the mountains above. The road was empty on a Sunday morning, and Páll took some risks he probably shouldn't have. He turned left off the main Stykkishólmur road onto the dirt track that led through the Berserkjahraun lava field to Bjarnarhöfn. Three minutes later, he was rattling over the cattle grid into the farm.

There were a couple of cars parked in front of the nearest building, a cottage with white concrete walls and a red corrugated metal roof. Páll knew that was where old man Hallgrímur lived; his son, Kolbeinn, inhabited the main farmhouse with his family. The front door of Hallgrímur's cottage was open. Páll slowed and scanned the farm. The cloud stooped low, embracing the lower flanks of the fell, from which fingers of snow stretched down to the fields. A waterfall spurted from a gash in the steep hill, feeding a stream that tumbled down towards the sea, hidden in the gloom. Páll could see one other dwelling – the main farmhouse – a large barn and a number of smaller farm buildings. The gaps between the buildings were cluttered with the usual farming bric-a-brac: machinery, fuel tanks, large circular hay bales wrapped in white plastic, and even a couple of old shipping containers.

Two red-and-white-coated Icelandic sheep dogs with tightly curled tails appeared, barking. But no people.

Then Páll remembered the little church, set a couple of hundred metres to the north of the farm towards the sea. He could just make it out through the mist, and he spotted Magnus, standing at the entrance to the churchyard, waving. A woman stood next to him, holding the bridle of a horse.

Páll considered driving over the field to the church, but common sense prevailed. If it was indeed a homicide, then chewing up the path to the crime scene was not a good option.

So he parked his car a few metres away from Hallgrímur's cottage and took a direct route to the church. There was no path over the field, but it would be important later to ensure that everyone approached the crime scene by the same way. Páll recognized the woman Magnus was with as Aníta, the farmer's wife, and therefore Hallgrímur's daughter-in-law.

'Hi, Páll, how are you?' said Magnus. He was a tall, red-haired detective in his mid-thirties with broad shoulders. Last time Páll had seen him he remembered feeling in awe of the tough cop from Boston, with his air of calm competence. But now Magnus's face was tense.

'What have we got?' Páll asked.

'Take a look.'

The church was little more than a black wooden hut, with its own red metal roof and a small white cross at the peak of the gable above the entrance. The door was open, and Páll looked inside. There were only half a dozen rows of pews. An ancient oil painting hung behind the altar, which was fenced in by an ornate white wooden rail.

In front of the altar lay the body of an old man. Páll recognized him. Hallgrímur.

A pool of blood spread across the wooden floor around the old man's head, reddening his wispy white hair, and licking his wrinkled face. His blue eyes were open.

'I'm sorry, Magnús.'

Magnus shrugged. 'I didn't know him that well. But I've got to admit it was a shock to find him here.'

'How long has he been dead?' Páll asked.

'Not for too long. He's still warm and rigor hasn't set in.'

'There's no chance he just fell, is there?' There were at least three or four cuts in the old man's scalp, and a dent high on his forehead.

Magnus shook his head. 'When I first saw him on the floor, that's what I assumed. But once I'd taken a closer look...'

Páll took a deep breath. 'When did you find him?'

'About twenty minutes ago.'

'Did you see who did it?'

'No. I didn't seen anyone until Aníta arrived about ten minutes ago.'

Páll stood still at the entrance and scanned the church. No sign of an obvious murder weapon. There was a footprint in the blood next to Hallgrímur's head, and a couple of red marks leading back to the entrance.

'Was that you?' He glanced down to Magnus's shoes.

'Yes. Sorry,' Magnus said. 'This is my grandfather. I was thinking more like a grandson than a detective. When I saw him lying there, I just went straight to him.'

'Of course,' said Páll. He surveyed the church. 'We should secure the scene.'

'Right,' said Magnus. 'If you get the tape, I'll help you. I figure I'm more witness than investigating officer here.'

They left the church and Páll approached Aníta, still waiting patiently at the entrance to the churchyard. She was a tall woman in her late forties, with high, finely lined cheekbones, and long plaited blonde hair. Although Páll knew who she was, they had only spoken a couple of times in the past.

'Did you see anything?' he asked her. 'Anyone leaving the church?'

'No. The only person I saw was Magnús up at the cottage, and he took me down here to show me Hallgrímur.'

'Who is at the farm now? Where's Hallgrímur's wife?'

'Sylvía? I haven't seen her today.' Aníta looked over towards the cottage. 'Her car isn't there. It's a Sunday – church, maybe? She goes more and more these days. My husband Kolbeinn is off

13

at basketball practice with Krissi, our son. Tóta, my daughter, is probably in the main farmhouse. She'll have only just got up. That's everyone who lives here.'

'What about you? What were you doing?'

'I went out for a ride for at least an hour, probably an hour and a half. I went round the far side of the fell, so I couldn't see the road over the lava field. It's too misty anyway.'

Páll glanced at the horse, and more particularly at the horse's hooves. They had churned up the damp grass just outside the gate to the churchyard. 'OK, well you and your horse had better move right away from here. Follow a route directly back to my car over there. Then go back to the farmhouse. We'll speak to you later.'

Aníta did as she was asked. As Páll and Magnus followed her and the horse, another two police cars screeched to a halt next to Páll's vehicle. Rúnar, the chief superintendent of the Stykkishólmur area, and two colleagues also in uniform, hurried down towards Páll.

Rúnar was a bald, bouncy man who looked younger than his forty years. Although chief superintendent was a high rank, and the area he covered from Stykkishólmur was a large one, there were fewer than a dozen policemen reporting to him, including Páll. But there was also a population of only a few thousand for them to police, and the crime rate was low. Local knowledge and peer pressure made sure of that. A murder was virtually unheard of.

'I'm surprised to see you here,' said Rúnar. 'I heard you were wrapping up that tourist case on the volcano.'

'I'm here in a personal capacity,' said Magnus. 'This is my grandfather's farm. I was just coming to visit him. And I found him dead.'

'I'm sorry,' said Rúnar. 'Show me.'

Páll left Magnus to show his boss the body, and opened up the boot of his car to dig out some tape. A raven croaked. And a telephone rang; it was coming from Hallgrímur's cottage.

Páll dropped the tape, ran inside and picked up the phone in the living room.

'Hello?' he said, out of breath.

'Afi? Is that Afi?'

Páll hesitated. *Afi* was the Icelandic word for grandfather, but the question was in English.

'Afi?' Again.

'No, Hallgrímur isn't here now,' Páll replied in English. 'This is the police. Something has happened to him. Who am I speaking to?'

Silence.

'Is this his grandson?'

The line went dead.

Páll replaced the receiver, frowning. He crossed the field to join Magnus and Rúnar at the church.

'I just took a phone call in the cottage,' he said.

'Who was it?' asked Rúnar.

'It was weird,' Páll said. 'Someone speaking English who asked for *Afi*. He hung up when I said Hallgrímur wasn't here.'

'His grandson?' said Rúnar.

'Must be,' said Páll. They both turned to Magnus.

'Do you have a brother?' Rúnar asked him.

Magnus took a deep breath. 'Yes, I do. Ollie. He's lived in America since he was ten. He speaks English; he's forgotten all his Icelandic. Hallgrímur has other grandchildren, but it must be him.'

'Is he in Iceland now?'

'Yeah. He's been staying with me for the last few days. Here, I'll give him a call.' Magnus pulled out his phone.

'Better not,' said Rúnar, reaching for his own phone. 'Páll, your English is better than mine. You call him back. What's his number, Magnús?'

'OK,' said Magnus. He dictated some digits. Páll punched in the numbers. It was a US dialling code.

There was no reply. Páll left a message, in English. 'Ollie, this is Páll from the police. We have some news about your grandfather. Please call me back on this number.'

Rúnar turned to Magnus. 'Do you know where your brother is now?'

'No, I don't,' said Magnus. 'He took off from my place in Reykjavík this morning. I don't know where he went.'

'Let's hope he calls back. All we can do now is secure the scene and wait for the Dumpling to arrive from Akranes.'

'The Dumpling?'

'Inspector Emil. He will be in charge of the investigation. I called him on my way. We'd better wait until he gets here.'

The Stykkishólmur police didn't have a detective on the payroll, so they had to borrow one from Akranes, a hundred kilometres to the south.

'Look, Rúnar,' Magnus said. 'I know I'm off duty, but do you want me to help with the case? It will take this Dumpling guy an hour and a half to get here.'

'I'm sure we could use someone with your experience,' said Rúnar. He blew air through his cheeks, thinking. 'But you're a witness on this one, and the victim is your own family. Better wait for Emil. He can decide whether it's OK for you to help us.'

Magnus's steady blue eyes examined the chief superintendent. He looked as if he was about to argue, but then he nodded. 'OK, I guess that's right. Have you requested the forensics unit from Reykjavík?'

'Not yet. I'll do that.'

'Aníta said that Tóta was the only one at the farm. It might be worth checking to see whether she saw anything. And making sure that there really is no one else here. Maybe the farmer at Hraun over there saw something.' Magnus pointed into the gloom to the east towards the lava field.

'Don't worry, Magnús,' said Rúnar with a touch of impatience, struggling to assert his authority over the junior but more experienced officer. 'We've got it covered. We'll talk to you when we need you.'

Magnus held Rúnar's gaze for a moment and then nodded again. Páll busied himself with tape as Magnus headed over to the farmhouse where Aníta was taking off her boots by the front door, watched by the two dogs. As she went on into the house,

Páll saw Magnus hesitate, then pull out his mobile phone to make a call.

Páll respected Rúnar, and the Dumpling was no dummy, but neither of them had anything like Magnus's experience. Procedure was procedure, but it seemed to Páll that they could use all the help from Magnus they could get.

CHAPTER THREE

'WHO WAS IT?'

Jóhannes and Ollie were on the cliffs heading back towards Arnarstapi, where they had left Jóhannes's car.

'The police. They want me to call them back.'

'You should do that,' Jóhannes said.

'Are you out of your mind?' Ollie checked his watch. 'It's quarter of one. Why don't you just take me back to the airport? I can still make my flight.'

'If it isn't cancelled.'

'I think flights to the States are still OK,' Ollie said, increasing his stride. The birds were wheeling and yelling under the rim of the cliffs a few yards to their left.

'They'll be waiting for you at the airport,' Jóhannes said.

'They might not be.'

'They almost certainly will be. And it will be a lot tougher explaining ourselves then than it would be now.'

'We could hide,' Ollie said. 'C'mon, Joe. This is a massive area with hardly anyone around. We must be able to find a hiding place in those mountains up there. Like those outlaws from history you were telling me about on the way up here. Gretel the Strong.'

'Grettir,' Jóhannes corrected him. He smiled wistfully. Ollie knew the idea of following in the footsteps of a saga hero would appeal to the schoolteacher. 'It took them twenty years, but they caught up with Grettir eventually. And they would catch up with us. No, Ólafur, you have to call them. We discussed this before.

We knew we would be interviewed. We just have to stick to our stories.' He paused. 'Well, modify them a bit. We can discuss that now.'

The path emerged into the open. 'Take a look at that,' Jóhannes said. 'Snaefellsjökull.'

Behind them and to the left the clouds had cleared above a perfect volcano-shaped mountain, with a soft white snowcap. A small pinnacle of rock thrust out of the glacier at the top, like a thorn or a question mark.

'Isn't it beautiful?'

Ollie looked. It *was* beautiful. And comforting, in some strange way. Stuck out here at the end of the Snaefells Peninsula, he felt safe. He really didn't want to go back to Bjarnarhöfn, or even Reykjavík.

'Are you sure there's nowhere around there we can hole up? Up by that mountain, perhaps?'

'Call him back, Ólafur.' Jóhannes was firm.

Ollie felt like a school kid. A defiant school kid.

'Ólafur?'

Ollie sighed and took out his phone. He was disappointed to see he had cell coverage. He called the number back.

Páll and one of the other constables had secured the scene. Magnus, Aníta and her daughter were in the farmhouse with the other constable. There was no sign yet of Kolbeinn, the farmer, or Sylvía, Hallgrímur's wife. The ambulance was still parked behind the police cars, although Hallgrímur's body wasn't going anywhere soon. It had to wait for the local doctor from Stykkishólmur, who was on his way, but even then the body wouldn't be moved for several hours, until the forensics team from Reykjavík had arrived.

And of course they were waiting for Inspector Emil, also on his way. Rúnar was finding it difficult to control his impatience, darting back and forth between the chapel and the farmhouse.

Páll's phone rang. He checked the caller's number.

The chief superintendent saw Páll take out his phone and trotted across the farmyard towards him.

'Ollie? This is Paul.' Páll used the English form of his name.

There was silence at the other end of the phone.

'Ollie?' Páll repeated. 'We need to speak to you soon.'

'Er, OK,' came the reply. 'Why?'

'I am sorry to inform you that your grandfather Hallgrímur has been murdered. At Bjarnarhöfn. And we need to speak to you about it. Where are you now? Are you in Reykjavík?'

'Er, no. I'm not too far away from you.'

'OK. Can you come right over?'

'To Bjarnarhöfn?'

'Yes, that's right. We must see you now.'

'Er... OK. I'll be there. About an hour, I guess.'

'Good. An hour?' Páll glanced at the chief superintendent to make sure he was following. 'See you soon.'

Páll hung up. 'He's on his way.'

A BMW four-wheel-drive sped into the farmyard and stopped by the police cars. Páll recognized the duty doctor and followed Rúnar over to greet him.

The doctor was about sixty, lean, bald, with a neatly cropped greying beard on his chin. A livid purple burn mark spread across one side of his face and over his nose. His name was Ingvar. Ingvar Hallgrímsson.

'I'm sorry about your father,' Rúnar said.

'They said it was murder?' said the doctor, opening the back of his car. 'I can't believe that.'

'It looks like it. Multiple head wounds. You can see for yourself.'

'Where?'

'In the church.'

'The church? What the hell was he doing there? I'll need forensic overalls presumably?'

'We've set up a crime scene. It's pretty badly messed up already, but do what you can to avoid making it worse.'

Ingvar grunted. Páll had worked with him several times before on a variety of untoward deaths, none of them murder. He was efficient and sharp-eyed. Despite his gruff exterior, he was a popular doctor. Patients loved him; when he told you what was wrong with you, you believed him. And when he told you he could fix it, you believed him too. When Páll's wife had started getting mysterious headaches two years before, she had been scared. Ingvar had sent her off to Reykjavík for a brain scan, the results of which were inconclusive, at least according to the specialist at the National Hospital. Páll's wife had been distraught, especially after she had spent a couple of hours on medical sites on the Internet.

Dr Ingvar had calmed her down. He had seen this kind of thing many times before. It was just a headache. It would go away. She believed him. It did.

'Any idea who killed him?' the doctor asked.

'Not yet,' Rúnar said. 'Magnús found his body. His grandson.'

'Magnús!' Ingvar looked surprised. 'I didn't know he was up here.'

'Well, he is. He's in the farmhouse now.'

'I understand he and his grandfather didn't get on?' Páll said.

'No. My father was a tough bastard,' Ingvar said. 'Tough on his family. Especially Magnús and his little brother Óli. They stayed here for a few years in the nineteen eighties when they were kids. And now there is Krissi, his youngest grandson.'

'Ollie's floating around somewhere too,' said Rúnar.

'I thought he was in America. How about Kolbeinn? Is he here?'

'I think he might be coming now.' Páll pointed to the lights of another four-wheel-drive piercing the mist. In a moment Kolbeinn arrived, with his son in the front seat next to him. Kolbeinn was bigger and sturdier than Ingvar, with fair hair greying at the edges and sharp blue eyes darting out of a weather-beaten face. He had the square jaw of his father. Every inch an Icelandic sheep farmer.

He jumped out of his car. 'What the hell's going on?' He

glanced at the ambulance, the police chief, his brother now suited in forensic overalls. 'Has someone been hurt?'

'It's Dad,' Ingvar said. 'He's been murdered.'

'No!' said Kolbeinn, stunned. Páll noted he was the first member of Hallgrímur's family who seemed genuinely distressed at the old man's death.

Inspector Emil sped along the flat lava plain between the mountains and the sea. The dramatic crater of Eldborg rose in front of him. To his left, the glacier that capped Snaefellsjökull shimmered in the sun. Little black balls of cloud bounced around the sky, spraying quick showers here and there, occasionally ramming into the thick cushion of grey that covered the ridge of mountains along the spine of the peninsula to the north. Emil's blue light was flashing but there was no one to see it.

He regretted not stopping at the N1 petrol station at Borgarnes on the way up for a hot dog. Or two. It would only have taken five minutes and would anyone have known? What was five minutes in ninety?

But Linda, his wife, would certainly have found out. Ever since he had stupidly shared the results of his conversation with his doctor a fortnight before, she had interrogated him every time he came home about the snacks he had had on the way. She could always tell when he was lying. Always.

She said she had his best interests at heart and no doubt she did. What the doctor had told him was scary. Emil was a heart attack waiting to happen. People had always been telling him this, but this time the look on the doctor's face had been one of genuine concern. Cut down on the food. Cut down on the drink. Exercise.

Exercise! How could he exercise? He was barely able to walk these days. His knees were giving out, although he hadn't mentioned that to the doctor. The poor man looked stressed enough as it was. Emil weighed close to a hundred and thirty kilos. Exercise would kill him.

Which maybe would be the best thing. At least Linda would get the insurance money and would be able to pay off the stupid loan they had taken out three years before to pay for the new barn. Ever since Linda had inherited her parents' farm she had wanted a new barn for the horses, but they couldn't afford it. Then one day she had come back from the bank brandishing an offer of a special foreign currency low-interest loan. He told her it was way too much, but she wouldn't listen. Her sister was borrowing, his brothers had both bought new summerhouses; they could afford a new barn.

And now the debt was rising. It was linked to something strange like Swiss francs or yen, and when the *kreppa* came, the financial implosion of 2008, the value of the loan had ballooned. They were behind. So far behind they could never catch up.

And Emil knew there was no way that he would pass his next medical due in July. So then they would be living on his police pension. The farm broke even at best. Yes, maybe he should just have a heart attack. That would solve everything.

Unfortunately, there wasn't another place to buy a hot dog before Bjarnarhöfn.

So, this was almost certainly Emil's last major investigation. There had been very few of them since he had transferred from CID in Reykjavík to Akranes after his wife had inherited the farm. He had been a good investigator once. At least as good as his old colleague Snorri Gudmundsson, who was now National Police Commissioner. However badly his body was wearing out, Emil's brain was still in good shape, he knew that. Although, if this was a homicide and the killer wasn't right there waiting to confess at the farm, he would have to draft in help from Reykjavík. They would probably send that jerk Baldur.

But then there was Magnús Ragnarsson. He intrigued the inspector. Snorri and his wife still occasionally visited Emil and Linda for dinner at the farm, and Snorri had a lot of good things to say about the Icelandic American. He had really shaken things up in Reykjavík. Inspector Baldur, who ran the Violent Crimes Unit, didn't like him much, which was a good thing as far as Emil was concerned. And now Magnus had found the body. Perhaps Emil could use him. That would be interesting.

He called the chief superintendent. 'Hi, Rúnar, it's Emil. I'll be at Bjarnarhöfn in about half an hour. Anything to report?'

'I'm keeping the family at the farmhouse until you arrive,' said Rúnar. 'The victim's grandson Ollie called the victim's house soon after he died. He's somewhere in the area, I'm not sure where. I've asked him to come here as soon as possible.'

'And forensics?'

'An hour behind you, I think. They've just set off.'

The forensics team had to gather in Reykjavík before heading up to the Snaefells Peninsula, so that was quick going.

'No obvious suspects, then?'

'Not yet.'

Rúnar was waiting for Emil in the farmyard. He and Páll showed the inspector the crime scene and the victim's body, then briefed him on what they knew so far. As Emil and Rúnar made their way back to the farmhouse they were stopped by a tall woman with long blonde hair.

Rúnar introduced Aníta, the farmer's wife, Hallgrímur's daughter-in-law. She seemed agitated.

'I don't know whether this is important, but I saw something that doesn't seem right the more I think about it,' she said to Rúnar, glancing back over her shoulder to the farmhouse.

'What's that?' asked Rúnar.

'Magnús. When I was riding back to the farm, I saw him through the window of Hallgrímur's cottage. He was washing up a mug.'

'Really?' said Emil. 'Are you sure?'

'Quite sure. He saw me, and rushed outside to tell me that Hallgrímur had been killed in the church.'

'Was Magnús staying in the cottage?' Emil asked.

'No. At least I don't think so. I've only ever met him once before, over ten years ago. I had no idea he was coming today. No one mentioned it; not Hallgrímur, nor his wife Sylvía. And he and Hallgrímur hate each other, so I was surprised to see him here.'

'Thank you,' said Emil. 'That's very interesting. I was just going to speak to him now. Is there somewhere we can talk privately?'

There were two large men sitting in grim silence in the kitchen: Kolbeinn and Magnus. Kolbeinn was pale and shaken, Magnus calm. Clutching mugs of coffee, Emil, Rúnar and Magnus followed Aníta through to a small study, and she left them with promises of refills if they needed them.

'We haven't met yet, but I've heard a lot about you,' Emil began with an amiable smile. 'They tell me you cleared up that case last week, the tourist who was murdered on the volcano?'

'That's right,' said Magnus. 'Made some arrests yesterday.'

'Good work. We don't get that kind of case very often around here. Although you were up this way last year, weren't you? With the fisherman from Grundarfjördur. And the murder today, of course.'

Magnus nodded.

'Are you staying here at Bjarnarhöfn?'

'No. I just came up by car from Reykjavík this morning. I was planning to drop in and see my grandfather. When I got here, I knocked on the door of his cottage. There was no answer, so I pushed the door and walked in. There was no one there. I saw that the church door was open and so I thought I would check it out. That's when I found him.'

'And you didn't see anyone else around?'

'No.'

'What did you do after you discovered the body?'

'Dialled 112. Then I went back to the cottage to see if I could find any evidence of someone visiting Hallgrímur.'

'And did you find anything?'

'No. Nothing obvious. But maybe forensics will spot something.'

The constable, Páll, had told Emil that Magnus had appeared tense when he first saw him, but he seemed cool now. Wary. Alert. Was this natural, Emil wondered? Possibly. Discovering a body would be very familiar to Magnus; discovering his grandfather's body would be a shock. It was difficult to predict what a natural response to such a clash of professional detachment and private grief should be.

'Aníta says that when she saw you through the kitchen window you were washing up a mug.'

'Huh.' Magnus thought a moment. 'I could have been washing my hands. I had got some blood on them. That must have been what she saw.'

Emil paused. 'Páll said he saw you make a phone call just after he and Rúnar arrived. Who were you calling?'

'The station,' Magnus said. 'Just checking in.'

'I see.' Emil smiled. Magnus smiled too. There was a long period of silence. Emil fondled a wart on one of his chins, the middle one.

Eventually Emil spoke. 'Do you have any idea who might have killed your grandfather?'

'No. Absolutely none. I didn't know him very well, and hardly know his family at all.'

'You think they might be involved?' Emil asked.

'I've no idea,' said Magnus. 'But it's a logical place to start.'

'Indeed it is,' said Emil thoughtfully. 'I'm just worried about that mug.'

'The mug?'

'Yes. When you were looking for evidence in your grandfather's cottage, did you find any?'

Magnus met Emil's eyes with a steady gaze. 'No. Only a Sudoku puzzle open on the table. I assume my grandfather was working on that.'

'No mug?'

'No, as I've explained, I wasn't washing up a mug.'

'There is a mug on the drainer by the kitchen sink,' Rúnar said.

'I'm sure there is. Maybe that's how Aníta got confused.'

'When we check the mug for fingerprints, which we will, will we find yours on it?' Emil asked.

'I don't think so,' said Magnus. Then he hesitated. 'Wait. I might have taken a drink out of it. After washing my hands.'

Emil just looked at him. Magnus looked back. 'If you've finished, Emil…'

But Emil hadn't finished. 'Why did you allow Aníta and her horse to mess up the approach to the church?'

'I wanted to show her the body.'

Emil grunted. 'Magnús, you must have seen dozens of murder victims in your time.'

'That's true,' Magnus said. 'Actually, that's probably an underestimate.'

'So you know how to examine a body without getting blood all over your shoes and traipsing it everywhere?'

'Yeah. When I'm in detective mode. But this was my grand-father we're talking about.'

'Were you fond of your grandfather, Magnús?'

Magnus paused, but kept his gaze steady on Emil. 'No. No, I wasn't. He was pretty horrible to my brother and me when we lived here. And he ignored me when I came back to Iceland after my father died.'

'When was that?'

'Ninety-six. When I was twenty.'

'And have you seen him since?'

'Just six months ago. When I was working that case up here. Rúnar will remember that. I stopped in, just for five minutes. We had words.'

'Harsh words?'

Magnus nodded slowly. 'There weren't many of them, but they weren't exactly kind.'

Emil stared at Magnus in silence. Then he hauled himself to his feet. 'Will you excuse me for a moment? I need to make a phone call.'

He left Magnus in the study and went outside into the yard. He pulled out his phone.

Rúnar followed him. 'You don't think Magnús has anything to do with this, do you? He's one of our top detectives in Reykjavík.'

Emil took a deep breath. 'I need to call the Police Commissioner.'

CHAPTER FOUR

JÓHANNES DROVE ALONG the south shore of the Snaefells Peninsula in sunshine, with the volcano rising majestically behind them. Then he turned north, up into the mountains that ran along the peninsula, and into thick cloud.

He and Ollie spent half an hour or so discussing what they would say, then lapsed into silence. As they crossed the pass, a cloak of dread enveloped Ollie. It wasn't just the forthcoming interview with the police. He was worried about that – the story they had concocted had some holes in it. That fear was a rational one. But there was a deeper, stronger terror that gripped him.

Bjarnarhöfn and the bleak landscape around it scared the hell out of him. It always had, and it always would.

A new road led up over the pass. But Ollie remembered the old mountain pass just to the east, presided over by a pinnacle of lava in the shape of an old woman with a sack of babies over her shoulder. The Kerlingin troll. The local legend was that if the children of Stykkishólmur were bad, then the troll would creep down to the town at night and steal them away. According to Afi, Ollie was always bad. And he had lived in constant fear of the troll.

Ollie couldn't see her through the cloud, but he knew she was there still, ready to pounce.

There was another ghost up in the hills that his grandfather had told him about: Thórólfur Lame Foot, a saga chieftain from the area who had been killed by one of his rivals and had never rested quietly since.

Eventually they descended and emerged from the cloud right by the Berserkjahraun, the berserkers' lava field. It had started to rain. The congealed lava twisted in a frozen tumult down to Breidafjördur, at a point between Bjarnarhöfn and the neighbouring farm of Hraun. Fantastic shapes writhed in the mist, nibbled at by moss.

'You know my father and your grandfather used to play here?' Jóhannes said. 'I'm sure you know the story of the Swedish berserkers who cut a path across the lava between our two farms and were killed by the farmer at Hraun?'

'Yeah,' said Ollie in little more than a croak. The story had thrilled Afi, and Magnus for that matter, but it was just another thing that scared the shit out of Ollie. The Swedish warriors had been buried in a cairn in the middle of the lava field. You could still see it a thousand years later. And as a child, especially on foggy days, Ollie couldn't help seeing them flitting between the lava pinnacles.

He felt a sudden yearning for the lush green of the Boston suburbs, his home. And a strong desire to see a tree. Just one fucking tree.

And there was the farm, coming ever closer through the rain. Bjarnarhöfn.

The scene of the four most dreadful years of Ollie's life. It wasn't really the beating that stuck with him. It was the terror. The dark cold cellar half full of rotting potatoes. The fell looming above and lava field surrounding them. The wet pyjamas. The fear that his grandfather had drilled into him as a six-year-old, and which had grown deep inside him to eat up his soul. Hallgrímur's rage primed to ignite at any moment. The inconsistency. The love glimpsed and then snatched away.

Ollie's mother was buried there, in the little churchyard. Presumably Afi's body was there somewhere too; the police wouldn't have taken it away yet. And Ollie should be safe now that his grandfather was definitely dead.

Ollie didn't believe in ghosts. At least not in America. But here, in the mists and loneliness of Iceland, how could he not believe in ghosts? How could he believe that now Hallgrímur was dead he would just rest quietly?

Jóhannes was slowing to cross the cattle grid at the entrance to the farm.

'Turn around,' Ollie said.

'No, Ólafur, we have discussed this,' Jóhannes said. 'You have to talk to the police.'

'Stop the car, then,' Ollie said, pulling the handbrake.

Jóhannes's car skidded on the dirt track and nearly went into a ditch.

'You idiot!' Jóhannes yelled. 'What the hell are you doing?'

At that moment a police four-wheel-drive approached them from the farm. It slowed to pass. Ollie caught a glimpse of the large figure in the back seat. Magnus. They exchanged glances for an instant, and then the police car went on its way.

'Shit! That was my brother,' Ollie said. 'They've arrested him.'

'It looks like it,' said Jóhannes.

'Look, Joe. If they interview me at Bjarnarhöfn, I'll screw it up. This place terrifies me. Let's get out of here.'

'And go where?'

'I'll call them,' Ollie said. 'I'll tell them I'll meet them at the police station in Sticky Town or whatever it's called. They won't argue. Seriously, man, I can't handle this place.'

Jóhannes hesitated, examining Ollie. 'OK. We'll go on to Stykkishólmur. You call the police. I'll go slow, give them time to do whatever they're going to do to your brother before we get there.'

Detective Vigdís sighed as she straightened the piles of paper on her desk. She glanced at her computer screen. There were virtual piles much bigger than those in the police servers.

Murder always generated paper. Computers hadn't made things better. They had just made it easier to produce more paper, cutting and pasting, copying, merging, collating, printing multiple copies. Computers could produce sheets of paper, but they couldn't read them. You needed poor dumb detectives for that.

The case had involved the murder of one of the volunteers for Freeflow, a bunch of Internet activists. Thanks to Magnus, and Árni, it was pretty much wrapped up. Except for the paperwork.

Ordinarily, Vigdís would have been up for it. She was diligent and hard-working, and she understood that careful preparation of a case was vital if the suspect was to be put away. But at that precise moment she should have been in Paris with her boyfriend. He had got there, but the volcano, and the case, truth be told, had kept her in Reykjavík. He hadn't been happy.

Where the hell was Magnus? Árni had a reasonable excuse – he had been injured making the arrests – but it was unlike Magnus not to be in bright and early. He was good at the paperwork. As he never ceased to tell them, in murder cases in the United States, you had to be.

Her phone rang. She picked it up. 'Vigdís.'

'Hey, Vigdís, how are you?'

Her heart leapt. 'Davíd! Where are you?'

'New York.'

'So you got out of Paris?'

'Got someone to drive me to Madrid and caught a flight from there. And I'm jet-lagged to hell.'

'At least you can get to Chicago, then.'

Davíd was Icelandic but he worked for a TV company in New York. Last time he and Vigdís had spoken he had made a big deal about a conference in Chicago he was speaking at, and how important it was not to miss it.

'Uh… the conference is cancelled. We were expecting a lot of people from Europe and they couldn't make it.'

Vigdís felt the anger rise inside her. 'Oh.'

'Hey, Vigdís, I'm sorry. Truly I am.'

The anger melted away. 'Yeah, well, I'm sorry I never got to Paris.'

'Am I forgiven?' Davíd said.

Vigdís laughed. 'Only if I am.'

'Good. Because I could get on a flight to Reykjavík tonight, I think. Would that be a good idea? It would only be for a couple of days. Can you still get time off?'

'I don't know.' Magnus had insisted that she take the vacation days she had originally booked, even when the Freeflow case had erupted. But without Árni, Magnus would need her. Where was he, anyway?

Davíd caught her hesitation. 'Can't you just hurry up and solve that murder case today?' he said.

'Actually, we've done that,' said Vigdís. 'It's the clear-up. Look, I'll see what I can do and call you back in an hour or so.'

'OK, but be quick. I don't want to lose the seat.'

She put the phone down and sighed.

'Who was that?'

She looked up. There was Árni, her young colleague, his arm in a sling. He was tall and painfully thin, with dark hair, a hyper-active Adam's apple and a ready grin.

'Davíd,' Vigdís said. 'He wants to get on a flight to Reykjavík tomorrow. But if I can't get time off, he won't come.'

'You're supposed to be on vacation anyway, aren't you?' said Árni. 'Magnús and I will cope. Where is he, by the way?'

'I don't know,' said Vigdís. 'Are you sure? What about your arm? Can you type?'

'It's my shoulder,' said Árni. 'I'll be fine. I'm sure Magnús will be too. Go ask Baldur.'

Vigdís grinned at Árni. 'OK, I'll have a go,' she said and headed for Baldur's small office.

Baldur was a detective inspector and head of the Violent Crimes Unit, for which Vigdís and Árni both worked. Technically Magnus reported directly to the National Police Commissioner's office, but in practice he had a desk in the unit. He, Vigdís and Árni made a pretty good team.

Vigdís knew that Baldur had initially opposed her appointment to the unit. It was only partly because she was a woman. It was mostly because she was black. In Baldur's eyes it was inconceivable that a black woman could investigate a crime in whiter-than-white Iceland.

The Commissioner had disagreed and forced Vigdís on the reluctant inspector. Vigdís had worked hard; she didn't want to let down the Commissioner's confidence in her. And she had earned Baldur's grudging respect. She was diligent and quick-thinking. She had a particular knack for finding connections in piles of unrelated information. He also liked the fact that her English was even worse than his own.

He listened to her carefully. 'Are you sure Árni can cope?' he asked.

'Quite sure,' said Vigdís.

Baldur had a thin, lugubrious face. He smiled so quickly that Vigdís nearly missed it. He was just about to speak when the phone rang. 'Baldur.'

He listened a moment, and then straightened up. 'Yes, Snorri, just one moment.' Snorri was the Commissioner. Baldur nodded. 'OK, Vigdís. That's fine. But do as much as you can today.'

Vigdís smiled again and left Baldur to the Commissioner.

She called Davíd right back and told him to book flights. After they had hung up, she turned to her colleague. 'Thanks, Árni. I owe you one.'

'No problem,' said Árni. Then his smile disappeared as he glanced over Vigdís's shoulder.

She turned. Baldur was standing there looking grimmer than usual, and Baldur usually looked pretty grim.

'What is it?' she asked.

'It's Magnús. He's being held at Stykkishólmur police station.'

'What?' exclaimed Árni. 'What for?'

'Murder. His grandfather.'

'Murder!' said Vigdís. 'That's ridiculous.'

'The victim was found dead at his farm this morning.'

'Well, Magnús can't have murdered him,' said Árni. 'He was here in Reykjavík.'

'No, he wasn't,' Baldur said. 'It was Magnús who found the body.'

'Is he under arrest?' Vigdís asked.

'Not yet.'

'Don't worry,' said Árni. 'If it's the Dumpling investigating, they'll never pin anything on him.'

'The Dumpling is sharper than he looks,' said Vigdís. 'I worked a case with him last year, a rape in Borgarnes.'

'Emil is just a lump of lard,' said Baldur. 'I remember when he was a detective here. But he's best buddies with the Big Salmon.' The Big Salmon was Snorri, the Commissioner.

'Whatever. They won't pin anything on Magnus because he's innocent,' said Vigdís. 'Wait. They don't want us to investigate him, do they?'

'No. The Commissioner is confident Emil can lead the investigation. He's going to get him some support from Keflavík. So it will be up to Emil to decide whether Magnus is really innocent.'

'Of course he's innocent,' said Vigdís. Baldur's suggestion that he might possibly not be angered her. She knew that Baldur resented the foreign interloper in his team with his big-city smart-arse American crime techniques, but you had to stand by your colleagues.

Which was no doubt why the Commissioner had insisted on someone from outside Reykjavík to investigate.

'The evidence doesn't look good so far,' said Baldur.

'What have they got?' Árni asked.

'I'm not allowed to discuss the case with you.'

Vigdís rolled her eyes. Then why had he mentioned the evidence? Just to wind them up? Baldur could be a real jerk sometimes.

'And in fact the Commissioner was very clear that none of us should communicate with Magnús until this is sorted out. Is that understood?'

'Jesus Christ,' said Árni in English as Baldur left the room. 'I didn't know Magnús was going up there.'

'Nor did I,' said Vigdís.

'There's no way he's guilty?' asked Róbert, another detective in the unit who had been listening in.

'Of course not,' said Vigdís. 'But that puts paid to my vacation. I can't leave all this with you, Árni.'

'Yes, you can,' said Árni. 'Our suspects are in jail on remand, no one's going anywhere for the next few days. Besides.'

'Besides what?' said Vigdís.

'If you have a few spare moments, since you are not on duty, you might be able to help Magnús.'

'Huh. Yeah, you're right.' She tapped on her keyboard, picked up the phone and dialled a number from her computer screen.

'Who are you calling?'

'Stykkishólmur police station,' said Vigdís.

Árni raised his eyebrows.

'Yes, hello,' said Vigdís, to the woman who answered the phone. 'Can I speak to Chief Superintendent Rúnar?'

She waited a moment. 'Rúnar? This is Detective Vigdís Audardóttir from Reykjavík Violent Crimes Unit. I understand you have my boss there. Can I speak to him?'

'I'm sorry, Vigdís, I can't allow that.'

'I won't discuss your case,' said Vigdís. 'But we made some arrests yesterday in a murder investigation, and I really need to check something with him.'

There was a pause. 'All right. Just a moment.'

She couldn't quite hear Rúnar's instructions to Magnus, but a few seconds later she heard his familiar strong voice on the phone. 'Hey, Vigdís, what's up?'

'Sorry, I know you're busy,' said Vigdís.

'Actually I'm sitting here twiddling my thumbs. Rúnar said you had a question on the Freeflow case?'

'Yes, I do.' Vigdís glanced at the top sheet of paper on her pile, a forensic report, and asked something pointless about it.

Magnus realized it was pointless but answered it anyway.

'Thanks, Magnús,' Vigdís said. 'By the way, Davíd's flying into Keflavík tomorrow morning, so I'm taking my couple of days off. Árni's out of hospital, so he can cover for me.'

'That's great,' said Magnus. 'I'm sure I'll be back at the station tomorrow. They've got to ask me the questions, but once I've answered them they'll let me go.'

'Do you want me to help you?' Vigdís said. 'Check something out? Get you a lawyer? I can come up and see you.'

'No,' said Magnus. 'I'm quite all right here. Don't worry about me; it'll sort itself out. Have a great couple of days.'

'But Magnús—'

'Vigdís. I said drop it.' Magnus's tone was stern to the point of being offensive. 'Do you understand me?'

'Magnús—'

But Magnus's voice was replaced by the chief superintendent. 'Detective Vigdís, I think you have finished here.'

'Yes, of course,' said Vigdís. 'Thank you.'

'Didn't want your help, huh?' said Árni as she replaced the receiver.

Vigdís nodded.

'He's a stubborn bastard.'

'Yes,' said Vigdís. 'He certainly is.'

CHAPTER FIVE

'YOU DON'T CARE that he's dead, do you?'

'Tóta, dear, that's a horrible thing to say.' Aníta was taking a batch of small cakes out of the oven. She was also brewing a new pot of coffee. There were a lot of people around, lots of coffee to drink and cakes to eat, and besides, baking was a favourite displacement activity for Aníta when she was upset.

Tóta was fifteen, and pretty, if in a slightly tarty way. Long blonde hair, a snub nose, pouting lips in a chubby face. She and her mother had shared a love of horses since soon after Tóta could walk, but for the last twelve months, horse rides had become more rare – only if the weather was good and Tóta was in the mood. Tóta had grown, her softness rearranging itself around her body in a way that interested boys. And she was interested in them.

Which was fine. There had been boys in Aníta's teenage years and men when she had gone down to high school in Reykjavík when she was sixteen. So many men. Such awful men, frankly. It was one of the major reasons she had returned to the Snaefells Peninsula. She hoped Tóta wouldn't make the same mistakes she had. But she could see that already Tóta would make mistakes; she was determined to do so, if only to anger her mother.

Tóta was sitting at the kitchen table, flipping through a magazine and waiting for the cakes. 'You hated him.'

'No, I didn't.'

'Well, you hardly ever said anything to him.'

'We had a lot of respect for each other.' By which Aníta meant they had kept their own distance.

Hallgrímur had doted on Tóta, frequently commenting that she reminded him of Margrét, his lost daughter. Aníta had never known Margrét, who had died before Aníta had married Kolbeinn, so she had no idea how true this was. Kolbeinn went along with it, but Aníta suspected that this was just to keep his father happy.

There was the sound of pounding on the stairs and Krissi barged in. 'Hey, Mum, are they ready yet? I'm starving.'

He was tall for a twelve-year-old, which was good for basketball, but he wasn't used to his own size yet, and had developed a tendency towards clumsiness. He was also becoming surly, but in a much more withdrawn way than Tóta. But at that moment he had pink cheeks and a wide grin on his face, like a little eight-year-old. Aníta felt a huge desire to hug him. So she did. He didn't resist.

'He's not sad either,' Tóta said.

'What about?' asked Krissi, innocently.

'Afi, idiot. Someone murdered him. Probably our psycho cousin. And you don't care.'

Krissi looked serious for a moment. 'Of course I care,' he said, glancing at his mother.

'Yes, of course he does, Tóta,' said Aníta, although actually she suspected Tóta was right. And although Tóta had shed tears, Aníta wasn't sure how sad she really was, either.

But the manner of Hallgrímur's death really was shocking. Murder. His blood spilled on the wooden floor of the little church. It was not the way for an old man to die, not even Hallgrímur.

Another death at Bjarnarhöfn. Another ghost. So many ghosts.

'So that was Cousin Magnús?' said Tóta. Magnus had spent some time with them in the kitchen before the police had whisked him away. Tóta had been little more than a baby the last time he had visited Bjarnarhöfn briefly. 'He's pretty hot.'

'Yuk,' said Krissi. 'He's your cousin!'

'I know,' said Tóta. 'I was just saying. Anyway, he's really old.'

Tóta had a point, thought Anita. In fact, she had warmed to Magnus as they had waited in the kitchen for the police. She doubted that he had really murdered Hallgrímur, but she didn't regret telling the police what she had seen. She was one hundred per cent sure that Magnus was washing up that mug in Hallgrímur's kitchen.

And the enmity that Hallgrímur felt towards his grandson was obvious. When Magnus had visited Bjarnarhöfn immediately after his father's death, Anita had done her best to welcome him. He was only twenty then, too young to lose both his parents. But Hallgrímur had wanted nothing to do with him and had forbidden Anita from even asking him to stay for dinner. So Magnus had found a room in a hotel in Stykkishólmur and then gone back to America. If he had intended to effect some reconciliation with his Icelandic family, he had failed.

Kolbeinn, as usual, had taken his father's side. There were three brothers – Vilhjálmur, Kolbeinn and Ingvar – and then Margrét, Magnus's mother. Vilhjálmur, or Villi as he was known to his family, had emigrated to Canada sometime in the 1970s. Ingvar had gone to Reykjavík to become a doctor, and then to France before returning to Stykkishólmur. Kolbeinn had stayed put and run the farm. Someone had to.

Kolbeinn was nearly fifteen years older than Anita, and she was his second wife, his first having run off with a fisherman from Akureyri. He was tall, strong and steady, if unimaginative. Anita had married him on the rebound from the string of imaginative disasters she had dated in Reykjavík. But she didn't regret her decision. After nearly twenty years she loved him still.

He was out fixing fences, preparing for the lambing season. The ewes were all indoors at the moment, but once they began lambing they would be let outside into the meadows around the farm, volcanic ash permitting. That was only two weeks away. Lambing was hard work, but totally absorbing, and the distraction would be welcome.

'I think Amma is here,' said Krissi, pointing out of the window. Indeed, her car, a small silver Opel, was parked next to

Magnus's green Range Rover outside her cottage and she was talking to the policeman standing guard there. There were even more people milling about than before; the forensics team from Reykjavík had arrived. It was raining.

'She looks upset,' Krissi said.

'I bet she is,' said Aníta. She left the cakes and rushed outside, trotting over to the cottage through the rain. The dogs followed her.

Sylvía was a small, tough woman in her mid-eighties, with short grey hair. Her expression was usually one of disapproval, but for once she looked distressed. Aníta hurried over and put her arm around the old woman's shoulders.

'The policeman says I can't see Hallgrímur,' she said. 'Where is he?'

'I think he's in the church, Sylvía.'

'But he can't be. There is no service there today. Besides, Hallgrímur never goes to church.'

'Is that where you were, Sylvía?' Aníta asked. 'At church?' In the last year or so Sylvía had started to go to church with increasing frequency. There was only one service a month at Bjarnarhöfn, given by the pastor at Helgafell, and she had started attending that. Now she often went into the new church at Stykkishólmur.

'Yes, dear. Why won't the policeman let me into my house?'

'I don't know,' said Aníta.

The fat detective was waddling towards them from the church. Aníta beckoned to him. 'Can my mother-in-law go in?'

'I'm sorry,' said the inspector. 'It's a crime scene. Can you take her over to the farmhouse? I want to have a word with her.'

'How long will it be a crime scene?' Aníta asked. 'The church I can understand, but Sylvía lives here.'

'We have to wait for forensics. It can be a slow old job. They might not release the cottage until tomorrow. She'll probably have to sleep at the farmhouse tonight.'

'Can she at least get her stuff? She'll need things for the night.'

'Yes, she can get those later. And in fact, I'd like her to check the cottage to make sure nothing is missing. But we must wait until forensics are set up here, OK? I'd also like to have a word with you in a few minutes. I need to understand a bit more about your family.'

'That's all right,' said Aníta. She turned to her mother-in-law, who was dripping in the steady rain. 'Come back to the farmhouse, Sylvía. Let's get you dry. The policeman says you will have to stay with us tonight.'

'Does he indeed? And Hallgrímur too?'

Oh, God, thought Aníta. She had been afraid that this would happen; half expected it, even. She suspected that her mother-in-law was in the early stages of Alzheimer's. She was a stubborn old bird at the best of times. If she didn't want to accept that Hallgrímur had been murdered, it would be difficult to persuade her. She glanced at the detective, who was watching the old woman closely. He seemed to understand what was going on.

'I'm afraid Hallgrímur is dead, Sylvía,' Aníta said as kindly as she could.

'Nonsense, dear. I expect he has gone into town for something. He'll be back soon.'

'No, Sylvía. You need to understand. He's been killed. In the church.'

'But he doesn't go to church,' said Sylvía, confusion written all over her face. 'I told you that.'

Aníta was suddenly aware of the large damp figure of Kolbeinn at her shoulder. He opened his arms, pulled his mother into his broad chest and rocked her, tears in his eyes.

Emil drove the twenty kilometres from Bjarnarhöfn to Stykkishólmur alone. He appreciated the time to think. And it would allow him to stop for five minutes for a hot dog at the petrol station on the edge of town.

Aníta had given him some useful background on Hallgrímur's family. It was clear that he was a nasty old man;

indeed, it seemed likely that he had been a nasty young man. He had also publicly rejected his grandson Magnus. He had been upset at the death of his alcoholic daughter and clearly hated Magnus's father.

That wasn't so unusual. Icelanders had lots of children, their extended families were big, and in any big Icelandic family there was always someone who made trouble. But that didn't mean that they were murdered.

Dr Ingvar had speculated that a possible cause of the murder was someone banging Hallgrímur's head repeatedly against the floor of the church. It was soft pine, but Hallgrímur was an old man: it wouldn't take much to kill him. Blows to the head with a blunt instrument were still a possibility, but no likely blunt instruments had been found. All would be clearer at autopsy, which would take place in Reykjavík the following morning.

Magnus had discovered the body. It was beginning to look as if he had disrupted the crime scene intentionally. Edda, the head of the forensics team, would give Emil a much better idea of that in a few hours. It may well be that they would find enough forensic evidence to pin the crime on Magnus, but somehow Emil doubted it. Magnus had involved himself so thoroughly in the crime scene that it would be difficult to prove that he was anything but a thoughtless, blundering bystander.

No, Emil needed a motive. He needed to find out more about Sergeant Magnús Ragnarsson.

Emil had had a difficult time with Hallgrímur's wife. She refused to accept her husband's death. She had been to church at Stykkishólmur, and Hallgrímur had been fine when she had left, doing his Sudoku puzzles. He must have gone off to see a friend or to choir practice. After much cajoling from her son Kolbeinn, the three of them had checked the cottage. Sylvía didn't seem to think that anything had been taken, but it was hard to be sure. There was a Sudoku book lying open on a table in the living room. Kolbeinn had checked the church: there was nothing missing from there either. So a surprised burglar, although not to be ruled out entirely, was looking unlikely.

Stykkishólmur police station was a modern white office block surrounded by car park, between the post office and the Bónus supermarket as you came into town. Half of the building was the magistrate's offices, and the other half the police regional headquarters.

Chief Superintendent Rúnar was waiting for him. 'Do you want to speak to Magnús now?'

'No,' said Emil. 'Let me talk to his brother first.'

'OK. But he doesn't speak Icelandic,' Rúnar said. 'I've got an interpreter standing by.'

Emil raised his eyebrows. 'All right.'

That was a pain in the arse. Emil was proud of his English, but in cases with foreign nationals where both the police officers and the witnesses spoke English, an interpreter was required for an official statement.

The interpreter was a young teacher from the primary school just down the road. He followed Emil and Constable Páll into the interview room where Ollie was waiting. The Stykkishólmur police had sensibly kept him away from his brother.

Ollie was a thin man with fine features, curly fair hair and a couple of days of stubble. He looked tense.

Emil smiled as he sat down. 'Good afternoon, Ollie,' he said in English. 'Do you want some more coffee?' He nodded to Ollie's half-full Styrofoam cup.

Ollie shook his head. 'No, but I'd like a smoke.'

'Sorry, Ollie. Not allowed these days.'

Ollie's fingers drifted to his coffee cup and he began to fiddle with it.

'Since I understand you don't speak Icelandic, we need an interpreter,' Emil said. 'I'll ask the questions in Icelandic, and although I'll probably understand your answers, we need it translated for the record.' He nodded to a recorder. 'This interview is being taped.'

'OK,' said Ollie, swallowing.

'Can I confirm that your name is Ólafur Hallgrímur Ragnarsson?' Emil switched to Icelandic, with the interpreter translating.

'Er, no. At least not any more. It's Oliver Hallgrimur Jonson. At least that's what it says on my United States passport, and I don't have an Icelandic one. My father was Ragnar Jónsson, but he found it too complicated that Magnus and me had different last names to him, so he figured we should all be Jonson. And I've always been happy to stick with that.'

'I see. Date of birth?'

'February second, 1978.'

'Address?'

'Five six one Stanton Street, Medford, Massachusetts, USA.'

'OK. And how long have you lived in America? You were born in Iceland, right?'

'Yes, I was born here. In Reykjavík. I moved to the States when I was ten. That's about twenty years ago. As you can see I've forgotten all my Icelandic. This is the first time I have been back.'

'Really? And how long have you been in the country?'

'I flew in Wednesday. Stayed with my brother in Reykjavík. I was due to fly back this afternoon, but I guess I'm going to miss my flight.'

'Sorry about that.' Emil smiled. 'But I'm sure you can understand.'

'I guess,' said Ollie.

'So where were you this morning at about ten-thirty?'

'When my grandfather was killed? You don't think I did it, do you?'

'I have to ask the question, Ollie. Of you and everyone else.'

Ollie nodded. Swallowed. 'I, er, I was at a place called Arnarstapi, something like that. It's further along the peninsula. I was with Joe, Jóhannes. He wanted to show me a cliff walk there. And the glacier. It was pretty cool.'

'I see. So it was a tourist excursion. Is Jóhannes a friend of yours?'

Ollie shook his head. 'I only met him a couple of days ago. We were actually coming up here to talk to my grandfather. But we were too early on a Sunday morning to disturb him, so Jóhannes wanted to show me the sights. Then I called Grandpa to tell him we wanted to see him, and that's when I heard he was dead.'

'I see. Why did you hang up? And why didn't you answer the phone when Páll here called you back?'

'I was shocked. I didn't know what to do. But when I thought about it a bit, I did call the police back.'

'I see.' Emil observed Ollie calmly. 'Are you always this nervous?'

Ollie shrugged. 'Sometimes.'

'You don't like talking to cops?'

Ollie laughed. 'It depends on the circumstances.'

'When we check your criminal record, what will we find?' Emil asked.

Ollie smiled ruefully. 'A couple of minor drug busts. Possession. I was questioned a couple years back about mortgage fraud, but they had nothing on me. They might keep records of that kind of thing, I don't know. But I'm not an international master criminal.'

Emil laughed at Ollie's attempt at humour. 'So why, after twenty years, did you suddenly want to see your grandfather?'

Ollie took a deep breath. 'That's a very good question.' He hesitated, drinking some of his coffee. 'Neither Magnus nor I liked our grandfather. He gave us a real tough time at Bjarnarhöfn, especially me. That's why I wanted to come here to be interviewed rather than there, the place still gives me the creeps. But after our father was murdered—'

Emil sat up. 'Murdered? I heard he had died, but I didn't know he was murdered.'

'Oh, yeah,' said Ollie. 'In 1996. I was the one who discovered his body.' He winced. 'It was in a house we were renting on the South Shore. Of Boston. As you can imagine, it freaked me out. Freaked us both out. Magnus became obsessed with trying to figure out who did it. He was twenty, I guess, at

46

college, but he nosed around asking questions. I figure that's why he became a cop.'

'And did they catch the murderer?'

'No,' Ollie said. 'He's still out there somewhere. And Magnus is still looking for him. Which is why I came to Iceland.'

'You were here to help him?'

'No. No, not at all. I was here to try to persuade him to stop. You see, he thinks there is a link between our grandfather and our father's death, and since he's been back in Iceland, he's been asking questions.'

'Was your grandfather in Boston when your father was killed?'

'No. Magnus says he has never left Iceland. Doesn't even have a passport. But there was another murder, here in Iceland, which had the same, what do you call it – MO?'

Emil nodded.

'Yeah, MO. Some guy called Benedikt something or other. He was a famous author. He was killed in 1985 in Reykjavík.'

'Benedikt Jóhannesson? I remember that,' Emil said. 'I helped out on that investigation.'

'And you didn't find the killer either, did you?'

'No,' said Emil. 'Didn't Benedikt come from up here some-where?'

'Exactly right. He lived at Hraun when he was a kid. The farm on the other side of the lava field from Bjarnarhöfn. He and my grandfather were neighbours when they were kids.'

'OK,' Emil said. 'That's a link, but a weak one.'

'It gets stronger, at least according to Magnus,' Ollie said. 'Back to the MO. Benedikt was stabbed in the back once and twice in the chest by someone who was right-handed. Dad was killed in the exact same way. So Magnus thinks the two crimes must be linked. And he thinks the link must be Grandpa.'

'But you don't?'

'I didn't. I mean it could be a coincidence, right? I thought that this was just Magnus's obsession and I wanted him to stop it. Anything that brings back that place does my head in. At first he listened, but then he said he was going to carry on regardless. So I came over here to try to persuade him not to. Which is where I met Joe.'

'Jóhannes?'

'Jóhannes Benediktsson. The schoolteacher. Benedikt was his father. In fact, Joe discovered his dead body as well. Back in 1985. Magnus turned him up from somewhere and we both met him last week. He has read all his father's books many times, and he thought that they implied there was a feud between our two families, with Grandpa right in the middle of it. A feud going right back to the 1930s.

'Magnus lapped this up, of course, but I was sceptical. But the more I thought of it, the more I thought Joe might have a point. So I went around to his house a couple of days ago and we talked about it. We figured we may as well go right up to Bjarnarhöfn and ask Grandpa straight. I could never have done that myself, I'm still scared of the guy, but with Joe I thought I could do it. So we drove up this morning.'

'I see,' said Emil. 'But why go with Jóhannes? Why not with your brother?'

'Well, that's what I thought of doing first,' said Ollie. 'Naturally. But Magnus is kind of weird about all this stuff. And I'd have had to admit to him I had changed my mind. He's a cop, and so he might have suddenly come over all official. So that didn't work. But I suddenly thought, wait a minute, maybe I could come up here with Joe? And so here we are.'

'And what was Magnús doing here?'

Ollie blew air through his cheeks. 'I've no idea. He made some big arrests yesterday, to do with that tourist who got killed on the volcano. I didn't see him. And we left early this morning, Joe and me.'

'So he might have been seeing Hallgrímur for the same reason you were?'

'He might,' said Ollie. 'I don't know. Have you asked him?'

'I will.' Emil leaned forward. 'Ollie? Do you think your brother could have killed your grandfather?'

'No!' said Ollie. 'Absolutely not.'

'Why not?'

'Because Magnus has devoted his whole life to finding murderers, not murdering other people.'

'Maybe that's what he was doing? He had found his murderer, the murderer of his father. And he was bringing him to justice?'

Ollie frowned. 'No,' he said, uncertainly. 'No way. Not Magnus.' He leaned backwards, folding his arms and shaking his head. 'Uh uh.'

They sat there, detective and witness, for half a minute. Ollie maintained his pose of denial. Emil thought, his fingers caressing the wart on his neck.

'Ollie?' he said.

'Yeah?'

'What time did you leave Reykjavík this morning?'

'About seven-thirty.'

'It takes about two, maybe two and a half hours to get from Reykjavík to Bjarnarhöfn. If you didn't want to disturb Hallgrímur on a Sunday morning, why did you leave Reykjavík so early?'

Ollie frowned some more. 'Er...'

Emil waited as Ollie floundered. Eventually he thought of something.

'I don't know. Joe just said he would pick me up at seven-thirty. It's his country. I just did what I was told.'

'I see,' said Emil. 'That will be all for now. Thanks for your cooperation.' He nodded to Páll, who turned off the recorder. Páll and the interpreter would have the job of writing up a statement and then translating it into English for Ollie to sign.

'Can I go now?' Ollie asked. 'I've missed my flight, but I'd like to go to Keflavík and try to get myself on another one.'

'We'll need you to hang around to sign the statement,' Emil said in English. 'And good luck with the airport. I saw pictures on the news and it looked like a zoo. Most of the flights have been cancelled and no one knows whether they are coming or going. But I think I would prefer you stayed in Stykkishólmur, at least for another day or so. In fact, I'll take your passport. You are a material witness in a murder investigation.' He held out his hand.

Reluctantly, Ollie reached into his jacket and handed his passport over.

CHAPTER SIX

EMIL STUDIED THE man in front of him.

Magnus was a different prospect to his brother. Taller, broader, tougher. Where Ollie had seemed nervous, Magnus now looked composed, fit and alert. His steady blue eyes returned Emil's appraising glance.

'I've just spoken to your brother,' Emil said.

'Is he here?' Magnus asked.

'Yes. But I can't let you see him.'

'I understand,' said Magnus. 'What did he say?'

'He said he didn't like your grandfather much. Apparently neither of you did.'

Magnus didn't respond.

'He told me about how you had spotted a connection between your father's death and the murder of Benedikt Jóhannesson.'

'He did?'

'Yes. And how you had discussed this with Benedikt's son.'

'I see,' said Magnus, nodding.

'Ollie thinks that you believed your grandfather was responsible for both the murders.'

'I'm pretty sure that he wasn't in America when my father was killed,' Magnus said.

'I said "responsible". I didn't say Hallgrímur committed the murders. There's a difference.'

'There is,' admitted Magnus.

Emil realized that a more direct tack was required. 'OK. So let's start with this morning. When did you leave Reykjavík?' He

51

glanced at Páll sitting next to him, pen at the ready. The constable's moustache really was a fine one.

'I won't comment.'

Emil looked at Magnus sharply. 'I don't want a comment. I just want you to answer a simple question.'

'And I don't want to answer it.'

Emil leaned back on his chair. It creaked alarmingly. He slowly leaned forward; collapsing a chair was not good interview technique.

'You're a policeman. There's been a murder. I need to know what all the witnesses' and suspects' movements were. You found the body. I have to know what you were doing.'

'Oh, I quite understand that,' said Magnus. 'But I don't intend to tell you.'

'Even what time you got up in the morning?'

'Even that.'

'I see.' Emil thought a moment. 'You do know the laws here in Iceland?'

'Yes,' replied Magnus. 'I did six months at the police college. I have read the Penal Code.'

'Then you know that there is no constitutional right not to incriminate yourself like there is in the United States?'

'Yes, I do.'

'You know that if you refuse to answer even the most straight-forward question about what happened today, it will be reasonable for me and the prosecution to assume that you are trying to hide something?'

'Yes, I know that,' said Magnus.

'All right. Let me go through the evidence against you,' Emil said. 'One. You discovered the body. We're not sure yet, but it seems that the victim hadn't been dead long when the first policeman arrived at the scene. That puts you at the scene at about the time Hallgrímur was killed.'

He glanced at Magnus, who made no response, just watched him coolly.

Emil counted off the points on his fingers. 'Two. You hated

your grandfather. You suspected that he had had your father murdered.'

Emil checked Magnus again. No response.

'Three. You easily have the strength to kill Hallgrímur, just by banging his head against the floor. Four, it appears that you did your best to disturb the crime scene. You intentionally got Hallgrímur's blood on your shoes, you allowed a horse to shit all over the approach, and you seem to have tampered with evidence in his cottage.'

Emil counted his thumb. 'And five, you are refusing to talk. I mean, think about that. All the evidence so far points to you murdering your grandfather. Now, if I'm on the wrong track, tell me about it. Give me your side of the story. We can check it out. If you are innocent, we can prove it. Do you understand me?'

'I understand you,' said Magnus.

'Well?'

'I'm not saying anything.'

'And you know the consequences of your decision?'

'The consequences are entirely up to you,' said Magnus.

Emil could see Magnus wasn't rattled. He had thought all this through. Emil had only come across one witness before who had been so reticent, and as a tactic it had worked very well. It wasn't an Icelander – they could always be persuaded to say something – but a Dutchman, many years ago back in Reykjavík, a hardened drug dealer who had been accused of arranging a mule to import drugs through the airport. If a suspect didn't tell a story, there was nothing to attack. Emil hadn't been able to make the case, and eventually they had had to release the Dutchman, who had got on the first flight back to Amsterdam.

'All right. In that case, Magnús, I'm arresting you for the murder of Hallgrímur Gunnarsson. Would you like to contact a lawyer?'

Magnus seemed unsurprised at the arrest, Emil thought, as though he was expecting it. Not just expecting it; as though he had planned it.

'Yes, I would. Sigurbjörg Vilhjálmsdóttir. If you let me have my phone back, I have her number on there.'

'OK. Páll, give Magnús the lawyer's number and let him make the call. And then lock him up.'

The waiting was driving Ollie mad. Eventually the police had produced a two-page statement for him to sign, which seemed accurate enough. In the meantime he had eaten two sandwiches from the supermarket opposite the station and smoked a packet of cigarettes. It had stopped raining, but it was damp and cold as he took another circuit round the car park. He had tried walking further, but as soon as he was more than a couple of minutes away from the station, he was drawn back.

He had done good, he thought. Stuck to the story that he and Jóhannes had agreed. Except he seemed to have inadvertently dropped his brother into it. The possibility hadn't occurred to him until the fat detective pointed it out; the idea of Magnus being involved in a crime was laughable. Ollie smiled at the irony that it was Magnus who was in trouble with the cops for once and not him.

Magnus would get himself out of it, he always did. Wouldn't he? This was a foreign country, a pretty weird country, operating under a strange set of rules. Ollie knew too well Magnus could be a pain in the ass. If the Icelandic police didn't like Magnus for some reason, perhaps they would turn on him?

It was too late now. Besides, Ollie had only told the truth, about Magnus at any rate. It was the story that Jóhannes would tell, and probably Magnus too. If Ollie had tried to hide Magnus's obsession about their father's death from the police, they would have discovered it soon enough anyway. And then Ollie would have been squarely in the frame, which is absolutely where he did not want to be. Magnus could cope with the Icelandic police much better than Ollie, that was for sure.

Ollie had had a difficult few days in Reykjavík with his brother. He had gone there to have a fight, and they had had one. But Magnus had refused to drop his stupid fixation with their father's death. Usually Magnus could be relied upon to support his little brother, as he had done so often over the years. But not this time, apparently.

Still, it had been nice to meet Magnus's landlady Katrín. Ollie smiled at the memory of the long limbs, the white skin, the black hair and eyeshadow. She was hot in a spaced-out, kooky way that kind of suited Ollie.

He heard a door bang and looked up. 'Finally!' Ollie said as he saw Jóhannes approaching him down the corridor. 'How did it go?'

'Wait till we are outside, Ólafur,' said the schoolteacher. He looked calm. It can't have been too bad, thought Ollie.

They left the station and crossed the car park to Jóhannes's car. 'All right, how did it go?'

'Satisfactorily, I think,' said Jóhannes, as they got into the car. 'I stuck to the script. There was just one difficulty.'

He looked disapprovingly at Ollie from under his thick white eyebrows.

'What did I say?' said Ollie, getting the message.

'That you didn't know why we left Reykjavík so early. That you were just doing what I told you.'

'So?' said Ollie. 'My mind went blank. I knew you'd have an answer.'

'Well, I did. But I said we discussed it on the way up and it was only then we realized that we were too early to see Hallgrímur, and that's why we took a diversion to Arnarstapi.'

'Did the fat guy spot the discrepancy?'

'He did. I said I'd initially told you what we were doing, but then we had discussed plans once we were on the road.'

'Sounds good,' said Ollie. 'Hey, I think I did well. It could have been a lot worse.'

'Yes,' said Jóhannes, smiling. 'Yes, you did well, considering.'

That cheered Ollie up. It was weird how he sought praise from this man he hardly knew. 'Where to now?'

Jóhannes started the car and turned towards the centre of

town. 'I'll drop you off at a hotel in Stykkishólmur. Then I'll head back to Reykjavík.'

'Reykjavík? Wait a minute. How come I have to stay here and you get to go home?'

'Because tomorrow's Monday. I have a class to teach. And they don't want you flying off to the States in case they have to interview you again. You are Magnus's brother, after all.'

Ollie looked anxiously out of the car window at the houses lining the road. This was going to be tough, abandoned in Stykkishólmur without Jóhannes. And it sounded like Magnus wouldn't be much help either.

As if reading his mind, Jóhannes soothed him. 'Don't worry. Act helpful. Stick to our story. Don't go off on any digressions. They'll let you go tomorrow.'

'OK,' Ollie said. 'OK. I'll call you and tell you what happens.'

'All right, but keep it short. Remember, they might be listening.'

'You mean bugging my phone?'

'I doubt it, but possibly. We can't take any chances, now can we, Ólafur?'

'No,' said Ollie.

They stopped outside a green building halfway down a low hill leading towards a harbour. Ollie could see the sea and islands ahead of him.

He hoisted his bag out of the trunk, and watched as Jóhannes turned his car around and drove off, south towards to Reykjavík.

He took a deep breath and entered the small hotel, feeling very alone.

Jóhannes was not even sure he would go in to school the following morning, but he was glad of the excuse to leave Stykkishólmur. After thirty years' teaching, he had been sacked the week before. The principal had said it was because of government spending cuts, but had made clear that Jóhannes had been chosen because he had refused to follow the national curriculum. Jóhannes had thought he was untouchable; he knew himself to be without doubt the best Icelandic teacher the school had ever had.

It was the shock of his sacking that had prompted Jóhannes to go back to a biography of his father he was planning, and led him to get in touch with Magnus and his brother. The principal had given Jóhannes only the afternoon off; he was supposed to continue teaching until the end of term. Jóhannes had just not turned up at school for the rest of the week. But given the day's events, it might be a good idea to show his face again.

He took a small detour on his way back to Reykjavík. A few kilometres south of Stykkishólmur he turned right on to Route 577, a rough road that ran along the southern shore of Breidafjördur. He passed several large prosperous farms, until he came to the one he was looking for: a collection of buildings on a knoll looking out over the sea towards the West Fjords.

Hraun. The place where his father was born. Not just his father, but his grandfather and his great-grandfather.

Jóhannes pulled over to the side of the road by the track that led up to the farm. He had no idea who lived there now, but whoever it was kept the place in good nick. The fences were standing straight and intact, a row of white hay bales ran along the bottom of the home meadow, and there was none of the junk lying about that you usually saw on an Icelandic working farm.

Jóhannes knew his family history. It was 1942 when his father Benedikt had left the farm. He had gone to high school in Reykjavík, while his widowed mother and sisters had moved into Stykkishólmur, where his mother had bought a dress shop.

He looked down to the lava field and across to the imposing snow-streaked lower slopes of the fell of Bjarnarhöfn.

Jóhannes knew the history of this place too. His favourite text at school was *The Saga of the People of Eyri*, which described the life and times of the first settlers in this area over a thousand years before. Some time in the ninth century, Björn the Easterner, the son of Ketill Flat Nose and the brother of Audur

57

the Deep-Minded, had been the first, pitching his sacred wooden pillars into the sea to let the gods determine where he should make landfall. The gods had chosen Bjarnarhöfn.

Jóhannes knew the stories of Björn, his followers and their successors intimately. Most of their farms were still standing a millennium later, including Hraun, which had been the home of Björn's great-grandson Styr.

Between Bjarnarhöfn and Hraun lay the tossing sea of stone that was the Berserkjahraun. It was this that had given the farm its name: 'hraun' meant 'lava'. Jóhannes was drawn to it. It was the backdrop to a couple of chapters in the saga, which were the favourites of every Seventh Form class he read them to.

He drove on a couple of hundred metres, parked the car and strode off to the edge of the broad channel of ancient lava, which was raised several metres above the ground. The rain had stopped but a thick layer of leaden cloud hung low above the shoreline. There was a breeze, there was always a breeze, but it was relatively gentle, and felt refreshing after the fug of the car.

He found the beginning of the Berserkjagata, the narrow path that the berserkers had cut through the lava between the farms of Hraun and Bjarnarhöfn. He followed it as it twisted through the congealed lava, spattered with grey, green and yellow moss. The path dipped and dived and turned. Strange shapes pirouetted: fists, fingers, arms, beards, tresses of hair, horses, pigs, trolls all caught in mid-movement. Although the lava had frozen three thousand years before, it seemed to be alive, like a still from an action film, just waiting for someone to press 'play'. There was no sound apart from the wind, and a cormorant calling in the small bay to his right.

The path led upwards for a few metres and then plunged down into a shallow amphitheatre in the middle of which was a noticeably man-made block of stone perhaps four metres by three. This was what Jóhannes was looking for. It was here that the two berserkers had been buried.

He stood still, letting the cool air touch his cheeks and the damp silence settle upon him. He felt at peace.

Berserker was the term the Vikings used for especially fierce warriors who could whip themselves up into a frenzy of violence in battle where they were no match for any normal man. Vermundur the Lean, who was the farmer at Bjarnarhöfn, had visited Norway and been given two Swedish berserker servants by the king there. He had brought them back to Iceland, but they had proven difficult to handle, so he had passed them on to his brother Styr, the farmer of Hraun on the other side of the lava field, who was famous for his bad temper.

Styr didn't have much more luck. But he did have a beautiful daughter, Ásdís, to which one of the berserkers took a fancy. The berserker demanded that Styr give Ásdís to be his wife. Styr was unhappy with this idea and, together with his friend Snorri from Helgafell, concocted a plan. He told the berserker that he could marry his daughter if the berserker and his fellow Swede cut a path across the lava field from Hraun to Bjarnarhöfn. The berserkers worked themselves up into a frenzy and did just that.

Afterwards, they were exhausted, and Styr let them bathe in his new bathhouse. While they were in there he closed it up with wet ox hides. The heat became unbearable and the berserkers rushed out, whereupon Styr ran them both through with a spear.

They were buried right where Jóhannes was standing.

There were feuds aplenty in saga times, Jóhannes thought. But from what he had read, and what Magnus the American detective had told him, there were still feuds today. If his calculations were correct, the first death had been in 1934. Followed by 1940. And then 1985. Possibly 1996. And now today, 2010.

He couldn't deny that there was something inside him that was stirred by the feud, that resonated with all those other feuds of saga times that he knew so intimately.

But they were dangerous, those old feuds, where neighbour slew neighbour. Styr himself had been involved in many, and had been killed as a result of one.

Jóhannes had his heroes from the sagas. Egill, the violent, ruthless warrior who slaughtered enemies from Norway to England to Iceland, and yet whose poetry was so beautiful that his captor, King Athelstan of England, set him free when he heard it. Grettir the Strong, who had survived as an outlaw for twenty years with his strength and cunning. Leifur Eiríksson who had sailed to Greenland and then on to Vinland, the grape-bearing shore of North America.

But Jóhannes knew he didn't resemble these men. The saga hero he most admired, the one whom he would most like to have been, was Njáll. Njáll was a lawyer and a peacemaker, who advised his bloodthirsty friends how to win their feuds through the annual parliament at the Althing, or by subterfuge or cunning, rather than simply with the sword or axe.

Njáll would have put a stop to this modern-day feud. Prevent it from festering. He would have figured out a way.

Jóhannes looked across at Bjarnarhöfn, where Hallgrímur Gunnarsson had lost his life only hours before, and where his family were at that very moment mourning him.

There should be no more deaths. Jóhannes knew what Njáll would do.

CHAPTER SEVEN

'HERE, TÓTA, TAKE this out to the policeman,' said Aníta, handing her daughter some of the *hangikjöt* and rye bread. It had somehow seemed right to serve this traditional smoked lamb dish for dinner. It was one of Hallgrímur's favourites. Also, they had a lot of it at the farm and there were plenty of people to feed.

As Tóta grudgingly took the plate outside to the poor policeman who was still guarding the crime scene, Aníta took her seat at the table. It was surrounded by her husband's family – Hallgrímur's family. Sylvía was there, of course, and Ingvar had driven back to Bjarnarhöfn from Stykkishólmur, with his French wife Gabrielle, whom Aníta liked. Plus one other surprise guest.

Villi.

He had arrived unannounced in the middle of the comings and goings outside Hallgrímur's cottage. He had flown in from Canada that day. He said that he had received a ticket from a friend in Toronto whose onward trip to Europe had been ruined by the volcano. He had been shocked to learn that Hallgrímur had been murdered that morning, but his arrival was a welcome distraction.

He was the eldest of the three brothers, probably sixty-four, Aníta would guess. She realized that he actually looked like an older version of Magnus. He had Magnus's broad shoulders and almost his height, but there was also something about the way he held himself, alert, watchful, that recalled his nephew. His hair, which had once been fair, was now a sandy grey.

He had just retired from a career in engineering, which had taken him all over the world from his base in Canada. He had worked for most of that time for mining companies, although he wasn't a mining engineer. His experience as a young man building roads and bridges in Iceland's rugged landscape had served him in good stead in the Yukon and Chile and New Guinea.

Aníta was pleased to see him.

'I didn't see any sign of ash in Reykjavík,' Villi said. His voice was a deep rumble. He still spoke perfect Icelandic, with just a hint of a North American accent. Once again, like Magnus.

'The wind is still blowing from the north,' said Ingvar. 'All the farms to the south of Eyjafjallajökull are covered in it.'

'It will ruin them,' said Kolbeinn. 'Once the fluorine gets into the soil, you have to bring all the livestock inside and keep them there. And just before lambing season too.'

'Did you see Hvolsvöllur on TV?' Krissi said. 'I was watching the news just now. It's pitch black in the middle of the day, just like night-time. And all the fields are covered in ash, and the people and the horses.'

'It must be horrible for the horses,' said Tóta. 'They should have brought them inside. Maybe we should bring ours in, Dad?'

'I hope to God it doesn't come this way,' said Kolbeinn. 'But I'm glad it brought you over here, Villi.'

'Hallgrímur will be pleased to see you, Villi,' Sylvía said. 'I think perhaps he is at choir practice. He'll be back soon.'

There was silence around the table. It was at least a decade since Hallgrímur had sung in the local choir. He had once had a fine baritone voice, but eventually ageing vocal chords had forced him out. It was as if Sylvía, unable to face today, was taking herself back in time.

Villi glanced at the others. Each one of them had tried to explain to Sylvía what had happened to her husband and failed.

'I'm sorry I missed him,' Villi said, swallowing.

There was a knock at the door.

'Hello?' called an unfamiliar voice.

The two dogs, who were lying in their corner of the kitchen, roused themselves and began to bark. Aníta got up and hurried to the front door. Tóta was there with a tall man in his fifties with a shock of thick white hair. Another policeman, perhaps?

'We're just having dinner,' Aníta said. 'Can we answer your questions tomorrow?'

The man frowned and then smiled. 'Oh, I'm not with the police,' he said. 'My name is Jóhannes. Jóhannes Benediktsson. My family came from Hraun, just over the lava field.'

'Oh, I'm sorry. Come in. Would you like some food?'

The phone had been ringing and they had had a couple of visits already from Hallgrímur's old cronies. Perhaps this man was one of them, although Aníta didn't recognize him at all.

Aníta introduced the man to the family around the table. Kolbeinn looked perplexed, but Ingvar seemed to register who the stranger was. 'You're Benedikt Jóhannesson's son, aren't you? The writer?'

'That's right. I apologize for disturbing you, and I won't stay long. I'm on my way back to Reykjavík, but it's very important that I speak to you all first. It's about Hallgrímur's death. His murder.'

There was silence around the table as they all stared at him. Aníta gave the man a seat and he sat down.

'First, let me say how sorry I am. I didn't know Hallgrímur. Indeed, I have never met him. But he was part of your family. And that's why I have to talk to you.'

He looked around the table, checking that he had got all their attention.

'Krissi, can you leave us now?' Aníta asked.

'No, let him stay,' commanded Jóhannes. 'It's important that all generations are here.'

Krissi stayed, eyes wide, eager to hear what the stranger had to say. Aníta didn't mind being contradicted. The stranger had a natural authority, and she wanted to hear him out too. Even the dogs' ears were pricked.

'I've spent some time researching my family,' Jóhannes went on. 'And through those researches I have learned a lot about your family. We have both suffered a number of untimely deaths. This is just the most recent.'

'What do you mean?' asked Villi.

'The first was in 1934,' said Jóhannes. 'At least, I think it was the first. My grandfather, also called Jóhannes, who was the farmer at Hraun, disappeared suddenly one afternoon. No one knew why or where he had gone. Perhaps he fell into the sea. There was a rumour he disappeared to America. But he left his wife without a husband and his children without a father.'

'I remember that,' said Sylvía, her eyes brighter than they had been all day. 'My brothers helped with the search.'

'My father wrote a novel called *Moor and the Man* in 1985, just before he died,' said Jóhannes. 'In it he describes how one farmer murders a neighbour because he has been having an affair with his wife. The affair and then the murder, or at least the disposal of the body, is witnessed by two small boys.'

'Wait a minute,' said Villi. 'Are you suggesting that our grandfather murdered yours?'

'I know that Hallgrímur read *Moor and the Man* and that he was upset by it,' Jóhannes said. 'You must have known that.'

'He hated that book,' said Sylvía. 'Did you write it?' she asked Jóhannes.

'No. It was my father, Benedikt.'

'Oh, I see. No, Hallgrímur didn't like that book at all.'

'That doesn't prove that our grandfather killed anyone, though,' said Kolbeinn.

'No,' said Jóhannes. 'It merely suggests it. Let's go on to 1940. Your grandfather, Hallgrímur's father Gunnar, rode to Ólafsvík for supplies. He had to go by Búland Head, which in those days was traversed by a treacherously narrow path. His horse slipped and he fell into the sea.'

'We know that,' said Kolbeinn. 'We've all heard how our grandfather died.'

'Yes. But you might not have known that my father was also

coming back from a confirmation in Ólafsvík that day. He said he never saw Gunnar. He was an honest man, and so everyone believed him.'

'So?'

'My aunt says that my father was indeed an honest man. Which is why he wrote about what had happened in a short story called "The Slip", once again written just before he died.'

'What happened in "The Slip"?' asked Krissi, who was listening in rapt attention.

'A boy is riding along a cliff edge. He passes a man whom he believes has raped his sister. He pushes man and horse into the sea.'

There was a stunned silence around the room.

'And now you think Gunnar raped your aunt?' said Villi.

'No. This was fiction. What I am suggesting is that your grandfather Gunnar killed my grandfather because he was having an affair with Gunnar's wife. Then my father...' Jóhannes hesitated. He swallowed. 'Sorry. My father pushed Gunnar off the cliff at Búland Head.'

'But you have no proof?' said Ingvar.

'That's right,' said Jóhannes. 'No proof. Now let's move on to 1985.' Suddenly the man's confidence stumbled. He took a drink of water.

'At this point, my father Benedikt knew he had a brain tumour. He thought he had only one year to live. He chose not to tell his family, but he did write the two pieces I have just told you about, the novel and the short story. Your father, Hallgrímur, read them. He didn't like them.'

'He didn't like them at all,' said Sylvía.

Jóhannes flashed the old lady a quick smile. She seemed to be taking it all in.

'But my father didn't die of his brain tumour. One evening, just after Christmas in 1985, Benedikt was murdered in his house in Reykjavík. Stabbed once in the back and twice in the chest by an intruder. I found his body. The police never discovered who did it. I'm sure you heard about it.'

Even Aníta remembered that one. She was in Reykjavík herself at the time, where it was all over the papers, and back home in Stykkishólmur they were talking about nothing else. Benedikt was a local boy, he had made good, they were all proud of him and shocked at his death.

'You don't think our father did that?' said Kolbeinn.

'I don't know,' said Jóhannes. 'Maybe. Maybe not. There's no proof.'

The Hallgrímssons exchanged glances; Aníta could feel the hostility to this stranger building around the table. But she wanted to hear more. The man's sincerity seemed genuine to her.

'In 1996, Hallgrímur's son-in-law, Ragnar, was murdered in America in exactly the same way as my father had been killed,' Jóhannes continued.

'That must be a coincidence,' said Villi.

'I don't know. Perhaps,' said Jóhannes. 'I'm not sure how that fits in, if at all. Do any of you have any ideas?'

His question was met by blank stares around the table.

'Anyway,' Jóhannes went on. 'That brings us on to 2010. Today. This morning, to be precise. When Hallgrímur was murdered. And that's why I'm here.'

'You think there's a connection?' Ingvar asked.

'I think there might be,' Jóhannes said. 'More importantly, some of you might think there might be.'

'What do you mean?' said Ingvar.

'I mean that we may have a family feud here, between my family of Hraun and your family of Bjarnarhöfn. Stretching from 1934 to 2010. I'm a schoolteacher, I've been teaching saga literature all my adult life. I know how dangerous these feuds can be. They can be passed down from generation to generation. And I think this one should stop. Now. Today. And we should all agree on that.'

'Well, I don't believe that there's any connection,' said Villi.

'That's good,' said Jóhannes. 'But I'm pretty sure your father did.'

Kolbeinn was frowning. 'What about you?' he said.

'Following through the logic of what you are saying, it's you who is most likely to have killed Hallgrímur. Or someone from your family.'

'I know. But it wasn't me. I've told the police where I was when Hallgrímur was murdered. I have a brother and a sister, but I haven't discussed any of this with them.'

'Did you tell the police what you've just told us?' asked Villi.

'No, it didn't seem relevant.'

Ingvar snorted. 'Sounds relevant to me.'

'I will tell them if they ask me. I don't intend to hide it,' Jóhannes added.

'Is that why Magnús came up here?' asked Aníta.

Jóhannes turned to her. 'Probably. I discussed all this with Magnús and his brother Ólafur last week in Reykjavík. Magnús is still determined to discover who killed his own father, and he thinks there is a link with my father's death. Perhaps he's right, perhaps he's wrong. I don't know.'

'Do you think Magnús could have killed Dad?' Kolbeinn asked.

'I've no idea. What I'm not trying to do here is the police's job. I don't care about murders in the past. I want to stop any more deaths in the future. And I want you to help me with that.'

'What about Óli?' asked Kolbeinn. 'The police said he called Dad this afternoon.'

'Yes. He was with me,' said Jóhannes. 'So I know he didn't kill Hallgrímur.'

'So you say,' said Kolbeinn.

Jóhannes shrugged. 'I suppose I'm here to declare peace between our two families. Will you accept my offer?'

The Hallgrímssons exchanged glances. Ingvar cleared his throat. 'Jóhannes, I can see you are a romantic at heart,' he said. 'But I think you have let your imagination run away with you. The Icelanders stopped feuding centuries ago. No one here even knew who you were before this evening, let alone wanted to start a feud to the death. Now, will you leave us alone? You are distressing my mother.'

All eyes turned to the old lady, who looked confused and was twisting a piece of bread on her lap. She was almost on the point of tears. 'I'm sure Hallgrímur can explain all this,' she said uncertainly.

Jóhannes frowned, opened his mouth, but thought better of whatever he was going to say.

'Tóta? Can you get *Iceland Idol* from last year on your laptop?' Aníta asked.

'Yes,' said Tóta. 'But I've seen it.'

'I know you like to see them several times,' said Aníta, staring straight at Tóta. The girl was smart; surely she would know what Aníta was asking of her.

Tóta hesitated, about to kick up a fuss, then glanced at her grandmother. 'Sure, Mum. Amma, would you like to come and watch it with me? It's nice to have company.'

'*Iceland Idol*?' Sylvía said. 'Oh, I don't think that's quite my kind of programme at all. But if you want the company.' She slowly followed her granddaughter through to the living room. There was something about that particular show that fascinated the old lady, although she would never admit it to anyone.

Jóhannes stood up to leave. 'All right. I've said my piece. Here, let me write down my number.' He had noticed a list pad on a dresser next to the table, and scribbled his name and number next to a half-formed shopping list. 'But remember: as far as I am concerned, this feud is over.'

CHAPTER EIGHT

THERE WAS A stunned silence after the man had left.

'He's a nutter, right?' said Kolbeinn.

'Not a complete nutter,' said Aníta. 'He seemed pretty sane to me.'

'I can remember your father getting worked up about those two books,' said Gabrielle. She spoke Icelandic perfectly, but with a strong French accent that Aníta rather liked. 'You were in Canada, Villi, but you remember that, don't you, Kolbeinn?'

'I don't know. I didn't always listen to Dad,' he said.

'Your mother remembered them,' said Aníta.

'Who knows what Mum remembers,' said Kolbeinn.

'No.' Aníta stood her ground. 'She wasn't making that up. And I'm sorry to say it, but I can imagine your father carrying on his own little feud.'

There was silence round the table. They knew she was right.

'Well, if there was a feud going on, perhaps this guy Jóhannes is just trying to get the final word,' said Kolbeinn.

'What do you mean?' said Aníta.

'He kills Dad. Then tells us there was a feud but it's all over. So we don't take our revenge.'

'He said he told the police where he was when Hallgrímur was killed,' pointed out Aníta.

'Maybe. We don't know that,' said Kolbeinn.

'You're jumping to conclusions,' Aníta said.

'I'm not saying he did it. I'm just saying we should consider the possibility.'

'So what are you suggesting?' Aníta said. 'You all take revenge on him?'

'If it turns out he is guilty, I know what Dad would do,' Kolbeinn said.

'But that's the whole point!' said Aníta, frustration with her husband boiling over. 'So does Jóhannes. He knows what your father would do. But your father isn't here now. We can make our own decisions.'

'Of course we can make our own decisions,' Kolbeinn snapped.

Aníta struggled to control herself. This was not a fight she wanted to pick with her husband on this night of all nights.

'Aníta's right, Kolbeinn,' said Ingvar. 'And although I still think Jóhannes is imagining things, he's right too. We don't want to start some kind of family war about it. And we should tell the police what Jóhannes told us.'

'Why?' said Kolbeinn. 'Jóhannes didn't.'

'Because the police need to have all the information they can if they are going to figure out who killed Dad.'

Kolbeinn shrugged.

'Do you think Magnús killed Hallgrímur?' Aníta said. 'I scarcely know him, but I do know Hallgrímur hated him. What is he like?'

'I remember him when he was here as a kid,' said Kolbeinn. 'I was still married to Thórunn then. It's true Dad gave him a hard time sometimes. But he took it well. Not like his little brother. Óli had no backbone.'

'Dad gave Magnús more than a hard time,' Ingvar said. 'Remember all those "accidents" he had at the farm? The bruises. The stitches. The broken arm. I didn't look at any of them myself, but at the hospital they were pretty sure they weren't accidents.' He turned to Aníta. 'So, yes, I suspect Magnús bore a grudge against Dad. But whether he did anything about it is up to the police to find out.'

Aníta glanced surreptitiously at the purple burn on Ingvar's face. It was supposedly the result of an accident when he was a boy, the details of which no one would explain.

Kolbeinn began to speak, but Aníta missed what he said. She thought she could hear something behind her. A murmuring. Angry whispers. She turned around, but she couldn't see anything.

She tried to focus on the conversation, which had moved on to the competence or otherwise of the local police. But she felt cold. A charge seemed to run through her body. She was sure there was someone behind her.

She turned again. Quickly. Nothing. She glanced at the dogs. They were both asleep, untroubled.

'What's the matter, Aníta?' Villi asked.

'Oh, nothing,' said Aníta.

'Have you seen something?' asked her husband.

'No, no. There's just a bit of a draught on my neck. It's nothing.' She turned to Villi. 'You should have called before you came. Mind you, given what happened today, I'm not sure it would make any difference.'

Villi coughed. 'I actually came because of Mum,' he said. 'I've had a few conversations with Dad about her. He seemed increasingly worried about her memory. I suggested I could come over to Iceland, but he was adamant I shouldn't. In the end I decided to come anyway without telling him. And I'm glad I did now.'

'So you didn't get given a free ticket then?' said Aníta.

'No.' Villi smiled. 'It was actually really difficult to get a flight.'

'I *thought* you couldn't transfer air tickets like that,' Aníta said. She returned Villi's smile. His warm brown eyes and deep rumbling voice seemed to her at least to reduce some of the tension around the table. 'Does Sibba know you are here?'

Sibba was Villi's daughter who worked in Reykjavík.

'No. It was all a bit of a rush and I didn't want to tell her I was coming and then not make it. I planned to call her when I got here. In fact, I should phone her tonight. Tell her what's happened to her grandfather before she sees it on the news.'

'You can use our phone if you like,' said Aníta.

71

'Thanks,' said Villi. 'But I've got my cell.' He glanced around the table. 'Mum is pretty bad, though, isn't she?'

'She is today,' said Aníta. 'This is by far the worst I've seen her. She's been forgetting things increasingly over the last six months, and it sometimes frustrates her. It really annoyed Hallgrímur. But this is the first time she hasn't realized what's going on around her.'

'A shock can do that with Alzheimer's,' Ingvar said. 'Shift it on a stage. A shock or an accident.'

'So it is Alzheimer's, then?' Aníta asked.

'Probably,' said Ingvar. 'It could be mini strokes, it's difficult to tell the difference. I'm surprised to see her this bad.'

'Isn't there anything you can do for her?' said Villi.

'You know I don't treat my own family,' said Ingvar.

'Why not?' demanded Villi. 'When you can see them falling apart in front of your eyes.'

Ingvar glared at his brother. 'I haven't been here very much over the last few months. And when I have she has seemed no more than forgetful.'

Aníta thought it was ironic that Villi had to fly all the way over from Canada to look after his mother, when he had a brother who was a doctor twenty kilometres away. But Ingvar liked to keep his distance. As he said, he insisted on not treating any of his family. He left that to his colleague Íris at the St Francis's hospital in Stykkishólmur. Aníta thought she could understand why. It would be very hard to maintain the conventional doctor–patient balance when the patient was Hallgrímur. And given what Ingvar had said about Magnus's injuries when he was a boy, maybe he was right to keep his professional distance. Ingvar was usually right.

Ingvar had scarcely visited Bjarnarhöfn at all over the last year or so, although Gabrielle had come riding with Aníta a few times. Aníta guessed that this was on account of Hallgrímur and possibly Sylvía, rather than Kolbeinn or her. She knew that Gabrielle hated her father-in-law. Aníta had asked Ingvar once why he lived in Stykkishólmur, leaving unspoken the point that it clearly wasn't because of his family. He said that it was the most beautiful place in the world. It was true that he loved to potter about the islands of Breidafjördur in his little boat, and Gabrielle was enthused by the desolate beauty of the Icelandic countryside.

'Speaking of Sylvía,' Aníta said, 'I'd better take her over to the cottage to get her things for the night. She can sleep in Tóta's room. You can have the spare room, Villi.'

'We should be going,' Gabrielle said. 'Thanks for supper, Aníta. It must have been difficult to cook for so many of us in these circumstances.'

Aníta smiled at her sister-in-law. Ingvar had met her while he was training in Paris. She was a nurse, and had worked in the hospital in Stykkishólmur, although she only covered there occasionally these days. She professed to love the Icelandic countryside, but she missed France, and she and Ingvar had bought themselves a small apartment in Paris four years before.

'We should go riding next week,' Aníta said. 'Before lambing starts. Give me a call.'

After Ingvar and Gabrielle had left, Aníta fetched Sylvía and they went outside to the cottage. It was a dark night, no stars, and the great fell behind the farm was just a looming shape. A light was on inside the one police car that still remained, parked near the cottage. Aníta noticed Magnus's Range Rover had gone, taken away by the police, presumably. The constable jumped out when he saw Sylvía and Aníta approaching.

'She needs to get her things for tonight,' said Aníta.

'All right,' said the constable. 'But I must be with her while she does it. And she'll have to point out what she wants and I'll get it for her. They haven't finished examining the place.'

The three of them entered the cottage, took off their shoes and then went through to Sylvía and Hallgrímur's bedroom. The bed was made, but the room wasn't quite as neat as Sylvía would have liked it, Aníta thought. The policeman put on gloves as an agitated Sylvía pointed out her nightclothes. She clearly didn't understand why she was doing this, but at least she didn't mention her husband.

'Are you here all night?' Aníta asked the constable as they were leaving. He looked seriously tired.

'No. Just till midnight. We don't really have the manpower to guard the place all night. But if you see or hear anything, call us right away, won't you?'

Aníta took Sylvía back to the farmhouse and got her sorted in Tóta's room. To be fair to her daughter, Tóta had put her recent awkward attitude on hold. Aníta really appreciated that; she must remember to praise Tóta for it. Although with her prickly daughter, Aníta would have to be careful how she did even that.

She went back downstairs to find Villi finishing the washing up. One of the dogs, Mey, was awake and watching him closely, hopeful for some scraps.

'You didn't have to do that,' said Aníta. 'Where's Kolbeinn?'

'Checking the sheep,' said Villi. 'He says a ram got in with the ewes last autumn and there's a chance you might get a few early lambs.'

'That's true,' said Aníta. Although it seemed to her that Kolbeinn was just trying to dodge washing up. She picked up a dishcloth and began to dry.

'At dinner, when Kolbeinn asked you whether you had seen something, what did he mean?' Villi asked.

Aníta glanced at her brother-in-law and could feel herself blushing slightly. 'Oh, nothing. I don't know what he meant.'

'Hmm,' Villi grunted. He looked as if he wanted to pursue the point, but changed the subject. 'You never told me how you managed to live here so long with my father so close,' he said. 'I escaped several thousand miles away, but you lived right next door.'

'It's true, I didn't. 'Aníta considered saying something about not speaking ill of the dead, but she realized it was pointless. Everyone in Hallgrímur's family knew what he was like. Besides which, she trusted Villi, and appreciated the opportunity to be frank. It was good to talk to him.

'It was really hard for the first year of our marriage,' she said. 'You might remember they were in the farmhouse then, and Kolbeinn and I were in the cottage. Hallgrímur used to boss Kolbeinn around, boss both of us around, and it drove me mad. You know how Kolbeinn has always been in awe of his father; well, he kept choosing his father over me, and that was unacceptable.'

'I can see that,' said Villi, placing a serving dish on the drainer for Aníta to dry. 'So how did you put a stop to it?'

Aníta smiled. 'I had a little word. I said, "Unless you leave me and Kolbeinn alone, I will take your son away. And there will be no one left to farm Bjarnarhöfn. If you let me run things the way I want to run them, then we'll stay. Kolbeinn will run the farm, with advice from you, and I will look after you and Sylvía until you both die."'

'I bet he didn't like that,' said Villi.

'Actually, he was OK with it. I think he respected me. And by and large we kept to each other's side of the bargain.' She shrugged. 'He wasn't all bad, you know. He loved playing with the kids; he was besotted with Tóta. I think his bark was worse than his bite. He had bad moods just like everyone else, but if you stood up to him, he was reasonable.'

'He could never resist a beautiful woman,' said Villi.

Aníta glanced sharply at him, and then turned away as she felt herself reddening again. She had to stop this blushing. 'I'm sure that's not it.'

'Oh, yes it is. My father fancied you. It was always obvious to me.'

'Don't be silly,' said Aníta, her eyes fixed on the saucepan in her hands. But she knew it was true. She had taken advantage of that fact to establish her own presence at Bjarnarhöfn. And what was wrong with that?

She wondered whether Kolbeinn had noticed. Probably not. The thought would have shocked her husband so much that he wouldn't have allowed himself even to conceive it.

'It's interesting how the three of you coped with him,' Aníta said. 'You ran away to Canada, Ingvar stayed close, but avoided him, and Kolbeinn couldn't break away. Of them all, I think you managed the healthiest relationship.'

Villi smiled. 'It's ironic that it was easier to keep in touch from thousands of miles away. We had some good visits.'

It was true that when Villi and his Canadian family came over every three or four years for Christmas or in the high summer, the atmosphere at Bjarnarhöfn lifted. And Aníta knew that Villi kept in touch with his parents on the phone.

'Then there was Margrét,' Villi said. 'Dad doted on her and she could never quite get away from him.' He sighed. 'Dad's death has sort of brought her back. At least to me.'

'I know how fond you were of her.'

'Oh, I loved her. And she adored me. She used to tag along after me on the farm when we were kids, watching me. She was in her twenties when I left Iceland. She hadn't started drinking then, although she clearly had a good time down in Reykjavík. Yes, it's terrible what happened to her. It was all Ragnar's fault.'

Ragnar was Margrét's husband. 'The affair?'

'With her best friend. That's what really set her off on the drink. At least that's what Dad always said.'

Aníta turned to put some of the dishes away. She found Villi's presence both comforting and disturbing at the same time.

Kolbeinn came in and took his boots off. 'No sign of any lambs, I'm glad to say. Have you two not finished yet?'

'Leave those to dry,' said Aníta, looking at the remaining pots and pans by the sink. 'Bedtime.'

CHAPTER NINE

VIGDÍS WORKED HARD that afternoon, but at five o'clock she called it a day. Árni and Róbert were coping well, and they were making real progress. Árni was even managing to type with his bad arm. She often had dinner with her mother on Sunday evenings, and she decided to drive straight out to her mother's flat in Keflavík.

Vigdís had been brought up in the town. When the Americans had arrived in Iceland during the Second World War, they had decided to build an airbase at the south-western tip of Iceland, near the fishing port of Keflavík. During the 1950s it had grown into a major base for the US Air Force, from which they could keep an eye on Soviet naval movements into the North Atlantic from the Arctic ports of Archangel and Murmansk. Iceland was an unsinkable aircraft carrier anchored at the perfect strategic location.

Money flowed in, and American soldiers and airmen, and there was plenty of work for the inhabitants of Keflavík. Vigdís's grandfather was a heating engineer, her grandmother managed a laundry facility, and her mother worked in a shop on the base. Where, at the age of twenty, she had met Vigdís's father.

Vigdís knew very little about her father. The mirror told her that he was black. Vigdís's mother was barely one metre fifty, whereas Vigdís herself was one eighty-five, so Vigdís guessed he was tall. But if Vigdís knew little about him, he knew nothing about her. In fact, he didn't even know she existed.

It was unfair, but Vigdís blamed her absent father. For abandoning her and her mother. For being American. And for being black.

It was difficult growing up a black kid in Iceland, especially if you didn't have a really good explanation. People assumed she was American herself. It was usual for an Icelander to greet her in a shop in English, although they usually did that only once. Vigdís's response was to deny her American heritage, to be every centimetre an Icelander. She was one of the few Icelanders her age who didn't speak good English. But she did have one favourite American movie: *White Men Can't Jump*. Vigdís was good at basketball.

Vigdís's mother, Audur, had done her best. She had held down a job at the base and brought up Vigdís. She had encouraged her to work hard at school, and been there for her when she was teased. She called Vigdís her 'blue beauty' – historically Icelanders were so unfamiliar with black people that they had called them 'blue'. Audur's father had coined the phrase, and she liked it, as did the little Vigdís.

Audur had had a couple of wobbles with drink, including a bad period the previous year, but she seemed to have got a grip on it now. She had always had boyfriends. She was an attractive woman: petite, with a small pointed nose, a sharp chin and short blonde hair. Some hung around for years, some came and went. If they were nasty to Vigdís, they went. Even now Audur was fifty-one, they were nosing around; there might even be one there this evening. Vigdís and her mother hadn't had dinner together for a couple of weeks, so Vigdís was a little out of touch.

The weather was brightening over the Reykjanes peninsula as Vigdís headed west towards Keflavík along the main road from the capital to the airport. In about twelve hours' time, she would be driving along this same stretch of road to see Davíd, as long as his flight wasn't screwed up by the volcano. Vigdís had been checking the Internet all afternoon. Although flights to Europe were still disrupted, flights between New York and Reykjavík were operating. Davíd was the brother of a friend of Vigdís who had gone to graduate school in America after university, and had stayed there. She had only met him for the first time the previous summer when he had spent a week with his parents in Keflavík. The moment they met she could tell he was interested in her. And she liked him.

With his work and her work it was difficult to see each other. They were trying, but the truth was they weren't really succeeding, which was why seeing him now was so important. The scheduled weekend in Paris had been a sort of make-or-break thing. And when Vigdís had put off going for a day because of the case, and then been stranded in Iceland by the volcano, it had almost been broken. Vigdís was pleased David had made a further effort; she didn't want to lose him.

She could see the white peak of Snaefellsjökull shimmering just above the horizon, way off to the north. She was struck with a pang of guilt as she thought of Magnus.

Vigdís liked Magnus and sympathized with him. They were equally mixed up, equally confused, just in different ways. She was biologically half-American, but believed herself to be 100 per cent Icelandic. Magnus was genetically 100 per cent Icelandic, but had spent two thirds of his life in America. Both of them didn't quite fit into their own country, and both of them found that fact uncomfortable.

She couldn't believe Magnus really had killed his grandfather, but things must look bad if the Commissioner had gone to the trouble to appoint a detective from outside Reykjavík to look into the murder. Usually it would have been one of the members of the Violent Crimes Unit, probably Inspector Baldur himself, who would have been assigned to help the local police.

Vigdís knew that Magnus had family up there in Snaefellsnes, although he had said very little about them. But a couple of nights ago, he had confided to her that he was having problems with his former girlfriend Ingileif, who had left him the previous autumn to go to Germany, but had shown up back in Reykjavík a few days ago. Things had gone well and then not so well, according to Magnus. Ingileif was probably still in Iceland somewhere. It was unlikely that she would have been able to get back to Germany, given the ash cloud.

Inspector Emil was a smart cop. He would soon realize Magnus was innocent and let him go. In fact, Magnus was probably driving back to Reykjavík at that very moment.

Unless Magnus wasn't innocent. He had quite a temper, and he had witnessed a lot of death in Boston over the years. Murder was perhaps not quite so outlandish to a man who was used to processing homicide victims on a weekly basis. Vigdís knew that there was tension with his Icelandic family, even though she didn't know precisely what it was. He was a very private man. Vigdís thought she knew him, but did she really?

She banished the doubts. She knew that Magnus would do anything for her, and for Árni for that matter, and she would do anything for him.

The airbase appeared on the left, now abandoned by the Americans and used solely as an international airport. She turned off to the right down to the town of Keflavík itself. Her mother's flat was on the first floor of a low white block. Vigdís rang the bell at the entrance to the building.

No reply.

She rang again. There was some disjointed noise and banging over the intercom, then she was buzzed in. She went up the staircase to the first floor. She was expecting to see her mother standing in an open doorway, but the door to her flat was shut.

Vigdís knocked.

The door was opened by someone Vigdís didn't recognize. He was probably in his thirties, with a dark beard and a beer belly sticking out over his jeans. He was holding a can of beer. Vigdís's nostrils immediately sensed alcohol and the sweet smell of marijuana. And male sweat.

Sex.

The man's eyes opened wide. 'Hey! Who have we here?' he said in English. He turned and called over his shoulder. 'Hey,

Audur! A friend has arrived. A gorgeous black friend. My name's Jerzy,' he said. 'What's yours?'

Vigdís's English wasn't very good and she wasn't sure exactly what the man had said, but she didn't like it. 'Where's my mother?' she said in Icelandic, and then pushed past the man. 'Mum?'

Her mother was sitting on the sofa with two bottles of red wine in front of her, one empty and one a quarter full. There was one glass. An empty pizza box lay on the dining table. The butt of a reefer drooped in an ashtray.

'Hey, Vigdís!' her mother said. 'Have a drink with us.' She pulled herself to her feet and tottered over. She stretched upwards towards Vigdís's ear. At least she was fully clothed. 'And don't tell him you are my daughter. He doesn't know how old I am.'

Vigdís scowled.

'Do you want a drink?' the man said in English. 'You speak real good Icelandic.' He placed one hand on Vigdís's arse.

Vigdís brushed it off. 'Mum. We were supposed to be having dinner together.'

'That's OK,' said her mother. 'I can call for more pizza. And don't call me "Mum".' The last in a ridiculous stage whisper.

Vigdís fought to control the tears. She hadn't seen her mother like this for at least a year. 'I've got to go,' she said.

'Oh, stay,' said the guy, this time in Icelandic.

Vigdís turned to him. Forced a smile. 'Hey. Come here,' she said. She took his hand and led him out of the flat into the hallway.

With a look behind him to Audur, the man followed.

He was a strong guy, a barrel chest and biceps showing beneath his T-shirt. But he wasn't ready for Vigdís. Once they were outside, she shut the door to the flat, spun round and pinned him up against the wall. She whipped out her ID.

'I'm Detective Vigdís Audardóttir,' she said. 'Listen, you Polish fuckwit. If I see you anywhere around my mother again, I'll bust you for possession, or having sex with a pensioner, whichever carries the longest stretch. Do you hear me?'

She wasn't sure how much Icelandic the man really understood, but he gulped and nodded.

'Good,' said Vigdís. She let him go and tripped him so he fell to the floor. Her cheeks burning as she ran down the stairs and out to her car.

She sat behind the driving wheel and banged it. 'Fuck! Fuck!' she exclaimed. And the tears rolled.

It was late, but Aníta couldn't sleep. She was lying in the big wooden bed in her bedroom, with Kolbeinn snoring gently beside her. The bedroom had once been Hallgrímur's, and his father's before him. There were some signs of Hallgrímur still in the room: a photograph of him fishing with a young Kolbeinn, and even one of his wedding day with Sylvía, she unrecognizable in the traditional *skautbúningur* – embroidered black jacket and long skirt with a tall white headdress and veil. Hallgrímur had the glare of an awkward bastard even on his wedding day.

Aníta had done her best to make the room hers, mostly by adding her grandmother's things: some framed tapestries, a photograph of her grandmother's own farmhouse thirty kilometres away just beyond Stykkishólmur, a rocking chair and even a small spinning wheel.

Aníta had been only one year old when her grandmother died, but nevertheless Aníta felt she knew her. Felt she knew her well.

She had dug out copies of *Moor and the Man* and the collection of Benedikt Jóhannesson's short stories, of which 'The Slip' was one. She read 'The Slip' first. It was only five pages long, but it conveyed the permanent simmering rage that the teenage boy felt towards his neighbour, and the sudden realization as he was passing the man on the cliff path that revenge was possible. Not just possible, inevitable. Could that neighbour have been Gunnar, who had slept in that very room seventy years before? It seemed to Aníta it could.

She turned to *Moor and the Man*, which was set in Reykjavík during the war, but included flashbacks to a rural childhood somewhere in the countryside. Chapter three was well thumbed; someone in the house had read it many times. And it was as Jóhannes had described: two boys witnessing one of their fathers committing adultery with the other's mother, and then later watching the cuckolded father dumping a heavy sack into a lake.

Aníta closed the book and turned off the light. She lay down beside her husband but couldn't get to sleep. Thoughts of Hallgrímur and Jóhannes and the goings-on at Bjarnarhöfn all those years ago swirled around her head.

And Villi.

Half an hour passed. Or perhaps it was an hour. She thought she could hear voices. She lifted her head from the pillow and listened.

Voices. Coming from downstairs.

Kolbeinn was in bed with her. Which meant it must be Villi. But who else was with him?

She got up and pulled back the curtain to check outside. The thick grey cloud was shredding. An almost full moon peeped through it, scattering pale sparkles on to the fjord. To the north she could see the green aurora slinking over the mountains of the West Fjords. The little church was clearly visible in the moonlight, as was the police tape fluttering at its entrance. They must have moved Hallgrímur's body by now, surely. Aníta shuddered.

It didn't feel like it.

Soon he would be brought back to the little churchyard and laid next to his ancestors, to his father Gunnar and his daughter Margrét. Maybe one day Aníta would join them. She shivered again.

The farmyard was empty, but she could still hear the voices.

Kolbeinn was asleep. She considered waking him, but decided against it. Just in case.

She went out on to the landing and slowly descended the staircase. The door to the kitchen was open. The only light inside came from the moon. She saw the silhouette of a small boy. Smaller than Krissi. Was it Krissi?

The voices were clearer. One of them she recognized.

'Go to bed now, boy. You heard nothing. Do you hear me? Nothing.'

Aníta stood completely still. What should she do? Scream? Grab the boy?

She felt fear. Not so much her own fear as the fear of the small boy. Was it Krissi?

He had moved out of her vision now, but a familiar figure had stepped forward.

Hallgrímur.

His face was illuminated by a flickering orange glow. He seemed to notice her for the first time and glared.

Then he turned towards where the boy had been and hissed, 'To bed, if you know what's good for you.'

'Stop!' Aníta shouted and ran forward into the kitchen. 'Hallgrímur, stop!'

But he wasn't there. Neither was the boy.

'Krissi?' she called out in a loud whisper.

And then she saw the glow. The orange glow.

Fire.

Hallgrímur's cottage was on fire. And outside it, standing only a few metres away, was Sylvía.

'Kolbeinn!' Aníta shrieked. She ran back to the staircase. 'Kolbeinn! The cottage is on fire! Come quick!'

Stopping only to pull on her boots by the door, she ran outside. The glow came from the window facing the farmhouse, which itself was out of sight of her bedroom. It lit up the small figure of Sylvía, her short white hair sticking up, staring, mesmerized.

'Stand back, Sylvía!' Aníta said, grabbing the old woman and pulling her back. The fire was intensifying in front of her eyes. The first signs of smoke curled along the edges of the window.

'Hallgrímur needed his dinner,' Sylvía said. 'He hasn't had his dinner yet.'

Aníta paused just for a second. What the hell was the old woman on about? She didn't have time to figure it out. She ran back to the farmhouse to meet Kolbeinn emerging from the doorway.

'You get the hose!' she shouted. 'I'll call the fire service!'

And she rushed into the house and dialled 112.

CHAPTER TEN

January 2010

THE PLANE BANKED low over the town of Cohasset on its approach to Boston's Logan airport. Magnus stared down at the snow-covered trees; he had read about the major dump the previous week. From the air, New England looked like a massive forest, extending as far as the eye could see; nothing like the neat patchwork of towns that appeared on the map, which in the real world were marked only by the round water towers on their stilts sticking high up above the trees.

So many trees! God, it was good to see them.

Magnus had felt no desire to cross-country ski in Iceland, but the clear blue sky, the glistening snow and all those trees made him want to put on a pair as soon as he landed.

The plane banked again, and lined up towards the runway squatting in Boston Harbor. The city stretched out to the left of the aircraft. The neighbourhoods where he had spent so many years cataloguing the dead bodies, getting to know the victims, figuring out who had killed them and why. A homicide investigation was like a process of reincarnation. First you found a body. Then you found its name. Then he or she became a murder victim. Then she became a person, a real person with a job, a family, hopes, fears, friends, lovers, faults. And enemies. And you began to work for that person, for that person's family. You had to find who had killed her and why.

And when you did find the killer, and the evidence against

him, and you did the paperwork right and he went to court and then to jail, it wasn't over. There was always another body. Another victim to get to know.

This cycle had become Magnus's life the moment he had joined the homicide unit seven years before. He could never get enough of it. And he was good at it – there were very few unsolved cases. If there was no evidence, he would keep looking. If the witnesses wouldn't talk, he would find a way to crack them.

Of course there was one unsolved murder. There was always the one unsolved murder. It might have happened before he joined the department, but it had pursued him throughout his career as a policeman.

Murder in Iceland was different. Magnus had been lucky: he had been involved in a handful of fascinating cases since he had arrived in the country nine months before. But the population was small, barely three hundred thousand people in the whole nation, handguns were banned, and serious crime was rare, at least when compared to a big US city. That was good for Iceland's citizens, but frustrating for Magnus. Three murders a year was not enough; it didn't take long for him to feel like climbing the walls.

That was part of the reason why he had decided to take a couple of vacation days to return to the States. He had been transferred to Reykjavík in a hurry, partly at the request of Iceland's Police Commissioner, but also because he had become a witness in a nasty police corruption case involving a Dominican drug gang. There had been a couple of attempts on his life, and his boss, Deputy Superintendent Williams, had grabbed at the chance to get him safely out of the country.

But the Icelanders had wanted someone for more than just a few months. The National Police Commissioner had made Magnus commit to staying in Iceland for two years, and so Magnus had spent six months at the police college learning the law. Magnus felt he owed the Commissioner, not least because Magnus's presence in Iceland had lured the Dominicans with their guns to Reykjavík, with the result that the Commissioner had nearly lost one of his own officers.

So, nine months down, fifteen to go.

That was one of the reasons for returning to Boston. To put in some face time. Keep up with the department's news. Make sure they hadn't forgotten about him. Headcount was a big issue these days; Magnus wanted to know they were still counting his head.

Magnus was uncertain what he felt about returning to the States. As an adolescent, and then as an adult, he had felt proud of his Icelandic heritage. He had kept up his language skills, read the sagas and returned with his father once a year to go hiking in the wilderness. He had always felt special among the other Americans. Different.

But when he had returned to Iceland, things had not been as easy as he expected. His Icelandic was very good, but not perfect. The people were reserved and he felt like an outsider, if only because he wasn't part of the intricate web of connections of family, school, university and job, which bound all Icelanders together. He found himself withdrawing from the others. He liked his colleagues, especially Vigdís and the hapless Árni, but he didn't socialize with them. For six months there had been Ingileif, but then she had left for a job in Germany.

The plane was on its final approach now, only a few feet above the cold grey sea.

Ingileif. Magnus smiled to himself. He missed Ingileif. Impulsive, unpredictable, insatiable. Gone.

But the real problem was the one there had always been; the unsolved murder. Magnus was twenty when he had been told that his father had been killed, stabbed in the hallway of the house by the shore he was renting for the summer. For a year or so Magnus had thrown himself into his own personal investigation, determined that if the police couldn't find his father's killer, he would. But he hadn't. No matter how many other crimes he solved in the Greater Boston Area, or indeed in Iceland, he hadn't.

But in Iceland he had turned up some interesting new lines of inquiry. Lines that his brother Ollie had insisted that he drop.

The airplane juddered as its wheels hit the tarmac.

That was the other reason for coming to Boston. To get Ollie to change his mind.

It was a Sunday night, so O'Rourke's wasn't too crowded.

'Cheers, Stu,' Magnus said as he raised his glass of Sam Adams.

'Skol!' Detective Stuart Riordan grinned as he raised his own glass. He was a short guy of about Magnus's age, with a neat beard and highly toned muscles. Magnus and he used to work out together in the police gym, but Magnus never quite pushed himself as hard as Stu.

'I'm impressed,' said Magnus. 'But it's actually "Skál".'

'Whatever. How's the beer over there?'

'Not as good as this,' said Magnus. Truthfully, it wasn't just the Sam Adams he missed; it was the couple of beers after a shift. In Iceland they thought you were an alcoholic if you had a beer on a Tuesday, but didn't care if you drank a couple of gallons on a Friday night.

'Meet any hot Eskimo babes?'

'Don't you mean cool Eskimo babes?' Magnus said. Stu liked to talk about babes, even though he was happily and monogamously married to a woman called Donna. Maybe because he was happily and monogamously married to Donna.

'I guess.'

'They don't have Eskimos in Iceland. I've told you that a dozen times, moron. They have Viking babes. They've had three Miss Worlds.'

'OK, so any hot Viking babes?'

Magnus thought of Ingileif. She counted. He smiled.

'Hey,' said Stu. 'Colby's history, then?'

Magnus nodded. Colby was the woman Magnus had gone out with for a couple of years in Boston. Until she had taken offence at being shot at in the North End.

'That's good,' said Stu. 'She was bad for you, man. She was stuck way up her own ass.'

'Yep,' said Magnus. 'She was.' Colby was a lawyer and wanted Magnus to be a lawyer. She didn't think much of Magnus's police buddies, or of his police buddies' wives or girlfriends. 'I think you'd like the Viking. You should come visit some time.'

'All those icebergs? No way. It's cold enough here.'

Magnus didn't push it. Stu had never left the United States, and now he and Donna had a kid they were in the week-at-the-shore vacation routine of their parents. Stu was actually a smart guy: there was nothing he didn't know about the American Civil War, and he and Magnus had talked for hours about the minutiae of American politics while hanging out in cars waiting. But he knew very little about the world outside the United States, nor did he care.

'Hey, Magnus! How the hell are you?'

Magnus looked up to see two more of his former colleagues approaching the table. Artie, a black detective, dapper even on a Sunday night, and Craig, an older guy with a comfortable roll over the waistband of his jeans.

'I'm doing great,' said Magnus. He stood up. There was a lot of hugging and back-slapping. Magnus liked it. He had always felt himself a little aloof from his colleagues in Boston, but the camaraderie and warmth made a pleasant change from Iceland. These guys were genuinely pleased to see him.

It was strange; he felt a different person here, speaking English. Different from the Icelandic cop, speaking Icelandic in Reykjavík. It was as if his personality changed in subtle ways, depending on which language he was using, even though he was just the same guy underneath.

'Hey, I'm sorry to hear about Jason, Stu,' said Artie, with a sympathetic frown.

'Yeah,' said Stu. 'He was engaged, too. Gonna get married in June. I was on the invitation list.'

The bonhomie was gone. 'Jason Hershel?' said Magnus,

remembering a tall young guy with a buzz cut who had joined Homicide a month before Magnus had left for Reykjavík.

'Yeah, that's the guy,' said Stu. 'A good kid.'

'What happened?' asked Magnus.

'You tell him,' Stu said to Craig.

Craig sighed. 'There had been a shooting in the D Street Projects. Turf war. Stu and Jason were just door-to-door canvassing. Jason knocked on the door, the punk let him in, panicked and shot him.'

'He wasn't even a suspect,' said Stu.

'Is he...' Magnus asked.

Stu took a deep breath. 'Yeah. Shot twice in the chest. Died in the ambulance on the way to hospital.'

'Did you get the punk?'

'Shot him as he ran down the stairwell,' said Stu. 'Didn't kill him, unfortunately. The fucker is already out of hospital. One of those times that makes you wish Massachusetts had the death penalty.'

Stu stared at Magnus. It was a discussion they had had on and off over the years. Stu for, Magnus against.

'Yeah,' said Magnus simply.

'What can I get you guys?' A waitress in a Bruins T-shirt hovered.

'Four beers,' Stu said. 'And I think we need some chasers, don't we, guys?'

'Hey, good to see you, Magnus.' Deputy Superintendent Williams leaned back in his chair. 'They finally threw you out of Iceland?'

'Not quite yet,' said Magnus, taking the seat in front of Williams's desk.

'I'm surprised. I got a couple of calls from their Police Commissioner over the last year. Sounded like he couldn't wait for me to take you off of his hands.'

'There were some awkward situations.'

Williams laughed, wrinkles spreading themselves over his worn black face. 'Yeah. There always were awkward situations with you. But he called back later and said he wanted to keep you.'

'I'm signed up for two years,' said Magnus. 'How's Soto?'

'Pedro Soto's still in Cedar Junction, and will be for a long time. The Dominicans up in Lawrence have gone quiet, at least for now. But it turns out Soto has a little brother with big ambitions, so that might change.'

'Figures.' You took one out and two more popped up in their place. That was the problem with the war on drugs. 'They didn't touch Colby, did they?'

'No. She hid out in the woods somewhere for a month. Smart girl. She should be safe now. But you may want to watch your back while you're over here. Soto's kid brother could be into revenge. It's not the same urgency as when they wanted to stop you testifying, but you never know.'

You never knew. Revenge was as powerful a motive on the streets of Boston as it had been in the farms of the Snaefells Peninsula a thousand years ago.

Or perhaps today.

'You want to come back early?' Williams said.

'Is there room for me? I hear things are tight.'

'You're a good detective. We need more like you, so yeah, there's room for you. Do you want me to haul your ass back here?'

Magnus hesitated. It had felt good to walk back into the homicide unit, say hi to his buddies, watch the guys working the phones, listen to the banter. He felt more at home here than he realized.

Yet he had given his word to Snorri. Did that matter much these days?

Yes, it probably did.

'Think about it,' Williams said, watching his confusion. 'How long you in Boston?'

'Just a couple days.'

'Well, give me a call before you head back. Maybe we can work something out.'

As he walked out of the police headquarters into Schroeder Plaza, Magnus's cheeks were bitten by the cold air and kissed by the gentle January sun. The sky was a brilliant winter blue, a blue that you never saw in Iceland. The piles of snow on the sidewalks were just beginning to fray at the edges. Magnus's eyes were dazzled by the sun bouncing off the brilliant white. He should have brought his shades.

There was no getting around it: the weather in Iceland was crap. When he had left Reykjavík, it was raining. And at this time of the morning it would still be dark.

His head was pounding. They had drunk way too much for a Sunday night. Magnus had paced himself, but Stu had knocked back chaser after chaser. Magnus was staying with him and Donna at their little house in Braintree. She had not been impressed when they had shown up at midnight. Magnus had helped Donna put Stu to bed.

'It's just since Jason was shot,' Donna had said. 'He's not normally like this. He blames himself.'

I bet he does, thought Magnus. Good cops blamed themselves when bad things happened. You couldn't help it.

Magnus had slept badly; he knew he would. It wasn't just the drink. He had shot and killed two men in his police career, neither of them innocent, both of them armed. In his waking moments, Magnus wished he had shot them more quickly. But when he was asleep... When he was asleep they died again in agonizing, tedious slow motion.

He knew a little drug store in the Back Bay, near where he and Colby used to live. It was only a mile away. Magnus jumped into his rented car and drove over there, parking right outside. He recognized the clerk, but she didn't recognize him as he bought some Tylenol. Rather than get right back into his car, he thought he'd take a short walk.

He found himself strolling over to his old apartment building. Well, not his, Colby's. A cop could never afford to live in the

Back Bay, but Colby could, with her job as a legal counsel at a successful medical instrument company on Route 128. OK, so it wasn't his, but he had lived there for a year. He stood on the sidewalk, remembering.

There had been good memories.

'Magnus?'

He turned at the familiar voice. There she was, wearing her favourite coat and pulling a small suitcase behind her.

Colby.

'I thought you'd be at work?'

She smiled and laughed. 'Well, that's nice. Wanted to make sure you missed me?'

Magnus winced. 'You weren't real happy with me last time we spoke.'

'You mean after I'd gotten shot at and you wanted to kidnap me and take me to Iceland?'

'Er, yes.'

'And then a psycho broke into this apartment and threatened me?'

'Yes. And that.'

'And I had to take off into the woods in Maine to make sure the psycho and his friends couldn't find me?'

'Well, there's that as well.' As well as the fact Magnus had refused to marry her. For most people, that would come down the list a bit, but nor for Colby.

Colby laughed. 'You're right. I was furious. I'm still furious. But I'm also cold. Shall we grab a coffee at Starbucks? I'll just drop this case in the lobby.'

Magnus noticed she hadn't invited him into her apartment. Their apartment. Her apartment. He was tempted to just say no, to walk away, but she seemed better disposed towards him than he expected. Also, he'd noticed a large sapphire ring on her left hand.

'Sure,' he said.

The Back Bay was crawling with Starbucks, and they went to the closest, just a block away. 'So why aren't you at work?' Magnus asked as they were standing in the line. 'Playing hooky?'

'I was supposed to be flying to Atlanta today, but the meeting just got cancelled, so I thought I'd drop my stuff back home before going back to the office. They won't miss me for an hour or so. How about you? Have you moved back to Boston?'

'Just here for a couple of days. Now I'm one of Reykjavík's finest.'

Colby laughed. 'You must be so proud.'

For a moment Magnus bristled, but Colby's brown eyes were shining.

'I am,' he said. And in some ways that was true.

They took their lattes over to a table. Colby asked him about life in Iceland. To Magnus's surprise, she seemed genuinely interested. He had tried to take her there with him on several occasions, but she had refused, citing the bad weather. But it was clear she had been listening more attentively than he gave her credit for. She was a smart woman.

She was also attractive. He had forgotten how attractive she was, especially when, like now, she was so animated, talking, smiling, teasing.

The coffee was long finished when Magnus pushed his mug to one side. 'I'd better be going. And you have a job to get to.'

'It's been great to see you,' Colby said. 'It would be a shame not to see you again before you go back. Are you around tonight?'

'I was planning to spend that with my brother,' Magnus said. 'And I'm flying back tomorrow evening.'

'Oh. OK,' Colby said, leaving the invitation hanging there.

'What would he think?' Magnus asked.

'Who?'

'The guy who gave you that ring.'

Colby glanced down at her fingers quickly and then put her left hand under the table. 'Oh, that's Richard. Richard Rubinstein. You remember him?'

'Not really,' said Magnus.

'Yeah, well.' Colby sighed. 'I don't think Richard and me is going to work out.'

'I'm sorry,' said Magnus.

'Yeah.' Colby shrugged. Looked down at her coffee. Then glanced quickly up at Magnus through a strand of curly dark hair. 'Do you want to take a look at the apartment? I've got some new curtains from Crate & Barrel. I think you'll like them.'

Magnus smiled. Thought. Then stopped thinking.

'You know me. A sucker for new curtains.'

CHAPTER ELEVEN

Monday, 19 April 2010

IT WAS CHAOS at Keflavík Airport. Vigdís had never seen it so full. The ash cloud was drifting back and forth across Northern Europe, occasionally opening up patches of airspace above Norway and Scotland. France, Germany, England and much of Central Europe was closed. Ironically, Keflavík itself remained open, protected by the prevailing wind pushing the ash to the south. It was a nightmare for the airlines: their schedules were a mess and all their aircraft were in the wrong place. The Icelandic staff were answering questions patiently. This was the kind of crisis Icelanders were good at, thinking on their feet.

Vigdís had checked Davíd's flight on the Internet before setting off to the airport but there had been no information on its status. She joined a small crowd peering at a monitor, and picked out Davíd's flight from New York.

Cancelled.

Vigdís felt her eyes sting. Her phone vibrated in her jeans pocket. A text.

Flight delayed then cancelled. Shall I try again tomorrow? D.

She texted back immediately: *Yes. Please try again. I really want you to come.*

She pushed through the crowds back to her car. She was surprised at how disappointed she was. She liked Davíd, liked him a lot, but they were not that close. They hadn't had the chance to be. That was the problem.

Finally the right guy had come along, and she hadn't been able to see him because of her stupid job and the stupid volcano. She liked her job, but she needed a personal life too. A relationship. Something.

She drove back towards home. She considered dropping in on her mother, making sure she was awake and ready to go to her work in the café. But she couldn't face it. There would be a row. She would feel even worse. Her mother would just have to look after herself.

So, work it was. She picked up her phone and called the station. To her surprise, Árni answered.

'You're in early,' she said. It was not yet eight o'clock.

'There's a lot to do,' said Árni. 'Has Davíd landed?'

'Flight cancelled,' said Vigdís. 'I thought I'd come in and help you out.'

'Hey, I'm sorry,' said Árni. 'I know you were looking forward to seeing him.'

Vigdís considered denying it. She wasn't big on emotion at work, but Árni meant what he said, and she appreciated it.

'Thanks. What's happening with Magnús? They said on the radio a farmer had been murdered in the Stykkishólmur area, but they didn't give any details.'

'They've arrested him,' said Árni.

'I don't believe it!'

'The gossip is they've got a good case.'

'Jesus. There's no way he did it, you know that, Árni?'

'Yeah, I know it. Hey, Vigdís?'

'Yes?'

'Maybe you shouldn't come in. I won't tell Baldur your boyfriend hasn't shown up. Maybe you should do some digging yourself? See if you can help Magnús.'

Vigdís stared out at the open road cutting through the brown rubble of the lava field ahead of her. At least that would take her mind off Davíd. 'Magnús told me pretty explicitly to back off,' she said.

'Of course he did,' said Árni. 'He's a stubborn bastard. But you know what he would do if you or I were in a similar fix?'

'I do.' Vigdís smiled.

'Tell you what. I'll sneak out of here and meet you at Café Roma at nine-thirty. We'll figure out how we can help him.'

It was a cool, moist morning. Aníta walked her mare Grána through the farmyard past the singed cottage. The building looked intact, the roof seemed to have held, although the window frames of the living room and kitchen were blackened. A smell of wet, stale smoke seeped through the damp air.

That was going to be one hell of a mess to clear up.

She waved at the constable, cosy in his police car, sipping the cup of coffee she had brought him earlier.

She touched Grána's flanks and the mare speeded up to a *tölt*, the unique gait, a kind of smooth trot, of the Icelandic horse. Aníta wanted to get out of there, into the open.

She was badly shaken. Hallgrímur's murder. The fire. And then seeing Hallgrímur himself the night before.

Like a lot of Icelanders, Aníta could see things. See people. Dead people. Ghosts.

She wasn't proud of it. In fact, it scared the hell out of her. It hadn't at first. Her grandmother, her mother's mother, had died suddenly when Aníta was one. Apparently her mother had been very ill in the first few months of Aníta's life, and her *amma* had cared for the baby. And after she died, she cared for her grand-daughter still.

When Aníta's parents caught their three-year-old daughter talking to someone invisible, at first they thought she had an imaginary friend. But it soon became clear that the little girl was conversing with her grandmother. They kept this knowledge within the family, and as Aníta grew older, the visits from her grandmother became rarer.

Until one night when Aníta was twelve, her grandmother told her to warn her cousin Sindri not to go out on the fishing boat that day. Sindri was four years older than Aníta, a good-looking and popular boy in Stykkishólmur, and another one of Aníta's *amma*'s grandchildren. So Aníta got up very early the next morning and rode her bike into town, down to the harbour where Sindri was preparing his friend's father's fishing boat to go out for the day. There was a brisk wind, and black clouds lurked on the western horizon, but then there were nearly always dark clouds lurking on the horizon.

Sindri was joking with the men. He was a tall, strapping sixteen-year-old who looked to Aníta more like a man than a boy.

He didn't know about Aníta's gift. What could she say to him? How could he possibly believe she was anything but a silly girl? What if the others went out on the boat, Sindri stayed behind, and nothing happened? She would feel so stupid. Humiliated. There is little a twelve-year-old girl fears more than extreme embarrassment. All the other kids would know, everyone would know. The teasing would unbearable.

Also, although Aníta had no doubts that she was talking to her grandmother, she wasn't sure that the old lady's warning was based on reality. She was a bit of a worrier, Aníta's grandmother, always fretting that she should be careful.

So Aníta turned and pedalled back to her farm.

Sure enough there was a storm. And Sindri was washed overboard.

Aníta told no one of her grandmother's warning, but the old lady was very angry with her. And the guilt was unbearable. She stopped eating, stopped doing her homework, her parents grew worried, but she never explained.

As she grew up, Aníta kept her talent quiet. Every Icelandic town had its 'seers', and Stykkishólmur was no exception. Women who spoke to hidden people, men who could look into the future. Aníta had no intention of becoming one of their number. On the winter of her fourteenth birthday, her friends became obsessed with the Ouija board, but Aníta wanted nothing to do with it, even though they all assured her she would be certain to get through to 'the other side'.

Her grandmother appeared with much less frequency. There had been a couple of warnings, which Aníta now heeded, and a message for Sylvía. Aníta had told Kolbeinn of her skill, and Sylvía when necessary. Both of them had accepted it, and kept the knowledge to themselves.

But last night was the first time Aníta had seen a ghost who was not her grandmother, and she didn't like it. At all. She had no desire to see Hallgrímur ever again.

The horses found it difficult to pick through the lava field, so Aníta rode along the edge of the Berserkjahraun, with the great lump of Bjarnarhöfn Fell rising above her. To her left, the clouds hovered above the tossing sea of lava and moss, frozen in cold anger. A raven hoisted itself into the air, croaking as it did so, soon to be joined by its mate. On the other side of the lava field, the farm of Hraun squatted on top of its knoll, and far in the distance she could see the holy bump in the landscape that was Helgafell.

It was good to be out in the fresh air. There was plenty to worry about when she got back to the farm, Sylvía top of the list. Aníta had left her preparing to go out to see to the chickens, which was Sylvía's normal early-morning routine. Sylvía was still remarkably strong for her age, unlike her husband whose energy had declined over the last few months. Perhaps Aníta had made a mistake? Perhaps Sylvía would set alight the chicken shed, or rather the chicken shipping-container. The metal wouldn't burn, but the straw would. Or even worse, she might return to the farmhouse and set fire to the kitchen. But Kolbeinn was out in the farmyard; he would notice if something went wrong.

No, Aníta shouldn't have left her mother-in-law alone. Sylvía was going to be a problem.

Aníta noticed a figure ahead hunched on a stone a few metres in to the lava field. It was a woman, with her back to her. She was wearing a long skirt, and a headscarf. She was dressed like an old lady, but she didn't look old.

Grána drew nearer.

'Hello?' Aníta called.

The woman turned. She had long plaited blonde hair, like Aníta. But she was quite a bit younger, probably in her mid-thirties, with clear features. She looked familiar to Aníta, but at first

Aníta couldn't place her. Tears streamed down the woman's cheeks.

'What's wrong?' Aníta said, nudging Grána towards the edge of the lava field. The mare didn't want to move.

'It's Jóhannes. He killed Jóhannes.'

'Jóhannes?' Aníta said. 'Who is Jóhannes?' But of course she knew.

'Jóhannes from Hraun.' The woman waved an arm vaguely in the direction of the farm on the other side of the Berserkjahraun.

Aníta recognized the woman. She had seen her face staring out of photographs in Hallgrímur's cottage. It was Marta: Hallgrímur's mother, Gunnar's wife, her husband's grandmother.

Aníta's first instinct was to turn Grána around and bolt for home, but the woman didn't look threatening. She just looked broken-hearted.

'Who killed Jóhannes, Marta?' Aníta asked.

The woman didn't seem to be surprised that Aníta knew who she was.

'My husband,' she said. 'Gunnar. And I have to pretend that I don't know what happened to him. All the neighbours go looking for him up in the mountains, when all the time he is at the bottom of Swine Lake! I know that and Gunnar knows that. But he still goes out with them.'

'I'm sorry,' said Aníta. And it was true, she felt a burst of sympathy for this woman sitting a few metres away from her. A woman who had been dead for forty years. Aníta looked across the lava field to the farm of Hraun, standing proud on its knoll.

'I come here to think about Jóhannes,' the woman said. 'To get away from that monster at home.'

Grána had had enough. She pinned back her ears and reared. Aníta kept her balance and fought to bring the mare back under control. The horse wheeled around a couple of times before Aníta calmed her down.

When she looked back into the lava field, Marta was gone.

*

Emil surveyed the police officers sitting around the table in the conference room in Stykkishólmur police station, which had been turned into an incident room. Someone had placed a large whiteboard along the wall opposite the door. It was empty; no one had had the time to write on it.

It was eight o'clock and none of the officers had got much sleep after the goings-on at Bjarnarhöfn. There was Rúnar, Páll and three more of the local police constables. Then the two detectives who had arrived the evening before to reinforce Emil: from Keflavík a small man in his twenties with prematurely thinning fair hair named Adam, and Björn from Akureyri, who was pleasingly chubby, at least to Emil's eyes. With Reykjavík out of bounds as a source of detective manpower, there were precious few other places to go for help.

Then there was Edda, the head of the forensics unit. At least Emil had been allowed to use them, even though they were based in Reykjavík. She was a head taller than him, with long legs, short blonde hair and an air of calm competence. Emil had worked with her on one of her first major cases, when she had spotted some fibres on a fence in the garden of a house in Akranes whose owner had been brutally assaulted by a burglar. It had led to a conviction that otherwise would probably never have been made. She was gorgeous then. And she was gorgeous now, even though she looked as tired as the rest of them.

Emil's stomach rumbled. The hotel in Stykkishólmur had been overwhelmed with the sudden influx of policemen and forensics technicians, and hadn't been able to come up with much of a breakfast that early in the morning.

'Let's start with the fire,' Emil said. 'How badly burned is the property?'

'The structure is still standing,' said Rúnar. 'The inside is badly burned, especially the kitchen and the living room. The desk has gone, as well as the computer. Plenty for forensics to work on,' he said to Edda.

'It's pretty clear that the old woman started it,' said Emil. 'She seemed to think that she was cooking supper for her husband.

She still doesn't understand, or refuses to understand, that he has been murdered.'

'Did she say how exactly the fire started?' Edda asked.

'No. I asked her, but I didn't get an answer that made any sense. We're relying on you to answer that question.'

'We'll work on it as soon as we get up to the farm this morning,' said Edda.

'Is it Alzheimer's?' Rúnar asked.

'Probably,' Emil replied. 'I spoke to Aníta, who said that Sylvía had been displaying signs of memory loss over the last few months, but nothing this bad. She has deteriorated rapidly since yesterday. I assume it was the shock of her husband's death.'

Emil remembered his own father, who had died only the previous year in the advanced stages of Alzheimer's. At first, the old man, a widower, had done his best to hide his condition from his children. But as his memory loss had become more obvious, he had become increasingly angry and impatient with anyone trying to help him. Against Emil's wishes, he had insisted on going out fishing in his boat by himself. One evening he had fallen in and spent half an hour in Faxaflói Bay clinging to his boat before a fellow fisherman found him, near death from the cold. The shock had definitely accelerated his decline.

The memory brought back for Emil the familiar feelings of guilt, anger and powerlessness. It would have been difficult, but Emil should have done more for his father. He hoped he wouldn't live long enough to suffer from Alzheimer's himself. Then he thought of his last consultation with his doctor: little risk of that, apparently.

'Can Aníta look after her?' Rúnar asked.

'I don't know,' Emil replied. 'I don't think she should be staying at the farm, at least for the next few days.'

'Páll, get on to Hanna at social services,' Rúnar commanded. 'And see if Dr Ingvar can help.'

Páll nodded.

That really is a very fine moustache, thought Emil. 'Do we have anyone at the farm now?'

'Yes,' said Rúnar. 'There's been a constable up there all night. Or at least since the fire.'

Emil let the silence linger to the point where it became awkward. Technically Rúnar outranked him, but he knew and Emil knew that the chief superintendent had screwed up. The crime scene must always be guarded until it was released, even in rural areas where there were no spare resources to do it. There was a reason for the procedure.

Emil waited until he saw two pink spots of shame emerge on Rúnar's cheeks and then moved on. 'OK, let's turn to the murder investigation. I interviewed Magnús yesterday afternoon, as well as his brother.'

Emil spent a few minutes recounting the results of the interview.

'So Magnús is definitely our top suspect?' Adam, the detective from Keflavík, asked.

'Definitely,' Emil replied. 'But we should keep an open mind. Let's go through the family.'

They ran through them one by one. Kolbeinn had dropped his son at basketball practice. Sylvía had been seen in the church at Stykkishólmur, where she had arrived at the ten-thirty service a little late. Ingvar had said that he was tinkering with his boat in Stykkishólmur harbour – that had still to be checked, but it should be easy to find witnesses. No one had seen Aníta on her horse, nor had anyone seen the daughter Tóta, who claimed, quite plausibly, that she was lying in bed on a Sunday morning.

In theory the neighbouring farm at Hraun had a clear view of the approach to Bjarnarhöfn over the lava field, and the farmer had been out on the home field checking his own fences before the lambing season. But the weather was so bad that he hadn't been able to see anything. He couldn't remember hearing Magnus's car approach, or any other, and there was no chance that he could have seen as far as Cumberland Bay on the far side of the farm where Aníta claimed to have ridden.

'OK, what about forensics, Edda?'

'The crime scene is a joke. Blood has been trampled everywhere. There was a horse hanging around for twenty minutes. Magnús's fingerprints are on everything, except those surfaces that have been wiped down.'

'Wiped down?'

'Looks like it to me,' said Edda. 'Unless the place was thoroughly cleaned very recently. There was a broom just outside the church with a set of Magnús's prints on it and no one else's.'

'You mean Magnús swept the church?' Adam asked.

'No, that's not what she means,' said Emil, stroking one of his chins. 'She means Magnús wiped the handle clean.'

'A broom handle like that should be covered with the prints of whoever usually uses it,' said Edda. 'Presumably Sylvía, or perhaps Aníta. They should still be there under Magnús's own prints. If they are not it means that someone wiped the broom handle down before Magnús touched it. Not necessarily Magnús. That's up to you guys to decide.'

'But he is an obvious possibility,' said Emil.

'The footprints are Magnús's, and he has blood on his shoes. Also some blood on the cuff of his shirt. We assume that's Hallgrímur's, but we will check it, obviously. We'll check his clothes more thoroughly in the lab back in Reykjavík.'

'Did you find anything in the church?'

'Some white hair, which is probably Hallgrímur's, but we will need to check. It could be Sylvía's. And this.' She held up a small round silver earring. 'The design is a flower. We need to find its twin.'

'I'll ask Sylvía and Aníta,' said Emil. 'The body has been taken to the morgue in Reykjavík. They'll do an autopsy today. Our best guess at the moment is that Hallgrímur's head was pounded into the floor by someone holding his hair. Which suggests anger rather than premeditation. A blunt instrument is a possibility, but we'll know more once we have heard back from the autopsy.'

'Could the broom have been the murder weapon?' asked Adam.

'I doubt it very much,' said Edda. 'It wouldn't have left those wounds. And there would probably have been some signs of blood, even if it had been wiped down. We'll take it down to the lab to be sure.'

'I think Edda's right,' said Emil.

'We started work on the cottage, but only in the kitchen,' said Edda.

'Magnús claimed he was washing blood off his hands and then took a drink from a mug. Aníta claimed she saw him washing it up.'

'No sign of blood,' Edda said. 'But the mug had been washed up and there were Magnús's prints on it.'

'It wasn't lost in the fire, was it?'

'Of course not,' said Edda. 'It's safe in our van.'

'Good. Can you check for Magnús's DNA around the rim?'

'To see whether he drank from it? Yes. It will take a while to get the results. Especially with the volcano doing its stuff.'

DNA needed to be flown to a lab in Sweden for analysis. Turnaround was frustratingly slow at the best of times. With the airspace full of ash, who knew when they would get the sample there, let alone receive it back?

'It might be useful for the trial.'

'You're pretty sure Magnús was lying about the mug?' Rúnar asked.

'I'm pretty sure Magnús is lying about a lot of things,' said Emil. 'I've arranged a hearing with the judge in Borgarnes this morning, and then we'll send him down to Litla-Hraun.'

Litla-Hraun, meaning 'Little Lava Field', was Iceland's only major prison, and it was where suspects on remand were held. It was on the south coast of the country, about a three-hour drive away on the other side of Reykjavík, which was going to be inconvenient.

'But, as I said, we need to keep an open mind. And I wouldn't be surprised if Magnús's brother Ollie is also involved in this somehow. Do you two speak English?' Emil asked his new assistants.

'I do,' said Adam confidently.

Björn shrugged, not wanting to admit to poor language skills.

'Good, because he seems to have forgotten all his Icelandic, and we may want to interview him again later. I'll go back to Bjarnarhöfn after the hearing with you, Adam. Then I'll head down to Reykjavík. I'd like to be present at the autopsy. And I need to find out more about Magnús.'

'What about the press?' said Rúnar. 'There's a guy from *Morgunbladid* downstairs. And RÚV have just arrived.'

Emil sighed. There was no way of avoiding the press interest; a murder was a big deal.

'Will you talk to them? But keep them away from the farm.'

He turned to the two detectives. 'Adam and Björn, double-check everyone's alibis. Look for any other witnesses. Björn, check the cameras on the Hvalfjördur tunnel.' Any car driving up from Reykjavík would be bound to go through the tunnel under the deep Whale Fjord, which had a toll at its northern entrance, with cameras. 'Look out for Magnús's Range Rover, and also Jóhannes Benediktsson's car.' He turned to the blank board behind him, staring at him with white insolence. 'And someone write something on that.'

As they broke up, Edda approached Emil and touched his sleeve.

'Do you know Magnús?' she asked him.

'No. I've never worked with him before.'

'Well, I have,' Edda said. 'Just last week I was up at a crime scene with him on Eyjafjallajökull. He seems like a good guy to me and I find it hard to believe that he's a serious suspect for this. But if he is, you should know that he is smart. Very smart.'

CHAPTER TWELVE

January 2010

MAGNUS OPENED HIS eyes.

Colby was lying next to him. Smiling. 'You were asleep.'

'Was I? For how long?'

'Only ten minutes or so.'

'Jet lag. Plus I went out last night with Stu and the boys.'

'Huh.' She raised herself up onto her elbows, leaned over and kissed his lips. Her breast brushed his arm. 'You think I'm a manipulative bitch, don't you?'

'No, I don't,' Magnus protested.

'Yes, you do,' said Colby. 'But you know why I went to bed with you?'

'Er...'

'It wasn't to get you to leave Iceland and come back to Boston. It wasn't because I want to start something again.'

'No?'

'No.' She grinned. 'It's because I wanted a really good fuck.'

'Really?'

'Yeah, really. And you know what?'

'What?' said Magnus.

'Now I want another one.'

An hour later, Magnus was heading south on Route 3. He was grinning. He couldn't help it. He remembered why he liked Colby.

She was right; he *had* thought her manipulative. When they were living together it was clear that she wanted to change him, get him to quit the police and become a lawyer, then earn a lot of money. She had wanted to marry him; he didn't want to be the man she would have insisted he become, so their relationship had broken up.

That, and the gangsters trying to kill her.

Magnus had to admit she had been pretty forgiving about that. He smiled again.

In Iceland he had met Ingileif and she had seemed to be everything that Colby wasn't. She didn't care what he did for a living, she didn't seem to take herself or him very seriously, and she was fun to be with. In fact, she teased him about what she called his rigid American views on what a relationship should be.

But that meant that when she had been offered a good opportunity in a gallery in Hamburg, he couldn't really stop her. Even though he wanted to.

While he had been growing up in America, Magnus was sure that Iceland, the country of his birth, was his spiritual home. And there was a lot he loved about the place. But was it really home? Was he really an Icelander? People like Baldur could never accept him as such. Whereas here he had friends, a lover. And the familiar day-to-day rhythm of homicide investigations.

But exactly how healthy was it to need *that*?

The snow was piled thick on the sides of the highway. The outskirts of Boston gave way to white trees with occasional glimpses of marsh. He was heading to the town of Duxbury, just a few miles north of Plymouth, and the place where his father had been murdered.

His father had been a mathematics professor at the Massachusetts Institute of Technology. The family – Ragnar, Magnus, Ollie and Ragnar's newish second wife Kathleen – lived in a small house in Cambridge, but for two summers, 1995 and 1996, Ragnar had rented a property in Duxbury from a colleague at MIT.

Magnus turned off the highway and along a winding tree-lined road towards town. Duxbury had been a prosperous shipbuilding centre two hundred years before, but then the bay had silted up and industry had left, leaving only the clapboard houses of the wealthy ship owners. Since then, not much had changed. The town was a network of small roads passing beautiful wooden houses and white churches, with occasional views of the marshes or the bay. It was the sort of place that would be called sleepy, yet even in winter there were runners and cyclists on the roads. An active bunch, the citizens of Duxbury.

Magnus drove past the harbour and the small group of stores bunched around a flagpole that constituted the centre of town, out on to Standish Point. This was a promontory in Duxbury Bay named after Captain Myles Standish, the leader of the Mayflower colony at Plymouth, who had built himself a house there. There were some fine large houses, but the property belonging to Ragnar's colleague was small and simple, clad in weathered grey wooden shingles, built sometime in the 1920s. It perched on the edge of the bay, facing out to Clark's Island – where the Mayflower had first made landfall – and the inland edge of the seven-mile spit of sand that was Duxbury Beach.

Magnus parked opposite the house. The air was crisp, but still. The sun shone brightly off the snow and the blue bay. An old Volvo stood guard outside the house; Magnus had no idea if the place was still owned by the MIT professor or his family.

Magnus himself had been in Providence at the time of his father's death, waiting tables. Ollie had been at the beach with his girlfriend. Kathleen had been… Well, Kathleen had been busy elsewhere. And Ragnar had been in the living room with a view over the bay, working on his math.

That's why they were there, really, so that Ragnar would have time to think. His subject was Riemann surfaces, an esoteric branch of topology, and he liked to link up with a couple of collaborators around the world. He had fixed up a modem so that he could exchange ideas with a British and a Canadian mathematician. Afternoons were his mathematics time.

Someone had come and knocked on the front door. Ragnar had let the person in. This didn't necessarily mean Ragnar knew him or her; in a small town it would be natural to let in a friendly-looking stranger with a plausible story. Ragnar had turned his back on his visitor, who promptly stabbed him.

No one had seen the murderer. Magnus looked up and down the small lane that led down to the water. It was hidden by trees and bushes that would have been even thicker in summer. He doubted whether he himself could be seen by anyone at that moment.

A neighbour *had* seen a man with a beard, whom Magnus had eventually tracked down, but this had turned out to be a bird watcher from Worcester, a small city to the west of Boston.

Magnus looked around. Had he missed anything? Had Sergeant Fearon, the detective who had led the investigation all those years ago, missed anything? Even now, with his years of experience, Magnus couldn't figure out what that might be.

Apart from one small piece of evidence. Which was why he had made an appointment to see former Sergeant Detective Jim Fearon.

The ex-policeman was sitting waiting for Magnus in the bakery just by the town's small harbour. He was in his early sixties with a grey moustache, a belly peeking out over his pants and kind blue eyes that didn't miss a thing.

'Hey, Magnus, how are yah?' He shook Magnus's hand.

'I'm doing great, Jim. Thanks for seeing me.'

'No problem. Anything Pattie can do to get me out the house.'

Magnus smiled. 'So how long have you been retired now, Jim?'

'Nearly five years. She still hasn't gotten used to it. I make myself scarce during the day. I've got a boat down here that I tinker with in the summer. Do some fishing.'

'Sounds like a good life.'

'Ah, the winter drags a bit, you know?'

They went up to the counter. Fearon ordered a complicated pastrami sandwich and Magnus splurged and ordered a lobster roll. They had lobsters in Iceland, just not as many as in New England. Another thing he missed.

Fearon took a bite of his sandwich. 'So you said you are only around for a couple of days? You moved out of the area?'

'Iceland,' Magnus said. 'I'm attached to the Reykjavík Metropolitan Police.'

'Gee. That must be different.'

'It certainly is. And it's been good to go back to where my family originally came from.'

'That's all I know about Iceland,' said Fearon. 'Your family.'

'You sound like you regret it,' Magnus said.

'Hey. We didn't solve the case. You're a cop now; you know what that's like.'

'I also know you tried pretty damn hard.'

Fearon smiled. 'With some serious prompting from you.'

'Sorry about that.' Magnus winced. 'In retrospect you were incredibly patient putting up with me. I must have been a pain in the ass.'

'You were. You acted like you were taking what happened to your dad well, but I could see it was real tough on you.' He wiped his lips with his napkin. 'My guess is you haven't quit being a pain in the ass, am I right?'

Magnus nodded. 'That's why I'm here. You see, while I was in Iceland I discovered a link between my father's murder and another one ten years before.' Magnus explained about the stabbing of Benedikt Jóhannesson.

Fearon listened closely. 'That must just be a coincidence, surely? I agree it's the same MO, but we're talking thousands of miles in distance.'

'True. But Benedikt grew up on the neighbouring farm to my grandfather Hallgrímur. Who, by the way, hated my dad.'

'Hmm.' Fearon considered this for a moment. 'It still could be a coincidence, but I see your point.' He frowned. 'But no one saw any Icelanders around here. And, as you well know, we've tried just about every avenue. There are no loose ends.'

Magnus took a deep breath. 'What about the DNA? On that strand of hair?'

'They analysed it to death, you know that. They couldn't get a complete sequence. No matches. All we know is its colour: blond.'

'Yes. You can only get the mother's mitochondrial DNA from hair, unless you've got a root. That made it hard to get a match, especially back in the nineties.'

'If you say so,' said Fearon.

'But if two people are related on the mother's side, you should be able to figure that out from the hair sample.'

Fearon frowned.

Magnus took out a pair of latex gloves and put them on. The middle-aged couple at the next table stared. Then he took out a sample envelope from his jacket pocket. His name was already written on it.

'Hey, Magnus, what are you doing?'

Magnus didn't answer. From another pocket he took out an envelope, opened it and extracted a cotton swab. He opened his mouth and wiped around the inside of his cheek. He popped the swab in the sample envelope and put it on the table between them.

Both men, and the couple at the neighbouring table, stared at the sample.

'Do they still have the hair?' Magnus asked.

'They should in theory. But you know what police files are like. It's thirteen years ago.'

'Can you take a look?'

'I told you, I'm retired,' said Fearon.

'And you never talk to your old buddies at the station?'

Fearon smiled. 'If we do have the hair, you want it reanalysed?'

Magnus nodded. 'See if the hair belonged to someone related to me on my mother's side. I think they can do that.'

Jim Fearon thought. 'I guess they can try,' he said. He came to a decision. 'OK. I'll see what I can do.' He grinned. 'You are still a pain in the ass, you know that?'

'I know it,' Magnus agreed. He shook his head. 'I'm sorry about all that grief I gave you about Kathleen.'

Fearon sighed. 'You were right, she wasn't telling you the truth. You just weren't right about why.'

The twenty-year-old Magnus had been perplexed as to why, after an initial flurry, the police seemed to have pulled back from investigating his stepmother. He knew that things were going badly between her and his father, and he didn't trust her an inch. What Fearon had discovered, and what he didn't tell Magnus for several weeks, was that at the moment Ragnar was murdered, Kathleen was in bed with an air-conditioning engineer from Pembroke, a neighbouring town. They had met the previous week when he had come round at her insistence to install a unit in the unconditioned house.

'You know I haven't seen her at all since then?'

'Probably a good thing,' said Fearon.

The ex-detective hesitated and then returned to his sandwich. Magnus picked up the hesitation. 'What is it?'

Fearon glanced at Magnus and carried on munching.

'Come on, Jim. Don't hold out on me now. After all these years, tell me, whatever it is.'

Fearon leaned back and nodded to himself. 'All right,' he said. 'Do you still see your brother?'

'Yeah,' said Magnus. 'In fact, I'm planning on seeing him tonight.'

'Oh.'

'Jim? Tell me.'

'You're right; there was a lot of tension between your father and stepmother. You probably noticed that it got worse a couple of weeks before he died.'

'I told you that at the time.'

'You did,' said Fearon. 'What you don't know is why it got worse.'

'I assumed she was having an affair. The air-con guy.'

'Not him. Your dad never found out about him.' Fearon paused and looked straight at Magnus. 'She'd slept with your brother.'

'What!' Magnus was stunned. 'He was only eighteen! She didn't even like him.'

'That was old enough for her. And turned out she did like him after all. High school had just finished. He had been drinking. He came home, your father was at work, she gave him another drink, she had a couple herself, and one thing led to another.'

'How many times?'

'They said three. I believe them.'

'And did Dad know?'

'Yes. She hadn't tried very hard to hide it. My guess is she let him find out. She wanted to hurt him. Anyway, she admitted it to him.'

'I can't believe it. Why would Ollie do something so stupid? With her, of all people?'

But he knew why Ollie would do it. He was vain at eighteen, and the idea of seducing an older woman would have appealed. Kathleen was about thirty-seven at that stage, and still attractive. Red hair, full body. But, Jesus Christ!

'Why didn't you tell me this then?'

'Kathleen and your brother begged me not to. They thought you wouldn't understand, that it would upset you. It wasn't relevant to the investigation; both Ollie and Kathleen's alibis were rock solid.'

'You thought I wouldn't understand?'

'Actually, I thought you would understand perfectly well. But I did think it would upset you. It seemed to me you and your brother needed each other. You know how it is in murder investigations.' Fearon caught Magnus's eye. 'The dirty secrets come out. A lot of the time you gotta confront the victim's family with all that filth. But if you don't have to do it, you don't. At least, I don't.'

Magnus did know what he meant. Everyone has a secret, and when a person is murdered, that secret comes out. Some of his colleagues enjoyed getting it all out into the open, shaking the tree to see what fell out. Magnus didn't. Often he had had to tell relatives brutal truths. So he understood why Fearon had dodged that task if he could.

'I missed all that,' Magnus said. 'I stayed up in Providence that summer after college ended, working in a restaurant. I had a girlfriend who was working in the city on some youth project and I wanted to spend the summer with her. But I remember coming over to Duxbury the weekend before, and there was a lot of tension in the house. They were all on best behaviour, but I could tell it was for my benefit. And I do remember my father being angry with Ollie, but he was often angry with Ollie at that stage. Ollie had gotten himself into trouble over drugs, I think. He had been very lucky not to be expelled from high school.'

'Yeah, I recall something about that,' said Fearon. 'But I think what really pissed your dad off was that his son was banging his wife. Can't really blame him.'

'Oh, Ollie.' Magnus shook his head. He had done his best his whole life to look after his kid brother, but Ollie always seemed to find new ways of screwing up.

CHAPTER THIRTEEN

Monday, 19 April 2010

THE SPOT WOULDN'T come out of the kitchen floor tile no matter how hard Aníta scrubbed. She had no idea what it was and she didn't care; she just scrubbed harder. It was good to be on her hands and knees *doing* something.

She was scared, as had been Grána. They had cantered back to the farmhouse from the lava field and Aníta had hurriedly unsaddled the mare and let her into the paddock with the other horses. Kolbeinn and Villi were working on one of the fences of what would become the lambs' meadow. Sylvía had come in from the chickens and was looking lost, so Aníta had put her in front of *Shrek* with Tóta, who thankfully hadn't complained that she was too old to see the film again. She knew things with Sylvía were serious and she was prepared to do her bit.

As Aníta scrubbed, she remembered Jóhannes's visit of the evening before and his claim that Hallgrímur's father Gunnar had killed his grandfather, also called Jóhannes. That was clearly whom the woman Marta had been talking about.

Perhaps it wasn't Marta. Perhaps Aníta had dreamed it all, prompted by Jóhannes's story? And perhaps Aníta had just dreamed about Hallgrímur? Dreams were supposed to be like that, weren't they? Rehashing and reordering in your sleeping brain the events of the previous day.

But you couldn't dream something in the middle of the day on a horse. A horse that had bolted at the same thing.

What scared Aníta most was that having seen two ghosts in less than twenty-four hours, she would soon see another. She really didn't want to see Hallgrímur again.

What she wanted was for her grandmother to appear. Tell Hallgrímur to leave her granddaughter alone. Give Aníta a bit of comfort.

She had told Kolbeinn about Hallgrímur's visit the night before when they had finally got to bed in the small hours of the morning, after the policemen and firemen had left. He had listened closely, accepting what she said, and then he held her tight until they both went to sleep. That was the thing about Kolbeinn. He was big, reliable, he loved her, he never doubted her and he was always there.

She heard barking outside. Someone was coming. Aníta allowed herself a brief smile. Wouldn't it be wonderful if her grandmother walked in?

'Hello!'

It wasn't her *amma*. It was Gabrielle.

Aníta's heart sank. She liked Gabrielle, but she wasn't sure she was up to the serious gossip session that Gabrielle would want to embark upon.

'Oh, leave that,' the Frenchwoman said as she saw Aníta on her hands and knees. 'That can wait.'

'It's just good to be doing something,' said Aníta, getting to her feet. 'Let me put this away and then I'll make us some coffee.'

'I wondered how you were coping,' Gabrielle said. 'I heard about the fire. And I saw the cottage just now. It's crawling with people wearing those funny plastic bags. Don't they know Sylvía started it?'

Aníta put away the scrubbing brush and bucket and made coffee while Gabrielle nattered on in her strong French accent. Actually, it was nice to have her there. Aníta didn't have to think too hard about what she was saying, or how she replied. She was sure Gabrielle's concern was genuine, but it was clear that her sister-in-law was excited by the drama.

'Can I have another one?' Gabrielle said, reaching for the plate Aníta had put out. 'They are delicious.'

Gabrielle was excited by the cakes too.

She had olive skin, big brown eyes and thick dark hair cut short. She wore a pretty green scarf around her neck. She was several years older than Aníta, but Aníta was jealous of the way she always managed to wear the simplest items with a hint of sophistication, even on a farm in the middle of nowhere.

'How's Sylvía?' Gabrielle asked.

'She's watching a DVD with Tóta now. But I'm worried about her. She seems really confused. She knows her house has burned down and she seems to know she did it, but she won't say how, and she doesn't seem to understand that Hallgrímur has died, let alone been murdered. I was hoping Ingvar would come over and look at her.'

'He's got a clinic this morning,' Gabrielle said. 'I know Villi called him earlier this morning and they were talking about getting her to see a specialist in Reykjavík. Ingvar is surprised she has deteriorated so fast.'

'But he's hardly spoken to her!' said Aníta. 'How could he know how bad she was before?'

'He said he'd come over later.'

'I hope so,' said Aníta. 'I mean, I know he's wary about treating his own family, but his mother really needs his help.'

Gabrielle nodded. 'He understands that now. Villi told him so this morning. Anyway, how are you? I thought you were bearing up well last night at dinner, but you don't look so good this morning.'

'I don't feel it,' said Aníta.

Gabrielle reached over and took Aníta's hand. Her fingers were surprisingly cold, but Aníta appreciated the gesture.

'When this is over, you and Kolbeinn should spend a week in our flat in Paris.'

Aníta smiled. 'That's kind of you, but you know we can't leave the farm.' Although actually the idea of running away abroad at that very minute sounded attractive.

'That's a shame,' said Gabrielle. 'Maybe later in the year. At least we'll be able to keep it now.'

'What do you mean?' said Aníta.

'The bank was all set to take it back. We had a big euro mortgage on it when we bought it, and after the crash we've had a lot of trouble keeping up with the payments on our flat and our place in Stykkishólmur.'

'Oh. I didn't realize.' Aníta had assumed that they were fairly well off, especially since Ingvar was a doctor.

'Yes. That's why Ingvar and his father fell out last year. Ingvar asked for some money and Hallgrímur said no.'

'I'd noticed Ingvar had seen less of him recently,' said Aníta. 'I wondered why. But then Hallgrímur had a pretty strange relationship with all of his sons.'

'You're telling me. In some ways Ingvar seemed almost to hate him. He wanted to keep his distance. And yet Hallgrímur had this power over him. It was irresistible. I mean, we had the whole of Iceland to live in and we chose Stykkishólmur. Ingvar did very well at medical school and was a star in Paris. He could have been a top surgeon at the National Hospital in Reykjavík by now. But we are here. Ingvar always says it's because he loves the area, but the reality is he couldn't tear himself away from his father. It's unhealthy.'

'He seemed to take Hallgrímur's death pretty well. They all did, apart from Tóta.'

'Don't be so sure. You know Ingvar; he always seems so cool and detached, never lets anyone see what he's thinking, even me. But he's a mess. He couldn't sleep last night. I woke up in the middle of the night to find him sobbing. He got up and drank half a bottle of brandy. He *never* does that.'

Aníta had never really liked Ingvar. She respected him, but thought him too cold, too arrogant. She expected more warmth from a family member; even Hallgrímur could be warmer than Ingvar. In fact, the doctor took after his mother more; ever since Aníta had first known her, Sylvía had seemed permanently detached from everything. It had always struck

Aníta as odd that a doctor could appear so little moved by humanity. She was glad, in a way, that Ingvar's father's death had had an effect. But Gabrielle was right: it *was* an unhealthy relationship.

'That burn on Ingvar's face wasn't really an accident, was it?' Aníta said.

Gabrielle glanced at Aníta conspiratorially and shook her head. 'Ingvar won't tell me what really happened, but I know his father had something to do with it. I'll bet he threw boiling water at his face when he was a little kid. And none of them are allowed to talk about it. Even now.'

'Villi was the smart one,' said Aníta. 'Escaping to Canada.'

'Yes. Although I sometimes get the feeling that Hallgrímur's power stretched over the Atlantic.'

'So why did Ingvar ask him for the money?' said Aníta. 'Hallgrímur was always going to say no, wasn't he?'

'He shouldn't have done,' said Gabrielle. 'Considering Ingvar was responsible for Hallgrímur making all that cash in the first place.'

'All what cash?' Aníta said. She was vaguely aware that there was some arrangement between Hallgrímur and his sons about who should have what, which had led to Kolbeinn taking over the farm, but she had never troubled to find out the details.

'You know Hallgrímur had a small quota in Stykkishólmur?'

'Yes,' said Aníta. 'But didn't he sell it?'

In the early 1980s fisherman had been given the windfall of a 'quota' or proportion of the total Icelandic fishing catch. This could be transferred, and many of the smaller fishermen, especially the part-time ones like Hallgrímur, had sold theirs to fishing companies for useful lump sums.

'He did. And Ingvar helped him invest it. He did spectacularly well. You remember Óskar Gunnarsson, the chairman of Óðinsbanki, who was killed last year?'

'Yes.'

'Well, Ingvar is good friends with Óskar's uncle who lives in

Stykkishólmur. He gave Ingvar a tip that Óðinsbanki shares were going to soar. Ingvar told Hallgrímur and he made several times his money on them.'

'But didn't all the banks go bust?'

'Not before the uncle told Ingvar to sell.'

'So how much does Hallgrímur have then?'

'I don't know precisely. Probably a couple of hundred million krónur.'

'No!' Aníta blinked. She hadn't thought at all about Hallgrímur's will. She hadn't even thought about what would happen to the farm, which she knew still belonged to Hallgrímur. 'Does Kolbeinn know this?'

'Probably not,' said Gabrielle. 'I know Hallgrímur wanted to keep their success a secret from everyone, including Sylvía and his other sons. And I have no idea how it will all be split up. But you can see why it was reasonable for Ingvar to ask his father for some of the cash he had made him.'

'Yes, I can,' said Aníta.

'Anyway. At least we should be able to keep the flat. Which is a great relief to me. I love Iceland, but I need that place in Paris to stay sane.'

'I should tell Kolbeinn this,' Aníta said.

'Actually, it's probably best if you don't,' said Gabrielle. 'He'll find out very soon himself, won't he? And it would be bad if he discovered it from me. I don't want to create tension between the brothers if Ingvar hasn't told Kolbeinn. I probably shouldn't have told you. It will only be for a few days. As soon as they look at Hallgrímur's bank statements it should all be clear.'

'If they weren't burned,' said Aníta.

'In which case, they'll ask the bank for them,' said Gabrielle.

'OK, I'll pretend I don't know when Kolbeinn finds out,' said Aníta.

'Thanks,' said Gabrielle. 'Now, I should go. And leave the housework alone for now. Give yourself a break. You Icelandic women don't know how to relax.'

Aníta tried not to laugh. Relax? No chance. But she appreciated her sister-in-law's friendship.

'Why don't you come over for a ride tomorrow morning?' she said.

Gabrielle smiled. 'Would you like the company?'

'Yes, I would,' said Aníta. She couldn't be sure, but there was probably less chance of meeting Marta if she had a chattering Frenchwoman with her. 'I would really like it.'

Árni was waiting for Vigdís when she arrived at Café Roma. It was around the corner from the police station and one of Árni's favourite haunts. Vigdís was amazed at how many of their pastries he could stuff into his mouth and still remain so skinny. He was wearing his sling.

'How's the shoulder?'

'Hurts a bit. I've taken some painkillers.'

'Shouldn't you be resting it?'

'A man's gotta type what a man's gotta type,' Árni said in American English.

Vigdís didn't precisely understand what Árni had said, but she laughed anyway. You had to laugh with Árni. He was tall and weedy and painfully thin, famous within the department for his cock-ups, but he was brave. There was no doubt Árni was brave, even when it came to typing.

'Sorry about Davíd,' he said.

'Yeah. He's trying to get on a flight tomorrow,' Vigdís said. 'It will only give us a couple of days, but that's better than nothing. Have you heard anything about Magnús?'

'No. Apparently Adam from Keflavík has been put on the case. I know him pretty well. I thought I'd give him a call.'

Vigdís knew Adam a little too and doubted he would be helpful. The rules on this one would be clear: don't talk to Magnus's colleagues. Adam was ambitious and he wouldn't want to break the rules on a high-profile case.

'I'm not sure that's a good idea,' she said.

'Can't hurt to try,' said Árni.

Vigdís shrugged. 'I guess not. But be subtle about it.' Fat chance of that, she thought.

'Also, I spoke to my sister last night,' Árni said. His sister, Katrín, was Magnus's landlady, who shared the small house in Njálsgata with him. 'You know Magnús's brother Ollie was staying there?'

'Yes,' said Vigdís.

'Apparently he left early yesterday morning, saying he was going to the farm where he grew up. A schoolteacher friend was taking him. Then Magnús rushed off after him.'

'That's interesting,' said Vigdís. 'That must be Bjarnarhöfn. Maybe I'll go and talk to her this morning. See if I can find out who this schoolteacher is. Also, I thought I would see if Ingileif is still in Reykjavík. I know she was planning to fly back to Germany, but her flight will have been cancelled because of the ash cloud. Magnús might have told her something useful. And I had another thought.'

'Oh yeah?'

'A few months ago Magnús asked me how to get hold of an old file: Benedikt Jóhannesson's murder in 1985. Do you remember that one?'

Árni looked blank. Vigdís had studied it at police college, and she would bet Árni had too. She'd also bet he had forgotten it.

'A writer who was murdered at his home in Vesturbaer,' she said. 'Stabbed. They never found the murderer.'

Árni shook his head, unable to remember. 'So why would Magnús want to read that?'

'Good question,' said Vigdís. 'Which is why I suggest you dig it out.'

'OK,' said Árni. 'I'll see if I can get hold of it this morning. We'll talk later.'

As they got up to leave, Árni paused. 'Oh, there is one thing I should mention. A guy called for Magnús last week. Some American detective. He said he had some lab results.'

'Interesting,' said Vigdís. 'Do you know what sort of results?'

'The guy wasn't specific.'

'And what did Magnús say when you told him?'

'Um...' Árni's Adam's apple started bobbing.

'Árni! You forgot to tell him, didn't you?'

'There was a lot going on,' Árni protested. 'We were in the middle of a case. It didn't seem relevant.'

'Árni! You are a moron.'

Árni winced. He didn't show any signs of disagreeing.

'Call this detective back after lunch. Find out what the tests were and why Magnús wanted them.'

They went their separate ways, with Vigdís muttering under her breath about the idiot she had to work with.

CHAPTER FOURTEEN

THE WARMTH AND the fragrant smell of hay and wool enveloped Aníta as she entered the large barn where they kept the ewes over the winter. The sheep, bellies swollen with unborn lambs, shifted and shuffled as they saw her. A gentle bleat rippled through the flock.

Aníta loved it in the barn, especially at this time of year. They kept the building scrupulously clean with hoses and a mucking-out machine, much easier than the old-fashioned hours with rake and fork. But it was the air of expectancy that hovered over the mass of warm wool that she felt was so delicious. A maternal mixture of excitement and nervousness, magnified four hundred times. One area of the barn had been kept clear for the lambing stalls. In a week or so, that section would be bustling. No one on the farm would get much sleep, but Aníta didn't mind. It was worth it for the joy of seeing the newborns twitch and flutter into the world.

Except when she lost a ewe, especially if it was an older beast whom she had got to know over several years, or one of the *forystufé*, the hardy, intelligent leader-sheep who steered the rest of the flock over the mountains and kept them out of trouble.

She waded into the flock, recognizing the different animals, all of which the family had named. Móses, one of the rams, had broken into the ewes' field the previous autumn. He hadn't been there long before he was discovered, and so far there was no sign of any early pregnancies. Aníta checked a couple of the ewes that she had spotted earlier that had seemed particularly restless, but no sign of any activity yet.

Good. The last thing any of them needed right then was to be up all night worrying about the sheep. The longer they could delay that the better. In fact, Aníta fervently hoped that the murder investigation would be tied up by the time the first lamb was born.

Perhaps it already was. The police had taken Magnus away after all. Could he really be a killer? Aníta thought not, but she didn't really know him. He did come from a world of gangs and guns and killing, and she knew that Hallgrímur had loathed him.

She stood among the rippling pond of wool and thought about what Gabrielle had said. Aníta had watched enough cop shows on TV to know that without realizing it, Ingvar's wife had let slip that her husband had a motive for murder. Now Hallgrímur had died, Ingvar would get his hands on some of the old man's millions. It was strange to think that Hallgrímur was so rich, but not at all strange to hear that he had hidden it from his family. *That* made perfect sense.

Perhaps Aníta should tell the fat detective what she had heard? She would be betraying Gabrielle's trust, and could get Ingvar into trouble. For all she knew, Gabrielle or Ingvar could have told the police about Hallgrímur's investments, and even if they hadn't, the detective would find out about it sooner or later. Aníta couldn't believe that the doctor had murdered his father. Yet if Ingvar *had* killed the old man, then of course he should be arrested. And if he hadn't, it should be easy for him to prove it. There was also Magnus to consider; Ingvar's guilt would prove his innocence.

There was no doubt that the right thing to do was to tell the police. But if she did that, Gabrielle would never forgive her. If Ingvar was guilty, that wouldn't matter, but if he was innocent, which he probably was, it most certainly would. Maybe there was a way of informing the police anonymously? The police always used anonymous informants on TV. But that was in London or New York; she wasn't sure her anonymity could be preserved successfully in somewhere as small as Stykkishólmur.

She left the barn, the two dogs at her heels. She had lots to do, but she wanted to check how Grána was. She had left the mare earlier that morning sweating in the paddock on the other side of the farm close to Cumberland Bay. She crossed the yard. The forensics van was parked outside the burned-out cottage; a technician in overalls was taking photographs of the exterior of the building. A couple of hundred metres out in the lava field, along the dirt road approaching the farm, she saw a group of cars parked precariously along the verge and half a dozen people staring towards her, some with equipment, held back by a policeman and some tape.

The press.

She was glad the police had kept them off the farm; she really didn't want to speak to them.

Villi was in the yard, standing by the pickup, looking lost. He waved to her. She couldn't help smiling when she saw him, and waved back a little too enthusiastically. She went over to him.

'Do you know where the fence posts are? Kolbeinn needs a couple of new ones. They seem to have moved since the last time I saw them thirty years ago, which isn't really surprising.' He laughed his deep rumbling laugh.

'Just in that shed behind the tarps,' Aníta said, pointing behind him. 'There's a whole pile.'

'I looked in there, but I must have missed them,' said Villi. 'Thanks.' He moved up close to her, too close, and touched her arm. For a moment she met his warm brown eyes. Then she broke away from him and hurried off towards the horses' paddock.

Why had she done that? Smiled at him? Let him come so close? Why had he come so close? They had agreed to keep their distance. And until now Villi had done so. He hadn't visited Iceland for four years.

He was in his sixties, for God's sake, and she was nearly fifty; this teenage flirtation was so stupid!

Yet for three days, four years before, it had meant everything to her.

It was August. Villi had just retired from the Canadian mining company that had employed him for twenty-five years, and had agreed to teach a semester at Reykjavík University. He had arranged to stay for a week at Bjarnarhöfn before term started. But, as he was driving there from the airport, Kolbeinn was taking their father in the other direction to hospital in Reykjavík for an emergency heart operation.

Villi decided to stay one night at Bjarnarhöfn with Aníta and the children and his mother, and then go down to Reykjavík the following afternoon to see his father in hospital. Aníta had been pleased to see him; she had always liked him and his company made a nice change. His mother, as usual, had seemed almost indifferent.

After lunch, Villi had asked if he could ride one of the horses up the fell. Aníta offered to come with him.

It was a gorgeous August afternoon, warm with only the slightest of breezes. As their horses climbed the flank of the fell behind the farm, they could see for miles: the bluish grey mountains of the West Fjords on the other side of Breidafjördur, the extraordinary yellow, brown and green towers of volcanic rock thrown up around the Berserkjahraun, Swine Lake lapping against the cliffs of rumpled lava, and over to the east the scattered white buildings of Stykkishólmur.

They talked. And talked. Aníta was very happy with her life on the farm, and her friends around Stykkishólmur. She had never regretted turning her back on the tumult of her life in Reykjavík, but she suddenly found herself craving the conversation of a wider world. Villi had a raft of fascinating stories to tell about his adventures with the mining company. And he was interested in her. Not in her life at the farm, but the time she had spent in Reykjavík, playing her flute, working in the record shop. She found herself talking about the series of unsuitable men who had invaded her life back then. Unsuitable, but interesting, dangerous even. She told Villi things she had never told

Kolbeinn, both because he had never asked and because she had never wanted to.

Villi was a lot like Kolbeinn: honest, dependable, strong. But he was smarter. And, amazingly, he seemed to understand her better.

They arrived back at the farm to hear that Hallgrímur wouldn't need to be operated on after all and would be returning to Bjarnarhöfn the following day, so Villi decided to stay on. The next morning, Aníta suggested another ride, with a picnic. Villi asked her to bring her flute. Sylvía ignored them.

The weather held. They went further and higher than they had the previous day, to a sheep's byre near the summit of the fell. Beside it was a grassy hollow with a view across the mountains to the peak of Snaefellsjökull itself. They sat and ate their sandwiches facing the beautiful white dome of snow with its tiny rock question mark right at the summit.

Aníta played her flute. It was at least a year since she had last picked up the instrument, and it took a few minutes to warm up. But she played Telemann, her favourite composer, and was amazed how she could remember the notes. Villi sat and listened, smiling at her. His smile did something to her playing. Her heart sang in time to the music.

Eventually she put down her flute. He reached over and kissed her. They made love, their naked skin chilled by the gentle breeze, but caressed by the sunshine. A pair of golden plovers peeped their support.

Afterwards, as she lay in his arms, she ran her hands over his chest, so similar yet so different to Kolbeinn's.

'You know, I've never done that before,' she said.

'Of course you have,' said Villi.

'No, I mean had sex with another man. Since I married Kolbeinn.'

Villi didn't reply. He just stroked her hair.

'You know it doesn't feel wrong. Up here, it doesn't feel wrong.'

But it *was* wrong, and it certainly felt wrong when Kolbeinn returned with Hallgrímur the next day. Villi and Aníta did a really good job of treating each other naturally, with casual amiability. Aníta was certain Kolbeinn had not noticed anything. Sylvía? Who knew about Sylvía? She seemed to treat Villi with mild disapproval, but that was no change from when he had first arrived. No one knew how much Sylvía saw of what went on around the farm. No one knew because Sylvía never told anyone anything. Secrets were safe with Sylvía.

Aníta managed to get hold of Villi alone a couple of hours before he left. They walked down to the little church. She could see in his eyes that he sensed her emotions.

'That was about the best afternoon of my life,' Villi said.

Despite her resolution to be stern with him, Aníta couldn't help but smile.

'But I know it shouldn't happen again,' Villi went on. 'I understand that. I'll keep my distance. It will be very difficult for me, but I will do it. I don't want to ruin your life.'

'Thank you,' said Aníta. She felt an urge to kiss him, but resisted it. Her fingers twitched with the desire to touch him, to hold his hand, but she clenched them. He *did* understand, she knew it. And she was relieved.

To Kolbeinn's dismay, Villi never came up to the farm again the whole time he was in Reykjavík, although Hallgrímur drove down to see him once, leaving Sylvía behind. It was easier, when Villi wasn't around, not exactly to forget what had happened, Aníta could never do that, but to keep it in a compartment, somewhere way up there on the fell, where it could stay safely out of her life. She was appalled at herself for sleeping with her husband's brother. But she knew she could never have betrayed him with anyone from the area. It was only because Villi came from a different country, a different continent, that she had been able to do it.

Sometimes, Aníta took Grána up the hill to that spot to remember. But she had never played her flute since.

She stood by the paddock and Grána trotted over to see her.

The mare seemed much calmer, yet still relieved to see her mistress. Aníta whispered nothings in her ear and patted her neck.

'Aníta!'

She turned to see the fat detective waddling over towards her, with a shorter, younger man at his elbow.

'Aníta, can we have a word?'

Emil accepted the cup of coffee offered to him and sat down at the kitchen table at Bjarnarhöfn. Whereas the previous day the kitchen had smelled of baking, that morning it smelled of bleach.

He was out of breath and his heart was beating unnaturally fast. The out-of-breath thing he was used to, but the heart worried him. He wondered whether he should be drinking caffeine. But one cup of coffee couldn't do any harm. Coffee was one of the few things not on the long list of items his doctor had given him to avoid.

After the morning's conference, he had driven down to Borgarnes, a small town halfway between Stykkishólmur and Reykjavík, to the court where a judge was hearing his application to hold Magnus in custody during the investigation. There were no difficult questions, and Magnus himself had said nothing. He hadn't even wanted his lawyer to attend. The police now had twenty-one days to gather evidence before they would have to appear before a judge again. In the meantime Magnus had been sent on to the prison at Litla-Hraun, where he would be held in solitary confinement.

There were still some cakes left, and Emil took one. Adam, sitting beside him, notebook at the ready, abstained. As Emil chewed, he examined the two women opposite him. Sylvía was clearly distressed. Her small brown eyes were staring at him and Adam with a mixture of fear and bewilderment. That didn't surprise Emil. Aníta, too, seemed to be suffering under the strain.

'Delicious,' said Emil, wiping his lips. Aníta smiled distractedly in acknowledgement. 'Now, do either of you recognize this?'

Emil gave a brief nod to Adam, who pulled out a clear plastic envelope containing the silver earring.

Sylvía leaned forward, studied the earring and shook her head.

Aníta glanced at the envelope quickly and then at Sylvía. 'You recognize it, Sylvía! Kolbeinn gave it to you a few years ago.' She turned to the detective. 'I know, because I bought them in Reykjavík.'

'Are you sure you don't recognize it, Sylvía?' Emil asked as gently as he could.

The old lady glanced at him with panicked eyes and shook her head again.

Aníta frowned. 'I'm afraid Sylvía is still very upset, Emil. I don't think she is thinking very clearly.'

Sylvía turned to her daughter-in-law with a scowl and then stared again at the earring, fascinated.

'Sylvía, we found this earring in the church yesterday morning. Do you know how it got there?'

Sylvía raised her eyes to the detective and shook her head quickly.

'Sylvía goes into the church quite a lot,' said Aníta. 'She cleans it, but she also goes in there to pray. She has done for the last couple of years. She could easily have dropped her earring there. The other is probably in her bedroom, if it hasn't been destroyed by the fire.'

'We will check,' said Emil. 'Now, Sylvía, I would like you to give us a hair sample.'

'What do you mean?' said Sylvía.

'A policewoman will cut just a tiny bit of your hair. Will you let her do that for us, please? We found some white hairs in the church as well, and we want to see if they are yours. Or they might be your husband's.'

'Hallgrímur never went to church,' said Sylvía.

'That's where he was found, Sylvía,' Emil said. 'Dead.'

Sylvía shook her head. 'Hallgrímur doesn't go to church. He will be back soon.'

'Do you really need to take the sample?' Aníta asked. 'You can see how upset she is.'

Emil nodded. 'We do. We can't force her to give it, but it would really help us if she did. I'll send a policewoman in in a moment. I would be grateful if you could persuade her to co-operate.'

He turned to Sylvía. He hated to ask her more questions, but he had to try one more time. 'Sylvía. How did the fire start last night?'

'I don't know,' said Sylvía. 'Hallgrímur was coming home late and he hadn't had his dinner, so I had to cook it for him. I was cooking dinner when the kitchen caught fire. I don't know why. And Hallgrímur still hasn't come home.'

Emil sighed. Sylvía's testimony was clearly unreliable anyway, whatever she said. But they had to ask the questions and write down the answers.

He drank the last of his coffee. Aníta and the two dogs followed him out of the farmhouse while Adam went off to find a female officer. Forensics technicians were bustling in and around the fire-damaged cottage.

'I'm sorry about that,' Aníta said as they walked across the farmyard to Emil's car. 'You can see she isn't thinking clearly at all. That earring is definitely hers.'

'Will you be able to look after her?'

Aníta shrugged. 'I think she should be somewhere else. This place clearly upsets her now. Ingvar said he would come over and take a look at her. Maybe she can go and stay with him.'

'If she does say anything to you about the fire, or about Hallgrímur, will you let me know?' said Emil.

Aníta nodded. Emil was about to get in the car when he registered the hesitancy in Aníta. The suppressed agitation. She was weighing up whether to tell him something.

He stood still.

'Aren't you leaving?' she said after a few moments.

'I'm waiting,' said Emil.

'For what?'

'For you to tell me something.' He raised his eyebrows.

Aníta blushed slightly. Fiddled with the edge of her sweater. Made a decision. 'Gabrielle came over to see me this morning,' she began. 'It probably has nothing to do with your investigation, but I feel I should inform you anyway. Just don't say it was me that told you. She said something interesting about Ingvar and Hallgrímur...'

Sigurbjörg Vilhjálmsdóttir, or Sibba as she was known to her friends and family, was preoccupied as she drove over the high heath to the south-east of Reykjavík. Pylons marched over the snow-spattered lava field towards a geothermal plant, crouching under a wrinkled mountain, belching billows of steam into the cold air. It was a clear day with pale blue sky and low sunshine dazzling off the streaks of snow.

Sibba was going to visit her cousin. In prison.

She had got the call the evening before. She was watching television with her husband. In the couple of years since the *kreppa* had taken hold, she had received a number of these calls at home and at odd hours from bankers or lawyers who had suddenly found themselves confronted by policemen asking difficult questions. Sibba was a lawyer, a partner of a firm with smart offices in Borgartún, a boulevard lined with swish modern bank headquarters that ran along the shore of Faxaflói Bay. She was a commercial lawyer, but increasingly her work had become criminal, as her clients had been questioned about their role in various alleged frauds that had taken place during the boom years in the first decade of the century.

But this phone call was different. This time she had been asked to defend a murder suspect. And the murder suspect was Magnús Ragnarsson, her cousin.

Sibba had been placed in a difficult position. Magnus had informed her who the victim was – her own grandfather,

Hallgrímur. She had resisted the urge to call her uncle at Bjarnarhöfn and find out what had happened, or even to ring her parents in Canada. She had refused to act for Magnus at first, pointing out the obvious conflicts and her lack of experience of murder cases, but Magnus had insisted. He said she was the only lawyer in Iceland he could trust to do what he wanted her to do.

She respected Magnus. He knew what he was doing. So, reluctantly, she had agreed to act for him.

That was the first strange call she had received that day. The second, later on that evening, had been from her father who said that he had arrived at Bjarnarhöfn that afternoon to find the place in uproar and his own father murdered. Sibba was so surprised to hear that he was in Iceland, and concerned about the conflict with Magnus, that she hadn't admitted that she knew already. That had been stupid. Her father would discover soon enough that she was defending the man accused of murdering her grandfather.

Sibba understood why her father hadn't told her he was coming to Iceland, but nevertheless she was a little miffed that he hadn't dropped in on her in Reykjavík on the way up to Bjarnarhöfn. She had a good relationship with him, and both her parents doted on her children, their grandchildren. Still, it would be a big help for Kolbeinn and Aníta to have her dad around. He was good in a crisis; he had faced them in mining camps all over the world. He would know what to do.

Sibba and Magnus had a lot in common. Like him, she had grown up abroad, in her case Toronto, only moving to the land of her ancestors when she graduated from law school. But they were not really close; Sibba had only realized that Magnus was back in Iceland when she had bumped into him in the street about a year before. He was eight years younger than her, but they liked and respected each other. The idea that he had murdered Hallgrímur seemed preposterous.

The road descended sharply, winding down a steep hillside. In front of her a broad plain stretched down to the sea, clear of snow at the lower altitude, dotted with farms. And in the far distance, at least seventy kilometres away on the other side of the plain, a plume of white rose high into the deep blue sky, and then bent over to the right as the north wind pushed it towards Europe. Beneath the white, and somehow quite separate from it, were smaller puffs of black. Ash. Not the fine high ash that was travelling across oceans high in the atmosphere, but denser stuff that fell to ground.

Eyjafjallajökull.

The sight took Sibba by surprise. She had watched the eruption on the news, and seen the disruption to local farms and to air travellers thousands of kilometres away. But she had yet to see the volcano itself.

She forced her eyes back to the road, with its switchbacks twisting down the steep slope, and then glanced quickly to the south. Along the shoreline she could see the ribbon of houses that made up the old trading port of Eyrarbakki, and at its eastern edge the white tower and buildings of Litla-Hraun prison.

She had been there a couple of times over the previous few months to visit bankers charged with financial crimes. It hadn't taken long to get them out, and none of her clients had yet been successfully prosecuted; this was new territory for the Icelandic legal system. But defending a murder charge would be an entirely different story. It was rare in Iceland once the police and prosecution had put together a case for a suspect in a traditional serious criminal trial not to be found guilty. There were no juries, and few loopholes to seek out.

She hoped Magnus's arrest had just been a dreadful mistake that would quickly become clear. Otherwise she would have her work cut out.

The prison was surrounded by a high wire fence. Sibba parked in a space outside the gates and introduced herself to the guard. She was led through to House Number One, a low white building fenced off from the others, where prisoners were held in solitary confinement. The building held a mixture of prisoners on remand and troublemakers from the main prison who had been sent there as a punishment. Conditions in the main prison were quite lax, but solitary was tough: no contact with other prisoners or visitors, one hour per day exercise alone in a walled courtyard. And this for citizens who had not yet been found guilty. The permanent residents, by contrast, had a shower in their cells, a wide-screen TV in the communal area of each wing, a gym, a snack shop, classrooms and plenty of social life.

The set-up was quite an incentive to confess, really.

Sibba was searched and then led into the interview room. She waited a moment and then Magnus came in. It struck her again how he looked like a younger version of her father: big, square-shouldered with red hair and an air of strong composure. He was wearing sweatpants and shirt, no doubt provided by the police.

He grinned when he saw her. She hesitated, torn for a moment between her role as cousin and lawyer, and then gave him a hug. The guard was surprised and made no effort to stop her.

They sat down and the guard left.

'I'm used to being in your chair,' said Magnus. They spoke in English, as they usually did. Neither Magnus nor Sibba's accent had any trace of Icelandic. 'It's weird to be on this side of the table.'

'This whole thing must be pretty weird for you,' Sibba said.

'It is.'

'How long have you been here?'

'Half an hour, maybe,' said Magnus. 'Haven't had time to decorate my cell yet.'

'Did you see the volcano on the way down?'

'Yes. Spectacular. Can't see it from my cell, though. Can't see anything from my cell.'

'How did the hearing go in Borgarnes?' Sibba asked.

'As you would expect. They've got me here for twenty-one days. I'm sure they will show you the paperwork.'

'You should have let me come,' Sibba said.

'You and I know there is nothing you could have done,' said

Magnus. 'It was a formality. The judge was always going to send me down here.'

'Possibly,' said Sibba. 'But before we start, I have to ask you. Are you sure you want me to act for you?' She looked closely at her cousin. 'I can find you another lawyer with more experience of violent crime.'

He smiled. 'No. I've thought this through. I want you.'

'But what about the fact that Hallgrímur was my grandfather too? You know my father showed up yesterday at Bjarnarhöfn? I'm going to have to explain to him that I am defending the man who is supposed to have murdered his own father.'

Magnus sighed. 'I know it will be difficult for you, Sibba, but I would really like you to represent me. I've thought about it hard. You are about the only person in this country I know who I can trust to do what I want. You and me are pretty similar. As you said, we both shared the same evil grandfather. You've been in this country a lot longer than I have, but I think you at least understand what it's like for me to be here.'

'Maybe I do,' said Sibba.

'Look. If I promise not to lie to you, will you promise to do what I instruct you to? As my lawyer?'

Sibba paused. This was getting strange. She was wary that Magnus was leading her into some kind of trap. But on the other hand, he seemed to need her. Sibba liked to be needed, by her family as well as by her clients. That was why she had become a lawyer in the first place. And although some of the bankers who had defrauded their shareholders out of millions needed her too, that was not quite so satisfying.

'OK,' said Sibba, pulling out a notepad. 'Let's start. Tell me what happened.'

In calm, clear tones, Magnus did just that. He explained how he had driven up from Reykjavík to see his grandfather, how he had found the body, how he had called the police, and how he had answered their questions. Sibba took detailed notes.

After he had finished, she looked them over. She realized that he had told her nothing more than what he had told the police.

Not one tiny bit more. Usually her clients had plenty to say that they hadn't included in their statements. Maybe Magnus had nothing to hide. But no one had nothing to hide, especially someone sitting in jail charged with murder.

'So what aren't you telling me?' she asked him.

He just shrugged.

She leaned forward. 'From what you've said, the case against you is pretty strong. The evidence is all circumstantial, but that can be enough. If the police and the judge are convinced you are guilty, they will find you guilty. There's no jury for us to bamboozle. You'll go to jail for a long time. Obviously you will be fired from the police force here. And when you get out, everyone in this country will know who you are for evermore: the American cop who killed his Icelandic grandfather. If you go back to the States, no police department there will take you with a murder conviction. Do you want all that?'

Magnus looked at her steadily, his expression grim. He blinked once, but he didn't answer. Why didn't he answer?

'There must be other details you know that you haven't told the police yet that can help establish your innocence. I need to know what those details are.'

Still nothing.

'You promised you wouldn't lie to me.' Sibba stared hard into Magnus's blue eyes.

He held her gaze. 'I did.'

'Very well, then. Why do the police think you are a suspect?'

'They say I tampered with the crime scene. They say I hated my grandfather, and that I believed he was responsible for my father's death. And I discovered the body, which means I could have killed the old man.'

'Did you?' Sibba asked.

Magnus didn't answer at first. 'Did I what?' he asked slowly.

'Did you tamper with the crime scene?' Sibba asked.

Magnus didn't answer.

'OK. Did you hate your grandfather?'

'You know I did,' said Magnus.

And that left the big question. The one that lawyers had to be very careful about asking their client. But Sibba realized that she couldn't defend Magnus unless she knew the answer.

'Did you kill Hallgrímur?'

CHAPTER FIFTEEN

Vigdís realized she had probably woken Katrín up. Árni's sister took an age to answer the doorbell of the brightly painted little house in Njálsgata. She was bleary eyed with the remains of the previous night's make-up staining her face. She was a tall woman with black dyed hair and a penchant for facial metal. So different from Árni. Vigdís didn't know her well, but she rather liked her.

'Hi. What do you want?' Perhaps Katrín was not so keen to see her.

'Sorry to disturb you. Did you hear about Magnús?'

'Yeah. My brother told me you've arrested him for murder. And if you're that stupid I'm not going to answer any of your questions.'

'Hold on, hold on,' said Vigdís, raising her hand to stop Katrín shutting the door on her. 'I've got a day off. I know Magnús didn't kill anyone. I'm here unofficially to help him prove it.'

Katrín blinked. Hesitated. 'Oh. OK. Come in. I'll make some coffee.'

The kitchen was surprisingly tidy, and Katrín began to fiddle with a coffee machine.

'Has anyone come around to speak to you yet?' Vigdís asked. 'Officially.'

'Not yet. I'll tell them where to go when they do.'

'Actually, it's in Magnús's interests if you answer their questions honestly. I believe the truth is that Magnús didn't kill his grandfather. So we want the police to figure that out.'

'Huh.' Katrín didn't sound convinced. 'What is it? The police in Stykkishólmur have their very own Árni? They must be stupid. Magnús would never kill an old man.'

'They must have strong evidence or they wouldn't have arrested him. But they are making sure that none of us in Reykjavík has anything to do with the case, so I don't know what that evidence might be. Which is why I want to talk to you. Magnús's brother Ollie has been staying here, hasn't he?'

The coffee maker began to bubble. Katrín sat down waiting for it to do its stuff. She lit a cigarette and offered Vigdís one. Vigdís shook her head.

'Yeah, he came the middle of last week. Magnús hardly saw him; he was working on that murder case. Ollie was a bit pissed off. I ended up entertaining him.'

Vigdís raised her eyebrows, wondering if Katrín meant what she thought she did. From the other woman's small smile, she saw that she did.

'What's Ollie like?' Vigdís said. 'I've never met him. A little Magnús?'

'Oh, no,' said Katrín. 'Ollie is a bad boy. Which is why I like him.' That little smile again.

'Did Magnús approve?'

'Of me fucking his little brother? I think he was a bit shocked. Ollie and I thought that was pretty funny.'

'And did Ollie talk much about Magnús?'

'No, not really. I mean, we joked about him a bit, but they have "issues", as the Americans like to say. Something to do with their father and their grandfather, all that shit. I wanted to stay well out of it.'

'That's a shame,' said Vigdís.

'Sorry. All I know was they were having some kind of argument. I could tell Ollie was upset, although he didn't want to talk about it. I didn't see much of Magnús last week. And then of course Ingileif showed up.'

'What happened there?'

'You know she's been in Germany for the last few months?'

Vigdís nodded.

'I think she just appeared unannounced. I didn't see her the first evening she came, but they spent the night together. Then they had some kind of row, I think.'

'Yes, he told me,' said Vigdís.

'Not a great week for Magnús, last week,' said Katrín.

'Except he made some arrests,' said Vigdís. 'That always makes him happy.'

Katrín shrugged. 'Whatever turns you on.'

'Árni said that Ollie left early on Sunday morning to drive up to Bjarnarhöfn with a schoolteacher. Do you know what time?'

'No. I rolled over and went back to sleep. But it was early. Six? Seven? Something like that.'

'Did you see the schoolteacher?'

'No. And I don't know his name. But I bet I know where you can find it.'

'Where?'

'Have you ever been in Magnús's room?' Katrín asked, that little smile hovering on her lips.

'Certainly not,' said Vigdís, trying to suppress a flash of anger. 'We are just work colleagues,' she added unnecessarily.

'Let me show you.'

They went up some narrow stairs into a bedroom with a bathroom off to one side. There was very little furniture. A bed. A desk. Two bookshelves. A closet. The bookshelves were full, with volumes overflowing on to the floor. A laptop was sitting open on the desk. Through the window was a view of the smooth spire of the Hallgrímskirkja thrusting up between the red metal roofs of the houses opposite.

There were two books on the bedside table: *Moor and the Man* by Benedikt Jóhannesson and *The Good Soldier* by Ford Maddox Ford. Vigdís was about to pick them up, but then decided against it. It was unlikely, but if a forensics officer came to take prints in the room, it would not look good if hers were on everything.

'Take a look at that.'

One wall was a patchwork of photographs, newspaper cuttings, drawings and Post-its in several different colours.

'Wow,' said Vigdís.

'Some men have pictures of women or football players on their walls,' said Katrín. 'And Magnús has this. I'll leave you to it.'

Vigdís stared at the wall. She could discern a pattern. One half dealt with the murder of Ragnar Jónsson, Magnus's father, in 1996 in Massachusetts. The other half centred on Benedikt Jóhannesson, the author who had been killed in 1985.

The space between was a mess of arrows and plain sheets of paper on which ideas had been scrawled and crossed out.

Vigdís took out her notebook and began to write.

It wasn't far from Magnus's house to the gallery in Skólavördustígur, which Ingileif still owned with a group of other female designers. Vigdís was betting that that was where Ingileif would decide to hang out when stuck in Reykjavík. And even if she wasn't there, someone at the gallery would probably be able to give Vigdís a clue where to find her.

Her phone rang just as she was about to enter the gallery. It was Árni.

'I called the American detective. His name is Jim Fearon.'

'It's a bit early, isn't it?'

'They get up early in America.'

'And?'

'Fearon said that the lab results were personal information. The only person he would speak to was Magnús himself.'

'Did you tell him that would be difficult?'

'Yes. I said that Magnús was in jail accused of murder.'

'You did what!'

'I figured Fearon would have to give me the information then. You know, he'd think I was investigating Magnús.'

'And did he?'

'No. He said in that case if the Icelandic police wanted the evidence they would have to go through the proper channels. That means Interpol, doesn't it?'

'Oh, Árni!' Vigdís couldn't control her frustration. 'Couldn't you have been a bit more subtle? Didn't I tell you to be careful?'

'That was with Adam. Although that conversation didn't go very well either. Anyway, we don't know what the lab tests were for. Maybe they were nothing.'

'Árni! What kind of detective are you? "Maybe they were nothing." Jesus Christ!'

Vigdís hung up. Árni and Vigdís had no chance of getting the information through Interpol themselves. They could tip off the Dumpling, but without knowing whether the lab results helped or harmed Magnus's case, that was a bad idea. Perhaps Magnus's lawyer would be able to help, whoever he was. Vigdís knew all the criminal lawyers in Reykjavík; she wondered which one Magnus had chosen. Worth finding out.

But first Ingileif.

Vigdís took a couple of deep breaths to calm herself down and entered the gallery. She was in luck. Ingileif was serving a customer, a Danish tourist. Vigdís was instantly reminded of the first time she had encountered Ingileif. It had been with Magnus in this very gallery. Ingileif was a witness in a murder inquiry, and Magnus had suggested they wait and observe her before talking to her.

At that stage, Vigdís had no idea that Magnus's interest would become more than professional. But Ingileif was undoubtedly attractive. Slim, blonde, very Icelandic, with a lively smile, Vigdís could see how Magnus had fallen for her.

Ingileif caught sight of Vigdís and flashed her a quick smile as she sold some earrings to the Danish woman.

'Hi, Vigdís!' she exclaimed as the customer left the shop. 'It's great to see you!' She kissed Vigdís on the cheek.

'I didn't want to interrupt,' said Vigdís.

'It's deathly quiet these days,' said Ingileif. 'The only hope is that some of the tourists who are trapped here by the volcano decide to go shopping. I thought it was bad when I left, but things haven't got any better.'

'I take it you're trapped here too?' Vigdís asked.

'Yes. I was supposed to go back to Hamburg on Friday, but my flight was cancelled. I'm trying not to get myself too worked up over it. I'll be helping out here until the ash cloud moves.'

'Can we talk?' Vigdís asked.

'Sure. But if a customer does come in, I'll have to do my stuff. What do you want to talk about?'

'Magnús,' said Vigdís.

Ingileif frowned. 'Oh, Vigdís! You're not some kind of messenger, are you? A peacemaker? That's a bit teenage even for Magnús.'

'He's in jail,' said Vigdís coldly. 'Charged with murder.'

'Oh, God,' exclaimed Ingileif. She put her hand to her mouth and blushed. 'Oh, I'm sorry. What did he do? Lose his temper? Beat up some criminal?'

'It was his grandfather.'

'Hallgrímur? He killed Hallgrímur?'

'Of course he didn't kill Hallgrímur,' Vigdís said angrily. 'How could you think he did?'

Ingileif blinked. 'I thought you just said he did. I'm sorry, I'm confused.'

Vigdís realized she was losing control. 'Yes. Sorry, I'll explain. The police in Stykkishólmur believe that Magnús murdered his grandfather at his farm at Bjarnarhöfn. I think they've got it wrong. So I want to help Magnús. I'm off duty now and this conversation is off the record.'

'OK, OK,' said Ingileif. 'I understand now. But it's still a lot to take in. Do the police have any evidence?'

'They must have some,' said Vigdís. 'Or they wouldn't have sent him down to Litla-Hraun. They are keeping his colleagues in Reykjavík out of it. But any help you can give me about Magnús's relationship with his grandfather, or his brother for that matter, would be very helpful.'

Ingileif frowned.

'What is it?' Vigdís asked.

'If there was any reason why Magnús might kill anyone, it

would be to do with his grandfather,' Ingileif said. 'That, and his father's murder.'

'I saw the wall in Magnús's bedroom,' Vigdís said.

'When?' asked Ingileif sharply.

'Just now,' said Vigdís. 'I've just been talking to Katrín. She showed it to me.'

'Sorry,' said Ingileif. She shook her head. 'Sorry. Yes. Magnús had a bad time as a kid at Bjarnarhöfn staying with his grandfather. As did Ollie. And since he's been back in Iceland he's begun to think that there is a connection between his father's murder in America and Hallgrímur. Magnús wanted to find out more, Ollie wanted to leave it alone; in fact, that's why Ollie came over to Iceland, I think, to persuade him to leave it all alone.'

'Did Magnús talk to you about all that?'

'Oh, yes,' said Ingileif. 'Many times.'

Vigdís took out her notebook. 'Do you mind if we go over some of the details?'

They spent an hour going over Vigdís's notes, interspersed with the odd visit from a customer. Ingileif was an expert at getting them to buy, Vigdís noticed: gentle with some, more forceful with others.

Eventually, they had finished.

'One last question,' Vigdís said. 'Did Magnús mention any lab results he was expecting? He got a call last week from an ex-detective, Jim Fearon, in the town where his father was murdered, saying he had some results for him. Árni took the call.'

'Meaning that the detective won't tell you what he's got?'

'Meaning that the detective wants a notice from Interpol before he tells us what he's got.'

'Oh dear,' said Ingileif.

'Yes. Oh dear.'

Ingileif shook her head. 'No, Magnús didn't mention anything to me about that.'

'OK,' said Vigdís. 'Thanks for telling me all this.' She shook her head. 'I thought I knew him pretty well, but he never said anything to me.'

'He's a private person,' said Ingileif.

'Yes,' said Vigdís. She was about to leave it there, but she couldn't help herself. 'But he did mention you.'

'Oh, yes?'

'Yes. We went out for a drink last Friday. He told me about the Turkish guy. And you blaming him for being jealous.'

Ingileif's eyes narrowed. 'I don't see what that has to do with you.'

'Magnús did,' said Vigdís. 'He was upset.'

'I'm sorry he was upset,' said Ingileif. 'But he knew what our relationship was. He's an American; he doesn't understand how life is in Iceland. You know, he thinks that a man and a woman seeing each other is the same as being married.'

'That's the thing,' said Vigdís. 'You were telling him that he was an uptight American putting too much emphasis on his relationship with you. When actually all you were trying to do was fix it so that you could fuck him and fuck someone else at the same time.'

'Vigdís! What is this?' said Ingileif. 'As I said, this has nothing to do with you. The poor guy is in prison. Can't you just focus on getting him out?'

'While you go back to Hamburg and your Turkish friend?'

Ingileif's face was bright red. 'Vigdís, I think you had better leave.'

It was all Ingileif could do not to scream at Vigdís as she left the gallery.

Who the hell did she think she was? OK, Magnus had confided in Vigdís more than he should, probably, knowing Magnus, after he had had more beers than he should. But what was he doing talking about their relationship with someone else anyway?

Ingileif paced around the small space, picking up a lampshade that was askew and putting it down again, more askew.

It was clear that Vigdís had a thing for Magnus. And it was

true that she was a beautiful woman. Tall, long legs, great body. Would Magnus care that she was black? Ingileif knew the answer to that.

How unprofessional! Lusting after the boss.

Ingileif remembered when Vigdís and Magnus had come into that very gallery. She had spoken to Vigdís in English, naturally assuming that she was a foreigner. Vigdís had been insulted and replied in Icelandic.

Ingileif winced. That had been embarrassing.

She stopped pacing. She blinked. She felt a tear run down her cheek, and then another, the anger leaking away.

She knew why she was so angry. Because Vigdís was right. She was right, damn her!

'Ingileif? Are you OK?'

It was Sunna, a painter, and one of the co-owners of the gallery.

Ingileif sniffed. 'Not really.' She coughed, trying to force back the tears, but she could feel them coming. 'I've had some bad news. Do you mind if I go out for a walk?'

'Er, no,' said Sunna, her face full of concern. 'No, go on. I'll look after things here.'

Ingileif blundered out. She stalked up the hill towards the big church and then turned down towards the bay.

She liked Magnus. She liked Magnus a lot. And she had hurt him; she knew that.

She had told herself that she wasn't doing anything wrong. She had never pretended that their relationship was serious. When she had told Magnus she was going to the gallery in Hamburg, he hadn't stopped her. He hadn't even *tried* to stop her; that wasn't how their relationship was. They had the freedom to spend time with each other or not as they chose. So when Ingileif had returned to Reykjavík and had chosen to spend time with Magnus, he had seemed happy.

Then she had told him about Kerem in Hamburg. She couldn't lie about that, could she? And he had been jealous, and, it had seemed to her, tried to use his jealousy to control her. She *said* he could make his own friends when she had gone to Germany; she had even set him up with a Facebook page, a necessity for a social life in Iceland. But there was nothing on it, of course.

She had thought that he had liked that about her, her spontaneity. He had mentioned an old girlfriend back in America who had wanted to force him to be someone he wasn't. Ingileif had never tried to do that. That was against everything she believed in.

She was down by the shore of the bay now, the breeze skipping in from the north-west. She turned along the bike path to the Höfdi House, the small white mansion that squatted between modern office buildings and apartment blocks at the edge of the main road that went along the water. She and Magnus had met there once, when she was still a witness to another murder. It was where she had realized that he was something more than a cop, and she knew that he had felt the same.

She had enjoyed their time together, but had he? She smiled to herself. Of course he had. It was their separation that was the problem.

For him, not her.

Because Ingileif knew Vigdís was right. Ingileif had always been in charge. She was the one who dictated the rules of the relationship, who delighted in keeping Magnus off balance, who confused and, yes, excited him. She knew that was one of the reasons that he liked her, but she had taken advantage of him. She had treated him badly.

Ingileif thought of the flash of jealousy she had felt towards Vigdís. Of course Magnus was jealous of Kerem. And if Kerem ever found out, he would be furious.

But if dropping in on Magnus as she had done the week before was wrong, then there were some difficult decisions to be made. She would have to choose between Kerem, or Magnus, or nobody. Ingileif's desire not to be tied down wasn't just a pose; she meant it.

Tricky.

But she would worry about that later. Right now, Magnus was in jail, and he needed her. She thought she had done a good job of hiding from Vigdís what she really knew about Hallgrímur's death. She wouldn't let him down.

CHAPTER SIXTEEN

OLLIE SPILLED OUT of his hotel into the street and headed downhill towards the harbour. He had spent a frustrating hour on the phone to Icelandair, before eventually rebooking a flight to New York for Thursday afternoon. Flights to Boston had been impossible, but frankly he would have accepted Moscow if it got him out of the damned country. He needed to escape his tiny hotel room, get some air, the semblance of freedom.

He felt trapped, alone and scared. He never should have come to Iceland. At least in America he seemed safe, even though he knew that the errors of his past were closing in on him. Here, his precarious position was much more obvious. He was stuck in some godforsaken town in a country he hated where they all spoke a language he didn't understand. He had no car and a volcano had trapped him on the island. And at any moment the police were going to arrest him.

The sun peeked through the clouds and a few rays sprayed the water in the harbour with a bright golden sparkle. Stykkishólmur had a small natural harbour, protected on the fjord side by a basalt rock of steep cliffs. Brightly coloured fishing boats bobbed and rattled, and a large ferry was manoeuvring its way past the rock, out towards the open water of Breidafjördur.

Ollie walked along the harbour wall, the breeze refreshing on his cheeks. The fjord was dotted with innumerable islands. From somewhere in his distant past Ollie remembered something his *amma* had told him. 'There are two things that cannot be counted: the stars in the night sky and the rocky islands of Breidafjördur.'

The thing was, Ollie was scared. Scared for his life. He remembered when the gangster had broken into his house in Medford and stuck that revolver in his mouth. He remembered the taste of the metal, the sound of the click as the man pressed the trigger. The feeling of relief and amazement when he realized there was no bullet in the chamber. The fear that there might be a bullet in the next one or the one after that. The man had wanted to know where Magnus was. Ollie had betrayed his brother then. Ollie had always betrayed the people closest to him. It was how he had survived.

He walked up the steep path on the rock to the seaward side of the harbour. The breeze was stiffer up there. He turned to look at the bright little town with its harbour, its fish factory, the hospital, the brightly painted metal houses – light blue, green, dark red, white, cream, peach – and on a bluff to one side of town, the space-age white church.

Why was it only he who was faced with these horrible choices, to betray or be killed? OK, he had taken a wrong turn or two back when he was a kid, but surely he had paid for those?

His phone buzzed. An SMS. Ollie checked it. He recognized the sender.

Meet me outside the church this afternoon. 4p.m.

Ollie looked at his watch. One-thirty p.m. Shit. He really didn't have any choice.

Sibba found a spot in the car park outside her office on Borgartún and entered the lobby. There was a fresh breeze, and the sun was dodging between the clouds.

Magnus hadn't answered her question. Which meant she probably shouldn't have asked it. If he had admitted that he had killed their grandfather, she would have had to withdraw from representing him there and then. But as it was?

She didn't know. She just didn't know. He was clearly hiding something, and that something could be that he had driven up to Bjarnarhöfn and cold-bloodedly murdered the grandfather whom he had hated since childhood. Or it could be something else. She didn't know. The police didn't know.

But she did know that Magnus hated their grandfather. She hadn't had as much of a problem with him; the old man had always been nice to her. Every few years, she and the rest of her family had made the pilgrimage to Bjarnarhöfn, often at Christmas. Icelandic Christmases were something special: the visits of the Yule Lads, singing carols around the tree on Christmas Eve, the candles and the gifts. Her grandmother was cold to Sibba and her little brother, but her grandfather was always eager to see her, eager to play. He had taken them out into the Berserkjahraun and told them wonderful stories of berserkers and the Vikings who had lived at Bjarnarhöfn and the farm opposite, she forgot the name.

She had enjoyed the attention. But as she grew older she began to notice the fear that everyone in the family felt towards Hallgrímur. His wife, her uncle Kolbeinn, even her own father. And the time she had visited as a teenager when Magnus and his little brother Ollie were staying there, it was clear Ollie was terrified. She remembered Magnus's misery mixed with stoicism; he was a brave kid.

She should resign. Yet Magnus needed her. If he had wanted an experienced criminal lawyer to negotiate a guilty plea, he would have hired one. But he had hired her, to do as he instructed. Which was what, exactly? It was hard to tell.

Sibba was becoming more used to criminal trials, or at least criminal investigations, but those all involved paper. Lots and lots of paper. Statements, financial records, articles of association of offshore companies, shareholder agreements, loan agreements, and e-mails. Hundreds, no thousands, of e-mails. The role of a lawyer was to read the documents and figure out which ones would help and which ones would hinder her client.

But in this case? Sibba wasn't entirely sure what to do. Magnus's strategy of simply refusing to answer any of the police's questions was probably a good one, but it didn't give Sibba anything to get her teeth into. The police were under no obligation to share any of the evidence they were gathering until after twenty-one days.

In the meantime, Sibba didn't even know whether Magnus was planning to plead guilty. Perhaps they could argue that Hallgrímur had accidentally fallen over? Or perhaps he had attacked Magnus and Magnus had pushed him away, so that the old man had tripped and cracked his head. That didn't seem to fit with the medical evidence, but that could be discredited with a little ingenuity. It would help that the victim's son had been the attending doctor. Or perhaps Magnus really had just shown up at Bjarnarhöfn to find his grandfather dead.

In which case, what was he hiding?

Sibba stepped out of the lift into the reception area of her law firm. The receptionist caught her eye.

'There's someone to see you.'

Sibba turned to see a tall black woman wearing jeans and a traditional lopi sweater sitting on a sofa. Who the hell was she? Sibba ran through her clients in her mind. She didn't really look rich enough to be a girlfriend.

'Good afternoon,' she said in English. 'I'm Sigurbjörg. I understand you are waiting for me.'

The woman stood up. She was a good thirty centimetres taller than Sibba.

'*Sael*,' she said. 'My name's Vigdís Audardóttir. Detective Vigdís Audardóttir. I am a colleague of Magnús. I believe you are representing him?' The woman's Icelandic accent was perfect.

Sibba raised her eyebrows. 'Do you have ID?'

The woman's lips pursed in frustration and she pulled out a Reykjavík Metropolitan Police identity card.

Sibba examined it. 'You had better come into my office,' she said.

They sat at Sibba's small conference table.

'Are you here in an official capacity?' she asked the detective.

'No, not at all,' said Vigdís. 'In fact, I am off duty at the moment. And I would be grateful if you wouldn't mention to the police investigators that I have come to see you.'

Sibba examined the woman opposite her for a moment. She looked sincere. Magnus had mentioned that the police were keeping officers from Reykjavík outside the investigation. She was inclined to trust the woman. At least she might learn something from her, if not from Magnus.

She smiled. 'Would you like some coffee?'

Vigdís nodded and Sibba asked the receptionist to bring some.

'I've just come from Litla-Hraun,' Sibba said.

'How's Magnús doing?' Vigdís asked.

'He'd only been there half an hour,' Sibba said. 'But he seems to have things under control.' She chose her words carefully, not wanting to give too much away. 'Do you have some information for me?'

'First of all,' Vigdís said, 'I know he didn't kill his grandfather.'

'Oh?' Sibba leaned forward. 'And why is that?'

'I've worked with Magnús for the last year. He solves murders; he doesn't commit them. It's just not his nature.'

'You're a detective,' Sibba said. 'That's not exactly great evidence, is it?'

'No. But you are a lawyer. It's useful to know whether your client actually committed the crime they are accused of, isn't it?'

'Sometimes,' said Sibba.

'Anyway. Please tell Magnús I'll do anything to help him. And if there is something I can do for you, just ask.'

'I will,' said Sibba. She realized Vigdís meant what she said, and she decided to be a bit more forthcoming. 'The trouble is, it seems like Magnús doesn't want much help.'

'Typical,' said Vigdís with a tight smile. 'I managed to call him just before he was arrested, and he told me to leave it alone. He can be stubborn. But he also might need me.'

'Perhaps you *can* do something for me,' Sibba said. 'Like give me some background.'

Vigdís described what Katrín and Ingileif had told her about Magnus and Ollie's movements in the days before Hallgrímur's murder. She also talked about the link that Magnus was trying to make between his father Ragnar's murder in 1996 in America and the murder of Benedikt Jóhannesson in 1985 in Reykjavík.

She pulled out the police file on the Benedikt case.

'Should you have this?' Sibba asked.

'Not really,' admitted Vigdís.

'In that case, please put it away. I don't want to see it.'

'I understand,' said Vigdís. 'Perhaps I can tell you some of the details of the case? I studied it at police college.'

'Good idea,' said Sibba with a smile. 'But put that file back where it belongs so that I can request it officially.'

Vigdís closed the file and slipped it into her bag. She explained how Benedikt had been found murdered by his son Jóhannes at his house in Vesturbaer. How he had been stabbed once in the back and twice in the chest by someone who was right-handed, just like Ragnar eleven years later. And how that same Jóhannes, a schoolteacher, had made contact with Magnus and Ollie the previous week and then driven Ollie up to the Snaefells Peninsula.

Sibba took detailed notes. She remembered that Magnus had asked her the previous year about the rumour within the family that Ragnar had had an affair with his wife's best friend, but she had had no idea how far Magnus's investigations had taken him. Why the hell hadn't Magnus told her all this that morning?

Vigdís then explained what she had gleaned from the wall in Magnus's bedroom about Ragnar's murder in the small town of Duxbury.

'There's one interesting lead that you might be able to follow up,' Vigdís said.

'Tell me,' said Sibba, pen poised.

'The detective in charge of the investigation in Duxbury back in 1996 was a Sergeant Jim Fearon. He called for Magnús last week, said he had some lab test results for him. Magnús never got the message, and when one of my colleagues called Sergeant Fearon back, the detective refused to give him any information.

Unfortunately my colleague told the detective that Magnús was under arrest for murder, and Fearon said he would only release the test results after an official request.'

'A blue notice?' Sibba said, mentioning the standard Interpol form.

'I guess so.'

'Do we have any idea what the test is about?'

'None. But presumably it has something to do with Ragnar's murder.'

'I'll talk to Magnús.' Sibba frowned.

'You're worried he won't tell you anything about it, aren't you?' said Vigdís.

Sibba nodded. 'Not an easy client, your colleague.'

Vigdís smiled. 'Not always an easy boss either. Maybe you could call Fearon yourself? Here is the number.' She handed Sibba a sheet from a notebook with a US number on it.

'Maybe I will.'

After Vigdís left, Sibba stared out of her window across the bay. Somewhere over there, a hundred kilometres away or more, lay the Snaefells Peninsula. At that moment the Snaefellsjökull was hidden behind cloud.

Sibba was pretty sure she could trust Vigdís. But could she trust Magnus?

There was one awkward phone call she had to deal with first. She dialled a Canadian number. A cell phone.

'Hi, Sibba.'

'Dad, I have something to tell you,' Sibba said. They spoke in English as they had always done since Sibba went to high school.

'Yeah?'

'I'm defending Magnus.'

'Really? Why are you doing that?' Sibba was relieved that her father sounded more puzzled than angry.

'He asked me to.'

'Is that OK? I mean, can you defend a relative?'

'We've discussed conflicts of interest and Magnus is comfortable.'

'You're the lawyer,' said her father. 'But if I were you, I would be pretty uncomfortable.'

As usual, her father took the common-sense approach.

'Am I going to get to see you?' Sibba asked. 'The kids would like it.'

'How are they?' said her father, his voice warm.

'They're both good.'

'Well, I'd like to see them too. Trouble is, I'm needed up here. Your grandmother is not coping well. Her Alzheimer's is much more serious than I thought. She won't even accept that her husband is dead.'

'I didn't know Amma had Alzheimer's.'

'That's why I came over,' said her father. 'Afi asked me to.'

'Perhaps I can come up there at the weekend?'

'I don't know when the funeral will be,' her father said. 'Presumably you could come up for that, eh?'

'That's going to be a problem,' said Sibba. 'There's a murder investigation. The police will want to hold the body.'

'I thought the autopsy was supposed to be today?'

Sibba shuddered. She didn't want to explain that the body would have to be kept in the morgue in case the defence lawyer demanded further evidence, especially since she was the defence lawyer.

Her father was right. Sibba was in a very awkward position.

The church in Stykkishólmur was seriously weird, like everything else in the country. Large for the small town, and painted white, it reminded Ollie of an ultra-modern reincarnation of some of the churches he had seen in New Mexico. It was isolated, on a rock on the edge of town. No one was about so he went inside. The painting behind the altar creeped him out. It was a massive picture of Mary and Jesus against a bright blue background staring at him. It was like they knew he shouldn't be in a church.

He went outside and lit a cigarette. He *had* to keep his shit together. He'd figure a way out of this mess; somehow he always did. He just had to keep his head clear and keep talking.

161

A car pulled up into the lot. Ollie straightened up. The car stopped a few feet away.

'Hi, Ollie.' A man got out of the car. 'I never thought I would see you back in Iceland.'

'Uncle Villi.'

There was something almost comforting in his uncle's deep Canadian accent, but Ollie wasn't comforted.

'Do you want to talk inside the church?'

'You've got to be kidding,' said Ollie. 'Let's stay out here.'

Villi looked around. There was no one about.

'Have the police spoken to you?'

'Yes.'

'And?'

'And I think I did OK. Don't worry; I didn't mention you at all. In fact, when they interviewed me I don't think they even knew you were in the country.'

'Good. I was thinking on the way here, if they check phone records they might know we have been in touch. Just say I am a concerned uncle, OK? Because I am worried about you, Ollie.'

'That's nice,' said Ollie, his voice laced with sarcasm.

Villi turned away from his nephew to look out over the town.

'Ollie. Now your grandfather is dead, there are only two people who know about your role in your father's murder, and that's me and you. Unless you told your brother?'

'There's no way I'd tell my brother that,' said Ollie. 'He'd freak out. He'd probably kill me.'

'Good,' said Villi. 'I'm not going to talk and I really hope you are not going to talk either. Because if you do, you won't go to that comfortable jail where they have sent Magnus. You'll be back in the States in a maximum-security hell. Your life won't be worth living.'

'You'll be there too, Uncle Villi.'

'Ollie, are you trying to threaten me?'

Ollie tried to hold his uncle's eyes but he couldn't. He swallowed, turned away towards the fjord, and took a drag on his cigarette. The damned thing was jumping about in his hand.

Villi sighed. 'Because actually, if I thought you were going to say anything, I might have to take what they call pre-emptive action.'

Ollie swallowed. 'What do you mean by that?'

'You know what I mean.'

Ollie did know. His psycho uncle would kill him, that's what would happen.

'No need to worry about me, Uncle Villi.'

Villi smiled. 'Excellent. So, tell me about this schoolteacher. He came to Bjarnarhöfn last night. He seems to think there's a feud between our family and his.'

'That is his theory. And he's not entirely wrong, is he? But he knows nothing about you, I promise.'

'Keep it that way, eh?'

'The police have let him go. He went back to Reykjavík last night.'

'Good.' Villi turned back towards his car. 'Now, enjoy your stay in Iceland. If I were you, I would get on a plane home as soon as you possibly can.'

'Don't worry, Uncle Villi. I will.'

CHAPTER SEVENTEEN

ST FRANCIS'S HOSPITAL in Stykkishólmur was an angular cream-coloured building down by the harbour. It had been founded by the Catholic convent next door, as part of their mission to save backward Protestant Iceland. The hospital was now run by the state, and was really too big for the three doctors and associated staff who worked there.

Adam argued with the receptionist who wanted him to wait until the last patient was seen before he spoke to Dr Ingvar. The patient in question, a stout woman in her sixties, glared at Adam as the detective insisted on priority. When a girl of about sixteen emerged from the consulting room, Adam walked right in.

The first thing that struck Adam about Ingvar was the purple burn mark across one side of his face and his nose. The second was the frown.

'Who are you?' he demanded.

Adam produced his ID. The doctor took it from him and examined it.

'Keflavík, eh?' He handed it back. 'Can't this wait until I have finished my surgery?'

'I'm afraid not, Ingvar. I have some questions I must ask you,' Adam said, lowering himself into the patient's chair. He was damned if he was going to let this doctor intimidate him. The Dumpling had gone down to Reykjavík, and Adam was pleased that he had been given this interview rather than Björn from Akureyri. He was determined to make the most of it.

He took out his notebook.

'You should have that mole on your forehead seen to,' said Ingvar.

Adam's fingers flew to his brow before he could stop himself. A small misshapen mark had appeared there a year or so before. What did he mean, get it checked? It couldn't be skin cancer, could it?

'Please make it quick,' Ingvar said. 'I really need to get back to Bjarnarhöfn to see my mother. Aníta says she is deteriorating.'

'She is,' said Adam, recovering. 'I want to speak to you about your father's finances.'

Ingvar sat back in his chair and raised his eyebrows. 'Yes?'

'I understand that you had been helping your father with his investments?'

Ingvar nodded. 'I had. I think I gave him some very good advice, actually.'

'From sources at Ódinsbanki?'

Ingvar hesitated. Adam realized the doctor was no dummy; he would know all about the insider trading and market manipulation investigations going on in Reykjavík.

'I think I have a good general overview of the financial markets. It's true that I recommended that my father invest in Ódinsbanki. And again that I told him to sell just before the peak.'

'Very impressive,' said Adam. 'And is it also true that you asked him for a loan as a result a few months ago? As an advance on your inheritance?'

'Where did you get this information?'

'Just answer the question please.'

Ingvar's disapproval was obvious. He leaned forward and fixed his eyes on the young detective. 'Very well. Yes, I did ask my father for a loan. Last August, I think. We have quite a lot of debt: a mortgage on our house here and another on our flat in Paris.'

Adam showed no signs of sympathy. 'And what did your father say to that?'

'He said no.'

'Did this anger you?'

'Yes, it did.'

'Would you say that there was tension between yourself and Hallgrímur as a result?'

'Yes, I would,' said Ingvar carefully.

Adam examined the doctor. He was cautious, but not nervous. He seemed to be in control. And expecting the next question.

'As a result of Hallgrímur's death, can you expect to inherit a significant sum of money?'

Ingvar smiled. 'No.'

'No?'

'No,' said Ingvar. 'Does that surprise you? Didn't your informant tell you that?'

Adam ignored the question. 'So what will happen to Hallgrímur's fortune?'

'He has no fortune,' said Ingvar. 'He sold when I told him to. The market fell a bit and one of his old buddies told him it was a good time to get back in. So he did. He bought a lot of bank shares, most of which are now worthless. Oh, he probably has some money, but not enough to bale me out.'

Ingvar shook his head in disgust. '*That's* what really made me angry. Not that he wouldn't give me a loan. I almost expected that from the old bastard. It was that he had been stupid enough to lose it all. He enjoyed telling me that the inheritance I had been counting on had disappeared. You can check this with my father's lawyer. And his bank.'

Adam wanted to ask why Ingvar hadn't told his wife about Hallgrímur's investment losses, but the question wasn't important. There were a dozen possible reasons, and he didn't want to confirm to Ingvar that Gabrielle was the indirect source of his knowledge. But Adam could tell from the way Ingvar was looking at him that he knew.

'I won't take up any more of your time.'

'Good,' said Ingvar. 'Now, please ask my next patient to come in.'

Adam felt a bit of a fool as he left the hospital. How was he to know that Hallgrímur had blown his profits? He hadn't actually been with Emil when Aníta had informed him of Ingvar's money problems, but Adam doubted that either she or Ingvar's wife knew about the old man's investment losses. He would verify that with Hallgrímur's bank, but he suspected that Ingvar was telling the truth.

The hospital was only two hundred metres from the harbour. Time to check whether Ingvar really was there working on his boat the previous morning when his father was murdered twenty kilometres away.

Emil had forgotten what a jerk Baldur Jakobsson was. He was in Baldur's office at police headquarters in Reykjavík, listening to the inspector doing his best to belittle him. Baldur wasn't being that subtle about it, either.

Emil was older than Baldur, and had been senior to him when Baldur had started in CID, but Baldur now outranked him. Baldur had stayed on in Reykjavík, whereas Emil had moved to Akranes to be near his wife's family farm. That was why Emil's career had been put on hold, yet here was Baldur acting like Emil was a failure.

'So, you haven't had any support yet from Keflavík?' Baldur was saying.

'Actually, they sent me a detective. A guy called Adam. Do you know him?'

'I've met him,' said Baldur. 'But not Thorsteinn? I would have thought he would have the right level of experience.'

Thorsteinn was an inspector in Keflavík's CID. Keflavík had more serious crime than Akranes, so Baldur was right, it would be natural for Thorsteinn to take charge. Except Emil knew he had the confidence of Snorri, his former colleague and the current National Police Commissioner.

'Not yet,' Emil said.

'Soon, I expect,' said Baldur.

'We do have a suspect in custody,' said Emil. 'One of *your* officers.'

'Magnús is not my officer. He just has a desk here. He reports directly to the Commissioner's office.'

'What's he like?' asked Emil. 'I hear he has been quite successful.'

Baldur didn't like that. 'It's true the team have had some successes over the past year. But it's a team effort. Like the arrests we made on Saturday. A team effort. And Magnús isn't really a team player.'

'No?'

'No. He likes to do things his way. Sometimes he gets lucky, but just as often he messes up the investigation. You should know something about Magnús.' Baldur leaned forward conspiratorially.

'What?'

'He's not really an Icelander. Sure, he speaks the language, but he's a Yank through and through. And a Yank policeman at that.'

'What does that mean?'

'It means he is used to violence. And I mean extreme violence. When he was in Boston he was dealing with violent death all the time. It means he demands to carry a gun, and my guess is if we let him carry one here, he'd use it. It means he doesn't ask the right people the right questions in the right way. It means he knows all these modern investigative techniques, but he doesn't know good old-fashioned police work.'

Baldur shook his head in disappointment at the way things had come to pass. 'He's here because the Commissioner thinks that Iceland is beginning to suffer the kind of crime that places like Boston experience every day. But you know what? I think that when the police start behaving like Magnús, the criminals will start behaving like gangsters too.'

'I see,' said Emil.

'What I'm saying is that an Icelandic policeman couldn't possibly commit murder. None of us could. But Magnús comes from a more violent world. To him, murder is different. It's day-to-day.'

'So you think he killed his grandfather?'

'I assume he did, which is why you've arrested him,' said Baldur. 'What I'm saying is, I'm not surprised.'

Emil felt almost sorry for Magnus. But maybe Baldur had a point. Maybe violent death was less extraordinary to Magnus than it would be to an ordinary Icelander.

'Do you mind if I question some of the detectives he has been working with? Find out what they have noticed over the last few days?'

'Not at all. He works with two of them, primarily. One is off duty, but the other is right here in the department.'

Baldur introduced Emil to Árni Holm, and then left them. Emil liked the young detective. He knew of him already – he was Thorkell Holm's nephew. Thorkell was the chief superintendent in charge of CID, which was no doubt how Árni had got his job in the Violent Crimes Unit. Where Baldur had been disparaging about Magnus, Árni was gushing in his praise. Such innocent, blind loyalty was touching.

Árni took Emil through everything that Magnus had done over the previous week in the investigation involving the Italian tourist killed on the volcano. Emil couldn't see a link to Hallgrímur's death, but unless he asked the questions, he wouldn't know for sure.

'Did Magnús talk about his family much?' Emil asked.

'Not really,' said Árni. 'He is quite private. I met his cousin once, a lawyer called Sigurbjörg Vilhjálmsdóttir, and I knew he had spent time with his grandparents in the Snaefells Peninsula. Also his brother from America is staying with him, but I'm sure you know that.'

So Sigurbjörg Vilhjálmsdóttir was Magnus's cousin as well as his lawyer? That was interesting. In Iceland's closed society it wasn't remarkable that a lawyer should act for her cousin. Unless the cousin had murdered their common grandfather. Now that *was* strange.

'Did he mention his father's murder in 1996?' Emil asked.

'No.'

'Or the murder of Benedikt Jóhannesson in 1985?'

Árni scratched his ear and shook his head.

'Are you sure, Árni?'

'Yes.' Árni nodded vigorously. 'Quite sure.'

'In that case, can you explain why the file is signed out under your name?'

'Er.'

Árni's eyes were wide, startled. Emil could see him trying to put together an explanation. Emil almost felt sorry for him.

'Take some advice, Árni. Don't lie to me. Whatever you do, don't lie to an investigating officer. Just tell me the truth.'

'I think I'll stick with "er",' said Árni.

Emil shook his head. 'Can I have the file please, Árni?'

'Er.'

Emil raised his eyebrows.

'The file is... somewhere else. I'll get it to you soon. Very soon.'

Emil's tone hardened. 'I don't know what you are doing with that file, Árni, or why it isn't right here on your desk. But wherever it is, I want it here in the next hour. Do you understand?'

'Yes,' said Árni crisply.

'Good. One last thing. Were you on duty here yesterday morning?'

'Yes,' said Árni.

'When did you hear that Magnús had discovered Hallgrímur's body?'

'Some time that morning.'

'Who told you?'

'Baldur. He got a call from the Commissioner.'

'Magnús didn't tell you himself?'

'No.' Árni noticed the expression on Emil's face. 'I mean...'

'Don't even try to lie about that,' said Emil. 'I understand your colleague Vigdís is on leave for a couple of days. I'd like to talk to her. Give me her number.'

Árni examined his phone and dictated some digits. Emil wrote them down and left.

The morgue wasn't far from police headquarters, just up the road on Barónsstígur, but Emil opted to drive. He slumped into the seat of his car, panting, and wiped sweat from his brow with the back of his hand. His heart was beating too fast again. He rested for a moment, and then took out his phone and called Björn in Stykkishólmur.

'I know it's early, but have we got the records on Magnús's mobile phone yet?'

'Just come in,' said Björn.

'That was quick.' Emil had only got the warrant from the judge in Borgarnes earlier that morning. Sometimes the phone company could take days to provide information.

'Told them it was a murder inquiry,' said Björn, with a touch of pride in his voice.

'Well done. Can you check what calls Magnús made after he discovered the body? That would be roughly eleven-thirty yesterday morning.'

'Sure. Hang on a moment.' Emil heard the rustling of papers. 'He called 112 at 11.29. Then nothing until 12.02.'

'What was that number? I bet it wasn't anyone at police head-quarters.'

'Let's see. An international call. The country code was forty-nine. Where's that?'

'That's Germany,' said Emil. 'Find out who is registered on that number as quickly as possible and call me back.'

Emil put down his phone. Who the hell would Magnus want to call in Germany?

Half an hour later, Emil was in the morgue, kitted out in scrubs, standing over a trolley bearing the pale, wizened body of an old man. The autopsy revealed nothing unexpected. The pathologist confirmed that the cause of death was cerebral bleeding following five blows to the skull. And fragments of wood in the victim's scalp suggested that these may well have been inflicted by the murderer banging the victim's head against a wooden floor. There were signs that three strands of hair had been pulled out by the roots.

There were plenty of other things wrong with Hallgrímur's body, but nothing that wouldn't be expected from moving parts that were more than eighty years old. In fact, for his age, he had been in good health. The one thing that caught the pathologist's attention was a couple of bruises on Hallgrímur's arm and legs, both a few days old, and signs of pinprick bleeds. The victim wasn't on any blood-thinning drugs, which suggested a possibility of leukaemia, a suspicion that would be quickly checked by analysis of the blood samples he had taken.

Afterwards, Emil went on to the house in Njálsgata where Magnus lived, a search warrant in his pocket. Magnus's landlady, an extraordinary-looking young woman named Katrín, turned out to be Árni's sister. Funny how the detective had failed to mention it. She was surly, but when Emil showed her his warrant, she gave a brief account of Magnus's comings and goings over the previous few days. She told him about his brother Ollie, his row with his ex-girlfriend Ingileif, and his departure in a hurry to follow Ollie and his schoolteacher friend north.

Then she took him upstairs to Magnus's room. She left Emil taking photographs of Magnus's wall.

He was writing up notes when his phone buzzed. It was Adam.

'How did you do with Ingvar?' Emil asked.

'Looks unlikely,' Adam said. 'He admitted that Hallgrímur had made millions on the stock market with Ingvar's help, but apparently he lost it all later. Ingvar was angry about that, but he doesn't expect to inherit anything.'

'His wife is in for a bit of a shock,' said Emil.

'I tried not to let on that was where we got the information, but I think Ingvar guessed. I checked with Hallgrímur's bank in town, who confirmed he had had a brokerage account there, but that he had closed it down when the shares in it became worthless.'

'What about the will? Do we know how much he had in his estate? And who he left it to?' The question had to be asked, but under Icelandic inheritance law, two-thirds of the deceased's estate had to be divided equally among 'forced heirs', meaning spouse and children. Only one third could be disposed of according to the deceased's will.

'I'll check,' said Adam.

'Anyone confirm that Ingvar was working on his boat at the time of the murder?' Emil asked.

'Yes. The harbourmaster. And the captain of the ferry, who is one of his patients and saw him.'

'That's pretty clear, then,' Emil said. 'Did Björn have any luck with the phone number?'

'It's a mobile phone, and most of those numbers are unlisted.'

'Damn! We'll have to get on to the German police.'

'No we don't,' said Adam. 'I dialled the number. Got put through to voicemail. It may be a German phone, but the owner is an Icelander, and her name is Ingileif Gunnarsdóttir.'

Emil studied the woman sitting behind the desk at the back of the small gallery in Skólavördustígur. Her colleague had agreed to leave them for a few minutes and had flipped the sign on the door to 'Closed'.

She was slender, pretty, with blonde hair hanging down in a fringe over her eyes. Emil noticed a small scar on her left eyebrow. She seemed cool and controlled but she avoided Emil's eyes.

Emil had simply called the number and asked to speak to her immediately. It had taken him less than ten minutes to drive from Magnus's flat to the gallery.

'You have no doubt heard that Magnús Ragnarsson has been arrested for murder?'

'Yes,' said Ingileif. 'Of his grandfather. But I don't believe it. It can't be true.'

'You were his girlfriend, I understand?'

173

'Yes,' said Ingileif. 'We met about a year ago. But then last autumn I went away to Hamburg, and we finished it.'

'Finished it? Didn't you spend the night with him last week?'

'Yes.' Ingileif smiled quickly. 'Yes, I did. But...' She glanced briefly at Emil and then away again. 'It wasn't a good idea. You see, I have a friend back in Germany, and Magnús didn't like that. So we had a bit of a row. I stormed out. I haven't seen him since.'

'And when exactly was that?'

'Er, Thursday night, I think. Yes, Thursday.'

'And you say you haven't seen him since?'

'Yes,' said Ingileif, raising her head.

'Have you heard from him?'

'No.'

Emil let the silence hang. 'Are you sure?' he asked eventually.

Ingileif's cheeks reddened. She seemed to feel it, because she rubbed them and then stared down at the surface of the desk.

'Not even yesterday morning?' Emil asked.

She looked up. 'No.' Stronger this time.

'The phone records show that Magnús called your number at 12.02 p.m. yesterday.'

The redness spread down towards her chin. Emil reeled her in patiently. He raised his eyebrows.

'I must have missed it. Although I didn't notice a missed call.'

'He spoke for seven minutes.'

'Did he?' Ingileif looked away at a painting of Mount Esja on the wall. 'Perhaps he was leaving a message.'

'For seven minutes? Did you hear one?'

'I didn't check.'

'Can you check now?'

Ingileif pulled out her phone and began to press buttons. Then she sighed and put it down. 'OK. Yes, he did call me.'

'And what did he say?'

She looked at him. Opened her mouth and closed it again.

'Ingileif, this is a murder inquiry,' Emil said gently. 'We already have plenty of evidence against Magnús, probably enough to convict him. There will be a trial and this phone call will be a key piece of evidence. You will have to take the stand and tell the court what Magnús told you. If you lie, it won't get him off the hook. But you will be charged with perjury. In fact, if you lie now, I will charge you with obstructing a murder inquiry. So think hard before you speak.'

Ingileif said nothing. The redness drained from her face. Then she bit her bottom lip and nodded.

'So what did Magnús say?' Emil asked again.

Ingileif coughed. 'He said he had just killed his grandfather.'

CHAPTER EIGHTEEN

January 2010

THE HOUSE IN Wellesley Hills didn't look big from the road, but as Magnus drove up the short driveway, he saw it was expensive. Snow lay across the carefully landscaped yard, and upon the cover of the fenced-in swimming pool.

It had taken him nearly an hour to find his stepmother's address. The process had involved using a public computer in Duxbury's library and calling her first husband, the one before Ragnar, whose name Magnus could remember. Kathleen was now Mrs Lichtburg, and she had clearly done well for herself. According to her former husband, Mr Lichtburg ran an investment-management boutique, whatever that was.

Magnus rang the doorbell. It was almost five o'clock and he had no idea whether Mrs Lichtburg would be in, but after a few seconds the door opened.

She was probably over fifty now, but she hadn't changed much. Red hair – coloured now, no doubt – a little make-up, expensive top and jeans. Well-groomed, thinner than Magnus remembered her.

'Yes? Can I help you?' She clearly didn't recognize him.

'It's Magnus.'

'Magnus?' She almost smiled, and then frowned. 'What do you want?'

'To talk to you about Dad.'

'Well, I don't want to talk to you. I was hoping I would never set eyes on you again.'

Magnus was about to protest vigorously when he stopped himself. She would just slam the door in his face. He forced a lopsided grin.

'Aw, Mom. That's not very nice! I've missed you.'

The idea of Kathleen being his mom struck both of them as absurd. Although for a couple of years she had indeed been his stepmother, he had never called her 'Mom', nor had she expected him to.

She laughed. 'Oh, all right. Come in. But only if you have a glass of wine.'

He followed her through into a large kitchen. There were photographs of kids graduating from something or other.

'These yours?' Magnus asked, although he knew that they were too old to be hers.

'They are Brian's. Stepchildren, you could say. Although I get on with them a whole lot better than I did with you.'

'Oh, you got on with Ollie OK, didn't you?'

Kathleen had her back to him as she took a bottle of wine out of the refrigerator. When she turned she checked his eyes to see whether he meant anything significant. Magnus gave no sign that he did.

'I was glad to get rid of the both of you,' she said, pouring two glasses. 'I was going to say, haven't you been able to forget your dad, but that's a bit cruel even for me. What is it? His estate? No, I know. You're still trying to solve his murder, aren't you?'

She sat at a stool at the island counter in the middle of the kitchen and Magnus sat opposite her.

He nodded. 'I've just been to see the detective who investigated the case down in Duxbury.'

'And he confirmed my innocence, I hope?'

'Oh, yes. He was quite sure where you were.' Magnus looked around the house. 'I see you didn't end up in Pembroke.'

'No, I most certainly didn't end up in Pembroke,' Kathleen said. 'Actually, I like where I am now.'

'I'm sure,' said Magnus.

'No, I don't just mean the money. Brian's a good man. And I think I'm a better person. There was ten years there where you could say I made some poor life choices.'

'Like marrying my dad?'

'And other things. Mind you, it was a mistake we both made. I thought he was good-looking, exotic, exciting. But it turned out that your father was dull. The only things he was interested in were math and Iceland.'

'That might be enough for some people,' said Magnus, who had been fascinated by his father.

'Maybe,' said Kathleen. 'But not me. And I could see him falling out of love with me in front of my eyes. I didn't like that.'

'So you started sleeping around?'

'As I say, I made some poor choices.'

'Including sleeping with my brother?'

Kathleen winced. 'You know about that?'

'Jim Fearon just told me. The Duxbury detective.'

'He promised me he wouldn't,' Kathleen said. 'But I guess it's a long time ago. To answer your question, that was a particularly poor choice of action.'

'And Dad found out?'

Kathleen nodded. 'He knew I had been sleeping with someone else. I told him it was his son. I was really angry with him about something, I can't remember what precisely now. Of course, what I was really angry with was that he didn't love me any more and I had been dumb enough to marry him.'

'And how did he take that?'

'He was furious. With me. With Ollie. He shut himself away with his math. It was all very unpleasant. And then someone killed him.'

'And you've no idea who?'

Kathleen flashed her green eyes at Magnus. 'No, Magnus, I have no idea who killed him. Ollie was at the beach; I was with the air-con guy. And if you think I hired someone to kill him, which, by the way, your detective friend seemed to believe for a day or two, you're wrong. I felt trapped, but there was an easy way out. Divorce. I had done it before – I knew how. We hadn't discussed it, but we would have done. I'm sure if your father hadn't died we would have been divorced within a year.'

'Do you remember seeing any Icelanders around in the days before my father died?'

'Icelanders?' Kathleen was surprised by the change in tack. 'No. What sort of Icelanders?'

'My mother's family, perhaps?'

Kathleen shook her head. 'No. Ragnar hated the whole lot of them, didn't he? And he didn't have much of his own family left. I never saw any of them.' She sipped her wine. 'I mean, he had a couple of Icelander friends in Boston. You might remember them. Gylfi at Boston College. That guy who worked at one of those biotech companies on Route 128, Haraldur, I think his name was? A couple of others he saw occasionally. I didn't have much to do with them.'

Those weren't the kind of Icelanders Magnus meant. He examined the woman whom he had hated so much for so long.

He still hated her.

He put down his glass of wine. 'I've got to go, Kathleen. I doubt we will see each other again.' He stood up.

'You don't like me, do you?' Kathleen said.

Magnus shook his head. 'No, I don't.'

For a moment there was something close to sympathy in his stepmother's eyes. Then it vanished.

'Well, you'd better fuck off then.'

Magnus sat in his car on Stanton Street in Medford. He had been there for two hours. It was dark and it was quiet. His feet were beginning to feel cold, so he turned on the engine. What would he do if Ollie didn't come home at all? His brother could easily be out with some woman all night. Magnus had decided not to give Ollie advance warning of his presence in Boston. He wanted the conversation that he knew would ensue to take place face-to-face, not over the phone from Iceland.

It had begun to snow, gently.

Two figures approached along the sidewalk, a man and a woman. Even though he couldn't see the man's face, Magnus could tell from his walk that it was his brother. The woman's arm was hooked through the man's. They were both wrapped up in coats and hats.

They stopped outside a small white clapboard house and Ollie opened the door. Magnus gave them five minutes, then rang the bell.

'Hey, Magnus!' Ollie said, his face splitting into a huge grin when he saw his brother. 'What the hell are you doing here, man?' He gave Magnus a hug. Magnus couldn't help smiling.

'Come in, come in,' Ollie said.

Magnus followed Ollie into the familiar ground-floor apartment. He had stayed there himself a couple of times, most noticeably when the Dominican gangsters had been after him the year before. A blonde woman was sitting on the sofa. Very pretty. Very young.

'Hey, Brandy, this is my brother Magnus.'

'Hey,' said the girl, giving Magnus a sulky glance. She didn't seem overexcited by the company.

'Hi, Brandy,' said Magnus.

'Can I get you a beer?' said Ollie. 'I got Sam Adams.'

'Great,' said Magnus, taking the armchair.

'Brandy, could you get us some beers, please?'

The girl went to do as she was told.

'How old is she?' whispered Magnus as the girl headed through to the kitchen.

'Old enough,' said Ollie. 'Believe me.'

'Tenant?' Magnus knew that Ollie owned a few properties that were rented by students at Tufts, the university just up the hill from his street.

'Tenant's best friend,' Ollie replied. 'So what are you doing back in Boston? You got your old job back?'

'Just here for a couple of days. Checking in with headquarters. Thought I'd drop by.' The girl returned with three bottles of beer and an opener. 'Is it OK if I stay the night?'

Ollie glanced at the girl, whose sulky expression deepened. 'Sure. You got a car out there?'

'Yeah. My stuff's in the trunk. I'll bring it in later.'

'How come you didn't call?' Ollie asked, turning back to Magnus. But there was a hesitancy in his tone, which suggested he could guess the real answer.

'Wasn't sure of my plans,' said Magnus.

'Huh,' said Ollie.

Magnus cracked the beer and took a swig. It was good.

'So, where you been today?' Ollie asked, with the look of someone who had a fair idea of the answer.

Magnus drew in his breath. 'Duxbury.'

'Duxbury, huh? Now why would you want to go there?'

The girl on the sofa was watching the two brothers carefully. She had noticed the tension rising.

'I had a chat with Sergeant Detective Fearon. You remember him?'

'Oh, man! Can't you just leave all that alone?'

'He told me something very interesting.'

'What?' Ollie framed the question in a tone that suggested he didn't want to know the answer.

'That you slept with our stepmother.'

'Oh, Jesus!'

The girl roused herself. 'You slept with your stepmother?'

'It was thirteen years ago,' said Ollie. 'I was just a kid.'

'And that makes it better? Isn't that, like, incest? Yuk.'

'Yeah, yuk,' said Magnus.

'Hey, I think I'll leave you two guys to chat about old times,' said Brandy. 'Later, Ollie. Maybe.'

Ollie let her go.

'Nice girl,' said Magnus.

'Magnus, what the fuck are you doing here?'

'I've come to tell you I am going to ask questions. About Dad's murder. Back in Iceland and here.'

'Oh, man! We've been through this before.'

'What, are you afraid I'm going to discover something unpleasant? Like you banging our stepmother?'

'Yes! Yes, Magnus. You'll drag it all up. Me sleeping with Kathleen. Dad getting killed. Kathleen having her affair. And then you're going to bring up Grandpa and all that family of weirdoes. Mom's death. God knows what else.'

'Maybe it's time to face it,' said Magnus. 'I've held off for years for your sake, but I can't do it any more. I've got to know who killed Dad. Don't you understand that, Ollie? It's been eating me up ever since it happened. It's the one big enormous unresolved issue that is destroying my whole life.'

'Magnus, you're strong,' said Ollie. 'You know that and I know that. And believe me, I appreciate it. You've helped me out so many times in the past. I need your strength.'

Magnus was quiet, watching his younger brother.

'But I'm not strong, Magnus. Never have been. Of course I'm ashamed of screwing Kathleen. It's one of the dumbest things I've done in my life, and God knows there are a lot of those. You know what's behind all this, Magnus, for you and for me?'

'Yeah. Dad's death.'

Ollie shook his head. 'No. It's Afi.' Magnus noted that his brother used the Icelandic name for their grandfather, rather than the American 'grandpa', which they had slipped into soon after they arrived in the States.

'Afi screwed me up. Screwed us both up. It was him who messed up Mom.'

'Yeah, and I have a strong suspicion that he was behind Dad's murder as well,' said Magnus. 'That's why I need to find out more. And if he was responsible, he should pay, even if he is in his eighties.'

Ollie sighed. 'You know it was about this time last year when that psycho came round here, looking for you? Put a gun in my mouth.'

'Yes,' said Magnus. 'Yes, I'm sorry about that.'

'Well, I don't doubt you are used to hit men sticking guns in your mouth, but I'm not. It shook me up. I did a few more drugs than I should of. I got drunk. I let things slip.'

Magnus nodded. He wasn't surprised. But that familiar feeling of guilt which was always lurking somewhere at the back of the room whenever he was talking to his brother was beginning to slink out into the open.

'Then a girlfriend told me I should go and see a shrink again. I said no, but she made me. So I went to this therapist. She spent the summer trying to get me to tell her about Afi and the farm and I spent the summer trying not to. Then you called up last September all excited because you had found some Icelandic links to Dad's death. You remember that?'

Magnus nodded. 'I do. But then you asked me not to investigate any more, and I said I wouldn't.'

'And thank you for that. It helped. Even so, things got weird back here. But it turned out this shrink knew what she was doing. I've started talking to her about Bjarnarhöfn. And you. And Dad. In fact, I saw her this afternoon.'

'Does it help?'

Ollie nodded. 'Yeah. I think for once in my life I might finally be getting my shit together. And that's big for me. I think I'm a pretty successful guy, really, but when things are going right, I screw them up, like I was doing it on purpose. Like in 2007, I could have sold all my properties for a big gain, but what did I do? I turned down the offer and borrowed money to buy more. I *knew* it was dumb, but I did it anyway. And that's what my shrink said to me. I won't let myself succeed.'

'So what are you saying?' said Magnus. 'If I don't back off you'll take drugs again? Or are you saying that I'm responsible for your greedy real-estate investments?'

Ollie took a sip of beer and looked at his brother coolly. 'No. I'm saying that I was on the edge, but now things are going well. I'm saying if you leave me alone to work on this, I can straighten myself out. And then you won't have to pick up the pieces any more. Here you are, trying to avenge Dad. But think what he would have done, what he would want *you* to do. It's your call.'

Magnus was facing the familiar situation. He, the strong, competent one, was being manipulated by his brother's uselessness.

But it had to stop. He had made the decision that it had to stop. He just had to go through with it.

'Ollie. When I get back to Iceland I am going to ask more questions. I'm going to find out whether Afi was behind Dad's death, and if he wasn't, I'm going to find out who was.'

'Please,' said Ollie.

Magnus stared at his brother. And shook his head. 'No. Sorry, Ollie. No.'

Ollie closed his eyes. 'In that case, fuck off. Just get the hell out of here.'

Magnus was about to say sorry again but stopped himself. It was time to stop saying sorry. He drained his beer, stood up and left.

He didn't go back to the car, but walked up the hill towards the university campus. Snowflakes were falling steadily. A thin layer of slush lay on the salted sidewalk, but on the verges soft new snow gently refilled the footprints that had been formed over the previous few days. There was scarcely anyone around.

That was twice in a few hours he had been told to fuck off by members of his family. He genuinely didn't care about Kathleen. And he had expected trouble from Ollie.

He was glad Ollie was getting somewhere with a therapist. Their father had sent him along a couple of times when Ollie was a teenager, but he had never really cooperated and so had achieved nothing. Ollie was probably right: their grandfather was behind his psychological problems. And although Ollie said that Magnus was stronger than him, there was no doubt that Magnus had his own issues. His obsession with his father's death went way beyond a natural desire to see justice done. It wasn't even revenge. Magnus wasn't really sure what it was. An attempt to restore order to his world? Some kind of guilt he felt towards his father, or his mother, or even Ollie?

A therapist would have a field day. If Magnus ever let one near him. Oddly, the one person who had gotten closest to understanding his obsession was Ingileif, and now she was gone.

He hoped that by solving the crime, he would deal with the

problem once and for all. That was what was driving him on; that was what drove him to do his day job of solving one homicide after another. But would it? The thought that it might not, that even if he knew who had killed his father and brought whoever it was to justice he still wouldn't be able to sleep easily, scared him.

Unlike Ollie, Magnus had always admired his father. Even when the boys had been abandoned at Bjarnarhöfn, Magnus had known that Ragnar would return for him, and he had. Ragnar had read the sagas aloud to Magnus every night; they had enjoyed those tales of medieval murder and revenge together. The saga heroes who sought justice for their relatives were Ragnar's heroes, as well as Magnus's.

And yet.

And yet Magnus knew that although his father was very proud of him, he wasn't worried about him, he was worried about Ollie. He had always been worried about Ollie, from when he had hauled the damaged little boy over to Boston, probably even to when he had discovered eight years later that his son was sleeping with his wife.

He had never said it, but Magnus knew that his father blamed himself for how Ollie had turned out. If Ollie really could sort himself out, once and for all, then his father would be happy. And if Magnus helped him do it, then he would be proud of his eldest son.

But was Ollie really sorting himself out? Could he ever sort himself out? Wasn't he just a lost cause?

Magnus stopped and turned around. He was close to the summit of the small hill, with Tufts University buildings around him. Through the snowflakes he could see the lights of Cambridge and, beyond that, the city of Boston glowing softly through the flakes.

Ollie was a lost cause as soon as Magnus gave up on him. There *was* no one else.

Magnus blinked as a flake fell in his eye. He stood still, letting the decision he was making wash over him. He knew what his father would want him to do.

He pulled out his phone and selected Ollie's number.

'Yeah?' his brother answered.

'You win, Ollie,' Magnus said. 'I'll quit asking questions. But on one condition. You keep seeing that therapist.'

Magnus could hear his brother exhaling. There was silence for moment.

'Thanks, bro,' Ollie said. 'Thanks.'

He hung up.

Magnus put the phone back in his pants pocket and hurried down the hill back to his car. He didn't want to stay with Ollie that night. It should be easy to find a hotel room.

Or.

When he got to the car, he started it up and headed for Harvard Bridge over the Charles to the Back Bay.

CHAPTER NINETEEN

Monday, 19 April 2010

ANÍTA STIRRED THE stew. She still felt agitated, and as night came closer her agitation increased. In the end she had walked down the track with Kolbeinn to speak to the press; it was clear they wouldn't go away until someone had done so. She had done all the talking, but she couldn't deny that it had helped having Kolbeinn's large presence beside her. She had managed to hold it together, but it had been difficult.

But she had had a good conversation with Ingvar that afternoon, who had agreed to fetch Sylvía the following day and have her stay with him and Gabrielle. He would try to take her down to Reykjavík to see a specialist gerontologist in the next few days. He wasn't sure to what extent her confusion was psychological, and to what extent the result of Alzheimer's or possibly mini strokes. He was clearly feeling guilty that he had neglected his mother over the previous few months, although, being Ingvar, he wasn't about to admit it.

So, one more night to get through. Aníta was still worried that Sylvía might start a fire. Villi was in the guest bedroom and Sylvía was sharing Tóta's room. Aníta had given her daughter strict instructions to wake her up if she heard her grandmother get up in the night. Aníta planned to hide all the matches in the house before she went to bed.

Once again, Tóta was watching *Shrek* with her grandmother. The dinner could look after itself for a few minutes, so

Aníta decided to go up to Tóta's bedroom, just to check Sylvía's stuff.

The room was reasonably tidy. Tóta was sleeping on a camp bed and Sylvía in Tóta's bed. Sylvía's clothes were neatly folded in the small suitcase they had taken out of her cottage the night before. Feeling slightly guilty, Aníta ran her fingers through the garments, feeling for a box of matches or a lighter. Nothing there.

Sylvía had packed a little wash bag that was on the bed stand. Nothing odd there either.

She ran her hands under the pillow. Nothing. She felt a bit stupid searching her mother-in-law's stuff for non-existent matches, but not half as stupid as she would feel if the old lady burned the house down that night.

She stood back. Her eyes caught the wooden corner of a small box under the bed. She bent down to take a look.

She didn't recognize it, but it was clearly very old – the dark-stained wood had split. It was perhaps twenty centimetres long. She hesitated before opening it. People put private stuff in boxes like that.

But what if there were matches in there? Aníta knew that it was partly that fear and partly just plain curiosity that made her open the box.

There were only a few small items inside. Two old brooches. A locket containing an old black-and-white photograph of a woman, who Aníta was pretty sure was Sylvía's mother. A tiny framed photograph of a pretty blonde girl of about eight: Margrét, Sylvía's daughter. Aníta examined the photograph for a moment and decided there was only a superficial similarity with her own daughter Tóta.

She heard heavy footsteps on the landing outside Tóta's room. Aníta had left the door open. She shut the box quickly as Villi poked his head around the door. He saw Aníta with the box on her knee.

'Oh, it's you,' he said. 'I thought it was my mother.'

'No, she's downstairs with Tóta,' said Aníta. She reddened. 'I was just checking to make sure Sylvía didn't have any matches or anything.'

'You don't think she'll start another fire, do you?'

'No. But I want to be sure.' Aníta considered sharing her discovery of the box with Villi, but thought better of it. It would show that she had been snooping. 'Frankly, the sooner she is at Ingvar's house, the happier I will be.'

'He said he would come tomorrow afternoon,' said Villi. 'I'll make sure he does.'

'Thanks,' said Aníta.

Villi hesitated. They looked at each other. Aníta felt a desire to throw herself into his arms, to explain everything: Hallgrímur's ghost, the woman in the lava field, her fear that Sylvía would burn the house down, everything. And to look through the box together.

But she resisted it. She sat motionless.

'See you later,' said Villi, eventually.

'Dinner is in about half an hour.'

Aníta waited a full minute and then got up to shut the door. She sat on Sylvía's bed and opened the box again.

There was an airmail envelope in the box. She lifted it up and underneath lay a single earring, the mate of the one the police had shown them that morning.

The envelope bore a United States stamp, and was addressed to Hallgrímur. Inside it was a postcard. She slipped it out.

Aníta knew she shouldn't read the card. There were no matches in there, she should just put everything away and replace the box under the bed. But she couldn't help herself.

What she read changed everything.

Villi stood staring out of the window of the small guest bedroom. He hadn't liked the guilty look on Aníta's face. He had hoped that his hesitation would prompt her to be forthcoming, and he sensed that it almost had. She was clearly snooping in his mother's stuff. But what had she found?

There was only one way to find out. He waited. The smell of stew wafted up from the kitchen. Aníta would have to return there at some point to see to dinner.

It was only about five minutes before he heard Aníta's footsteps hurry along the landing and down the stairs. He slipped out of his own room and into Tóta's. It took him only a few seconds to locate the box under Sylvía's bed.

He found the little pieces of jewellery. And the envelope, addressed to his father in his own handwriting.

He pulled out the postcard and scanned the writing on its back, even though he could remember what it said.

Shit! What the hell was he going to do now?

Dinner was difficult. Villi did his best to play that traditional Icelandic role, the successful relative from the west returning home to his family. He managed to keep his air of calm, even when Aníta started asking who was where in the winter of 1985. Villi insisted that it was the following year, 1986, when he had brought his family over for Christmas. That was before Aníta's time; she hadn't married Kolbeinn until the early nineties. Kolbeinn didn't contradict him. Neither, thank God, did Sylvía.

After dinner, Villi excused himself and went out for a walk, striding west towards Cumberland Bay. The clouds had mostly gone and the sun was dipping down towards the horizon. The shadow of the snow-topped Bjarnarhöfn Fell darkened the Berserkjahraun behind him. A small group of Aníta's horses ambled across their paddock towards him.

What was he going to do with her?

Life was so much easier in Canada. There he was the man he wanted to be. A well-respected retired civil engineer, reliable, honest, not exactly a pillar of his local community, but someone most people liked. He had been a good husband, almost faithful. He had brought up two decent children with good jobs and nice kids of their own.

But here in Iceland... Here in Iceland he was something else. A murderer.

He was nineteen. It was the night of the *sveitaball*, the summer dance in Stykkishólmur. He got drunk; all the kids got drunk. It was a lovely summer's night, one of dusk rather than darkness, when the sun rolled under the horizon for a couple of hours before rolling up again, unnoticed. He had kissed a girl; he couldn't even remember her name. He had taken her off to a cove a few hundred metres away from the dance. She had come willingly.

So had her boyfriend. Villi could remember *his* name: Atli. He was a year or so younger than Villi and quite a bit smaller. Just as drunk. And angry as hell.

He had jumped Villi on the path down to the cove. They were maybe ten metres above the sea. It had all been over in seconds. Atli had swung at Villi, who had parried his blow, and stumbled backwards. Atli had shoved Villi hard and Villi had nearly fallen. The anger had risen in Villi – the bastard had nearly killed him! Atli lunged again, and this time Villi moved out of the way. He hooked his own foot around Atli's and Atli fell.

There were rocks down below and the sea rose in a swell against them. Villi looked down at the body of Atli, which was being thrust against the rocks in a macabre rhythm. Atli seemed to be head down in the water. There was no easy way down there, and besides, it looked dangerous. Villi knew how drunk he was: if he went down to try to help Atli, he would probably fall in too.

The girl had run away back up the path. She was just as drunk as the two boys. Villi turned and hurried after her.

That was his mistake. If he had only stayed, tried to fish Atli out of the water. Even if he had failed he could kid himself that it was all an accident, it was all Atli's fault, that Villi had done everything he could. But because he walked away, he couldn't rid himself of the memory of hooking his foot around Atli's.

Villi had killed another boy. From that fact, everything else had followed.

Villi reached the shore of the inlet that was known as Cumberland Bay after the English traders from that county who used to put in there in the Middle Ages. Now there was just grass and cormorants.

It was strange to see Aníta again. She was still beautiful, although she must have been nearer fifty than forty. He remembered those three magical days. For him it had been a form of escapism; not escape from his respectable life in Canada, but from those other memories that Bjarnarhöfn brought back. Atli.

And his father.

He didn't give a damn about Ollie. The snivelling little bastard deserved all his troubles. But Aníta. Oh, Aníta! What the hell was he going to do about Aníta?

Vigdís jogged down the hill from her apartment building towards the harbour. She lived in the fishing port of Hafnarfjördur, a few kilometres south-west of Reykjavík, just off the highway to Keflavík.

It was nine o'clock and still light. Vigdís was amazed how quickly the evenings lengthened in April: it was less than four weeks since the equinox. What Icelanders laughably called 'The first day of summer' was only three days away. The last weather report she had seen had forecast a 30 per cent chance of snow.

It had been a bad evening. After a panicky phone call from Árni, she had met him in Café Roma to return the Benedikt file, and then she had headed out to Keflavík to see her mother. She had cooked them both an early supper of pasta. Things weren't too bad: there was no sign of the Pole, her mother had only been ten minutes late to work that morning, and she seemed cold sober. But she had drunk 'just one glass' of red wine at supper. There was three-quarters of a bottle left when Vigdís had gone home.

Her mother had insisted that the night before had been a one-off. But Vigdís had learned enough about her mother to know that a one-off became a two-off, which became an every-night, which became an every-day.

The thought sent shivers down her spine. Was she kidding herself to believe that her mother could ever kick the habit?

She ran along the edge of the harbour, a natural cove formed by the lava flow from a prehistoric volcanic eruption. A massive blue trawler was unloading its catch on the far side. The town was just a bunch of buildings plonked on top of a lava field. The cold anger of the earth was never more than a couple of metres below you in Hafnarfjördur.

Tomorrow morning she would be up early to drive out to the airport at Keflavík again. This time she really hoped Davíd would be there. She needed cheering up.

She ran around the harbour and up the lava hill on the other side. The details she had quickly read that afternoon in the file on the murder of Benedikt Jóhannesson jogged around her mind. The investigation, led by Inspector Snorri Gudmundsson, who had gone on to become National Police Commissioner, was thorough. Vigdís had been unable to spot any leads that should have been followed up but weren't. Family members had been investigated, including Benedikt's son, Jóhannes the schoolteacher, as had all known local burglars. Nothing. There wasn't even any forensic evidence that might yield results to modern analytical methods in a cold-case review.

Unlike the Duxbury murder eleven years later. Vigdís was sure that the lab results the American detective had referred to related to that. If there was to be a breakthrough, that was where it would come from. If only Árni had been more tactful! Now the detective knew Magnus was a murder suspect, Vigdís doubted he would give up whatever information he had to anything but an official request.

At least after her day of asking questions, and particularly looking at Magnus's wall, Vigdís had a pretty good idea what Magnus knew. How he was piecing together the evidence relating to his father's death. How he might suspect that his grandfather was involved. Why, indeed, he might go up to Bjarnarhöfn to see him.

To do what exactly? To confront him? Or to kill him?

Vigdís kept the pace up as she ran up the hill back towards her apartment building, past the twisted lava garden that, according to its owner, was teeming with hidden people, that parallel invisible population that many Icelanders believed inhabited the rocks and stones around them. Although she passed it almost every day, Vigdís had yet to see one.

OK, so that was Magnus. But what about his brother Ollie? Vigdís wasn't completely clear why he had suddenly decided to come to Iceland. And then why he had taken off up to Bjarnarhöfn with the schoolteacher. Magnus had probably been asking himself the same question. There was a photograph of Ollie pinned bang in the middle of his wall with a yellow Post-it bearing a large question mark stuck over his face.

Why was Magnus so stubborn? Surely after all they had been through over the last year he would trust her. He might be a private person, a bit grumpy sometimes, but she thought of him as a friend. So why hadn't he opened up to her? Allowed her to help him?

Then the awful thought hit her. Maybe the real reason was the obvious one. Maybe Magnus had killed his grandfather after all.

Aníta was scared to go to sleep. But she was also exhausted. The thoughts that had been jumping around her head all day had pummelled her brain to the point where it just wanted to quit. Her husband was snoring gently beside her. Kolbeinn always slept well.

'Aníta. Aníta.' The whisper woke her. She must have drifted off.

She opened her eyes, and across the room saw the familiar figure of her grandmother sitting in her rocking chair, her form faint in the dim moonlight that seeped into the room through the curtains.

Aníta sat up. 'Amma? Amma, I am so pleased to see you. I am so frightened.'

'So you should be, Aníta, dear,' her grandmother said in the tone of an adult admonishing a child. 'So you should be.'

'I saw Hallgrímur last night. Downstairs. With a boy. I thought it was Krissi, but it wasn't.'

'No, it wasn't Krissi,' said the old lady. 'It was another boy. But don't worry. I have told Hallgrímur to leave you alone. He won't bother you.'

'Oh, thank you, thank you, Amma.'

'But I have come to warn you. You must leave Bjarnarhöfn first thing in the morning. The very first thing, do you hear me? You must listen to your grandmother this time, Aníta, dear.'

'Why? Why must I leave?'

'Please don't ask questions, Aníta, just promise me you will leave. Do you promise me?'

'Yes, I promise you. I promise you, Amma.'

'Good.'

Aníta turned to her husband and shook him awake. 'Kolbeinn. Kolbeinn! Amma is here.'

But when she turned back towards the rocking chair, the old lady was gone.

Kolbeinn snorted, opened his eyes and grimaced. 'What is it, Aníta?'

'Amma. Amma was here.'

He hauled himself on to his elbows and leaned back against his pillow. Aníta could see in the darkness he was blinking.

'What? Where?'

'She was in the rocking chair just now. I was talking to her.'

'Well, that's better than Dad, I suppose.'

'Much better,' said Aníta. 'But she said we should leave. First thing tomorrow.'

'What? Why?'

'She didn't say. But she made me promise.'

'And did you?'

'Yes.'

Kolbeinn cleared his throat. 'What about the sheep? They'll be lambing any day soon.'

'Yes, I know,' said Aníta. 'But Amma said. I promised.'

'Look, Aníta. Be reasonable. Our livelihood is out there in the barn. We can't take them with us. We can't leave them alone. I know you can… see things, but we can't leave here just like that.'

Aníta nodded. She knew you couldn't ask a farmer to abandon his sheep. But she had promised.

'Perhaps I'll go. Take Tóta and Krissi with me.'

'And leave me by myself? Now, of all times?'

'Villi is here. He can help.'

Kolbeinn rubbed his face. 'Aníta, no. Absolutely not. We both have to be here for the lambing. And so do the kids. We need their help. I'm sorry, but no.'

Kolbeinn never said no to Aníta. But she understood why he was saying no now. And yet. And yet Aníta had ignored her grandmother before with terrible consequences. Kolbeinn didn't know about that, and Aníta didn't want to explain it to him.

'We'll talk about it in the morning,' she said.

'The first lambs could be here in the morning,' Kolbeinn replied, and rolled over with a loud grunt, facing away from his wife.

CHAPTER TWENTY

EMIL STARED OUT of the window of the tiny office he had been given in the National Police Commissioner's building. It was another clear day, and he could easily see the tall chimney at Akranes over the bay. The snow across the long ridge of Mount Esja glimmered in the morning sun. He munched one of the two *kleinur* he had bought on the drive in to Reykjavík, and sipped a cup of coffee.

His chest felt fine, which was a relief. At breakfast, his wife had hit him with an estimate for the repair of the roof of the new barn, which was more than they could afford. Unless they stopped making the payments on the mortgage. A lot of people were doing that these days, the banks weren't fore-closing yet, but it was something Emil really wanted to avoid if he could.

The office was at the end of the corridor that housed the International Department, one floor down from where the Commissioner himself sat. It had been half full of junk: stacked chairs, cables and cardboard storage boxes, but Emil had shoved them all to one side to make a little space for himself. He had a phone, and a computer from which he could log into the police system.

He heard the door open behind him and a small man with thick silver hair and bright blue eyes bounded into the room. Emil hauled himself to his feet.

'I've found you!' The Commissioner stepped forward and held out his hand.

Emil shook it and grinned. He had always liked Snorri. 'You have. Thanks for the office. I needed somewhere to base myself in Reykjavík, and I couldn't really do it at headquarters.'

'It's small, but at least there's a view,' said the Commissioner. 'How's Linda? Still busy with the horses? Is she bringing them in?''

'You mean because of the ash?' said Emil. 'So far she's kept them outside. As long as the wind sticks from the north, we should be OK. But she's ready to move them if things change.'

Snorri looked for a free chair, decided against untangling the two in the corner, and perched on the desk. 'How's the case going?'

For a moment Emil hesitated. Baldur had been right: technically Magnus reported directly to the Commissioner, and so technically the Commissioner should be kept out of the investigation. But then Snorri was the boss, the 'Big Salmon' as he was known, and more importantly, Emil trusted him.

'Magnús is at Litla-Hraun. I'm building up a case. Still some leads to follow up.'

'Are you sure he did it?' Snorri asked, watching Emil closely.

'It's looking that way,' Emil said.

Snorri sighed. 'Pity. I liked him. And I liked what he was doing here. But if he did murder his grandfather, make sure you put him away. The case against him has to be watertight.'

'I understand,' said Emil.

'I know I can rely on you,' said Snorri. 'Keep Kári informed.' Kári was the senior prosecutor. 'And let me know if you need more resources. It's difficult without using Metropolitan Police officers, but I could get Inspector Thorsteinn from Keflavík involved.'

With that he bustled out.

Emil appreciated that the Commissioner had made the effort to come and find him, rather than summoning him upstairs to his office. He was a good guy, Snorri. But he had been bearing a message: don't screw this up.

He checked his watch. Nearly eight o'clock. Time to call Stykkishólmur.

Adam, Björn, Rúnar and Edda were all gathered in the conference room they were using as an incident room at the police station in Stykkishólmur. They were on a speakerphone.

'I hear Magnús confessed?' Rúnar said.

'Yes, to his girlfriend, Ingileif,' Emil said. 'I've got a signed statement from her.'

'Have you gone back to Magnús?' Rúnar asked. 'See what he had to say about that?'

'No,' said Emil. 'I'll leave him stewing in Litla-Hraun for a while. I don't want him or anyone else to find out what Ingileif told us. I'd like to build the case against him and then confront him with overwhelming evidence.'

'OK, so what do we do next?' said Adam.

'We focus on Magnús's brother and the schoolteacher. I don't know what they were doing up in the Snaefells Peninsula, but I'm sure they haven't told us the whole truth. Any luck with the Hvalfjördur tunnel cameras?'

'Yes.' It was Björn's voice. 'Jóhannes's car came through at 8.06. Magnús an hour and a half later at 9.40. The timings match their accounts.'

'All right,' said Emil. 'We need to find the connections between the three of them and Hallgrímur's murder. Did they know what Magnús was going to do? Did all three of them plan it? Maybe one of the two of them killed Hallgrímur after all? We pull them in and make them sweat for twenty-four hours. See what they tell us. I'll take Jóhannes, since he is here in Reykjavík. Adam, you go find Ollie; see what you can get out of him. I might have a go with him myself after I have interviewed Jóhannes.' That would mean another long drive up to Stykkishólmur, but it would be worth it. In all this, Ollie was probably the weakest link. 'Anything on the Hallgrímssons?' he asked. 'How do their alibis hold up?'

'Ingvar's alibi holds for Sunday morning,' said Adam. 'Two witnesses at the harbour.'

'What about the other two?'

'I checked with the basketball coach,' said Björn. 'The boy Krissi was there on Sunday.'

'And his dad?'

'I assume he must have been, or else how would Krissi have got there?'

'Don't assume. Check. What about Villi?'

'We know he drove direct to Bjarnarhöfn from Keflavík Airport,' said Adam.

'Do we know when his flight landed?' said Emil.

'Er. No,' said Adam.

'OK. Check that and double-check it with the airline.' Emil wasn't surprised at the young detectives' slips. They were inexperienced and the focus of the investigation was on Magnus. But he knew from experience that if you only saw what you expected to find in an investigation, you missed vital leads. 'Edda, anything more from the crime scene?'

'Nothing from the murder scene. But the cottage fire looks like arson. Pretty amateurish arson.'

'Really?'

'Yes. A curtain was soaked in cooking oil in the kitchen, and some papers were soaked in more oil and scattered around and set alight in the living room. The irony is that cooking oil is a lousy accelerant. It was the living-room sofa that really got things going.'

'Cooking oil isn't an accelerant? I didn't know that,' said Emil.

'Neither did whoever set the fire,' said Edda. 'Which isn't really surprising; most people would think it was. But in fact some of the curtain didn't even burn. I can't think why anyone would pour cooking oil on a curtain unless they thought it would start a fire.'

'No,' said Emil. 'Interesting.'

'It must have been Sylvía,' Adam said.

'The question is, did she know what she was doing? She's very confused.'

'Shall I go ask her?' Adam said.

'No, not yet. She's not going anywhere. We'll need to be very careful about an interview. We should do it in the police station with a psychologist and a lawyer present. If Sylvía is prosecuted, it will all turn on what state of mind she was in when she set the fire.'

'I'll organize it,' said Adam.

'Bring in Ollie first,' said Emil.

As Emil hung up, there was a knock at the door and a tall black woman entered. Emil had only spoken to Vigdís once or twice, but she was Reykjavík's most easily recognizable detective.

'Hi, Vigdís, thanks for coming in. If you can extract a chair, please sit on it.'

Vigdís untangled a chair from the corner and pulled it up to Emil's desk.

'*Kleina*?' Emil offered her his second pastry, and when she shook her head, took it himself. 'So. Tell me about Magnús.'

'No, you may not come in.'

The deputy governor of Litla-Hraun was a tall man with kind eyes and a soft voice. They were in the car park just outside the high prison fence, and he was standing between Ingileif and the pedestrian turnstile just to the side of the vehicle gate.

'I want to see the governor,' Ingileif said. 'I demand to see him.'

'He is a she,' said her deputy. 'And she is not here. It won't make any difference. Magnús is in solitary confinement. He is not allowed any visitors apart from his lawyer. And the police.'

'But I'm his girlfriend! I have a right to see him.'

The big man shook his head. 'I am sorry, Ingileif. You don't. It's that simple.'

Ingileif tried to push past him, but he was unmoveable. She felt tears spring to her eyes. The man was so big! She stood in front of him and shoved hard at his chest. He raised his arms but didn't budge.

'Why don't you leave now?' he said, so softly it was almost a whisper.

'Fuckwit!' Ingileif muttered and turned on her heel. She ignored her car and stomped off towards town. Her cheeks were burning and she was breathing heavily. She was *so* angry. Didn't they realize she had to talk to Magnus? She absolutely *had* to.

It had never occurred to her that they wouldn't let her in. She had been prepared to wait, all day if necessary, that was why she had driven down there so early, but she hadn't been prepared to be turned away. She had things to explain to Magnus. Things he had to hear.

Until that moment she had done a very good job of keeping calm. She knew Magnus was in a bad situation, but she trusted him to get himself out of it. With her help. She felt guilty about how she had treated him, about what she had said. But somehow she had thought that if she could only show him how much she cared about getting him out of there, if they could discuss what she could do to help him, it would be all right.

It was partly seeing the prison itself. The place where he would spend many years of his life if things went wrong. It would destroy him.

She didn't want Magnus destroyed. She couldn't let him be destroyed. She had to do something for him, *anything*.

The small town of Eyrarbakki ran along a road just parallel to the sea. A hundred years before, it had been the foremost trading port on the south coast; farmers would travel for days to trade there with Danish merchants. Many of the old houses from that period survived, prosperous by Icelandic standards of the time, clad in red, blue and green painted corrugated metal. Between the road and the sea ran a three-metre-high grassy bank, a defence against wind and tide.

The town was quiet, with only the occasional car passing Ingileif, carrying someone off to work somewhere. She dodged a bunch of nine-year-old girls meandering across the road on bikes on their way to school. She cut up between two houses on to the sea wall, the highest land for miles around. The sky was clear and there was a gentle breeze coming in from the ocean. Over to the east she could see the plume of the volcano stooping and stretching southwards. Only the week before, Magnus had been up there, investigating a crime. A raven, sitting on the bright blue metal roof of one of the houses, croaked at her.

She checked her phone for Vigdís's number and found it.

'Hi, Vigdís, it's Ingileif.'

'Oh, hello.'

Vigdís sounded flat, Ingileif thought, as flat as Ingileif felt.

'How is the evidence against Magnús?' This was Ingileif's way of asking whether Vigdís had heard about Magnus's confession to her.

'Not good,' said Vigdís. 'I have just been talking to the investigating detective. They seem to think they are building a strong case.'

'Has Magnús himself said anything?'

'From what I understand he's refusing to talk,' said Vigdís. 'Why, do you have some more information?'

It sounded as if the fat detective, for whatever reason, hadn't told Vigdís about Magnús's confession. Good.

'No, I haven't,' said Ingileif. 'But is there anything I can do to help?'

Vigdís sighed. 'I don't think so.'

'Any news from the detective in America about the lab results?'

'Nothing. He's not giving us anything without an official request. Which is a pity. I think that's our most promising line of inquiry. At any rate, it's about the only one we've got.'

'Can I try and speak to him?' Ingileif asked.

'I don't see how that will help,' Vigdís said. 'Sibba, Magnús's lawyer, called him and even she didn't get anywhere.'

'What was the guy's name again?' Ingileif asked.

'Jim Fearon,' Vigdís said. 'But really, there's no point, Ingileif. Just leave it to us.'

'All right,' said Ingileif. But as she walked back to her car through Eyrarbakki, Ingileif had no intention of just leaving it to them.

*

Vigdís walked out of the Police Commissioner's building and turned left to where she had parked her car, further along the shore of the bay. Her conversation with Emil had depressed her. Although he hadn't been specific, it was clear that he was pretty certain of Magnus's guilt. He wasn't on a fishing expedition; he already had good evidence. Vigdís had been happy to tell him all she could about Magnus, on the theory that the more of the truth Emil knew, the more likely he would be able to figure out that Magnus was innocent.

If he really was innocent.

It was all very well for Ingileif to offer to help, but there was nothing she could do. She would just have to live with her guilt. Vigdís was beginning to worry that there was nothing any of them could do.

The morning had started off early and badly. She had woken at five and when she checked her computer she saw Davíd's flight had been cancelled. Again. While she was speaking to Emil she had received a text message from him to call her.

She paused, staring out over the bay towards Mount Esja, and selected his number. It was probably only five in the morning his time, but so what? She had had to wake up that early herself.

'Hello?' His voice was thick with sleep.

'Hi, Davíd. I can't believe your flight was cancelled again! Why was that? Most of the other flights from America are getting through.'

Davíd sighed. 'The airspace is clear. But apparently all the planes are in the wrong place. It's going to take days to sort it out.'

Vigdís swallowed. She hardly dared to ask her next question. 'Can you come tomorrow?'

'No,' said Davíd. 'No, I'm sorry, Vigdís. I've got a meeting on Thursday back in New York I can't miss. It didn't really make sense to fly over today, and it makes no sense at all tomorrow.'

Vigdís couldn't say anything.

'Vigdís?'

'Yeah. Yes, sorry. OK. I get it. We'll talk later.'

She hung up. Couldn't he cancel his damned meeting? Use the

volcano as an excuse? From what she heard on the news the whole world had been disrupted by the volcano, so why couldn't he disrupt his piddling little meeting?

She knew she wasn't being fair. It was she who usually cancelled, changed plans, missed trips.

She had to face it – she and Davíd were never going to make it. She would end up like her mother: fifty, alone, picking up fat Polish guys ten years younger than her. Except she wouldn't have a daughter to scream at her.

What now? She couldn't really cry off work any longer. She may as well turn around and head back to Hverfisgata and the police station. She called Árni.

'What's up, Vigdís?'

'Davíd's flight was cancelled. Again,' Vigdís said.

'Hey, I'm sorry.'

'I think I'll come in this morning,' she said. 'I just spoke to Emil. It doesn't look good for Magnús.'

'Did he tell you about the confession?'

'Confession? What confession?'

'There's a rumour going around that Magnús confessed to the murder. To Ingileif. She told the Dumpling about it yesterday afternoon.'

'Ingileif?' Vigdís thought back to her phone call a few minutes earlier and Ingileif's request to do anything she could to help. 'I don't believe it! The bitch.'

CHAPTER TWENTY-ONE

JÓHANNES STOOD IN front of the class of thirteen-year-olds and put everything he could into his performance. His ability to transfix a group of teenagers with his readings from the sagas was legendary. Despite that, or in his view because of it, he had been given the sack the week before. The principal was a slave to the national curriculum; Jóhannes wanted to set his pupils free to delight in their nation's great literature. The principal was a moron.

He was still supposed to see out the term. And he was determined if there was one thing he did in the weeks left to him, it would be to bring the sagas alive to all of his students.

He was reading 'The Tale of Thorsteinn Staff-Struck'. The piece was off-syllabus, but so what? It was a short saga, less than a dozen pages, but it recounted the feud between two neighbouring farms, Sunnudal and Hof. Thorsteinn, the son of the farmer from Sunnudal, had been struck by the staff of a worker from Hof and had been reluctant to take any action in revenge. But Thorsteinn was goaded on by his old and blind father, and blood flowed.

There was a fault line running between Sunnudal and Hof in the tenth century, just like there was between Hraun and Bjarnarhöfn in the twentieth. And probably the twenty-first.

Jóhannes was coming to one of his favourite passages. He lowered his voice, combining menace with weakness as Thorsteinn's aged father spoke these words to Thorsteinn: 'I would rather lose you than have a coward for a son.'

Was that what Hallgrímur's father had said to Hallgrímur, he wondered? Indeed, Jóhannes remembered how as a child he had once asked his own father why people today didn't take revenge as they used to in the sagas, and been told: 'Sometimes they do.'

Jóhannes was immensely proud of his father, whom he considered one of the greatest novelists Iceland had produced, certainly better than that rambling, self-important communist, Halldór Laxness. His father had shown him what was important in life: education, literature, truth, moral self-confidence. In his own novels, and in his response to the sagas they read together, Benedikt had recognized that there was a place for revenge, even in modern Iceland.

Jóhannes realized that his pause for effect had become much more, and he looked up to see his class's reaction.

The children were transfixed. But standing listening with them, at the back of the classroom, was a very fat man wearing a baggy suit.

Inspector Emil.

'Can I help you?' Jóhannes said, lacing the question with disapproval. He had worked hard to build the magic; an interruption would disperse it in seconds.

The man pushed past the desks towards him. Jóhannes glared at him, raising his bushy white eyebrows. Jóhannes's eyebrow-enhanced glares could stop a child dead in his tracks, and usually had the same effect on adults.

But not this time.

'Jóhannes, I would like you to come down to the police station with me.' The combined intake of breath from the class was audible. 'I have some questions I want to ask you about the murder of Hallgrímur Gunnarsson.'

Adam and Páll made their way towards Páll's patrol car parked outside Stykkishólmur police station. They were going to pick up Ollie at the small hotel near the harbour where he was staying. Adam's phone rang.

'Adam.'

'It's Aníta from Bjarnarhöfn. I have something I would like to discuss with you. I think it might be related to Hallgrímur's murder.'

Adam thought for a second. Ollie could stew in a cell for a bit. It would do him good, get him in the right frame of mind. But Adam wanted to be there when Ollie was picked up, see his reaction. Then he would go on to Bjarnarhöfn.

'All right. I'll be with you in an hour or so.' He hung up and turned to the mustachioed constable. 'Let's go.'

Ollie looked down over the cliff edge to a small beach. It was just around the headland from the harbour. A few boats were pulled up on the sand to the grass above the high-water mark. There was very little he remembered from his childhood in Stykkishólmur, but he had the feeling he had been in that exact spot before.

It was amazing how little he recalled of his life before the age of ten. There were things at the farm that his conscious brain had tried to black out, but what was extraordinary was how good a job his unconscious had done of obliterating everything. He had been to school in the town, he'd had friends, but he could scarcely remember them. There was a tall, thin boy with buckteeth, but he couldn't for the life of him remember his name. Maybe the two of them had stood on that cliff together twenty-odd years before.

He clambered down the cliff path and perched on a rock a few feet away from the tiny waves nibbling at the sand.

He was scared. So scared. And it was just getting worse.

Uncle Villi just never left him alone. Wherever he went, whatever he did, Uncle Villi would pop up with his veiled threats. And Ollie believed the threats. There were a lot of dead bodies to back them up: Benedikt Jóhannesson, his own father, Afi.

Ollie had the feeling that Uncle Villi was losing patience with him. And when that happened, Ollie would be added to the list.

He couldn't wait to get on that plane on Thursday. That is, if the police let him go. The police *had* to let him go by then, surely?

Ollie felt the panic rise in him. Maybe they wouldn't. Maybe Uncle Villi would get him first. He had to get out of this damn town somehow!

Could he hire a car? Stykkishólmur was far too small to have an Avis or a Hertz, but there must be some guy in a gas station somewhere who would rent him a car. And then what? He could drive into the empty interior of Iceland where no one would find him.

He wished Jóhannes was still around. He would know where to hide out, all the places from some damn saga. Who was that outlaw – Gretel the Strong? Something like that.

His eyes fell on the boats. One of them, a twelve-foot skiff, had an outboard motor attached. Perhaps he could just get in that and head out over the Atlantic. The States were thousands of miles away. Greenland was too cold. How about Ireland? How far was Ireland? He had no idea.

He was being ridiculous. He had puttered around the coast of Maine in a motorboat in the past, but he wouldn't survive a night in an open boat in the North Atlantic.

He hopped off his rock and climbed back up the cliff path. He wished he could talk to Magnus. This was the kind of situation where he really needed his older brother to help him out. Magnus would figure out something. But Magnus had his own problems. The police had taken him away, God knows where. He would be little use to Ollie.

Besides, Ollie had a different fear when it came to Magnus. Not a physical fear, but a fear that his elder brother would one day find out what Ollie had really done.

A short distance beyond the cliff top, Ollie was back in town. As he approached the hotel, he saw a large police four-wheel-drive draw up right outside. A uniformed officer with a big moustache accompanied by a smaller man in jacket and jeans jumped out and strode in through the entrance.

It was clear they were coming for Ollie.

Ollie halted and took a deep breath. Keep calm. Tell them nothing. Tell himself he had nothing to hide and then hide it.

When Ollie had been interviewed before, the knowledge that the big schoolteacher was in the same building had helped calm him, and he had managed to keep quiet. But Jóhannes was gone now and Ollie was in much worse shape. His nerves were frayed. He could almost feel the fear and the panic mingling like an unhealthy fuel mixture deep inside him, combining, expanding, ready to explode.

If the police hauled him back to the station he would tell them everything, he knew it, he could feel it.

And that would be bad. That would be very bad indeed.

Ollie turned on his heel and jogged back towards the cliff path. He scrambled down to the cove, which was still empty. He dragged the skiff down to the water and waded after it. Once it bobbed free of the sand, he jumped in.

It was several years since he had piloted a motorboat, but the engine looked familiar. He pulled the cord. A cough and then nothing. He tugged again. Still nothing.

He sat facing the engine, studying it, trying to remember. The shift lever was in neutral and the throttle on 'start'. He recognized the primer bulb and squeezed it. He spotted a knob that was almost certainly the choke. Pulled it all the way out. Tugged at the cord.

Success!

He pointed the boat out into the fjord.

'How are you doing, Magnus?'

Sibba examined her cousin, sitting across from her in the interview room at Number One House in Litla-Hraun. He had shaved and he looked clean. He seemed calm.

'I'm OK, Sibba. I get time to think in here, which is good. Not much exercise, just one hour a day walking around a little yard. But the prison staff are pretty friendly.'

'Do you need some more clothes? I can get some from your house if you like.'

'Yeah. That would be good. Just jeans and T-shirts. And underwear.' Magnus grinned. 'Sorry about that.'

'That's what lawyers are for,' said Sibba with a small grin. 'Sorting underwear. I do it for the children; I can do it for you. No word from our friend Emil?'

'No, nothing. He is letting me stew while he builds a case. He knows I'll say nothing anyway.'

'I've been in touch with Vigdís,' Sibba said. 'She has offered to help.'

'I know. I told her not to,' said Magnus.

'Why?' Sibba asked.

Magnus hesitated, considering his answer. 'She's better off staying out of it. I don't want to bring her down with me.'

'She doesn't care. I get the impression she would do almost anything for you.'

'Precisely. Is Davíd here? Her boyfriend?'

'No. His flight was cancelled again.'

'Poor Vigdís.'

Sibba nodded. 'She did tell me that a detective called Jim Fearon from Duxbury called Árni a few days ago to say that he had some lab results for you.'

Magnus leaned forward, and for the first time Sibba saw interest flickering in his eyes.

'Really? Did he give them to Árni?'

'No. Fearon insisted on talking to you directly. Then Árni called him back and said you were in jail. Fearon said in that case he would only release the results through official channels.'

'Árni said what! Why did he do that?'

Sibba shrugged. 'I think he thought Fearon would be more likely to tell him the results.'

'Idiot!'

'I called Fearon myself. Said I was your lawyer. No dice. We only get the results the official way or not at all.'

'Yeah, I'm not surprised. Fearon is actually retired, so he

probably shouldn't have seen the results himself. He will have gotten a buddy to request them for him. So now he's trying to cover himself and his buddy.'

'So the question is, should we go through official channels? I could tell Emil I knew the results existed. Then he could send an Interpol blue notice. The Duxbury police would probably release them. I've no idea how long it would take.'

Magnus mulled it over.

'Of course, as a defence lawyer I'm wary of asking for evidence when I don't know where it will lead,' Sibba said.

'Meaning?' Magnus asked.

'Meaning will it incriminate you?'

Magnus didn't answer her, or at least didn't answer that question. 'Thinking about it, we don't tell Emil, at least for now. I'd love to know what those results are, but don't forget if the Icelandic police do get them they are not required to disclose them to us until the three weeks from my arrest are up. And I doubt very much that Emil would disclose them. So let's wait a couple of weeks. Then maybe we tell him.'

'Are you sure?' Sibba asked.

Magnus nodded.

'This is so frustrating, Magnus. Here I am supposed to be defending you, but you won't give me anything to go on!'

'I know,' said Magnus. 'And I'm sorry. But I'm not saying anything. Not to the police, and not even to you.'

Aníta tightened the girth under Sól, the horse that Gabrielle liked to ride. She checked her watch: it was twenty past nine. Gabrielle was late, but then Gabrielle was always late. Aníta didn't mind. She was nervous about the call she had just made to the police. She knew it was the right thing to tell them about the postcard of Sylvía's she had found the night before. She wasn't sure herself what it meant. That was part of why she had called them. She would rather they figured it out than her. She was afraid of what would emerge.

She heard a car approaching along the dirt track to the farm and saw it was Gabrielle's. The press had gone. It had been sensible after all to talk to them the day before; now they had no reason to hang around at the farm. She could tell from the morning paper that they were still interested in the case, but they were bugging the police in Stykkishólmur. Luckily the volcano had kept the story off the front page.

Gabrielle pulled up close to the horses. Aníta was surprised to see that she wasn't wearing her riding boots. Then she saw her face.

Gabrielle was not happy.

'Aníta!' she said. 'You told the police, didn't you?'

Aníta stepped away from Sól to face her sister-in-law. This was going to be difficult.

'Yes. Yes I did, Gabrielle. And I'm sorry.'

'What do you mean, you are sorry? I *asked* you not to tell anyone!' Gabrielle looked over her shoulder towards the cottage where forensics technicians were still at work, and a police constable was reading the paper in his car. They were too far away to hear anything, but Gabrielle lowered her voice to an angry whisper anyway. 'When I said, "Don't tell Kolbeinn", I didn't mean, "Do tell the police".'

'I know. But the more I thought about it, the more I was sure it was important evidence. I *had* to tell them. And I asked them not to say where the information came from when they spoke to Ingvar. Did they tell him it was you?'

'No. But whatever you may think about Ingvar, he's no dummy. He knew it was me. And he was angry. I can't say I blame him. I trusted you and you let me down.'

'But if he's innocent, it won't matter.'

'Of course he's innocent, you fool! It turns out that Hallgrímur lost all the money that Ingvar made him. So there's nothing! We'll have to sell the flat in Paris after all.'

'Oh. I'm sorry. Look, Gabrielle, I really am sorry. Do you want to come riding with me after all?'

'No, I don't.' Gabrielle turned back to her car, muttering something in French.

Aníta watched Gabrielle's car speed out of the farmyard, scattering a couple of chickens on the way. One of the forensics technicians stopped and stared, then turned towards Aníta. The policeman had put his newspaper down to see what was going on.

Aníta guessed that it was as much the fact that there was no money left as Aníta's betrayal that had upset Gabrielle. Of course Gabrielle was correct; Aníta had been foolish to expect the police to keep the source of their information from someone as smart as Ingvar. But she still thought she had done the right thing. She just should have figured out a better way of doing it.

And what about the postcard she had found? What trouble would that cause? More, probably. Well, that was their problem, the whole damned family's, including Gabrielle.

Aníta unsaddled Sól, but decided to take Grána out herself. Marta didn't hold quite the terror that she had the day before. The woman in the lava field might be creepy, but she wouldn't actually hurt Aníta.

Sylvía emerged from the chicken shed and stared at her. Aníta waved, but the old woman's expression didn't change. Thank God Ingvar had finally promised to come and fetch his mother that afternoon.

As she hoisted herself up on Grána, Aníta thought about the old woman and the postcard. She wasn't surprised that Sylvía had hoarded it and not told anyone about it. There was a lot that Sylvía must have seen over the years that she hadn't talked about. From when her own children were small. From when Magnus and Óli were staying at the farm. Other things that Aníta couldn't even guess at.

Aníta had noticed a change in Sylvía in recent years. A slow change. It had coincided with Sylvía beginning to attend church. She had always shown up for the occasional service at the little church at the bottom of the farm, but a couple of years before she had begun to go to the big church at Stykkishólmur, at first every couple of months or so, and then more frequently. Aníta also occasionally found her just sitting in the Bjarnarhöfn church, staring at the old altar painting, the one of the Last Supper that was supposed to have been given by grateful Dutch sailors who had been shipwrecked nearby. Was she praying? Or just thinking? Was there a difference? Aníta didn't know.

During that time Aníta got the impression that Sylvía was trying to become more involved in the family around her. She seemed a little less aloof. It was partly because of that that Aníta had decided to pass on the enigmatic message from her grandmother: 'Open your eyes and see what is in front of you.' Aníta had no idea what it meant, but Sylvía had. And she had taken it seriously, not doubting Aníta for a moment.

Sylvía had known Aníta's grandmother when she was alive. She had spoken very little about her, but she did say that she was always worth listening to. That she knew things.

Aníta and Grána headed along the edge of the lava field. Which brought Aníta back to the warning she had received the night before. The instruction to leave Bjarnarhöfn first thing in the morning. It was already past that time.

How could she ignore such an explicit warning? But on the other hand, how could she follow it? Kolbeinn was right: there was a barn full of pregnant ewes to think about.

Aníta passed the point where she had seen Hallgrímur's mother the previous day. There was nothing; just a pair of ravens wheeling among the twisted fingers of lava. It was a clear day and she could see over the Berserkjahraun to the farm of Hraun on its knoll. The family who had lived there for the last seventy years had had nothing against the inhabitants of Bjarnarhöfn, but the family before that? The family of Jóhannes, and Benedikt and the other Jóhannes?

She *had* to persuade Kolbeinn to let her go. Perhaps she should speak to Villi about it. He had disappeared somewhere in his rental car after breakfast. Aníta hadn't told him about her grandmother, but she was sure that he would take her seriously. But then there was Sylvía's postcard. She couldn't really trust Villi until she understood what that really meant. She couldn't trust any of them.

Fear clutched at her chest.

What was she thinking? She had to do what her grandmother had instructed her. She had to leave. She had to leave now!

She turned Grána around. The mare seemed to sense her mistress's rising panic and skittered over to one side away from the lava field. Then a rock embedded in the slope of the fell behind them erupted in a spurt of lava fragments. An instant later Aníta heard a sharp crack that echoed off the stones. She recognized the sound of a rifle shot.

Grána surged forward and Aníta bent low, letting the mare go her own way. Something hit her chest so hard it almost knocked her out of the saddle, just as she heard another crack. There was no pain, yet she could feel the strength seeping out of her. She just had to hang on, hang on until Grána got back to the farmyard. Hang on...

CHAPTER TWENTY-TWO

OLLIE HEADED NORTH-EAST out of Stykkishólmur, keeping a sharp eye out for rocks and skerries, and also giving a wide berth to other boats. He was wearing a fleece on top of a cotton shirt, but he was cold out on the water. He gritted his teeth. Time to be a tough Icelander. Or even a tough New Englander, for that matter.

The engine was powerful, and the skiff made good speed, but Ollie didn't want to open the throttle all the way in the slight chop. He headed for the nearest bunch of the 'countless islands of Breidafjördur', hoping to put some of them between himself and the town. After about half an hour he slipped behind a strip of grass and rock. There was another island, and another. In the distance he could see the mountains behind Stykkishólmur, and also hills from some other chunk of mainland in the opposite direction. He had no map. He had no idea where he was.

He came to what seemed to be a slightly larger island, with a small hill at its centre. A single house stood cold and alone a few yards inland. The building looked derelict and uninhabited.

Ollie found an inlet, out of the line of sight of the open water, slowed the engine right down and nosed the boat in among some rocks. He jumped out and heaved the skiff up to the stony shore. There was nothing to tie the painter to, so he dragged the boat over the stones. It was hard work, and God knows what damage he was doing to the hull, but he had no choice if he didn't want the boat to drift off at high tide. It wasn't completely hidden, it was impossible to hide a boat on a mostly flat, treeless island, but at least it was only visible from a channel between two islands, and then only at a certain angle of approach.

With the engine off, Ollie could hear the seabirds: whistles, whoops and chuckles. They swooped and flitted, eager, busy, ignoring him.

His feet and ankles were wet and cold. In fact, all of him was cold. He walked over the grass to the small house. It was more of a cabin, really. It had a rusted metal roof and wind-bleached grey wooden walls. The door sported a large padlock, but the window right next to it was broken.

He climbed in. There were two rooms downstairs – a kitchen and a living room – and some simple furniture. The stairs themselves looked dodgy, so Ollie didn't try them. There was an old rug on the floor. Ollie wrapped himself in the rug against the cold and sat on the floor, wondering what the hell he was going to do next.

After they failed to find Ollie at the hotel, Adam and Páll drove slowly around the centre of Stykkishólmur, looking out for him wandering around. After twenty minutes or so, Adam decided to go on to see Aníta at Bjarnarhöfn, leaving Páll and another constable to extend the search for Ollie. At this stage, Adam still thought Ollie was out somewhere for a walk. There were only a finite number of places he could go without transport.

The sky was clear and the visibility good as Adam reached the Berserkjahraun and turned off towards Bjarnarhöfn. The sun glinted off the snow on the fell above the farm and the sharp ridge of mountains along the backbone of the peninsula. The lava field itself was quiet, although there was a vehicle of some kind pulled over a hundred metres or so in from the road to Grundarfjördur. Some movement caught his eye, and Adam spotted a horse bolting along the edge of the lava towards the farm.

A riderless horse.

Adam put his foot down, spraying stones on all sides as he sped towards the farm. The horse beat him to it. As Adam careered into the farmyard he noticed the forensics van and a police car parked outside the cottage. He scanned the fields and saw Kolbeinn carrying a fence post across one of them.

Adam was driving his own car, which was not too robust, but he swerved into the open gate of the field and drove towards Kolbeinn, flashing his lights and hooting his horn. Kolbeinn dropped the post and jogged towards him.

Adam rolled down his window. 'There's a horse back there, loose without its rider! I saw it galloping in from the lava field.'

Kolbeinn glanced back at the horse, which was shying in the farmyard.

'Aníta!' he said. 'That's Grána! Aníta was riding her. She must have fallen! But Aníta *never* falls.'

'Looks like she has now,' said Adam.

'I'll take the truck,' said Kolbeinn, running towards the Toyota pickup parked near the gate.

'I'll follow you in the police car,' said Adam. 'It's got a first-aid kit.'

He spun his car around and drove back to the yard, where the constable was waiting, standing by his own vehicle, watching what was going on. Adam leaped out of his car.

'Get in and follow him!' Adam shouted, pointing to the pickup, which was already nearly at the farm entrance.

He jumped into the police Hyundai and the two men took off after the Toyota, keeping good pace with it even though the ground was rough.

'That horse was bleeding from its rump,' said the constable, a man in his forties whose name was Gudjón, Adam remembered. 'It was in a right state.'

'Did you see Aníta ride out?' Adam asked.

'Yeah. About half an hour ago,' said Gudjón, wrestling with the wheel as his vehicle nearly rolled. 'I'd put that seat belt on if I were you.'

Adam did as he was told. Ahead, in a hollow right next to a rock, he could see what could either be a long dark stone or...

'Is that her?'

'I think so.'

It was.

Kolbeinn rushed towards his wife and was about to pick her up when Gudjón stopped him.

'Wait! Let me take a look. Grab the first-aid kit, Adam!'

She was breathing, just. She had a gash on the side of her skull and blood seeping out of her chest.

'Christ! She's been shot!'

Adam left the kit with Gudjón and ran back to the police car to radio for an ambulance.

It took twenty minutes for Emil to find an empty room in the Police Commissioner's office installed with the necessary equipment for a recorded interview. As he was negotiating access to it, he got a call from the pathologist. The doctor had done the complete blood count, and his suspicions were correct. Hallgrímur had leukaemia. Undiagnosed, according to his medical records. The blood count suggested that the disease wasn't yet in an advanced stage, but it was likely that Hallgrímur would have been showing signs of fatigue.

Emil wasn't sure whether that discovery had any significance. A terminal illness could cause sufferers to do things they might not have done otherwise, but only if they knew they had got it. He would double-check that Hallgrímur hadn't mentioned his cancer to anyone. His heart sank at the idea of asking Sylvía that question.

Eventually, he found the room with video-recording equipment, switched it on, and seated Jóhannes. The schoolteacher appeared calmer than he had when Emil had confronted him in the classroom.

Emil had quickly reread the statement that Jóhannes had given him two days before. He was watching for discrepancies.

'Now, Jóhannes, tell me again what you did on Sunday morning, from when you woke up.'

Jóhannes told him. Slowly, clearly and in detail, like a school-master describing a particularly complicated historical event.

Emil took notes, occasionally asking for more details. The greater the level of detail, the harder it was to lie consistently.

There were patches of vagueness, in particular the conversation with Ollie on the way up to the Snaefells Peninsula.

'Did you speak to Magnús at all that morning?'

'No,' said Jóhannes.

'Did Ollie?'

'No.'

'You sure?'

'Yes. He would have told me if he had. Or I would have seen him do it. He wasn't out of my sight the whole trip.'

'I see,' said Emil. He changed tack. 'So, tell me why you suddenly decided to go on a little tourist trip.'

'We were going to be too early, like I told you before.'

'How early?'

'I don't know. A couple of hours. We decided it would be best to wait until Hallgrímur was up and awake. It was Sunday morning.'

'But Hallgrímur is a farmer. He doesn't have a lie-in, surely? Even on a Sunday.'

'We didn't know. We thought he did.'

'Who thought he did?' Emil asked. 'You? Or Ollie?'

Jóhannes hesitated. 'I don't remember.'

'Of course you do,' said Emil.

Jóhannes regained his composure. Shook his head. 'No, I don't.'

'So how did the subject come up? You were driving along. You suddenly say, "It's too early to see the old man. Let's go for a walk along the cliffs"?'

'Something like that.'

'How like that?'

Jóhannes was silent. Emil waited. Then Jóhannes shook his head again.

'I can't remember.'

'Funny it's that bit you can't remember,' said Emil. 'You can remember the rest of the trip perfectly well.'

Jóhannes shrugged.

'Never mind,' said Emil. 'I'm sure Ollie will tell me when I ask him later on today.'

For a moment, doubt flickered in Jóhannes's eyes, and then it was gone. 'I'm sure.'

'And why did you suddenly decide to call Hallgrímur?'

'To tell him we were on our way. And before you ask me, I've no idea why Ollie panicked when the police answered the phone.'

'Why not?'

'Why not what?'

'Why don't you have any idea? I mean, didn't you ask Ollie?'

'Yes. He said he didn't like talking to the police.'

'His exact words?' said Emil, making a show of writing it down.

Jóhannes folded his arms. 'I think I've said enough.'

'I don't think you have,' said Emil. 'I have plenty more to ask you.'

'I want to speak to a lawyer.'

'But why do you want to do that? I thought you said you knew nothing about Hallgrímur's murder?'

'Because you clearly don't know anything either. And I don't want to create any misunderstandings. Implicate myself or Ollie in error.'

The inspector tried a few more questions but Jóhannes wouldn't budge. A pity, but Emil had got what he wanted: a detailed statement with which to confuse Ollie. Unless by some miracle Jóhannes was indeed telling the truth and nothing but the truth, Emil was confident Ollie would slip up.

Emil left Jóhannes in the interview room and went off in search of a constable to take the schoolmaster over to the cells in police headquarters and to arrange a lawyer. Unsurprisingly, it was proving impossible to keep the whole Reykjavík Metropolitan Police away from the investigation.

He was talking with the custody sergeant when his phone rang. 'It's Adam.'

'What is it?' Emil was alerted by the urgency in his subordinate's voice. He sounded breathless.

'It's Aníta. She's been shot. She was riding by the Berserkjahraun. She's alive but badly injured. A bullet in the chest and she hit her head when she fell off.'

'Any idea who shot her?'

'No. I saw a vehicle in the lava field earlier, which seems to have gone. It wasn't Kolbeinn because he was working in the field when I arrived just after it had happened. But Ollie wasn't at his hotel when we went to pick him up.'

'Where is he, then?'

'We don't know,' said Adam. 'Páll is looking for him in Stykkishólmur.'

'Well, go find him!' Emil took a deep breath. 'I'm on my way up there. Keep me posted.'

Who could have shot her? Ollie was an obvious suspect. But Jóhannes wasn't. And neither was Magnus, safely tucked up in his cell two hundred kilometres away at Litla-Hraun.

Damn! Emil just didn't have the resources to do the job properly. He'd need more help from somewhere. Time to swallow his pride.

He picked up the phone on his desk. 'I need to see the Commissioner,' he told the woman who answered. 'Right now.'

CHAPTER TWENTY-THREE

ADAM WAS TRYING hard to keep a clear head. He had left Kolbeinn and Gudjón with Aníta and driven back to the farm in Kolbeinn's pickup and then out on the track through the lava field. The vehicle he had seen earlier was no longer there. At least he didn't think it was. It was difficult to be sure because it had been parked in a hollow in the lava, which was only visible from a certain angle. So he drove all the way back to the main Grundarfjördur road, and then found a small track back into the Berserkjahraun.

That must be the road. There was definitely no sign of a vehicle of any kind there.

He tried to remember what make the car was. He couldn't, other than that it was some kind of dark-coloured four-wheel-drive. Or was it silver? Damn it, he was a police officer, how could he be vague about the colour of a vehicle he had seen less than twenty minutes before?

He decided not to drive down the track for fear of messing up tyre marks or other forensic evidence, so turned back to the farm. Edda was waiting for him, with another technician.

'What can I do?' she asked.

'How many people have you got here?'

'Three. I've sent Sigga up to where Aníta was shot.'

'OK,' said Adam. Usually the forensics people didn't show up to a crime scene until well after everything had calmed down, but in this case, he may as well make use of them.

'On my way here, I thought I saw a vehicle parked in the lava field to the south of where Aníta was shot. I've just been back up there and it's gone. But seal off the track and see if you can find any evidence.'

'OK. Where exactly was it?'

Adam described the location and how to get there. 'And be careful. If you see anyone, don't tackle them, OK?'

As Adam said this, he realized that Edda had considerably more experience and seniority than he did. But after a moment's hesitation she smiled.

'OK. Have you told Emil?'

'Yes. He's coming right up.'

'He's going to need more resources,' Edda said. 'A *lot* more resources. Give me a call if you need one of us back here.'

With that, she left.

Adam scanned the horizon anxiously for flashing blue lights. He thought he could see the white of an ambulance on the road in the far distance. He resisted the urge to call Gudjón to check whether Aníta was still alive.

What should he do next? His brain was scrambled. Slow down. Think. Rúnar the chief superintendent would be there in a few minutes; he would know what to do. Adam hoped he would bring Björn, the detective from Akureyri. He could use some support.

'Hey, you!'

He turned to see Sylvía bustling over towards him. This wasn't going to be fun.

'Hey, you! Are you a policeman?' Sylvía's eyes were concerned and frightened.

'Yes.'

'What's happened? Tell me what's happened. Is Aníta all right?'

'She's been shot,' Adam said. He tried to keep his tone soft, but he couldn't keep the panic out of his voice.

'Shot? What with?'

Sylvía's brown eyes were focused. She was definitely understanding what Adam was saying.

'A rifle, we think.'

'Who shot her? Is she all right?'

'We don't know who shot her. And she is alive. An ambulance will be here soon.'

'Oh, no!' Sylvía shook her head. 'Poor Aníta. Poor Aníta.' She turned back to the house, her head still shaking.

The news seemed to have shocked Sylvía into clarity. Adam considered taking advantage of her mental state to ask again about the fire. But Emil had been quite explicit that they should wait for proper interview conditions before questioning her further, so he decided to leave it.

Besides, a car was approaching the farm, a small Peugeot. Adam recognized Villi, one of Hallgrímur's sons.

He flagged him down.

Villi lowered his window. 'What's happened?'

'I'm afraid Aníta has been shot.'

'No! Is she OK?'

'I think so,' said Adam. 'Kolbeinn is with her. She's out by the lava field.'

'I saw the police car out there. I wondered what it was. I must go to her.'

'I'd like to ask you a couple of questions first,' Adam said.

'Later.' Villi opened the door.

'No, now,' said Adam firmly. 'I mean right now.'

Villi sighed with impatience. 'OK.' He stood next to his car, looking down on the young detective.

'Where have you just come from?' Adam asked.

'Swine Lake.'

'Swine Lake? Where's that?'

'Just over the other side of the main road at the other end of the Berserkjahraun.'

'What were you doing there?'

'Going for a hike.'

'A hike? Did anyone see you?'

'What is this?'

'It's an interview following an attempted murder. Now just answer the question.'

Villi frowned. Shook his head. 'I don't know. I didn't see anyone. I don't know.'

'Do you know where Ollie is?'

'My nephew Ollie?'

'Yes.'

Villi shook his head. 'No idea.'

'You didn't see him at Swine Lake or in the lava field?'

'No,' said Villi. 'Why, do you think *he* shot Aníta?'

'It's too early to say who shot her. Do you mind if I take a look in your car?'

'Do I have a choice?'

Adam peered into the front, opened the rear doors and checked the back seat and then popped the boot. No rifle, but he would get Edda to do a thorough analysis.

'Now please wait in the house,' Adam said. 'Don't leave the farm until we have had a chance to question you properly.'

'This is stupid,' muttered Villi, with a worried glance over to where Aníta lay. But he got back into his car and parked it outside the farmhouse.

Adam was glad to see two sets of flashing lights approaching – a police car and, about a kilometre behind, an ambulance.

'Hey, Constable!'

Sylvía was hurrying towards him. She seemed agitated.

It was all Adam could do not to tell her to get lost. 'Yes, Sylvía, what is it?'

'I have just unlocked the gun cupboard,' she said. 'Kolbeinn's rifle is missing.'

Ingileif stared out of the aeroplane window at the old American radar installations that lurked at the perimeter of Keflavík Airport. The view swung as the aeroplane lined itself up on the runway. The engines whined and the aircraft began to roll.

Ingileif felt tense but excited. Things were definitely going her way. Keflavík was a zoo, but two delayed planes for Boston were leaving in quick succession. The Icelandair reservation system was a tangle of cancellations, re-booking and overbooking. It was up to the people on the spot to ensure that the planes were filled fairly. One of the supervisors was a good friend of Ingileif's from her hometown of Flúdir, who had found her a seat without actually having to bump someone with a guaranteed reservation.

She was on a wild goose chase, she knew, and an expensive wild goose chase at that. But she felt lucky. More importantly, she was doing something for Magnus. She was trying. Even if she didn't succeed she would know that at least she had tried.

Ingileif didn't know exactly what Magnus's game was. She had been walking up Skólavördustígur on Sunday morning when he had called. She could tell right away from the tension in his voice that it was important. She had shut up and listened.

'Ingileif. There is something I'm going to tell you. I want you to remember it. And if the police ask you about it, then tell them. But not right away.'

'I don't understand,' said Ingileif.

'No, I don't expect you to understand. Just do as I ask. Please.'

It was a weird request. But Magnus wouldn't make it without a reason.

'OK.'

'I have just killed my grandfather,' Magnus said.

'What!'

'I don't know what I'm going to do. I can't think straight.'

'You sound as if you are thinking straight.'

'No, I don't.' Magnus paused. 'I need to talk to you about it. Can I see you?'

'Er.' Ingileif hesitated. She knew Magnus. She knew this wasn't how he would talk if he really had just killed his grandfather. The tone wasn't right. He wouldn't kill his grandfather anyway.

So what was he doing? He'd asked her to tell the police something that wasn't quite true. He couldn't admit to her it wasn't true or she would become his accomplice if she knowingly passed on what he said. He was protecting her. But he was also asking for her help.

He didn't really need to see her. He needed a credible reason to call her.

'I don't think that would be a good idea, Magnús,' she said. She tried to keep her tone neutral, devoid of emotion, willing him to understand that she knew what he wanted her to do.

'OK,' he said. 'I thought I'd ask.' He sounded unsurprised, pleased even. 'Thanks, Ingileif.'

Then he had rung off.

She had done what he had asked, or at least what she *thought* he was asking her. She had played the fat detective along, let him think that he had broken her resistance, and then told him about Magnus's confession.

Why Magnus wanted her to do that she had no idea. She just hoped to God that he knew what he was doing. It seemed to her that he had intentionally got himself stuck in prison on a murder charge, and if he wasn't very careful he would be stuck there for a long, long time.

The flight time to Boston was four hours and fifty minutes. She was too tense to read and too tense to do nothing. She dug out her iPod, selected some Bach and closed her eyes.

He needed her help and she wouldn't let him down. She would fix things. She smiled. She felt lucky.

Emil slowed as he came to the police checkpoint just to the east of Vegamót, the restaurant and petrol station at the turn-off to Stykkishólmur on the south shore of the Snaefells Peninsula. There was a small queue of two or three cars and a truck waiting for the constable to let them through.

Emil recognized the constable. He slowed his car and wound down the window.

'No luck, Hinrik?'

'No one remotely like Ollie Jonson.'

This was one of only two roads off the peninsula. The other was a dirt track that ran along the north coast.

'What about the N54?' Emil asked.

'The guys from Búdardalur have got that covered.'

The truck hooted, followed by two of the cars. The constable ignored them.

'I suppose he could have passed before you got here?' said Emil.

'Rúnar called Borgarnes. They set up something just north of the turn-off for the N1,' said the constable. 'That would have caught him, even if he had driven south directly.'

'Oh, yes, I saw it,' said Emil. 'Do you have a weapon?'

'No.'

'Well, if he does come by, and he waves a rifle at you, let him see you are unarmed and don't try to stop him.'

Hinrik nodded.

The policeman didn't look nervous, although he had every right to be scared. It was probably best if a lone policeman didn't have a sidearm anyway, thought Emil. A cop with a gun would only encourage Ollie to shoot first.

'Come on!' yelled the truck driver. 'Stop chatting, we've got places to go!'

'I'll let you get on with it,' Emil said, marvelling at how impatient people were, even here, in the middle of nowhere. He pulled away and turned north over the Kerlingin Pass towards Bjarnarhöfn. He was the first in a strung-out convoy. Several minutes behind him would be Baldur and a couple of detectives, followed by a van with a small number of uniformed officers, and then, when they had mustered, the Viking Squad.

Emil had admitted he needed help, and he and the Commissioner had decided that there should be no conflict if the Reykjavík Violent Crimes Unit investigated Aníta's shooting, since Magnus was definitely not a suspect. Emil himself would continue to investigate Hallgrímur's murder. Clearly Emil and Baldur would have a lot of information to share, but Emil thought it highly unlikely that Baldur would try to steer the investigation away from Magnus. He wasn't so sure about his detectives, Árni and Vigdís, although Emil would much rather deal with them than Baldur.

The Commissioner couldn't afford to part with many uniforms. They had already despatched all the spare officers they had in the capital to Hvolsvöllur to help with the volcano. And cuts in police numbers following the *kreppa* in 2008 meant that there were very few spare officers anyway.

But if Ollie really had gone into hiding with a rifle, they would need every man they could get. Which was why the Commissioner had summoned the Viking Squad, Iceland's SWAT team. Emil knew there were a small number of firearms in Stykkishólmur police station, but not nearly enough for every officer. Rúnar and his men would have to be very careful.

Once again, there were two or three vehicles from the press parked a short distance before Bjarnarhöfn in the lava field, but Emil ignored them. Rúnar and Adam were waiting for him outside the farmhouse. They led him in to the living room, passing Kolbeinn and Sylvía in the kitchen.

'I take it no one has found Ollie yet?' asked Emil.

'Not yet. We've set up roadblocks. Gudjón is driving the roads, and Páll is looking in Stykkishólmur. That's all we can do for now.'

'How's Aníta? I think I passed her ambulance on the way up.'

'She's alive, but critical. Unconscious. They've decided to take her down to Reykjavík. Stykkishólmur hospital couldn't deal with her.'

'Forensics found anything?'

'Not so far,' said Rúnar. 'No bullet casings from where they think the shooter's vehicle was, but he was probably positioned somewhere further in the lava field. Nor have they found any of the bullets themselves, although the one that hit Aníta is still probably inside her – there was no sign of an exit wound. They'll dig it out at the hospital, no doubt.'

'Do we know what the weapon was yet?'

'We have a good idea,' said Adam. 'Kolbeinn's .22 hunting rifle is missing from his gun cupboard.'

'No idea when it was taken?' asked Emil.

'Kolbeinn last noticed it was there two weeks ago, when he

took out the shotgun it's kept with. He has a licence for both guns, by the way. The cupboard had been unlocked and locked again, by someone who knew where the key was kept: in a drawer in the hallway.'

'That could have been any of the family, presumably,' said Emil.

'But not Ollie,' said Rúnar.

'Good point.'

'Villi was going for a hike around Swine Lake when the shots were fired,' said Adam.

Emil had seen Swine Lake as he descended from the mountain pass down towards Bjarnarhöfn. It was about a kilometre long, shaped like a hook, and was bordered on one shore by black sand and on the other by the Berserkjahraun lava flow. It wasn't far from there to the part of the lava field where Aníta had been shot, but a hundred-metre-high conical pile of volcanic detritus stood in the way, obstructing the line of sight.

'Really?'

'Do you want to speak to him? He's upstairs in his room. We decided to keep him away from Kolbeinn. We had Edda examine his hands for gunpowder residue. Nothing.'

Emil shook his head. 'We had better leave it to Baldur. He should be here soon. He will be leading the investigation into the shooting. What about Kolbeinn?'

'He was mending fences in a meadow close to the farm,' Rúnar said. 'Constable Gudjón was in his car and could see him the whole time. Kolbeinn wants to go down to Reykjavík with his wife, but we haven't let him. He's in the kitchen.'

'Better wait for Baldur for that too,' said Emil. 'And the kids?'

'At school,' Rúnar said. 'But Gudjón said that Gabrielle, Dr Ingvar's wife, showed up just before Aníta went out riding. Aníta had saddled up a horse for her. They had a massive argument, Gabrielle drove off in a huff, and Aníta went out riding by herself.'

'Gabrielle can't have shot Aníta, surely?' said Adam.

'Why? Because she's a woman?' Emil threw in some sarcasm. 'Not strong enough to pull a trigger?'

'Sorry,' said Adam, sheepishly.

'Looks like Baldur will have some leads to follow,' said Emil.

'There is one other thing about Villi,' said Adam. 'Björn checked on his flight on Sunday morning. It landed at 6.32 a.m.'

'And he didn't get here until the afternoon, did he?'

'Just after two.'

'Interesting,' said Emil. 'It would take, what, two and a half, three hours to drive from Keflavík to here?'

'That's about right,' said Adam, who had done that drive on Sunday night himself.

'So that's three or four hours unexplained. You know, I think I will have a quick word with Villi before Baldur gets here. Can you fetch him?'

A couple of minutes later Villi appeared in the living room. He looked worried.

'How's Aníta?' he asked.

'Still alive, as far as we know,' said Emil.

Villi breathed out. 'Good.' He stared straight at Emil. 'Now. What can I tell you?'

'A colleague of mine will be here in a moment to ask you some more about what you were doing this morning,' said Emil. 'But I just want to ask you quickly about Sunday. What time did your flight land at Keflavík?'

'Early. Half past six. Maybe seven o'clock.'

'Why didn't you tell us that before?'

Villi shrugged. 'You didn't ask me, I suppose.'

'You told us you drove here directly from Reykjavík.'

'I don't think I did,' said Villi.

'Well, you implied it.'

'I didn't mean to.'

Emil took a deep breath to calm his impatience. It had been Adam who had originally interviewed Villi, and he clearly hadn't done a thorough enough job of it.

'All right. So what did you do between six-thirty and two o'clock on Sunday?'

'I hung out in Reykjavík,' Villi said. 'Had breakfast at the

Grey Cat. Walked around. Had another cup of coffee some-where.'

'Where?'

'Kaffitár on Bankastraeti.'

'Why did you do that? Why didn't you drive straight up here?'

Villi shrugged. 'It was my first time back in Reykjavík for a while. I wanted to look around, enjoy the place.'

'Do you have receipts? From the cafés?'

'No,' Villi said.

What a surprise, thought Emil.

'That's going to make it difficult for us to check your story.'

'You could ask the people serving then. They probably wouldn't remember me at Kaffitár, but they might at the Grey Cat. And I paid by credit card.' Villi pulled out his wallet and showed them a Bank of Montreal card. 'Will that help?'

'It might,' said Emil. 'May we take this? We'll return it later on today.'

'Sure,' said Villi, and passed it over.

Emil heard a car, or perhaps two cars, drawing up outside. 'Wait here a moment,' he said.

He left Villi in the kitchen and stepped out into the farmyard to see the tall, lean figure of Baldur approaching him, with Vigdís and Árni in tow.

'OK, Dumpling,' said Baldur. 'Tell me what the hell is going on here.'

CHAPTER TWENTY-FOUR

OLLIE WAS COLD. His fingers were cold, his feet, which were still wet, were cold; his whole body was cold. The rug was just an old piece of carpet. He was warmer with it than without it, but that wasn't saying much.

He was hungry. And thirsty. He had only had a cup of coffee and a bowl of Cheerios for breakfast – he had steered clear of the weird Icelandic yoghurt – and that had seemed an age ago. He checked his watch. One-thirty. Lunchtime, he thought. His stomach rumbled in agreement.

Come on, he told himself, man up. So it was lunchtime? It was possible for humans to miss lunch and not die. The cold wasn't enough to kill him either. At least not yet.

He would at some point need food and drink and warmer clothes. And that would probably mean a trip back to Stykki to borrow or steal. But it would be good to avoid the town if he could. Ollie had little idea of the local geography. He knew he was east of Stykki, and Bjarnarhöfn was west. And further to the west along the coast, beyond Bjarnarhöfn, was the town of Grundarfjördur. But that was a long way in a motorboat.

What about the other direction? He had absolutely no idea. There seemed to be some mainland to the north of him; there was definitely a mainland-sized hill. That couldn't be the West Fjords, could it? The West Fjords was the fist with outstretched fingers that reached out to the ocean from the top left of Iceland on the map. Surely that was further away from Stykki than the hills Ollie could see? Was there some settlement over there in that piece of land, whatever it was? Ollie had no idea. Knowing how empty Iceland was, probably not.

Which meant Stykki. After nightfall. Which around here, even in April, was pretty late. The idea of manoeuvring the boat through the sharp skerries at night scared him.

At least they hadn't found him yet. He had been on the island for three hours or so and hadn't heard any searchers.

God he was cold. And stiff.

Outside, the sun was shining weakly from a pale blue sky. Maybe he would be warmer out there, especially if he walked a bit. Got his blood circulating. He might even dry his legs a little in the sun; stuck under the rug they were going to stay damp all day.

He crawled out from underneath the rug and hopped out of the broken window. It was just possible to see Stykki in the distance. But there was a low hill at the centre of the island that obscured the view, so Ollie decided to keep to the eastern shore, out of sight of the town, or, more importantly, any boats puttering in and out of the harbour.

It was good to stretch his legs. The island was treeless and would have felt deserted if it wasn't for all the bird life. Ducks, cormorants, geese, little white birds, even smaller brown birds, were all over the place. It was comforting, in a way.

After walking for twenty minutes, he found a rock in the lee of the hill and sat down, stretching out his legs to the sun.

His thoughts turned for the hundredth time to how he had gotten himself into this mess.

It was during the series of blazing rows with his father after Kathleen, stupid bitch, had told Ragnar about her and Ollie sleeping together. She had wanted to hurt his father and had succeeded in that. But she had also seriously screwed him.

At some point, when he was screaming at his father, he had yelled that his mother's family were a bunch of murderers. Then, when his father had asked him to explain, instead of shutting up like he should have done, he did just that. He said how, when he was seven years old, he had come into the kitchen at Bjarnarhöfn very late one night and overheard Afi and Uncle Villi talking about how a man called Benedikt had been stabbed. They saw him and Afi had threatened him never, ever to tell anyone what he had heard.

That was probably their mistake, because Ollie wasn't sure exactly what he had heard. Except when people started talking about a writer called Benedikt who used to live at the next-door farm of Hraun who had just been murdered in Reykjavík. He remembered two nights later, when the family were discussing it at the dinner table, glancing at Afi. Afi's glare said it all. Never, ever mention what he had heard to anyone.

And he hadn't, until that moment when he had lost his temper and thought, what the fuck?

Ragnar had questioned Ollie closely about what he had seen and heard. He was frustrated at Ollie's vague replies, but in fact Ollie wasn't really sure. All he could clearly remember was Afi's reaction.

Ragnar said Ollie should talk to the authorities in Iceland. He said he would fly the two of them over there to see the police in Reykjavík. Ollie had no desire to fly to Iceland. He refused. Ragnar said he would call Afi and find out what had happened. And if he didn't get an answer that satisfied him, he would fly out to Reykjavík himself without Ollie.

Then Uncle Villi had suddenly shown up from Toronto at their house in Cambridge and suggested he and Ollie go for a walk. None of the rest of the family was in; it was the day before they were all due to go off to Duxbury for a month.

Uncle Villi had driven Ollie down to the Fresh Pond nearby. They had walked and talked. Ollie had tried to persuade Villi that he had refused to go to Iceland with his father, and he promised that if the police ever did ask him what he had heard, he would claim not to remember anything.

This wasn't enough for Uncle Villi. He said that Ollie had to stop his father going to Iceland, otherwise he, Ollie, would die. Uncle Villi was quite convincing about that. It was partly his own strength of character, but it was also that Ollie knew Uncle

Villi was Afi's representative. And even though it was many years since Ollie had seen his grandfather, he was still scared of him. More than scared – terrified. Mortally terrified.

Uncle Villi had not been satisfied. A week later, he accosted Ollie in the beach parking lot at Duxbury. He asked Ollie when his father was alone in the house. Ollie told him every afternoon; that was when the rest of the family left him to do his math.

And then, two afternoons later, his father had been stabbed.

Ollie was at the beach with his girlfriend, so he had an alibi. But he felt guilty, guilty as hell. He was an accessory, a conspirator. He felt like he had murdered his father himself. It was his information that had allowed it to be done.

He knew he should speak to the police about what he had told Uncle Villi. Or speak to Magnus, which was more or less the same thing. But he also knew what the result of that would be. He would go to jail. Probably not for as long as Uncle Villi, but still for a few years. It would ruin his life.

And he would never be able to look his brother in the eye again.

Uncle Villi had reminded him of this fact on and off through the years. He had made it clear that if Villi was ever arrested for the murder of Ragnar, he would bring Ollie down with him. Sometimes Ollie thought he would call Uncle Villi's bluff. But Ollie was a lousy poker player. Whenever he called another player's bluff, it turned out they weren't bluffing after all.

So he had stayed quiet. Throughout all the investigation by the police, and by his brother, he had stayed quiet.

And then his asshole brother had started digging again. Asking questions in Iceland, where the answers lay buried. Ollie had used every strategy in his book to get Magnus to back off. Although Magnus seemed the decisive brother, Ollie could manipulate him. Use his own weakness against him. When Ollie claimed that Magnus's continued investigation into their father's murder would screw him up worse than he was already, Magnus knew it was true.

For several months it had looked as if Ollie had succeeded. Magnus had listened and promised to drop it. But then he had changed his mind. Which was why Ollie had come to Iceland; a last-ditch attempt to shut him up.

And why Uncle Villi had followed him.

Ollie heard an engine in the distance. At first it was a gentle hum, almost inaudible among the cries of the seabirds, but it was getting louder.

Shit!

He looked around the island. It was bare. Nowhere to hide, and he was easy to spot from the water.

He sprinted back towards the house. As he reached the door, the sound of the engine was louder, but the craft, whatever it was, was still out of sight.

Ollie dived through the window. At least they wouldn't be able to see him from the fjord now. But if they came ashore they would be certain to search the house.

He decided to risk the stairs, which creaked alarmingly as he climbed them. A rotten board split.

Upstairs were two bedrooms, each with two beds, just damp mattresses on metal frames. Ollie dived under the biggest of them and listened.

The engine sound dimmed. For a moment Ollie thought that the boat had gone away, but then he heard voices. They had found the skiff!

The voices got closer. They reached the door. Two men, speaking Icelandic, so Ollie had no idea what they were saying. There was a series of crashes and then the sound of splitting wood as the front door shattered.

He could hear footsteps downstairs. Then the creak of the staircase.

From beneath the bed, Ollie saw a pair of black boots enter the bedroom. And a moment later a friendly face behind a large, bushy black moustache.

'Hi, Ollie. How are you?'

'Fucking freezing,' said Ollie.

*

'Forty-seven, forty-eight, forty-nine, fifty!'

Magnus's arms collapsed from underneath him as his chest hit the floor. His arms burned, his chest screamed. Time to torture his stomach.

He rolled on to his back, put his hands beside his ears and sat up. 'One, two, three—'

'OK, Magnús, time's up!'

Thank God for that, thought Magnus, as he flopped on to his back. Sweat was pouring from his forehead and seeping over the front of his T-shirt.

The warder, a stocky woman with short red hair and a friendly smile, stood over him.

'Come on, up you get! I've seen people do exercises in here before, but nothing quite like you.'

'Clears my mind,' said Magnus.

They were in the small exercise yard. Four white-painted walls, no windows, a basketball hoop and a roof of steel bars and translucent plastic. An hour a day was all the solitary prisoners were allowed in there. Magnus had decided to make the most of it – get his adrenalin going, sharpen his body and his mind.

He hauled himself to his feet and the warder led him to his cell. There were ten cells in the solitary wing. Two of them, he knew, housed the people he had arrested only three days before. He had no idea who occupied the others.

As the door clunked behind him, he flopped against the wall and slid to the ground, still panting.

The warder, whose name was Heida, was the only person he had spoken to all day. He knew he was going to be stuck in solitary for a while. The usual period was three weeks, at which point he would get to see a judge again, and his lawyer would be given the evidence amassed against him. But in murder cases, he could be in there for months.

It was frustrating not knowing anything about how the investigation was going. He had been impressed by the detective in charge of the investigation, Emil, and very glad that they hadn't let Baldur have a go at him. He knew what Emil would be doing – letting Magnus stew while he built up the case. But Magnus really wanted to know what evidence they had gathered already.

And what had happened to his brother.

He had spotted Ollie with Jóhannes in the car approaching Bjarnarhöfn on Sunday afternoon. He had no way of knowing whether Ollie was under arrest too. He might even be in a cell a few metres away at Litla-Hraun. But he thought not. If they had strong evidence that Ollie had killed their grandfather then they would have had to let Magnus go.

Magnus looked around his cell: at the bed, the pillow, the duvet, the desk, the stool, the toilet and the red plastic sink. He was doing all this for his stupid little brother.

He wondered whether the police had got his confession out of Ingileif yet. He hadn't heard anything, which was frustrating, but then he didn't expect to hear anything. Unless Emil was totally incompetent, he should have checked Magnus's phone records and asked Ingileif about the call. He was confident that Ingileif knew what he wanted of her, and confident that she would do it. She was smart, that woman, and a quick thinker. God knows what she thought he was up to, but he trusted her not to believe that Magnus had actually killed his grandfather.

Whereas Ollie almost certainly had. Maybe with the help of Jóhannes, the schoolteacher. Maybe it was actually Jóhannes who had staved in Afi's head, but if that was the case, Magnus was sure that Ollie would have been right there beside him.

As long as Magnus remained the prime suspect, Ollie might get away with it. Eventually, volcano permitting, they would let him fly back to the States. It wouldn't be impossible to get him back, to extradite him to Iceland, but it would be difficult. And Ollie was smart enough to get himself a good lawyer back in the States.

So at that point, Magnus would have to try to negotiate his own freedom. Deny his confession.

At the time, in the half-hour or so after he had discovered Hallgrímur's body, it had seemed like a good idea. Because he hadn't actually killed Hallgrímur, he knew that there was no evidence that would conclusively prove that he did. If he had been in the United States, with a good lawyer, he was confident that the case would collapse.

But Iceland was different. Sibba was right: if the prosecutor and the investigating detective were convinced that a suspect had committed a crime, it was more than likely he would be convicted. Magnus didn't think that Emil or the prosecutor, in this case probably Kári himself, were crooked. But they were effective. And as a quasi-foreigner, no one would be too unhappy to see him take the rap.

In which case he would be moving next door, into the permanent wings.

So why did he do it? Why did he cover up for his brother? He detested cops who covered up for friends or relatives.

It wasn't exactly because he was glad that Afi was dead, although he was. Magnus had read the sagas many times. He understood revenge. But he had also seen enough revenge-related killings on the streets of Boston to know that they were wrong. Ollie had been wrong to do what he had done.

But Ollie wasn't an evil person. He was an unreliable loser of doubtful morals, but that was different. It was Afi who had turned Ollie into a murderer. It was Afi's responsibility, his fault. He had paid with his life. And, in a way, Ollie had already paid with his.

It was Magnus's destiny to look after Ollie.

It had been good to talk to Ingileif. To feel that she was on the same wavelength as him. When he eventually got out of here, he would go see her again, whatever she said, wherever she was – Hamburg or Timbuktu.

But when? When would that be?

Three weeks? Or fifteen years?

CHAPTER TWENTY-FIVE

EMIL RAN HIS eyes over Jóhannes's statement, preparing himself for Ollie's interview. He was sure Jóhannes was hiding something. And he was fairly confident Ollie would tell him what.

Baldur was further down the corridor of Stykkishólmur police station, interviewing Gabrielle with Vigdís. Emil had spent half an hour with him going through what he knew of the family at Bjarnarhöfn. Baldur had also interviewed Villi, who had stood by his story that he had been walking around Swine Lake, but now remembered that he had seen a young couple while he was there. Also his car, a rented Peugeot, was definitely not the vehicle that Adam had seen parked in the hollow.

But the rifle and its bearer were still out there somewhere. The Viking Squad was hanging around in the station, watching TV, waiting to be called out. It was a shame that the manpower couldn't be used in the search, but Rúnar had insisted that the squad be kept at the station in readiness, in case the shooter popped up somewhere, shooting.

One thing was certain: Ollie could not have shot Aníta. Páll had done a good job of tracking him down with the help of the coastguard. He had been noticed by the locals as he had taken the boat out into the fjord, and indeed the owner of the skiff had reported it missing. When Aníta was shot, Ollie was out on the water.

Emil led the interpreter and Adam into the interview room. Ollie was hunched up in his chair, cradling a cup of coffee in his hands.

'Hello, Ollie,' said Emil in English. 'Must have been cold out there?'

Ollie grunted.

Emil turned on the recording equipment and the laborious interview started, with everything being translated back and forth from Icelandic.

'Now, Ollie, take me through again everything that happened on Sunday morning.'

The details came thick and fast. They matched what Jóhannes had said very closely, except Ollie's recounting of why they decided to go to Arnarstapi. In Ollie's version, Jóhannes simply told him they were going there and didn't tell him why. Emil let Ollie talk, and wrote everything down.

When he had finished, Emil asked him another question. 'When did you last speak to your brother?'

'Magnus? I don't know.' Ollie frowned. 'I suppose not since last Thursday. Although I've been staying with him, I didn't see him on Friday or Saturday.'

'Did you phone him?'

'No.'

'Are you sure?'

Ollie paused. 'Yeah. I'm sure.'

'If we look at your mobile phone records, which we will do, will we find any calls to him? Any texts?'

'No.'

Emil would bet that Ollie was telling the truth on that, at least as far as the phone records went.

'Why didn't you talk to him?'

'He was busy with the case he was working on. And we had had an argument. About whether he should ask more questions about Dad's murder, and Joe's father, the writer. He was determined; I didn't want him to.'

'In that case, why did you and Jóhannes want to go up to Bjarnarhöfn to talk to your grandfather?'

Ollie didn't answer for a moment. He sipped his coffee. Then he spoke. 'Because I felt more comfortable with Jóhannes than

with my brother. Jóhannes is kind of reassuring; my brother is a
nut job when it comes to anything to do with Dad's death.'

'Do you know what this is?' said Emil, waving the sheets of
paper he had brought in to the interview room with him.

Ollie shook his head.

'This is Jóhannes's statement that I took from him in
Reykjavík this morning. I asked him the same questions I asked
you. This is what he said about deciding to go to Arnarstapi.'
Emil read out three different passages, all of which contradicted
Ollie. 'You see, I don't believe that you and Jóhannes took a
detour just to go for a walk on the cliffs.'

Ollie shrugged. 'Whatever.'

'I think you were supposed to meet Hallgrímur there. That's
why you called him at the farm. He wasn't there and you wanted
to know why.'

Ollie shifted in his chair. Emil could see that he was thinking,
trying to decide whether to change his story, weighing up the
pros and cons.

Help him along. 'I don't think you killed your grandfather,'
Emil went on. 'But it's hard not to mark you down as a chief
suspect when you and Jóhannes are lying so blatantly. All I
need is an explanation about why you were there. The real
explanation.'

Ollie seemed to come to a decision and smiled quickly. 'OK.
You are right. We were planning to meet Hallgrímur there. We
wanted to talk about Dad's death. We had questions to ask him.'

'OK. But why meet him there? Why not at the farm?'

Silence. Emil waited.

'I couldn't face going back to the farm. You know what a
miserable childhood I had there. Jóhannes mentioned Arnarstapi
as a neutral place.'

'I see,' said Emil. Ollie seemed to relax a touch. It was Emil's
turn to think. 'I still don't see why you chose Arnarstapi. Why
not a café in Stykkishólmur? Or Grundarfjördur? Both places
are quite a bit closer.'

Ollie shrugged. 'I don't know. Ask Jóhannes.'

'What is it about Arnarstapi? There are those cliffs there, aren't there? The path to Hellnar. That's a quiet place where you couldn't be seen. A good place to pitch someone into the sea.'

Ollie frowned. 'What do you mean?'

'Both you and Jóhannes had good reasons for wanting Hallgrímur dead,' Emil said. 'You hated him because of what he had done to you as a child. Jóhannes hated him because he thought he had murdered his father. You didn't want to ask him questions. Jóhannes maybe, but not you. You wanted to kill him.'

'I don't know what you are talking about,' said Ollie.

'Yes, you do. The plan was to lure Hallgrímur out to Arnarstapi, kill him, and drop him off the cliffs into the sea. Wasn't it?'

'No,' said Ollie. 'Is your theory he drove out there, we killed him, then drove him back to Bjarnarhöfn and dumped him in the church? That makes no sense.'

'*That* doesn't make sense. But you intended to kill him, he didn't show up and then Magnús killed him instead. That makes sense.'

'No, it doesn't.'

'Did you know Magnús was going to kill the old man?'

'I told you, I haven't spoken to Magnus for days,' said Ollie. 'And actually, I don't believe my brother did kill him.'

'You don't, huh?' Emil said. 'Is that because you killed him after all? Killed him and then drove out to Arnarstapi afterwards? You know we can use the phone records to check exactly where you were when you made those calls to Hallgrímur?'

'Then I suggest you should do that,' said Ollie. 'That way you will know I was miles away when my grandfather was murdered.'

Emil rubbed the middle of his three chins. It *almost* made sense, but not quite.

'Can I go back to Reykjavík now?' said Ollie. 'I want to make sure I get my next flight out of this stupid country.'

'No,' said Emil. 'We can hold you for twenty-four hours

without going to see a judge. And given your previous attempt to run away from us, you'll spend the night in the cells right here.'

Ollie winced and closed his eyes.

'We'll talk again,' said Emil. 'But if it isn't later on today, have a good night.'

Back in the incident room, Emil got Björn to check on Ollie's phone records. And on Villi's as well – that gap in Reykjavík needed to be substantiated. And he told him to take another look at the Hvalfjördur tunnel cameras, in case it was possible to identify the time that Villi's rental car passed through the tunnel.

Baldur strolled in, carrying a cup of coffee, and took a seat opposite Emil.

'How did it go with Ollie?' he asked.

'He was lying,' said Emil. 'I think that he and the school-teacher meant to lure Hallgrímur out to Arnarstapi to kill him.'

'Any proof?'

'Not yet.' Emil didn't want to talk too much more about Ollie's actions on the Sunday; it was more relevant to Hallgrímur's death than Aníta's shooting. 'How about Gabrielle?'

'She was very angry with Aníta, although she's distraught now that Aníta's been shot. At least she *seems* to be.'

'What was the argument about?'

'What you guessed. Her husband figured out that she was the source of the leak to us about his dispute with Hallgrímur over the loan. She had no idea that Hallgrímur had lost the fortune Ingvar had made him. So she was angry about that and she was really angry with Aníta for coming to us.'

'Makes sense,' said Emil.

'It's a pity your guy let out Gabrielle was the source,' Baldur said.

Emil ignored the criticism. 'Was she angry enough to shoot Aníta?'

'Don't know,' said Baldur. 'She claims that she drove straight back home. She doesn't think anyone saw her, but we will check with neighbours.'

'Do we know where Ingvar was at the time of the shooting?' Emil asked.

'He was seeing a patient out at a farm. We are checking with the farm now.'

'And anything more on Villi?'

'Trying to locate the witnesses. Villi thought they looked like tourists, so we are checking the local hotels. Nothing yet.'

Baldur was asking the right questions, Emil thought.

Baldur sipped his coffee. 'Aníta is still an attractive woman, isn't she? I've never met her, but I've seen her photograph.'

Emil pictured the tall farmer's wife with the clear skin and long blonde hair. 'Yes, she is. She has a way about her.'

'Could she be someone's lover?'

'I suppose so.'

'Is she?'

Emil was taken aback by the question, and then immediately felt foolish. 'I have no idea.'

Baldur pursed his lips. 'What about Gabrielle? She has a certain way about her too. And she's French. I wouldn't be surprised if she had a lover as well.'

Emil wanted to pick up Baldur on his shameless stereotyping, but the inspector had a point. A good point.

'Maybe Aníta had a lover?' Baldur went on. 'Maybe Gabrielle did? Maybe it was one of the brothers: Kolbeinn or Ingvar. Maybe there's a love triangle, or love rectangle.'

'I didn't consider that,' said Emil. 'But even if that was the case, I don't see what that might have to do with Hallgrímur's death.'

'People in town will know who is screwing who, won't they?' Baldur said.

Emil nodded. 'Talk to Rúnar. If he doesn't know, he will know who does.'

'I will.' Then Baldur frowned. 'You know, maybe there is someone else out there, someone we don't even know about. A jealous lover with a rifle, looking for revenge.'

*

It was just getting dark when Ingileif pulled out of the Avis parking lot at Logan airport in her small hire car. She decided to trust her map reading rather than the mysteries of the GPS, and set off through the maze of tunnels and highways out of Boston.

She had only been to America once before in her life, to New York, and she hadn't driven then. She found the sheer scale of the place daunting. There were so many cars, so many people, and, as she got out of Boston, so many trees. She could feel her confidence waning as she neared the exit for Duxbury. What if this Jim Fearon guy flat-out refused to speak to her? What would she do then? Just turn around and drive back to Logan? She thought of the time and the tens of thousands of krónur she would have wasted.

But at least she would have tried.

She took the Duxbury exit and paused several times to study the print-out from Google Maps she had brought with her. Fearon's address had been easy to find: there was only one entry under that name in Duxbury in the directory she had consulted on the Internet. He lived in a place called Tinkertown, which seemed to be a neighbourhood in Duxbury reached through a twisted network of wooded roads.

She finally came to the address and pulled up outside a small, neat wooden house with a boat on a trailer in the yard. She took a deep breath and rang the bell.

The door was answered by a forbidding woman in her sixties, tall, thin with blonde hair and a lined, freckled face. But when she saw Ingileif, she smiled, an unexpected burst of warmth.

'Can I help you?'

'My name is Ingileif. Ingileif Gunnarsdóttir. May I speak to Jim?'

The woman yelled over her shoulder. 'Jim! There's a young woman to see you.'

Jim Fearon eyed Ingileif with suspicion. He had grey hair, a silver moustache, and a comfortable middle.

'Yes?'

'Hello, Mr Fearon,' said Ingileif, holding out her hand and launching into her prepared spiel. 'I am Magnús Jonson's girlfriend and I have just flown in from Iceland today to talk to you. May I come in?'

'My, what a long way!' exclaimed Mrs Fearon. 'Of course you can come in.' But the suspicion in her husband's eyes deepened.

'Come on, then,' he said, and led Ingileif into the living room. 'Have a seat.'

'Is this some kind of police business?' said Mrs Fearon.

'I expect so,' said the former detective.

Ingileif smiled at the woman and nodded.

'I'll leave you to it, then,' Mrs Fearon said, and withdrew to the kitchen area, but she was still within earshot.

'So you are Magnus's girlfriend?' said Fearon.

'Yes. We've been going out for almost a year. Since he arrived in Iceland.'

'Lucky guy,' said Fearon.

Ingileif smiled.

'You're not a lawyer or a police officer, then?'

'No. No, I promise you I'm not.' But Ingileif could see that Fearon didn't trust her assurances. 'As you may know, Magnús is in custody in jail at the moment, accused of murder. He heard that you had some important evidence for him, some lab results, and he asked me to get them from you.'

'Did he?' said Fearon.

'Yes,' said Ingileif. She swallowed. She could feel her cheeks warming up. Damn it! Why did she always blush when she lied?

The detective noticed. Of course he noticed.

'He can't come himself, you see,' Ingileif added unnecessarily.

'Did he tell you who I am?' Fearon asked.

'Yes. You are the detective who investigated Magnús's father's murder here thirteen years ago.'

'Did he tell you I am retired?'

'Er, yes,' said Ingileif unconvincingly.

'And did he tell you what the lab results were about?'

'No,' she said. 'But he said they were important. So please can you give them to me, so that I can take them back to Iceland and pass them on to him?'

Fearon studied Ingileif's face carefully. Ingileif became more uncomfortable.

'I'm sorry, Inga…'

'Ingileif.'

'Yes. Ingileif. I'm sorry, Ingileif. I just don't believe you. I don't know why you are here, but I do know you are not telling me the truth.'

Ingileif's shoulders slumped. The optimism and energy that had lifted her over the Atlantic left her. It was late, she was tired, and she had made an enormous fool of herself.

She sighed. 'You're right. I went to see Magnús this morning at the jail in Iceland. They wouldn't let me in to see him – he's in solitary confinement. One of his police colleagues told me about the lab results and that you wouldn't release them without proper authorization, and I thought I could persuade you. I am persuasive, you know. Usually.'

Fearon smiled for the first time. 'I don't doubt it. But you are not a very good liar.'

Ingileif returned his smile, nervously. 'No. But I suspect you were a good detective.' She felt a tear appear in the corner of her eye. 'I'm not even Magnús's girlfriend any more. We've split up.'

Fearon got to his feet. 'I'm sorry you've wasted your journey.'

Ingileif rose also and nodded. 'And I'm sorry I wasted your time, Mr Fearon.'

She held out her hand and Fearon shook it. He ushered her towards the door.

'Wait a moment, young lady,' said Mrs Fearon. 'Did you really come all the way from Iceland this morning?'

Ingileif nodded. 'I drove here straight from the airport.'

'And where are you going now?'

'I don't know. I suppose I will find a hotel somewhere.'

'Have you eaten?'

Ingileif had been too tense to eat anything on the plane. She shook her head. 'Not for hours.'

'Then why don't you stay here? I've got some meatloaf left over from dinner. Do you like meatloaf?'

Ingileif had no idea what meatloaf was, but nodded.

'You don't mind, do you, Jim?'

Fearon smiled, unwilling to stand up to his wife's hospitality. 'As long as we don't talk about lab results.'

And they didn't. They sat in the kitchen as Mrs Fearon, or Pattie as she asked to be called, warmed up the meatloaf. Ingileif liked Pattie, who had all kinds of questions about Iceland. She had a friend who was nuts about Icelandic knitting patterns, and she had tried some herself. Ingileif knew a lot about the subject, and the conversation became quite detailed. Pattie claimed that she had always wanted to travel to Iceland and hinted that it was only her husband's lack of imagination that had stopped her.

The meatloaf turned out to be delicious. Jim Fearon clearly thought so, helping himself to more. Ingileif found herself relaxing in the warm welcome of the kitchen. The Fearons were parents and grandparents. Ingileif had lost both her own parents and her brother. She had left her homeland to go to live in Germany. She suddenly realized how much she missed family, home.

'It's strange thinking of Magnús growing up here,' she said. 'I never know whether to think of him as an Icelander or an American. Neither does he, for that matter.'

'His father's death hit him badly,' said Fearon.

'He hasn't got over it,' said Ingileif. 'It drives him on in almost everything he does. I sometimes worry that if he ever did really discover what happened to his dad there would be a huge hole in his life. He wouldn't know what to do with himself.'

'Tell me about him,' said Pattie. 'I can see you are very fond of him.'

'Can you?' said Ingileif. 'Yes, I suppose I am.' She paused. 'He's a good man. He cares about me. I mean really cares about me. I tease him about it sometimes, about how serious he can be, but I suppose I like it really. I just can't admit it to myself.' She pulled herself up short, marvelling about how she was saying things to these two perfect strangers that she could scarcely say to herself. But thousands of miles from home in this little house in the Tinkertown woods she felt safe.

'I was having a bad time when we met last year. Magnús helped me a lot. He's a private person and I'm not really, but I think the two of us understand each other. I've had lots of relationships, but Magnús is different. He knows who I am. And he likes who I am.' She smiled. 'I'm sorry, I must not be making any sense.'

'Oh, yes you are,' said Pattie. 'So what went wrong? If you want to tell us.'

Ingileif did want to tell them. She wanted to tell someone.

'It was my fault. I went to work in Germany. I think Magnús wanted to continue the relationship, but I didn't. I don't like to be tied down. I sort of think Magnús does. And now... Now he's locked up in jail and they think he murdered someone. Which he didn't, by the way. I'm quite sure he didn't.'

She paused to see whether she had convinced the retired detective. He showed no sign of it, although he was listening closely.

'So I came over here to help him. To show him and me that I...' She stopped. The Fearons stayed silent, letting her say what she wanted to say. 'I suppose that I love him.' She took a deep breath. 'I'm an optimistic person; I believe in myself usually. It never really occurred to me that you wouldn't give me the lab results. But of course there's no reason why you should. I don't know if they are important, anyway. It may not even matter.'

'Oh, I think they are important,' said Fearon quietly.

Ingileif glanced at him. 'Oh, I wasn't trying to get you to tell me, I promise.'

Fearon laughed. 'I know.' His blue eyes, suspicious before, now twinkled. 'That's the point. But I will tell you. And you should find a way to tell Magnus.'

Vigdís went to bed early. She was staying in the same small hotel in Stykkishólmur as Ollie. In fact, her room was only two down the corridor from his, empty for the night. Despite her early start that morning, and several nights of poor sleep, her brain was tumbling. Davíd, Magnus, Baldur. Although technically she was restricted to working with Baldur on the attempted shooting of the farmer's wife, she had picked up some information about Hallgrímur's murder and Magnus's supposed role in it.

It didn't look good. And however long she tossed things around in her sleep-deprived brain, it didn't become any better.

She must have gone to sleep eventually because her mobile phone's insistent tone woke her up. She checked her watch before answering. One-thirty.

'Yeah?'

'Vigdís? It's Ingileif.'

Vigdís sat up, the urgency and excitement in Ingileif's voice jolting her to wakefulness. 'What is it?'

'I'm in America. In Duxbury.'

'You're where?'

'Yeah. I, er, I flew to Boston this afternoon. And now I'm at Jim Fearon's house. The detective who worked on Magnus's father's murder.'

'OK,' said Vigdís.

'He can't give me the lab results he had for Magnus, but he did tell me what's in them. If I tell you, can you get the message to Magnus?'

'Um. Yes. I can call Sibba, his lawyer. She can go see him at Litla-Hraun.'

'Good,' said Ingileif. 'Because I think he'll want to hear them.'

CHAPTER TWENTY-SIX

Wednesday, 21 April 2010

SIBBA WAS FIDGETING with her pen as Magnus walked into the interview room at Litla-Hraun. She smiled when she saw him, and stood up to kiss him on the cheek, but Magnus could feel the tension.

'You're early,' he said. It was barely past eight o'clock.

'I've got some news. Lots of news,' Sibba said.

'Good, I hope.'

Sibba sat down and looked Magnus in the eye. She took a deep breath.

'Aníta was shot yesterday. She was taken down to the National Hospital in Reykjavík. She's alive but in a bad way.'

'Shot? Where? By who?'

'In the Berserkjahraun on her horse. A rifle. And they have no idea who shot her. At first they thought it was Ollie, but it turned out it couldn't have been.'

'Will she make it?'

Sibba shrugged. 'I don't know. She was shot in the chest. It was Kolbeinn's rifle, but they know he wasn't responsible; he was working on the farm in view of the police at the time. And Ollie was on an island in Breidafjördur.'

'What was he doing there?'

'Hiding from the police. They caught him, though.'

'I'm sure they did. Is he under arrest?'

'He is being held for questioning. About Grandpa's murder.'

Magnus paused, taking it in. He liked Aníta. In fact, with the exception of Sibba, she was the only one of what remained of the maternal side of his family he did like. Why would anyone want to shoot her?

'You seem to have good information,' he said.

Sibba glanced at a computer on her right. 'Do you know how to work this thing?' she said. 'Is it switched off?'

'You mean is anyone listening?' The computer controlled the recording equipment in the interview room. They both knew that it was absolutely forbidden for the police to listen in to discussions between client and lawyer, but they also knew of a recent case where the recording equipment had 'accidentally' been left on in an interview room. Magnus got up to check the computer.

'It's off,' he said.

'Good,' said Sibba. 'I don't want anyone to hear this. You're right – I do have a good source. They've drafted in Inspector Baldur to investigate Aníta's shooting, and he has taken Vigdís with him up to Stykkishólmur. She told me.'

'She should be careful,' Magnus said. 'She could lose her job.'

Sibba nodded. She took another deep breath. She was definitely anxious.

'There is something else Vigdís told me.'

'Yes?'

'Ingileif is in America. Duxbury. She saw the detective you spoke to.'

'In America! How the hell did she get there?'

'She seems quite resourceful, your girlfriend.'

'She is,' Magnus said. 'Don't tell me Jim Fearon gave her the results?'

'He did,' Sibba said. 'Or at least he told her what was in them; he didn't give her a hard copy.'

'And?'

Sibba paused. 'The mitochondrial DNA suggests that the hair found in the house where your father was killed belonged to a close relative on your mother's side, and it wasn't you or Ollie. As you probably know, the DNA in hair only allows analysis of the mother's genes.'

A broad grin spread across Magnus's face. 'Well done, Ingileif,' he said. Then he glanced at Sibba and the grin disappeared.

Magnus stood up and walked over to the window. There was a view north of the little car park outside the prison, over the flood plain to the snow-streaked ridge of hills above the towns of Selfoss and Hveragerdi.

'You know, this is the only room in Litla-Hraun where I can see the outside world.'

Sibba was silent.

He turned. 'Sibba, I have two important questions for you. I remember that you and your family came to visit us at Bjarnarhöfn one Christmas.'

'That's right. We came over to Iceland for Christmas several times, but only once when you were living at Bjarnarhöfn.'

'I don't remember what year it was. Do you?'

'I do, actually,' Sibba said. 'I was sixteen, so it was 1985. Christmas 1985.'

'Benedikt Jóhannesson was killed on December twenty-eighth 1985.'

Sibba frowned

'And is your father right-handed?' Magnus asked.

'Yes.' Sibba's frown deepened. 'Wait a minute. What are you suggesting?'

'Your father—'

'No! The visit is a coincidence. It's got to be a coincidence. And eighty per cent of the people on the planet are right-handed.'

'I take your point about being right-handed. But I remember Fearon saying the hair colour was blond, and your father had blond hair before it went grey.'

'Fair. Light brown, really,' Sibba said. 'Once again, like many people.'

'I think they also described it as "sandy",' Magnus said. 'And you really mean "like many Icelanders". But the key point is that it's a pretty big coincidence that a close relative of my mother's was in the house with my father in Duxbury in July 1996, and your father was at Bjarnarhöfn in December 1985.'

'He never left the farm, I'm sure. He didn't go down to Reykjavík. I would have remembered.'

'Two hours down, an hour there, two hours back. You wouldn't have remembered unless he told you, and he wouldn't have told you.'

'Dad isn't a killer!' Sibba protested. 'You know him. He'd never kill anyone.'

Magnus looked at his cousin. He had seen it so many times before in his career – children denying that their parent was a murderer, refusing to contemplate the possibility. On the other hand, he was pretty sure that was why Sibba had been so tense. She knew what Fearon's DNA analysis implied.

He touched her arm. 'I'm sorry.'

She shook him off. 'No! I won't accept that. It's just circumstantial. You can't make a case against him.'

'Not yet,' said Magnus. He returned to the chair opposite his cousin.

Sibba glared at Magnus. 'Now I'm definitely going to have to resign as your lawyer.'

Magnus nodded. 'Thanks for what you've done so far, Sibba.'

'But I haven't done anything!' Sibba's voice rose in frustration. 'You wouldn't let me!'

'You did what I asked you to do, even when it didn't seem to make any sense.'

Sibba shook her head and shrugged. 'So who do you want to replace me?' She paused for a moment, running through the possibilities. 'What about Kristján Gylfason?'

Magnus had sparred against Kristján before. He didn't like him much, but he was one of the best criminal lawyers in Reykjavík.

'Maybe.' He nodded. 'But first can you do one last thing for me?'

Sibba collected herself, once more the lawyer. 'What is it?'

'Call Emil. Tell him that I have some information for him that he is going to want to hear. But tell him I will only talk if he brings me up to Stykkishólmur. No video link from here. No interviews at police headquarters. Stykkishólmur or nothing.'

Sibba nodded. 'I'll tell him.' She hesitated. 'Magnus?'

'Yes.'

'Now I'm not acting for you, can I make an observation?'

'I guess.'

'You didn't kill Hallgrímur, did you? You think your brother did. You're covering for him.'

'I don't know who killed our grandfather, Sibba,' Magnus said. 'But I fear it was someone very close to one or other of us.'

Half an hour later, Magnus was sitting in the back of a police car in handcuffs, speeding northwards along the banks of the broad river Ölfusá towards Selfoss. Over to his right he could see the high bent plume of Eyjafjallajökull. He marvelled at how Ingileif had managed to defy the volcano that seemed to have grounded the rest of the world.

It was clear, despite Sibba's protestations, that her father, Magnus's uncle Villi, was a suspect for the murder of Ragnar, and of the writer Benedikt Jóhannesson. Magnus could see that. Sibba could see that. Would Emil?

Magnus realized that the moment he had been waiting for for thirteen years was close. Very close. Soon he would know for sure who had murdered his father. The excitement bubbled up within him. He was grateful that Emil had agreed to his request to be driven up to Stykkishólmur. Given what he now knew, he would have found it very hard to stay cooped up in Litla-Hraun. He might be in handcuffs, but at least now he was moving – moving north towards the Snaefells Peninsula and an answer.

Of course, even if Villi had murdered two people in the past, it didn't necessarily mean that he had killed Hallgrímur. Hallgrímur's killer might indeed have been Ollie, who was at that moment being grilled by the police. And, in fact, Magnus would still be their prime suspect. But there must be some connection between those earlier murders and Hallgrímur's, and Emil would be in the best position to find it, with some help from Magnus.

The police car bypassed Reykjavík, dived through the tunnel under Hvalfjördur, and sped along empty roads through heaths and lava fields beside the remote and beautiful western coastline. Magnus remembered that other trip along the same route, taken thirteen years before at a much slower speed on a bus from Reykjavík to Stykkishólmur. It was a couple of months after the murder of his father, and Magnus had decided to travel to Iceland to build bridges with his mother's family.

It had been tough settling down back at Brown. It had been the beginning of his junior year, and he found himself skipping classes. He had begun drinking. His girlfriend tried to support him, but he pushed her away. He felt alone, lost and angry. So he skipped some more classes and bought a ticket to Reykjavík.

Ollie thought Magnus was mad to go back to Iceland. But the country of their birth had always meant more to Magnus than to his brother. And now that their father was gone, it was as if Magnus had been cast adrift in America. It was his father who had spoken Icelandic with him, who shared his enthusiasm for the sagas, with whom he walked once a year in the mountains of their homeland. But Magnus believed it was also his father who had been the impediment to a rapprochement with his mother's family. Now he was gone, Magnus thought that perhaps he could form some kind of link with his uncles, and even his grandparents. He had to try.

Magnus remembered how on the bus he had gone through the two notebooks he had filled with thoughts about his father's murder. At that stage Magnus was still focused on Kathleen; no one had yet told him about her alibi in the air-con engineer's bed. He had stopped the driver as the bus descended over the Kerlingin Pass to the main Grundarfjördur–Stykkishólmur road, and jumped off. He shouldered his backpack and walked across the Berserkjahraun towards Bjarnarhöfn.

He hadn't warned them that he was coming; he knew they would just try to put him off. A feeling of dread gathered around him as he walked through the lava field and remembered his miserable childhood years at the farm. The yard was empty, so he knocked on the farmhouse door. He was surprised to see it opened by a tall, attractive woman in her mid-thirties with long blonde hair. Aníta.

Once Aníta had figured out who he was, she ushered him in to the kitchen and plied him with coffee and cakes. Her distress and sympathy at the death of his father was heartfelt. She explained how she and Kolbeinn had taken over the farmhouse from Kolbeinn's parents, who now lived in the cottage, and the warmth of Aníta's presence made the kitchen feel entirely different than it had when it was his grandmother's domain.

Kolbeinn dropped in a few minutes later. He was much as Magnus remembered him: tall, square-shouldered, reserved. His sympathy was more sparingly given, but was genuine nonetheless. He seemed pleased that Magnus had come.

They had chatted for almost an hour when Magnus spied through the window an old lady with white hair staring at him. His grandmother. Magnus saw hesitation turn to recognition in his grandmother's eyes. Magnus tried a smile. She turned and scurried off towards the cottage.

'She's going to tell Hallgrímur,' Aníta said.

'He's not going to like you being here,' said Kolbeinn.

'I'm ready for him,' said Magnus, turning over in his mind the little speech he had prepared about reconciliation and family.

They were silent for a couple of minutes, waiting.

Then Magnus heard rapid footsteps in the yard, and the door was flung open. In strode a short familiar figure, white hair sticking up, blue eyes blazing. And in his hands was a shotgun.

Aníta let out a small cry.

'Magnús? Are you Magnús Ragnarsson?' Hallgrímur spat out the words more as an accusation than a question. The gun was pointing upwards.

Magnus realized that although his grandfather was instantly recognizable to him, he himself had changed a bit since the age of twelve.

Magnus stood up slowly. 'I am your grandson, yes.'

'Hallgrímur, put that gun down,' said Aníta.

'Well, kindly leave my property,' Hallgrímur growled, ignoring her. 'Now.'

'I have come to talk to you, Afi. Now my father is dead, I hoped I could—'

'I said leave!' Hallgrímur lowered the gun so that it was pointing at Magnus.

'Put the gun down!' Aníta repeated.

Kolbeinn stood and moved towards Magnus. 'I can drive him into Stykkishólmur.'

'Do that,' snapped Hallgrímur.

'He just wants to speak to you,' Aníta said. 'He is your grandson, after all.'

'Go!' Hallgrímur said. 'And don't ever come back here again, or I will shoot you myself. And if I don't, my son will.'

So Kolbeinn had driven Magnus into the middle of Stykkishólmur and dropped him off. Magnus had bought a bottle of Scotch on his way into the country at duty free at Keflavík Airport as a peace offering to his grandpa. He walked along the harbour wall, found a good spot, dug the bottle out of his backpack and began to drink.

As Magnus stared out of the police car at the silver flatness of Faxaflói Bay, a thought struck him. He had always assumed that by 'my son', his grandfather had been referring to Kolbeinn. But maybe he hadn't. Maybe he had been referring to another, much more dangerous Hallgrímsson.

Villi.

*

262

Villi manoeuvred the car down the steep slope to the shore of the lake. A clang rang out above the sound of the engine as the floor of the Peugeot dropped on to a sharp rock. He should have hired a four-wheel-drive.

Swine Lake looped around the Berserkjahraun in a hook. The day before, Villi had parked at the northernmost tip of the lake, nearest the main road. And he had been seen. This time he had driven on along a rough track to a part of the lake out of sight of any road.

He parked down on the sand by the water. In the summer people fished for brown trout here. Indeed, he and his brothers had done that themselves, many decades before. But in April the only visitors to this spot would be particularly hardy hikers. And the odd eagle.

He climbed out of his car and strolled along the shore of the lake on a beach of black volcanic sand. It was a beautiful spot. The lava here was twenty metres high, a crenulated wall of frozen magma that had created the lake several thousand years before. The lake itself that morning was a bluish shade of grey, reflecting the sky above. A crisp breeze blew in from the fjord to the north.

Villi was angry. He was angry about Aníta. Kolbeinn had called that morning to say that they had operated on her, and it looked like she was going to pull through, although she was still unconscious. Villi knew that his anger stemmed from guilt. If only Aníta hadn't decided to snoop in his mother's stuff in the first place.

Villi was losing control. Somehow, since Ragnar's death thirteen years before, he had managed to keep a lid on things, or at least to scare Ollie into keeping a lid on things. But Magnus was always the weak link. Villi believed that Ollie had done his best to prevent his brother from asking difficult questions, and indeed Ollie's ability to manipulate Magnus was impressive. But when it had become clear that Magnus was not to be put off any longer, Villi had sent Ollie over to Iceland for one more try. The news from Ollie had been bad, and so Villi had warned his father that he could expect a visit from Magnus at any time, and told Hallgrímur to refuse to say anything.

But Hallgrímur didn't like being told what to do. He said that if Magnus came to see him, he would explain how Ragnar had deserved to die. How Ragnar had mistreated Magnus's mother Margrét, how he had slept with Margrét's best friend. He even muttered about telling Magnus about the feud with Benedikt of Hraun's family.

Villi didn't know whether the old man was losing it or whether he was just playing games, taunting his son as he so loved to do. But he knew he had to be stopped. Which is why Villi had flown to Iceland unannounced. The story about checking on his mother's dementia was just an excuse.

But Villi had lost control, as Aníta's shooting showed. Somewhere, a long way in the past, he had taken decisions, bad decisions, from which he had never been able to recover.

The obvious one was not turning back to help Atli when he had fallen into the cove the night of the *sveitaball*. But perhaps there had been another chance.

For when Villi had scrambled back up the cliff that night he had met his younger brother Ingvar, who was then sixteen. Ingvar denied seeing anything, but Villi swore him to secrecy anyway.

Atli was discovered by another couple an hour later, floating face down in the cove. The girl who had been with Villi said nothing. Villi said nothing. And Ingvar, if he had seen something, said nothing.

Or nothing to the police. It became clear, two years later, that Ingvar had told their father.

Why had he done that? You would have thought that Hallgrímur would have been the last person in the world Ingvar would have told. But Villi never underestimated the power of Hallgrímur not just to make his children confess, but also to realize they were hiding something. Villi couldn't really blame Ingvar. It was inevitable.

He still didn't know how much Ingvar had seen. But it was clear that Hallgrímur knew Villi had killed Atli. His father didn't say much – just the odd bitter or cruel comment when he was angry. Just enough to show Villi that he knew and that Villi was in his power.

Somehow Villi should have stood up to him then, before it was too late.

Villi was the eldest son, but he couldn't face the idea of becoming the farmer of Bjarnarhöfn and living his whole life in Hallgrímur's shadow, so he decided to study engineering. Hallgrímur was disappointed, but engineering was a good career, and Kolbeinn was a good substitute. The move to Canada had been more difficult. Villi and his new wife were absolutely determined to put the Atlantic Ocean between their new family and Villi's old one. Hallgrímur disapproved, and at one point seemed close to raising the threat of what he knew about Atli and the night of the *sveitaball*, but Villi had promised to visit home often, and Hallgrímur had let him go.

And he had built a new life, a decent life, a life where he could look at himself in the mirror in the morning when he shaved and like the man he saw.

But all along his father had always known what kind of man Villi really was.

A murderer.

One thing had led to another, Hallgrímur had made sure of that. Benedikt. Ragnar. Ollie. And even though Hallgrímur was gone, even though Villi himself was sixty-four, on the brink of old age, he was still not free of the web that his father had woven.

He had gone too far. He had gone way too far. He hated himself, or at least that part of himself that had become involved in murder, that part that however hard he tried he seemed unable to erase.

He looked down at the water, tiny waves lapping against the volcanic sand.

His cell phone buzzed. He was amazed he had coverage, even here.

'Yes, Ingvar,' he said.

'Are you at the lake?'

'Yes.'

'I'll be there in ten minutes.'

Villi waited for his brother, the anger boiling inside him.

CHAPTER TWENTY-SEVEN

MAGNUS SAT IN the interview room in Stykkishólmur police station marvelling at how fat Sergeant Emil was. Obesity was becoming a real problem for some detectives in Boston, but Emil was certainly the heaviest detective Magnus had seen in Iceland. Adam, sitting next to him, pen and notebook at the ready, looked positively emaciated by comparison.

Somewhere in the building, Magnus knew, was his brother. What he didn't know was what his brother had already said.

'I don't like being dictated to, Magnús,' said Emil sternly.

'I'm sure you don't, and I apologize. But at least you haven't had to drive all the way down to Reykjavík, and this will be much better than a video interview.'

Emil grunted. 'Where's your lawyer?'

'I've fired her. Not her fault. You'll see why in a minute.'

'Do you want another one?'

'I'll be OK for now,' Magnus said.

'All right,' said Emil. 'Talk to me. And I hope what you have to tell me makes dragging you up here worth it.'

So did Magnus. 'By now I am sure you have discovered that I have spent much of the last thirteen years investigating the death of my father.'

'I've been to your flat. I've seen the wall,' said Emil.

'Good. In that case you will know that I believe there is a link between the murders of Benedikt Jóhannesson in 1985 and my father in 1996.'

'Same MO,' Emil said. 'Stabbed in the back and then the chest.'

267

'Right,' said Magnus. 'You may or may not have discovered that I recently asked a retired detective in the town in America where my father was murdered to go back and reanalyse a strand of hair found at the scene.'

'Go on.'

'He did so and now has the results. It turns out that the DNA belongs to a close relative of my mother – but not me. Or Ollie, for that matter.'

'I see,' said Emil.

'I'm sure you have met Villi, my Canadian uncle. I understand that he suddenly showed up here the day Hallgrímur was murdered. You have probably interviewed him.'

'We have.'

'He has lived in Toronto for many years. He lived there when my father was murdered. It's easy to get from Toronto to Boston, or easy by North American standards. It's a quick flight, or if you wanted to make sure there were no records of your trip, you could drive it. Probably take nine or ten hours, something like that.'

'You're saying that your uncle Vilhjálmur left the hair in the house where your father was murdered? Are you also saying he flew over to Iceland to murder Benedikt Jóhannesson?'

'Benedikt was killed a few days after Christmas in 1985. Villi and his family came to Iceland that year. They stayed with us at Bjarnarhöfn. With my grandfather, who hated Benedikt and hated my father.'

'That *is* interesting,' Emil said. 'But how does that relate to Hallgrímur's murder?'

'It can't be a coincidence that Villi suddenly shows up from Canada the day Hallgrímur is killed, can it?'

'It could be,' said Emil. 'Let's just say for the sake of argument that you are right. Villi killed your father and Benedikt. And let's assume that he did that with the encouragement of your grandfather. That would give you a motive to drive up to Bjarnarhöfn to kill Hallgrímur.'

'But why would Villi suddenly show up?' Magnus said.

'Villi says he was still in Reykjavík when Hallgrímur was killed,' Emil said.

'And was he?'

'We're checking it. But right now you remain the number-one suspect for murdering your grandfather.'

'I thought as much.'

'Did you kill him?'

Magnus hesitated. He had to deny murdering Hallgrímur or how could he possibly get Emil to take his Villi theory seriously?

'No.'

'And why should I believe that?'

'I didn't tell you about a conversation I had with Ingileif on Sunday shortly after I discovered my grandfather's body,' Magnus said. 'I'm sure you have already spoken to her about it.'

Emil didn't answer. He just waited.

'I'll take that as a yes,' said Magnus. 'You probably heard that I told Ingileif I had just killed my grandfather.' He glanced at Emil. No response. 'Well, that wasn't true.'

'You lied to your girlfriend?'

'Yes,' said Magnus.

'Now why on earth would you do that?' said Emil.

This was getting difficult. Magnus couldn't admit to trying to take the police off the scent of Ollie, since that would be committing a crime in itself. But he was becoming doubtful that Ollie had in fact killed Hallgrímur.

'I don't know,' he said in the end.

'You don't know! That's absurd,' said Emil. 'You confessed to the murder, Magnús. I've got to have a better reason to ignore that confession than "I don't know".'

He had a point. But he was also smart enough to figure out what Magnus was doing, that Magnus was covering for his brother. Magnus couldn't make that link too overtly. But...

'How's my brother?' he asked.

'He's right here in the police station helping us with our inquiries,' Emil said.

'A helpful guy, Ollie,' said Magnus. 'What did he say?'

'What did he say about what?'

'What did he say about our grandfather's murder?'

Emil snorted. 'Magnús, you are a detective. I'm not going to tell a suspect what a witness said.'

'Unless it's in your interests to do so,' Magnus said.

'And why would it be in my interests?'

'I don't know,' said Magnus. 'Is Ollie a witness or a suspect?'

Emil paused, easing the flesh of his gently wobbling chins. Adam, the young detective, looked at his boss in bemusement. But Magnus knew that Emil knew that Magnus was covering for his brother. And Emil realized that Magnus couldn't admit to it.

The detective came to some sort of decision.

'We've heard back from the phone company,' he said. 'At 10.25 a.m. Ollie made a call from his mobile to the phone in Hallgrímur's cottage. He was on the D54 about twenty kilometres to the west of Vegamót when he made that call. He made another call at 11.49 a.m. from a location near Arnarstapi, which is about fifty minutes to an hour's drive from Bjarnarhöfn. We know that Hallgrímur was murdered sometime before 11.29 a.m. when you called 112 after discovering his body. The timing is too tight – it is physically impossible for Ollie to have driven to Bjarnarhöfn, murdered Hallgrímur, and then driven off to Arnarstapi.'

A wave of relief washed over Magnus. His little brother wasn't a murderer after all.

'So it *was* Uncle Villi.'

'Or you,' said Emil.

Árni walked the familiar corridors of the National Hospital. It was only a couple of hundred metres from the police station on Hverfisgata, and it was a regular haunt for officers seeking victims or perpetrators recovering from the effects of their crimes.

'Hi, Árni, how are you?'

Árni recognized the surgeon who had patched him up a year before, a woman in her mid-forties.

'I'm OK. No leaks.'

'That's good to hear. Duct tape works every time.'

'How is the victim?'

'She's in a worse way than you were. It was a hollow-point bullet. It's made a mess. She's conscious and she should pull through, but she's tired. Ten minutes only.'

'But I need to take a full statement,' Árni protested.

'Ten minutes. I agreed to the interview so that you can ask the key questions. A full statement comes later.'

Baldur wouldn't like that. But although Baldur wasn't a good man to displease, he was up in Stykkishólmur, and Árni liked to do what doctors told him.

'OK,' he said. 'I'll be quick.'

Aníta was lying in a bed surrounded by tubes and instruments. A large man with a tired face was sitting on the chair next to her. He stood up to let Árni take the seat.

'Are you a detective?' he asked.

'Yes, Árni Holm. And you are Aníta's husband?'

'Kolbeinn,' the man muttered, every inch a farmer out of his element.

'I just want a word with your wife. I won't be long. Would you mind waiting outside?'

Kolbeinn paused to protest, thought better of it, and bent down and kissed his wife. 'Back in a moment, love,' he said.

'Hi,' Árni said after Kolbeinn had left.

'Hi,' the woman replied. Her face was creased and smudged with fatigue. And pain, probably.

'Just a couple of questions,' Árni said. 'Did you see who shot you?'

'No.'

'Do you know where the shots came from?'

'Somewhere in the lava field.'

'OK.' Árni wrote down the reply. 'Did you notice anyone in the lava field before the shots were fired?'

Aníta nodded. 'I saw a woman there yesterday.' She paused, looking confused. 'What day is it? I mean the day before I was shot. Marta.'

'I see,' said Árni. 'And who is Marta?'

'Marta is Hallgrímur's mother.'

Árni stopped writing. 'Hallgrímur Gunnarsson?'

'Yes.'

'But she must be over a hundred?'

'No. She was a few years younger than me.'

'Ah. OK. Do you have any idea who might have shot you?'

'Hallgrímur, perhaps.'

Árni blew out through his cheeks. 'Aníta, Hallgrímur died on Sunday. He was murdered.'

A frown of frustration creased Aníta's brow. 'I know, I know. I mean his ghost. Perhaps his ghost fired the rifle.'

Árni nodded. 'Perhaps.' He had stopped writing. The woman was clearly raving. But in a panic Árni realized that he should still write everything down, even if it didn't make sense. This was a statement that people would definitely want to see. So he resumed scribbling.

'Er, have you any idea why someone would want to kill you?'

'No,' said Aníta. 'I thought Hallgrímur liked me.'

'Yes. OK.' Árni wrote down the words. 'Could the person who killed Hallgrímur have shot you?'

The woman blinked twice. 'I don't know. Isn't that your job to find out?'

'Yes, yes of course,' Árni said. He was getting flustered. He knew his dumb questions would be written down for all to see as well as the witness's dumb answers. Also, time was running out. 'Did you know anything? Had you discovered anything that might lead to the killer's identity?'

Aníta slowly shook her head. Then she blinked again. 'Wait a minute. I found a postcard. It was from Boston. It's in a box under Sylvía's bed at the farm. It could be that.'

The doctor returned. 'That's enough, Árni. You can see Aníta is tired.'

'Just a minute,' Árni said. 'What did the postcard say, Aníta?'

'It was from Villi. I don't remember the exact words. Go find it. You can read it yourself.'

'No more questions,' the doctor said.

'Just a couple more—'

'I said no more questions, or I'll use that duct tape on your mouth. Now please leave.'

Árni knew when he was beaten. He closed up his notebook. 'Thanks for your help, Aníta,' he said. 'I'll be back for a longer chat later on.'

Constable Páll drove down the by now very familiar track towards Bjarnarhöfn. He had been detailed to pick up Villi and he had two armed members of the Viking Squad accompanying him. He was nervous, but also excited. He was confident he could handle whatever situation developed.

The farmyard was empty. The forensics people had finished with the cottage and the church for the time being and were out in the lava field with a couple of uniformed officers. Police tape still surrounded Hallgrímur's burned-out cottage.

Villi's car was not visible. Páll debated with the two members of the Viking Squad what to do. In the end they decided that he would go into the farmhouse alone, and the other two would wait for him. If Villi was armed, then waving weapons around would alert him. Otherwise there was no real reason to think this wasn't just another in the long line of visits to the farm by the police over the previous few days.

Páll knocked on the door. There was no answer. He knocked again, opened it and shouted, 'Hello!'

'Wait a moment!' It was a girl's voice. After a few seconds, Tóta appeared. 'Hi. Sorry, I was upstairs.'

Her eyes were rimmed with red. Poor kid, thought Páll. He imagined how his own children would feel if their mother was in hospital.

'I took the day off school,' Tóta said. 'Because of Mum. It was stupid, really. She's in Reykjavík in hospital and Dad won't even tell me how she is. His phone is switched off. Have you heard anything?'

'No,' said Páll, trying a smile. 'And that's good news. I would have heard if something bad had happened. And your father has probably been told to keep his mobile phone switched off. They think it interferes with hospital equipment.'

'All he needs to do is step outside and call me,' Tóta said.

Páll didn't answer her. She was right. 'I'll tell you what, I'll get a message to the hospital to ask him to give you a ring.'

'Thanks,' said Tóta.

'Is your uncle here?'

'Villi? No, he's gone off somewhere. He left about an hour ago.'

'Did he say where he was going?'

'No. He said he would be back in a couple of hours.'

'Hmm.' Páll thought. 'Did you see him leave?'

'No. Why?'

'Do you know whether he had packed a bag?'

'Why would he do that?' Tóta asked, her eyes widening. 'As I told you, he said he would be back.'

'Can I just have a quick look in his room?'

Tóta looked as if she was about to argue, but seemed unable to summon up the energy to go through with it. She shrugged and led him up to a bedroom. It was neat, except for a suitcase on the floor containing a pair of shoes and a couple of items of clothing. Páll opened the closet. A jacket was draped on a hanger.

'Is this your uncle's?'

'I think so,' said the girl.

No sign of departure, Páll thought. He returned to his colleagues in the car and radioed in to the police station.

'Let's try Swine Lake,' said Páll. 'He might just have decided to go there for another walk, like he did yesterday.'

They drove back to the main road and then down to the northern tip of the lake where Páll knew Villi had parked the day before. Nothing. As they were driving back to the main road, they passed a lone walker.

It turned out he was German, but he spoke English. He said

he had noticed a car parked down by the other side of the lake. He had not seen anyone near it, but then it had been about a kilometre away. Oh, and he had heard what sounded like a shot about half an hour before.

Páll drove rapidly back over a rough track. In a few minutes he spotted the car – he recognized it as Villi's hired white Peugeot.

As Páll drove closer towards it one of the Viking Squad cried out and pointed. There was something floating in the lake behind the vehicle. It looked a bit like a log.

But it wasn't.

It was a body.

Emil knocked on the door of the room that Baldur had requisitioned as his office. It was lucky that the Stykkishólmur police station was undermanned. It had been built in more bountiful times, when it was assumed that the Snaefells Peninsula would need a well-staffed headquarters. Since then, following the *kreppa*, police numbers in the region had been cut. But they still had the desks and the chairs.

Vigdís was sitting with him.

'I just spoke to Magnús,' Emil said.

'On the video link with Litla-Hraun?' Baldur said. 'I thought he wasn't talking.'

'No, right here. And he decided to talk.'

'You brought him up here?' said Baldur, beefing up the incredulity.

'He wanted to talk; I let him.'

Baldur shook his head. 'Watch him, Emil, or he'll run rings around you.'

Emil ignored the comment. Baldur was right: there was a chance that Magnus was manipulating him. On balance, he didn't think so. He perched his backside on a desk. It creaked, but Emil was confident it was strong enough to hold him.

'He told me about his uncle, Villi.'

'The Canadian? I spoke to him yesterday.'

'Magnús suspects him of murdering Magnús's father and Benedikt Jóhannesson.'

'So what?' said Baldur.

Emil told the inspector about the evidence from the retired detective in Duxbury, and the fact that Villi was visiting Iceland when Benedikt was murdered.

Baldur seemed unimpressed. 'None of this is corroborated. We just have Magnús's word for it.'

'True, but we can corroborate it, and Magnús knows that.'

'So are you suggesting that Villi killed Hallgrímur? I thought you had Magnús's confession for that.'

'Which he denies now.'

'He denies it? Of course he denies it! What murderer wouldn't?'

'He doesn't deny making it. He just denies that it is true. He says he misled his girlfriend.'

'Jesus Christ,' Baldur muttered.

Emil noticed Vigdís smiling at this. He realized that he had gone too far discussing the case against Magnus with the police from Reykjavík.

'My point is, we know that Magnús didn't shoot Aníta because he was tucked up in Litla-Hraun at the time. And we know that Villi was in this area. So he might be a suspect in your investigation.'

'We should bring him in,' said Vigdís.

Baldur scowled at her.

'I've sent Páll out to Bjarnarhöfn to fetch him,' said Emil.

'And you expect me to interview him?' said Baldur.

'We both should, probably,' said Emil. 'But I would have thought—'

Baldur's mobile phone rang. He answered it before it had a chance to ring twice. Emil watched.

'Yes... Yes... Yes...' The corners of Baldur's mouth pointed even further downwards. 'You think it's suicide? Don't touch anything. I'll be right over.'

Baldur looked up to Emil and gave him a quick, joyless grin. 'Villi was found floating in Swine Lake. He had been shot once by a rifle fired from close range. The rifle is at the scene. Páll says it looks very much like suicide.'

Emil watched speechless as Vigdís and Baldur grabbed their coats and headed for the door.

CHAPTER TWENTY-EIGHT

MAGNUS HAD BEEN alone in the cell for two hours, but already he was finding it more difficult than the two days he had spent at Litla-Hraun. His brain was buzzing. Villi had killed Benedikt and his father and probably Hallgrímur too. Ollie was off the hook, yet Magnus still didn't understand what the hell he and Jóhannes were doing on the Snaefells Peninsula. Magnus himself was still very much on the hook, although he believed he had gone a long way towards persuading Emil that he was innocent.

Ingileif had done her stuff, as he always knew she would. The false confession had achieved its purpose of keeping the focus of the investigation away from Ollie and on to Magnus, but it now turned out that the whole thing had been unnecessary. Magnus would have to be careful how he extricated himself. His attempt to mislead Emil had clearly obstructed the investigation; if Emil chose to make an issue out of it, Magnus would be out of a job in Iceland, and they might not take him back at the homicide unit in Boston after all. At least he hadn't lied directly to Emil, as had been his first idea; confessing through Ingileif was much less of a sin. And it was easier to claim later that he had lied to his girl-friend than that he had lied to the police. Or at least so he hoped.

He was getting ahead of himself. If the evidence against Villi for Hallgrímur's murder didn't stack up, then he would keep his status as prime suspect. He wasn't out of jail yet.

He heard the sound of heavy footsteps, some wheezing and a key jangling, and the cell door opened. It was Emil himself. They must be short of constables.

'Magnús. We need to talk. Come on.'

Magnus followed Emil's wide buttocks on their slow journey up the stairs to the interview room. The detective was puffing heavily and his face was red. He slumped into a chair in the interview room, and Magnus sat opposite him. Magnus noticed that Emil didn't turn on the recording equipment. That was a serious lapse of procedure, but Magnus assumed Emil knew what he was doing.

'Things are moving fast,' said Emil. 'But I have no idea in which direction.'

'What's happened?'

'Villi has killed himself. Blown out his brains at Swine Lake. Baldur and Vigdís are there now.'

'Wow,' said Magnus. 'Well, that's an admission of guilt. Did he leave a note?'

'Not one we have found. We haven't checked Bjarnarhöfn yet.'

'So we don't know whether Villi killed Hallgrímur as well as Benedikt and my father?'

'Actually, we do,' said Emil. He was still breathing heavily from the effects of the stairs. 'He didn't.'

'He didn't?'

'We have two transactions from his credit card in Reykjavík timed at 8.35 and 11.16. And the camera at Hvalfjördur recorded him leaving the tunnel heading northwards at 12.32, at least an hour after you found your grandfather's body.'

'Oh,' said Magnus. 'So if it wasn't Villi and it wasn't Ollie, who the hell did kill Hallgrímur?'

'You are the obvious candidate,' said Emil. 'And you are still under arrest for that murder. But just for fun, if we assume that it wasn't you, who else could have killed him?'

'Just for fun? Is that why the recording equipment is off?'

'Maybe,' said Emil. 'I think I can use all the help I can get.'

Magnus stared hard at Emil. He could tell the fat detective's instinct was that Magnus was innocent, but he also knew he couldn't admit to it.

Magnus thought.

Emil waited.

'Have you been to the scene of Villi's suicide?' Magnus said eventually.

'No,' said Emil.

'Don't you think you should go?' said Magnus. 'And take me with you?'

Keflavík Airport was as chaotic as it had been just over twenty-four hours earlier when Ingileif had left it. Once again at Logan she had blagged her way on to an overbooked departing flight, taking a seat that had become available at the last minute. She had at least slept for a few hours on the aeroplane.

She was very pleased with what she had done for Magnus. She was confident that Vigdís would have got the message through to him at Litla-Hraun. She just hoped it would make a difference.

Perhaps they had let him out already? It was a bit much to hope for, especially given what she had told the police about his admission that he had killed his grandfather. But things seemed to be going her way. She still didn't know what he was up to with that confession. She was sure it wasn't true; she just had to trust that he knew what he was doing. She was desperate to see him, wherever he was.

She called Vigdís's number.

'Hi, I can't talk much now. What is it?' said Vigdís.

'Is Magnús still in jail?'

There was a pause on the other end of the phone. Then Vigdís said one word: 'Stykkishólmur.'

Ingileif realized immediately that Vigdís couldn't let whoever she was with overhear that she was talking about her colleague. 'You mean Magnús is in Stykkishólmur now?'

'Yes.'

'Is he free?'

'No. Not yet. Where are you?'

'I'm back in Iceland.'

'That was quick. I've got to go.'

'OK, Vigdís. Thanks.'

Ingileif rang off and made her way to the car park. Her friend María wouldn't mind if Ingileif borrowed her car for another day, she was sure. Because she was going to take it up to Stykkishólmur.

Vigdís hurriedly put her phone away and avoided the quizzical glance of her boss standing next to her.

They were at Swine Lake, and Vigdís had just finished erecting the tape around the primary crime scene. The body had been dragged in from the lake and laid on a plastic sheet, but a reddish brown stain was still visible in the water where blood had spread out from the mess of soggy tissue that was once Vilhjálmur Hallgrímsson's head. The doctor, not Ingvar this time but his less experienced colleague from the hospital, Íris, had pronounced him dead. It didn't take any specialist training in forensic medicine to do that. Edda and her team were hard at work checking the area immediately around Villi's hired Peugeot. They were working against time; rain was on its way, and it would be impossible to protect the whole area. One of them was erecting a tent to prevent rain falling on the already soaked body.

'Who was that?' Baldur asked.

'Árni,' said Vigdís, keeping her gaze away from Baldur and on to the tight black clouds to the west. 'It was nothing.'

Her mobile rang again. She checked the display: Árni. She glanced at Baldur.

'Hello again,' she said.

'Again?' said Árni, perplexed.

'What have you got now?'

'I spoke to Aníta,' Árni said, and proceeded to tell Vigdís about the farmer's wife's confused statement, and the postcard that was under Sylvía's bed.

Baldur was watching her closely, and when she had finished, Vigdís relayed what Árni had told her.

'Why didn't he tell you all that the first time he called?' Baldur asked.

'I was wondering that myself,' said Vigdís. 'Sometimes I don't understand Árni.'

'Sometimes?' snorted Baldur, and went over to talk to the doctor.

Magnus recognized the spot from his childhood. A strip of volcanic sand about fifty metres wide lay between the high wall of lava and the lake. A group of police vehicles were parked on the track from the road above the lake. Farther on, just before the track met the volcanic sand, stood a small white vehicle and, a short distance from that, a forensic tent. People were milling around, most of them in forensic overalls.

The sky and the lake were a dark grey. It was about to rain.

Emil parked his car next to the others and led Magnus along the marked corridor towards the crime scene. Magnus was glad to see that despite the presumption of suicide, they were following the proper procedures for a murder.

'Hey, Magnús!' Vigdís grinned as she approached him. 'Great to see you. Have they released you?'

'I'm afraid not,' said Magnus, returning her grin. It was good to see an unequivocally friendly face.

'I thought Magnús might be able to give us some help,' said Emil.

'Good idea,' said Vigdís. 'Do you want to see the body, Magnús?'

'Hold on, Vigdís,' said Magnus. They were standing at the perimeter of the primary crime scene, about twenty metres from the edge of the lake. 'Is Baldur around?'

'He's up there, with a hiker who saw Villi's car earlier.' Vigdís pointed up towards the frozen lava wall at the top of which stood two figures.

'He won't be happy with me poking around,' Magnus said. 'I don't want to get you into any more trouble than you are in already. Just describe the scene to me.'

'OK,' said Vigdís. 'The body was floating about twenty metres from the shore when we got here. You can see the rifle there; no one has touched it yet.'

About two metres from the lake edge, a bolt-action hunting rifle lay pointing away from the water towards Villi's car.

'Kolbeinn's?'

'Same model. Ballistics will confirm it. But for now we can assume it was Kolbeinn's.'

'Any casings?'

'One, at about the point you would expect it to be had the rifle been pointing towards the lake. No bullet found as yet, but that's hardly surprising. It will be out there somewhere.' Vigdís waved vaguely over the water.

'So the idea is Villi pointed the gun at himself, pressed the trigger and the gun recoiled away from him?'

'And he fell backwards into the lake.'

'Where was the wound?'

'It just about blew his head off.'

'Any gunshot residue on his hands?'

'None that we have seen yet. But it could have been washed off in the water. Edda thinks once she gets a close look at his hands, she should find some traces.'

'And the body is in the tent?'

Vigdís nodded.

'Hi, Magnús. I'm glad they have finally let you go.' Magnus turned to see the tall figure of Edda approaching him in forensic overalls, smiling, her short blonde hair hidden beneath a hairnet.

'He's still under arrest,' said Emil. 'But I thought he might be able to help us.'

Edda's smile slipped from her lips. 'All right,' she said, carefully. Magnus couldn't blame her caution.

'Vigdís told me how they found the scene,' he said. 'Anything to suggest it wasn't suicide?'

'No,' said Edda, but Magnus detected a touch of hesitation in her voice. 'Can't see any gunshot residue on the hands, but maybe I just need a closer look. Also, you would expect less with a rifle than a handgun.'

'What about blood spatter?'

'There is none,' Edda said. 'I suppose it must all have been blasted backwards into the water.'

'Hmm. You would have thought something would have gone sideways on to the sand.'

'Yes. You would,' said Edda. 'We've looked and haven't found anything yet. Maybe it didn't.'

'Any sign of anyone else at the scene?'

'No. There are signs of just one person moving around here. They all look like the victim's footprints.'

'Do you have a photograph of the victim?'

'Yes,' Edda said. 'I took my own. Here.'

She pulled out a digital camera, flicked through the images on the display at the back, and then handed it to Magnus. There were several of the body floating in the water, and then of what remained of Villi's head. A mess of bloody pulp. He was unrecognizable.

Magnus winced. He had seen suicides before. Shots in the head from close range were never pretty.

Then he looked again. The bottom right-hand jaw was still intact. 'Was the entry wound to the left, do you think?'

'Yes. The left cheek, or possibly temple.'

Magnus was silent. Vigdís, Emil and Edda all watched him.

'Villi was right-handed,' Magnus said eventually.

'How do you know that?' asked Emil.

'His daughter told me.'

Edda frowned. 'But this is a rifle, not a handgun.'

'Still applies,' said Magnus.

'Are you sure?'

'Quite sure. I had one of these three years ago in Boston. You can look it up in the literature.'

'What are you talking about?' asked Vigdís.

'It is very rare for a right-handed suicide to shoot himself in the left temple,' said Edda, who had been trained in forensics at the FBI Academy at Quantico. 'At least with a handgun. Think about it. But Magnus claims it is also rare with a long-barrelled weapon.'

'That's right,' Magnus said.

They turned at the sound of a vehicle speeding across the sand towards them. Baldur jumped out.

'What the hell is *he* doing here?'

'I thought it would be useful to bring Magnús to the crime scene,' Emil said. 'And I think it has been.'

'Why?' Baldur said.

'Magnús has doubts that this was a suicide.'

'Of course he does,' Baldur sneered. 'And does he say why?'

'Villi was right-handed and shot himself in the left temple.'

'So what?' said Baldur. 'If the victim was shot by someone else, how come we can't see any signs of anyone else at the scene? Answer me that?'

Baldur stared at Magnus. It was a good question. Magnus shrugged.

'Take him away, Emil. We don't have any time to waste. It's going to rain in a moment and then all the evidence will be washed away.'

'OK. Sorry to get in your way, Baldur,' said Magnus in as conciliatory tone as he could muster.

Edda looked at him thoughtfully. Magnus knew he had sown doubts.

'Baldur is an arsehole,' said Emil as they walked back towards Emil's car. 'Always was. So you think it might not be suicide?'

'The blood spatter, or lack of it, worries me, and so does the entry wound. But Baldur has a point. How could someone get to this soft sand and murder Villi without leaving a trace?'

'Could they have brushed away their tracks?' Emil said.

'Difficult to do. Especially difficult to do without Edda noticing,' said Magnus. 'She's good.'

He stared at the lake. Behind it rose the steep sides of the mountains that ran along the spine of the Snaefells Peninsula. Stone, moss, streams and, higher up, snow. Hallgrímur had taken him and Ollie fishing here a few times when they were boys. Ollie had hated it, and in truth Magnus didn't enjoy it much. They had caught a few trout, though.

But they hadn't driven down this track. They had parked around the corner somewhere, out of sight of where they now were.

'Come on,' said Magnus. He led Emil at a brisk pace down to the side of the lake at a point further to the west of the crime scene. Rain began to fall, just a few drops. Emil panted to keep up with Magnus.

'See how shallow it is here?' Magnus said. And indeed the sand slid gently down under the water. 'It would be very easy to wade a few feet out in the lake, pulling a body behind you.'

'I see what you mean,' said Emil. 'But from where?'

'Here, I'll show you,' Magnus said. Further along the shore the frozen lava jutted out into the lake like the tower of a medieval walled city. There was only a narrow strip of sand a couple of metres wide at that point. Magnus led Hallgrímur round the rock and there, out of sight of Villi's Peugeot and the rest of the crime scene, was a small beach at the end of a very rough track.

'Careful,' said Magnus. 'Follow my footsteps.' There were two sets of fresh tyre tracks. And where the tracks halted, footprints. A mess of footprints, leading down to the lake edge. Magnus moved carefully towards the point where the footprints stopped, examining the sand. He noticed a small brown stain. And another. And a shred of something pink that was probably brain tissue.

The rain was coming down harder now. In a couple of minutes most of the evidence would be gone.

Magnus turned and ran back around the lava battlement. 'Edda! Get your camera!' he shouted. 'Quick!'

CHAPTER TWENTY-NINE

MAGNUS AND EMIL stood back and watched Baldur direct operations. To be fair to the inspector, he was quick to appreciate what Magnus's discovery meant. Someone else had driven down to the lake, met Villi there, shot him with the rifle from close range, and dragged his body around the lava promontory to stage a suicide, returning the same way. He had then driven Villi's car round to where he had dumped the body and left the vehicle on hard rock, where no footprints would show. It had almost worked.

In the meantime there was evidence to be preserved from the rain. The bloodstains, the footprints and, in particular, the two sets of tyre marks: Villi's and those from the murderer's vehicle.

Vigdís paused by Magnus and Emil. 'Well done,' she said. 'Did you know it wasn't suicide before you got here?'

'I didn't know,' Magnus said. 'Villi could have chosen suicide as the easy way out. On the other hand, this kind of thing can be staged.'

'By whom?' Vigdís asked. 'And why?'

'To tidy things up,' Emil said. 'If we had bought the suicide, Villi might have been blamed for everything. Hallgrímur, Ragnar, Benedikt. The real killer would have got away with it.'

'If that's right, it suggests that Villi didn't murder those people,' Magnus said. 'Or at least not all of them.'

'And it's likely that whoever shot him also shot Aníta,' Vigdís added. 'By the way, it can't be Kolbeinn. I got a call from Árni in Reykjavík who says Kolbeinn is at the National Hospital with his wife. And Aníta said something interesting. Something about a postcard she had discovered under Sylvía's bed at the farm. From Villi. She thinks it might be important.'

'Important enough to be shot for?' Emil asked.

'You could go and see,' said Vigdís.

Magnus glanced at Emil. 'I don't think anyone would miss us here,' he said.

It took them ten minutes to get to the farm. Tóta let them in, surprised to see her cousin Magnus.

'Have you heard anything about Mum?' she asked.

'She's conscious,' Magnus said. 'She spoke to a policeman earlier this morning.'

'That's good,' said Tóta, but the worry didn't leave her face.

Neither Emil nor Magnus told Tóta about her uncle Villi. There would be time enough for that.

'Can you show us Amma's room?' Magnus asked.

'She was sharing with me in my room, but she's not here any more. She's gone to stay with Uncle Ingvar.'

'Can we take a look?'

Tóta showed them her room. Magnus checked under the bed. 'Did she leave a box here?' he asked.

'No. I know the one you mean, though. She took it with her.'

'Thanks,' said Magnus, and he and Emil left the girl, Magnus feeling guilty that they still hadn't told her about Villi.

It was raining as they hurried through the farmyard back to Emil's car. They sat in the vehicle and stared out across the meadows to the little church where the first murder had taken place only three days before.

'Villi's dead. Hallgrímur's dead. Kolbeinn is in Reykjavík. I was talking to you in cosy Stykkishólmur police station,' Magnus said. 'So that leaves one person who could have shot Aníta.'

'Who?'

'Ingvar.'

'Ingvar?' Emil rubbed a chin. 'He was seeing a patient at a farm somewhere at the time of the shooting.'

'Was the alibi checked out?'

'Vigdís was going to check it this morning,' said Emil.

'Give her a call,' suggested Magnus.

Emil pulled out his phone. Magnus leaned over so that he could hear both sides of the conversation.

'Hi, Vigdís. It's Emil.'

'Did you find the postcard?' Vigdís said.

'Sylvía took it with her to Ingvar's house,' Emil replied. 'We have a question about Ingvar's alibi for when Aníta was shot. Did it check out?'

'Not very well,' said Vigdís. 'I went up to the farm earlier this morning. It's over towards Grundarfjördur, only about seven or eight kilometres from Bjarnarhöfn. The farmer is ancient, well over eighty. His wife was the one Ingvar was visiting. She is bedridden with lung cancer; I don't think she has long to live. The husband was definite that Dr Ingvar had visited them in the last couple of days, but at first he thought it was on Monday. Then he changed his mind to Tuesday, and said it was some time in the morning. His wife had no idea. He's unreliable; a defence lawyer could easily drive a truck through his statement. And rightly so, the old bastard.'

'You don't like him?'

'He called me a monkey. A police monkey. He thought it was funny. I know some of these people have never seen a black person before, but that's no reason not to treat me like a human being.'

'Nice,' said Emil.

'It's Ingvar, isn't it?' said Vigdís.

Emil glanced at Magnus, who nodded. 'It's looking that way,' he said. 'I think we'll go along to Ingvar's house now.'

Ingvar lived in a neat blue house with a white metal roof in the middle of Stykkishólmur, on the old main street that sloped down to the harbour. Gabrielle answered the door. The doctor wasn't at home, but Sylvía was. She was in the living room, knitting. She looked out of place among the doctor's stylish furniture; a solid countrywoman perched on the edge of an expensive leather armchair. Outside was a view over brightly painted rain-swept roofs to the fishing boats bobbing in the harbour.

'Hello, Magnús,' Sylvía said. To Magnús's surprise, she gave her grandson a small smile.

The two detectives sat next to each other on a white leather sofa. Magnus glanced at Emil, who nodded.

'I have some bad news, I'm afraid, Amma.' Magnus could feel Gabrielle tensing. Sylvía frowned. 'Villi is dead. He was shot at Swine Lake this morning.'

The news seemed to physically strike Sylvía. She reeled backwards, dropping her knitting needles. She brought her fist to her mouth and bit it. Villi was her eldest son. Magnus wanted to put his arm around his grandmother, but couldn't quite bring himself to. Even in her grief, Sylvía's demeanour said 'hands off'.

'My God,' said Gabrielle. 'You police must really catch the man who is doing all this. Who is next? Ingvar? Sylvía? Me? I want this house protected.'

'That's not a bad idea,' said Emil. 'Although we are using every man available to try to solve this case.'

'Well, you are not doing a very good job of it,' said Gabrielle.

'Amma?' Magnus said softly. 'Amma? I have a question for you.'

Sylvía blinked at her grandson. Her mouth was open, her face white. But she knew him and she knew what he was saying.

'Aníta said you had a postcard from Uncle Villi to Afi in the box under your bed. Can we see it? I think it might be important.'

'Snooping in my things, was she?' Sylvía said.

'Yes. We think it might be why she was shot,' Emil said.

'It might be,' said Sylvía. She hesitated, pursing her lips, gathering scrambled thoughts. Her eyes focused, brightening. 'You know, Magnús, you were the best of the bunch after all. Hallgrímur said so, when you were a boy. I think he actually liked the way you stood up to him, at least at first. But when you went off with Ragnar he took it as a betrayal. Which makes no sense. You were only twelve.'

'And you, Amma? What did you think of me going?'

The old woman sighed. 'I didn't think anything of it. That's what I did then. I didn't think.'

The room was silent. Gabrielle was listening intently to her newly awakened mother-in-law.

'I've changed now. Too late, but I've changed.' She looked directly at Magnus. 'It was our little church at Bjarnarhöfn that did it. Strange, it had been standing there for over sixty years of our marriage, and I had ignored it, but one day I was cleaning it and I was tired and I just sat there. It was peaceful. I looked at the cross and the old Dutch painting, and I began to think. I felt brave enough to think.'

'Think about what, Amma?' Magnus asked.

The old lady smiled. 'About everything. About our family. About you, Óli, my sons. Margrét. And about my husband. I thought a lot about my husband.' She chuckled. 'I even started going to the church at Stykkishólmur and praying. Can you imagine me, Magnús, praying?'

She got to her feet. 'So the answer is yes, I can show you the postcard.'

She left the living room and they heard her making her way up the stairs.

'This is extraordinary,' Gabrielle said. 'This is the best I have seen her since Hallgrímur died. It's as if the news of Villi's death has unscrambled her brain. Is that possible?'

'I don't know,' said Emil. 'My father had Alzheimer's, and although he had good and bad days, he never made this much of a recovery.'

Sylvía returned within a couple of minutes, clutching an envelope. She passed it to Magnus. The envelope sported a United States stamp and was addressed to Hallgrímur Gunnarsson in block capitals. Although the postmark was smudged, Magnus could make out the year: 1996. Inside was a postcard. The picture was of Harvard Yard in Cambridge. Magnus flipped it over and read:

> Óli very scared but will keep quiet. No one knows
> Ingvar was here. Magnús has no idea but is talking
> about going to Iceland to see you. I still think it was
> wrong – wrong and unnecessary. I will keep Óli in line.
> He seems to listen to me.
>
> Villi.

Magnus glanced at his grandmother. 'You know what Villi means when he says, "I still think it was wrong", don't you?'

Sylvía didn't respond. She was waiting for Magnus to say it. So he did.

'He's talking about my father's murder.'

She nodded. 'I think he is.'

'When did you find this?'

'Only a couple of weeks ago. I went through Hallgrímur's old papers. There was this and some other letters from Villi to him over the years. The card is in Villi's writing, but the address is disguised in block capitals, so I wouldn't recognize it when it came in the post, presumably.' She sighed. 'I wasn't really surprised. I had seen all this going on in front of my eyes for years. This was just proof of what I had denied to myself.'

Gabrielle stood up and looked over Magnus's shoulder to read the card. 'But it mentions Ingvar. It says he was in Boston with Villi!'

'When my father was murdered,' Magnus said.

'That can't be right,' said Gabrielle.

'Can you remember where he was that summer?' Magnus asked her.

'No, not specifically. He used to go to the occasional conference in those days. And a couple of those were in the United States. Florida. New Jersey. I don't remember Boston.'

'Do you keep your old passports?' Magnus asked. 'In those days they stamped entry and exit dates, I think.'

Gabrielle nodded. 'Yes. They are all in a drawer in our bedroom.'

'Can you dig out Ingvar's from that time?' Magnus asked.

Gabrielle hesitated. 'I'm not sure I should.'

'Look, we can get a warrant for it if we need to,' said Emil. 'But if your husband was never in the US when Ragnar was murdered, the old passport will prove it.'

'All right.' Gabrielle left the room.

'So what happened?' asked Emil.

'Ingvar travelled to the United States to murder my father,' Magnus said. 'No doubt with Hallgrímur's encouragement. It looks as if Villi was a reluctant accessory.' He hesitated. 'And it also looks as if my brother knew about it. It was Villi's job to make sure he kept quiet.'

Magnus fought to control the anger that he could feel erupting within him. All those years when Magnus had been trying so desperately hard to figure out what had happened to his father, Ollie knew. It was unbelievable. But he could think about that later. Right now he had to keep his thoughts together, his mind clear.

'Did you know all this, Amma?'

'I slowly came to realize it,' she said. 'It was only when I found that postcard that I was absolutely sure.'

'So why didn't you tell the police?' Emil asked.

Sylvía looked at him steadily, but didn't reply.

'The Alzheimer's was all a sham, wasn't it?' Emil said. 'It was just a means of covering up what you knew. And was that why you started the fire?'

Sylvía put her hands together on her lap and stared ahead. You could almost feel the stubbornness spreading through the room.

Gabrielle returned, clutching a bright blue Icelandic passport with the corner clipped.

'I haven't looked,' she said, handing the passport to Magnus.

Magnus flipped through the pages. 'Here we are. "U.S. Immigration. 210 Newark. July fourteenth 1996."'

Gabrielle's eyes opened wide. 'Newark is in New Jersey, isn't it? That must have been the conference there I was telling you about. It's not Boston.'

'You can easily get to Boston from Newark on the Amtrak,' Magnus said. 'Or hire a car. Or fly.'

'Yes, but that's not proof that Ingvar actually did it,' Gabrielle said.

'You were living here in 1985, weren't you?' Magnus said. 'I remember seeing you at Bjarnarhöfn when I was a kid.'

Gabrielle frowned and nodded. 'Yes, we moved here in 1980. But that's hardly suspicious, is it?'

'And is your husband left- or right-handed?'

'Right,' said Gabrielle. 'Just like everybody else. So what?'

'So you are saying Ingvar killed Benedikt Jóhannesson?' Emil asked Magnus.

'And my father. With Hallgrímur's encouragement. And he shot at Aníta. And he killed Villi this morning.'

'What about Hallgrímur?' Emil asked.

'Probably him too,' Magnus said.

'No!' Gabrielle protested. 'You are making too many assumptions here!'

'Shush, Gabrielle,' Sylvía said. 'They are right, my dear. I'm afraid you are married to an evil man. Just like me. You must accept it. Don't deny it like I did for so long.'

'Ridiculous!' exclaimed Gabrielle.

'Where is your husband now?' Emil asked her.

'At the clinic, I think.'

Emil pulled out his phone and called the station.

CHAPTER THIRTY

TEN MINUTES LATER Emil and Magnus pulled up outside the hospital car park. Detective Björn had come from the police station to sit with Gabrielle and Sylvía to make sure that neither of them warned Ingvar. Emil had taken Gabrielle's mobile phone. The four members of the Viking Squad were in their van outside the hospital.

Emil turned to Magnus. 'I don't know what I'm doing dragging you around everywhere with me, but it's been useful so far.'

'I can't go in with you, can I?' Magnus said.

'No. I'd like to leave you here. Will you give me your word you won't run?'

'Of course.'

'Good. But I'd better cuff you. I hope you understand.'

Magnus did understand. Emil grabbed some handcuffs from the boot of the car and secured them on Magnus's wrists. Then he took one of the Viking Squad with him into the hospital, leaving the others in the van outside.

They were out in five minutes. The squad member ran to the van, and in a few seconds it was speeding up the hill. Emil waddled out at a slower pace. He opened the car door on Magnus's side.

'Not there?' Magnus asked.

'He told his receptionist he was going to see that farmer's wife with lung cancer again.'

'That makes sense,' said Magnus. 'Especially if he was actually at Swine Lake. He could well have gone straight on to the farm to establish his alibi. Are we going?'

'No,' said Emil. 'If he's there, they'll bring him in. But he might well not be. And I want to think.'

'Never a bad thing to do.'

Emil unlocked Magnus's cuffs. 'Walk with me.'

Magnus climbed out of the car and stretched. It had stopped raining and the grey clouds had been tugged like a torn curtain eastwards, leaving a clean blue sky. A breeze blew in from the sea. They walked slowly down to the harbour.

'We still don't know who killed Hallgrímur,' Emil said.

'Ingvar's alibi is solid?'

'I think so. My detective Adam checked it out. The harbour-master here and two others saw Ingvar working on his boat all Sunday morning.'

'Which leaves?'

'You, Magnús.' Emil frowned at him. 'It still leaves you. You were at Bjarnarhöfn when Hallgrímur was killed. No one else was, except maybe Tóta. It's conceivable that Aníta could have doubled back from riding, but I don't see why she would want to kill the old man. But you had a motive. And everything we learn makes that motive stronger.'

'I didn't kill him, Emil.'

'Help me here, Magnús. You've got to do better than that.'

'Are we going to see the harbourmaster now?'

'I am,' said Emil.

The harbourmaster's office was on the quay by the harbour itself. Emil left Magnus and went in. Magnus waited outside and watched him through a large window, chatting with a bearded man in his fifties.

Magnus understood what Emil meant. In his position, he would conclude that Magnus was the only suspect as well.

He gazed around the harbour at the fish factories, the harbour wall, the tall island of basalt that acted as protection from the sea, the big ferry waiting to go out to the island of Flatey and the West Fjords beyond, the host of little boats and, back up the hill, the brightly coloured houses of the town.

You couldn't actually see the space-age church of

Stykkishólmur from the harbour, but it was up there, behind the convent and the hospital from where they had just come.

The spark of half a thought ignited in his brain.

Emil emerged from the harbourmaster's office. 'You didn't run,' he said.

Magnus grinned. 'I wondered why you didn't cuff me.'

'There is nowhere to go,' Emil said. 'But if you had run, I would have known you were guilty.'

'Not much I can say to that,' said Magnus. 'Any holes in the harbourmaster's statement?'

'No. Ingvar was definitely at his boat between ten-thirty and eleven-forty-five on Sunday, and possibly longer. That's his boat there.' Emil pointed to a jaunty little craft about fifty yards from the harbourmaster's office. 'Which still leaves you.'

Magnus took a deep breath. His half thought was growing. 'What about my grandmother?'

'Sylvía? What about her? You don't think *she* killed her husband.'

'You said she wasn't at the farm. Where was she? At church?'

'Yes,' said Emil. 'At church here in Stykkishólmur.'

'Are you sure?'

Emil frowned. He pulled out a notebook. 'Yes. She did go to the service. It starts at ten-thirty. Apparently she was a little late.'

'How late?'

'I don't know,' said Emil. 'But that little old lady can't have been strong enough, surely?'

'I remember her being a very strong middle-aged lady,' Magnus said. 'And Hallgrímur was a very old man.'

'With leukaemia,' said Emil. 'Blood tests at the autopsy showed he had undiagnosed leukaemia. So he would have been physically weak.'

'Shall we go up to the church?' Magnus suggested.

The vicarage wasn't far from the large white church with its swooping bell tower, and the pastor was in. She was a plump, dark-haired woman of about thirty-five who knew who Sylvía was, and had noticed her arriving late at the service.

'How late?' Emil asked.

The woman concentrated. 'I remember the hymn we were singing. That would have been about forty-five minutes in.'

'So that would have been when? Eleven-fifteen?'

'Yes, about that,' said the pastor.

'That's not "a little late",' said Emil. 'That's very late.'

The pastor nodded. 'I do remember something else.'

'What was that?'

'Sylvía was flustered. She's usually so calm, almost cold. But she seemed in a bit of a rush. And she spilled some hymn books as she came in. That's why I remember it.'

'Did you speak to her afterwards?'

'No. She did stay in her seat praying for quite a long time after the service. Everyone else had gone and I went to talk to her. When people pray, there's often a reason. But she didn't really answer me, and left. That's fine. I'm here if my congregation wants me, but I don't want to get between them and God.'

'Thank you,' said Emil.

They left the vicarage. Emil paused by his car and pulled out his notebook. 'OK, so let's look at the timings. You called in finding the body at eleven-twenty-nine.' Emil hesitated. 'I believe you told us that you made the call right away. I'm not asking you to change your statement right now. But for these purposes, what time can we assume is the latest that Hallgrímur was alive?'

'I got to Bjarnarhöfn twenty minutes before that. So that would have been about eleven-ten,' Magnus said. 'And I didn't see Sylvía's car, so if she left the farm, it would have been before then.'

'And we know that Hallgrímur was alive at ten-twenty-five, because that's when the phone records say that Ollie called him.'

'So Sylvía *could* have killed him just after that and left by eleven o'clock. It would take her about twenty-five minutes to half an hour, I would think, to drive from the farm to the church here.'

'So if she left a little before eleven, she could have got here at about eleven-fifteen?'

'She could.'

The two detectives stood in silence.

'My grandmother can be quite stubborn,' said Magnus. 'Shall I talk to her? I think she might tell me what happened.'

The hostility in Ingvar's house was palpable. Björn answered the door. Sylvía was still in her place on the edge of the armchair knitting. And Gabrielle was pacing up and down, glaring.

'Have you arrested him?' she asked.

'Not yet,' said Emil. 'He wasn't at the clinic. But we will pick him up shortly.'

'You are making a dreadful mistake, you know,' said Gabrielle. 'And I want some proper protection. This man you left me with doesn't even have a gun. I don't know how you can call yourselves policemen when you don't carry guns. If this were France, at least he would be armed.'

Magnus had sympathy with Gabrielle's point of view, but kept quiet.

'We do have firearms in the area,' Emil said. 'In the meantime, would you mind leaving us alone with Sylvía for a few minutes, please, Gabrielle? Björn will keep you company.'

'Keep me company? Watch over me, more like,' Gabrielle muttered. She turned to the young detective. 'Come on. Let's go outside. Have you got a cigarette?' Björn reached inside his jacket pocket. 'And don't listen to her lies about my husband!'

Emil and Magnus took their seats.

'Poor woman,' said Sylvía. 'She can't believe what she knows is true.'

'Amma?' Magnus said. 'I have a question for you.'

Sylvía put down her knitting for a moment. Magnus noticed she was working on the chest of a traditional *lopi* sweater. He wondered who it was for. Tóta, perhaps?

'What is it, dear?'

She used the word *elskan*, a word used by grandmothers all over Iceland through the centuries to speak to their grandchildren. Except Magnus could not remember his grandmother ever using it for him.

All Magnus's professional instincts were screaming at him not to do what he was about to do. In America, it would be fatal to a case not to warn a suspect of their rights. A confession wrought from a confused old lady without a lawyer or a warning would never stand up in court. In Iceland the rules were different and, of course, Magnus needed to clear his own name. But still the policeman in him felt that he was taking advantage of a vulnerable suspect.

But he was also a son and a grandson. And he needed to find out the truth about his family.

'Amma. Why were you late for church on Sunday?'

Sylvía was silent for a moment. 'Your grandfather was correct, Magnús, dear. You were the brightest one in the family. You and perhaps your mother. Ingvar always thought he was so clever, but I was never convinced.'

'Amma?'

Sylvía looked out of the window into the small back yard, where puffs of cigarette smoke were hovering over Gabrielle and the detective. She sighed.

'I was... detained at the farmhouse.'

'What happened, Amma?'

Sylvía glanced at Magnus and at Emil, who had slid out a notebook.

'The phone rang. I was in the bedroom; Hallgrímur was in the living room doing his Sudoku. I came through to answer it, but Hallgrímur had already picked it up. I could tell it was Óli. Hallgrímur glared at me. I knew he didn't want me to hear, so I went back into the bedroom and picked up the phone in there.'

Sylvía licked her lips, remembering. 'Óli can scarcely speak Icelandic and neither Hallgrímur nor I speak much English, so the conversation was difficult. I think I heard someone prompting Óli in the background, an Icelander, but Hallgrímur didn't seem to notice. Anyway, Óli said that he wanted to meet Hallgrímur immediately, or he would speak to the police about Ragnar's murder and the murder of Benedikt from Hraun. He said he knew that Hallgrímur and Villi were involved in both murders. He wanted Hallgrímur to meet him along the cliffs at Hellnar.

'It took a few minutes for Hallgrímur to understand what Óli was saying, but in the end he agreed to meet Óli at Hellnar. They hung up. I waited a couple of minutes and then went through to the living room.'

Magnus and Emil listened closely, Emil scribbling in his notebook.

'I think I must have made some noise at the end of the conversation, because Hallgrímur was staring at me when I came in. "Did you hear that?" he asked me.

'I should have just said "no", or said I had heard something but didn't understand it. That had been my reaction our whole married life. But something snapped.'

Sylvía's speech was quickening and colour was appearing in her cheeks.

'I mean, I had heard my husband virtually admit that he had been involved in murdering two people. I suspected it already – you've seen the postcard. I just couldn't pretend I hadn't heard what I had just heard. I was suddenly angry, *so* angry. I had let him get away with his wickedness for years. So I started yelling. I called him a murderer. I told him he was an evil, evil man and he would go to hell. I told him he had made our family evil – Villi, Ingvar, Óli. I told him God would judge him and he couldn't hide from that.'

Sylvía swallowed. 'He was shocked at first, that I would stand up to him. I had never shouted at him like that. Of course I had been angry with him before, countless times, but always I used to say nothing. Then he said, "Don't talk to me like that, you old cow." And I told him I would go to the police and tell them everything he had done. "Don't you dare!" he shouted. "If you go to the police, I will kill you too!"

'I couldn't stand being in the cottage with him a moment longer, so I stormed outside, slamming the door. I found myself going down towards the church. I just wanted to sit in there, to pray, to ask God what I should do.

'I never turned to see whether he was following me, but he must have been because I had been in the church for less than a minute when he burst in, waving the broom. He started hitting me with it. A couple of years ago, that would have really hurt, but he was a very old man, nowhere near as strong as he used to be, whereas I...' She gave a small smile. 'I seem to be stronger than him now.'

'What happened?' said Magnus.

'He hit me with the broom. I pushed him over, so he fell on the floor. And then I was overcome with rage. I jumped on him, grabbed his hair and banged his head on the floor. Several times. He was screaming, there was a crack, and then he went quiet.'

She took a deep breath. 'He was dead. I didn't know what to do. I fled. I got in my car and drove away. To church. I thought if I got to the church in Stykkishólmur, maybe I could say that I had been there for the whole service. But when I crept in, I knocked over some hymn books and everyone saw me. And when I was sitting there in the pew, thinking, I realized that I must have left my fingerprints all over everything. But somehow you didn't seem to notice,' Sylvía said to Emil.

'Because your grandson did such a good job of messing up the crime scene afterwards,' said Emil.

'Why did you do that, dear?'

Magnus was about to explain about how he was covering for Ollie, but caught himself at the last minute. That was an offence he did not want to admit to. 'I was looking for evidence,' he lied lamely.

Emil snorted.

'So, I killed your grandfather, Magnús. I know it was a sin, and I have repented and asked for God's forgiveness. He was an evil man. It was God's will that he should die a nasty death, and I suppose it was God's will that I should bring that about.'

She smiled at Magnus. 'I'm glad you escaped him. He ruined his family, our children. They always did what he wanted. He drove poor Margrét to drink, and stopped her going to America with Ragnar. Villi and Ingvar wanted to get away from him, but they couldn't. Hallgrímur seemed to have some hold over Villi, I don't know what. And although Ingvar tried to keep his distance, he couldn't manage it. Hallgrímur could always bend him to do his will. It might have been Ingvar who killed Benedikt and Ragnar, but you can be absolutely sure that Hallgrímur put the idea in his head, some story about family loyalty, revenge for past deaths, a feud. You heard that schoolteacher, Benedikt's son, talking about how his own grandfather had been killed by Hallgrímur's father, and then how Benedikt had pushed Hallgrímur's father off a cliff on his horse. I think all that was true. And that would be enough for Hallgrímur to fire up his sons to take revenge.'

Sylvía shook her head. 'And I watched it. I watched it all and did nothing.'

'Was Ingvar angry about the loan?' Emil asked.

'Oh, Hallgrímur told me all about the loan,' Sylvía said. 'He thought that was very funny. That Ingvar believed he was going to inherit all that money and he was actually going to get nothing.'

'Yet Ingvar still did what Hallgrímur told him?' Emil asked.

'Oh yes,' Sylvía said. 'That's how he controlled Ingvar, don't you see? That's how he controlled all his children. Playing with them. Dangling something in front of them and snatching it away. Ingvar may be sixty, but he would still do anything for his father's approval. The tougher Hallgrímur was on him, the more desperate Ingvar was for praise. Kolbeinn was like that too. And Margrét. And Hallgrímur knew it too. He loved it.'

'What about Kolbeinn?' Magnus asked.

'Kolbeinn is a good man,' Sylvía said. 'And not too bright. He just did what his father told him, but I don't think he knew what his father and brothers were up to. Neither did Aníta. You know, her grandmother sent me a message once: to open my eyes and see what was in front of me. I listened to that message. Aníta's grandmother was a wise woman.'

'Was? Is she dead now?' Emil asked.

'Oh, she's been dead at least forty years,' Sylvía said. Emil frowned, and wrote down her words anyway. 'Ingvar shouldn't have shot Aníta. I am surprised Villi allowed that. Villi and Aníta...'

'Yes?' said Magnus.

Sylvía hesitated. 'Villi and Aníta liked each other. Villi will have been angry at Ingvar for shooting her, I am sure.'

'Why did you start the fire in the cottage?' Emil asked.

'I wanted to destroy the evidence. I knew that there would be letters from Villi to Hallgrímur, perhaps from Ingvar too. And you police have all these scientific methods. But I also wanted to destroy Hallgrímur. I wanted to get rid of his things, of his possessions, of him. He was an evil man. He's in hell now, I know he is.'

'And your memory?' asked Emil. 'You are not suffering from Alzheimer's?'

'Yes, I think I am beginning to. And when I came back to Bjarnarhöfn from the church at Stykkishólmur, I was confused. I couldn't believe what I had done, and I didn't understand why no one was arresting me. Then I saw everyone was treating me like a muddled old lady, not like a murderer, so I played up the confusion.'

'You don't sound confused now,' said Emil.

'I'm not,' said Sylvía.

Emil showed her his notes. 'In that case, if I take you to the station and type them up into a statement, will you sign it?'

Sylvía nodded.

'Thank you. Now will you follow me, please?'

Sylvía hesitated. 'I have one question before we go.'

'Yes?' said Emil.

'Are you allowed chickens in jail?'

CHAPTER THIRTY-ONE

THEY HAD JUST squeezed into Emil's car, leaving Detective Björn with Gabrielle, when Emil's phone rang.

'Yes... Yes... Let me think. I'll call you back.' Emil put down his phone and turned to Magnus. 'Ingvar wasn't with the old farmer. He had been there this morning, but the farmer can't say when.' Emil frowned. 'I wonder where he's gone.'

'He doesn't know that we know Villi's death wasn't suicide?' Magnus asked.

'He shouldn't do,' said Emil.

'Which means he is probably still hoping he's in the clear.'

'So he could be coming back to the clinic?' Emil said.

'Why don't you give him a call?' said Magnus. 'Tell him you want a second opinion about Villi. Tell him to meet you at Swine Lake. He'll be bound to come. Then there will be plenty of people around to arrest him.'

Emil grinned. 'Not a bad idea.' He turned to Sylvía. 'I'm sorry, but I am going to have to take you back into the house with the other detective for a few minutes.'

'I hope you catch him,' said Sylvía.

Emil hurried Sylvía back into the house.

'You drive,' he said to Magnus as he returned to the car. 'I've got some calls to make.'

Magnus switched seats and drove Emil's car out of town towards the Berserkjahraun and Swine Lake.

Emil's first call was to Ingvar. The doctor answered after the second ring. The conversation was brief and matter-of-fact.

'He said he'd do it,' Emil said to Magnus with a grin.

'Where is he?'

'I don't know. But he said he'd be at Swine Lake in fifteen minutes.'

'Excellent.'

Next was Baldur. Magnus could only hear Emil's side of the conversation. It was clear there was some initial prevarication from the inspector, but then he seemed to understand Emil's plan and go along with it.

Then Emil called Rúnar to tell him the plan and arrange for one of the few policemen still available to come to Ingvar's house and escort Sylvía back to the station.

They passed the small hill of Helgafell and accelerated over the long stretch of fast road towards the Berserkjahraun. Bjarnarhöfn Fell was clearly visible ahead. A lone car passed them in the other direction. Magnus thought he recognized the driver, if not the vehicle, and twisted around to look.

'Who was that?' asked Emil.

'No one,' said Magnus, turning his attention back to the road ahead. But if he hadn't known she was in America, Magnus would have sworn he had just seen Ingileif.

Tóta lay on her bed staring at the ceiling, Dikta blaring in her ears from her iPod. She wished Uncle Villi would come back. She even wished Amma was here so they could watch *Iceland Idol* together. And most of all she hoped that her dad would call from the hospital with news about her mum.

She felt alone. Alone and scared. Tears welled up in her eyes.

She had been so angry with her mother after Afi had been murdered, angry with the lot of them. It seemed to her that she was the only one who really cared that he had died; even Amma didn't seem too bothered, unless perhaps the shock of it had tipped her over into old-biddy confusion. It had been good for Tóta to have her grandmother to look after.

But then her mum had been shot too. The idea that her mum

might die scared the hell out of Tóta. And made her feel guilty. She and her mum had been so close when they were younger; all those horse rides they took together. Tóta used to think that her mum was beautiful; now she was embarrassed by her mother's long hair at her age. It made her look like a hippy. Mum had shown interest in the boys that Tóta had started to go out with, but Tóta had kept her away from them. They were her business, not her mother's.

But now that she was in hospital, Tóta wanted her mummy back. Whole and in one piece.

Then her cousin Magnus and the fat detective had arrived, asking questions about Amma. Something was up, and Tóta didn't know what. But couldn't they just have stopped and rung the National Hospital like the constable with the moustache had promised to do? And hadn't.

She felt as much as heard the door bang downstairs, the music coming through her earphones was so loud. She ripped them off and ran to her window. She was expecting Uncle Villi, but it was Ingvar's BMW downstairs. He ought to know how to get in touch with a hospital!

She made her way along the landing and down the stairs. She heard banging, the sound of a cupboard door opening and closing. The noise came from just outside the kitchen.

The gun cupboard.

She stopped on the stairs. Craned her neck down so that she could see along the hallway.

Uncle Ingvar was standing by the open gun cupboard with his back to her. He was breaking open Dad's shotgun and loading it with a couple of cartridges.

Someone had taken the rifle from that very cupboard before and used it to shoot her mother. Could it have been Uncle Ingvar?'

Maybe. Tóta didn't know. But she did know that Ingvar wasn't taking the shotgun in such a hurry because he had a sudden desire to shoot ptarmigan.

She crept back upstairs to her room. Picked up her phone and dialled 112.

She told the woman who answered what she had seen. The police would be there in a few minutes.

She put down her phone. There was a creak just outside her bedroom. There, in the doorway, was her uncle, carrying the shotgun. And pointing it straight at her.

Magnus was passing the turn-off to the Kerlingin Pass and the road to Reykjavík when Emil's radio sprang to life. It was Rúnar's voice.

'Emergency call received from Bjarnarhöfn. The girl Tóta has reported seeing Ingvar taking a shotgun out of the gun cupboard there. Is anyone nearby?'

Emil snatched the mic. 'Emil here. We are on the D54 going through the Berserkjahraun. Heading over there now.' He put the mic down. 'Bjarnarhöfn! Now!'

As the radio chattered with other officers acknowledging the call, Magnus sped past the track to Swine Lake and turned on to the dirt road through the lava field for Bjarnarhöfn. Most of the police officers at Swine Lake, including the Viking Squad, were on their way.

'Damn it!' said Emil. 'We should never have left the shotgun there after that rifle was taken.'

Dead right, thought Magnus. 'Let's hope that Ingvar doesn't realize Tóta is at home.'

Emil's vehicle bucked as Magnus drove it over the loose stones. Magnus lost traction as he rounded a bend too fast but got control back just in time to avoid hurtling into the rocky lava.

'There he is!' Magnus said.

Ahead, a BMW four-wheel-drive was speeding towards them. Magnus flashed his lights but kept his foot on the accelerator.

'What are you doing?' said Emil.

'Playing chicken,' said Magnus.

'Are you sure that's a good idea?'

The two vehicles were hurtling towards each other on the

narrow track at a closing velocity of well over a hundred kilometres an hour. The other car showed no signs of slowing.

Magnus was good at games of chicken. The secret to victory was conspicuous, unwavering determination. He maintained his speed.

They were five seconds away. Four. Three.

Emil shifted in the seat next to Magnus.

Two.

Ingvar wasn't wavering either. It suddenly occurred to Magnus why. For Ingvar, a head-on collision at high speed and instant death wasn't such a bad option. It may, in fact, be the best option.

Magnus took his foot off the accelerator and swerved to the right.

As did Ingvar.

The two vehicles dealt each other glancing blows. Emil's spun around and careered off the track into the lava field, bucking twice before ending nose-down in a small depression.

The seatbelt bit into Magnus's shoulders as he was flung forward and then whiplashed back into his seat.

He felt blood dribbling down his forehead and into his eye. Next to him, Emil was groaning. Magnus's brain was fuzzy.

It took him a moment to figure out where he was, which way was up. Then he shoved open the car door and clambered out.

On the other side of the track, about twenty yards into the lava field, was Ingvar's car, leaning drunkenly on one side.

Two figures were running through the sea of stone: a man behind and a girl in front. And the man was pointing a shotgun at the girl.

Ingvar. And Tóta.

Magnus ran after them.

The stone and moss were slick with rain. Magnus slipped, twisted his ankle and fell, but rolled on to his feet again in one motion. His ankle hurt as he chased after Ingvar and Tóta. They had joined a narrow path through the cold lava, the Berserkers'

Path, and were making faster progress. They stumbled over the crest of a hillock, between writhing statues of gnarled stone, and disappeared from view.

A few seconds later Magnus reached the path and followed them. As he crested the rise, he saw Ingvar and Tóta standing in the middle of a depression of moss and congealed stone about thirty yards across and twenty feet deep. Standing next to the cairn of the two dead berserkers.

Ingvar was pointing his shotgun at Tóta, who was weeping silently.

Magnus slid down the slope of the hollow along the Berserkers' Path.

'Stop right there!' Ingvar shouted.

Magnus stopped. And then took a pace forward.

'I said stop! Or I'll blow her head off!'

Tóta let out a loud sob.

'OK, OK,' said Magnus, raising his hands. He stopped. 'Mind if I sit down?'

'All right,' said Ingvar. He was breathing heavily, his eyes shining, the burn mark on his face blazing purple.

Magnus sat on a stone just to the side of the path and kept his eyes on Ingvar. He was about ten yards away.

'This is it, Uncle Ingvar. The police are on their way. There will be about twenty of them here in a few minutes, including the Viking Squad with guns. Your car is a write-off. There's no way out of here.'

'I've got Tóta,' said Ingvar. 'I can negotiate.'

'No, you can't,' said Magnus. 'You are in a godforsaken corner of a godforsaken island cut off from the rest of the world by a volcano. I'd say you are stuck.'

'What about you, Magnús?' said Ingvar. 'Aren't you stuck? You murdered Dad. Now you will have to pay for it.'

Tóta was watching Magnus with her eyes wide.

'I didn't kill him,' said Magnus. 'Your mother did. Sylvía.'

'That's not true!' protested Tóta.

'Yes, it is,' said Magnus. 'I'm sorry, Tóta, but Amma killed

310

Afi. She had her reasons, you could almost say good reasons, but she is a murderer.'

'I don't believe you!' said Tóta.

'Neither do I,' said Ingvar.

'It's true.' The voice came from above and behind Magnus. All three of the people standing around the cairn turned to see Emil panting on the rim of the hollow, his face red, wheezing audibly. 'Sylvía did kill Hallgrímur.' He bent down, fighting to regain his breath.

'Let Tóta go and give yourself up,' said Magnus. 'She hasn't done anything wrong.'

'Neither have I,' said Ingvar. 'It was Villi who killed Benedikt Jóhannesson and your father. Then he killed himself.'

'It wasn't suicide, Ingvar. Forensics can prove it. We found the spot where you drove down to the lake and the place where you shot Villi. When we examine those clothes you are wearing now, we'll find traces of Villi on you.'

'Did you shoot my mum, Uncle Ingvar?' Tóta asked, through sobs.

'Of course he did,' said Magnus. His eyes hardened. 'And he stabbed my father. Didn't you? They found a hair at the house in Duxbury where you killed him. It was yours, wasn't it? Back when you had some hair.' In those days Ingvar was not as bald as he was now, and his hair had been a sandy blond.

'I had to,' said Ingvar. 'To protect the family.'

'You mean Afi told you to.'

'I was a good son,' said Ingvar. His voice caught as he said it. 'In the end.'

The anger welled up inside Magnus. A good son? Here, finally, was the moment for which Magnus had been waiting for his entire adult life. He was face to face with the man who had murdered his father, the man who had ruined his life, ruined Ollie's life, changed everything for both of them. And how did his father's killer justify what he had done? He was a good son!

Magnus hated Ingvar with every sinew of his body, more than he had ever hated anyone before.

But he had to remain calm, for Tóta's sake. Focus on her. Change the subject to something less charged.

'How did you know we were on to you, Ingvar?'

'I called in to the clinic. My receptionist said that the police had been looking for me, and some of them were armed. I knew that wasn't just a casual call for more questions.'

'You should have given yourself up then,' said Magnus. 'There's nothing you can do now. Killing Tóta won't achieve anything.'

In the distance Magnus could hear sirens. Ingvar really didn't have any options. But the key was to make sure that nobody died.

Magnus glanced at the cairn next to Ingvar and Tóta, a square solid block of stone, covered with a tablecloth of intricate patterns of moss in many shades of green, splashed with brown and orange. Under there lay the bodies of the two berserkers that had been killed over a thousand years before. The two Swedes from long ago who had loomed so large in Magnus's childhood at Bjarnarhöfn, and presumably in Ingvar's. It was as if those bloodthirsty warriors had dragged Ingvar to this spot.

The doctor took a deep breath. 'You are right.' He paused. Seemed to come to a decision. 'I've got two barrels here. One for me. And one for you. You first, I think.'

He pushed Tóta away. She stumbled on a tangle of twisted rock and fell.

Too late, Magnus realized he had made an error. If it had been plausible that Villi should take his own life, how much more plausible would it be that Ingvar, cornered as he was, would take his? And take Magnus with him.

Magnus was too far away to jump Ingvar, too close to get away from him.

'Ingvar—'

Behind him, Magnus heard a gasp and the sound of a heavy weight rolling down a slope. He turned to see Emil tumbling to the bottom of the hollow.

Magnus rushed over to him.

'Stop, Magnús!'

Magnus ignored Ingvar and knelt over the detective, who had come to rest on his side. With a heave, he rolled him over on to his back, all the time expecting to hear the report of the shotgun and feel a hail of lead striking him.

'He's not breathing!' Magnus said. He pulled back Emil's jacket, placed his hands on Emil's chest and started pumping. Emil was so large and so fat he wasn't sure he had the right place. Was it the fourth or fifth rib down?

Nothing.

He pressed harder and then tried mouth-to-mouth.

Still nothing.

He turned to Ingvar. 'You're a doctor, Ingvar. Help me here and *then* blow your own head off. Help me save him!'

Ingvar hesitated. He began to raise the shotgun towards Magnus. Then hesitation left him: he laid the gun down on the cairn, and ran over to where Magnus was scrabbling at Emil's chest.

He pushed Magnus out of the way. Pressed into the rolls of fat around Emil's neck, searching for an artery. Pulled back his shirt, felt with his fingers through the fat for the right spot, placed both hands on his chest and pumped. Again. And again. Then he too tried mouth-to-mouth, and then pumped again.

Magnus sat back and watched.

'Call the police, Magnús! Tell them to bring a defibrillator down here. They should have one with them. If this works, he'll still need shocking.'

Magnus reached into Emil's jacket pocket and found his phone. He made the call.

After about thirty seconds, Ingvar glanced up at him. 'It's working! I'm feeling something!' More mouth-to-mouth. Emil's eyes flickered. Ingvar kept on pumping.

A minute later Ingvar stopped. He was sweating and breathing hard. He straightened himself and leaned back, still on his knees. 'You take over for a minute,' he said to Magnus.

Magnus was just beginning to move back towards Emil when

a loud bang went off in his ears, and the back of Dr Ingvar's head erupted all over his last patient.

Magnus turned in shock. The fifteen-year-old schoolgirl was standing astride the cairn, holding the shotgun, her face expressionless.

'Tóta?' Magnus said. 'Why? Why did you do that?'

'He killed my uncle. He killed your father. He shot at my mother. He probably killed Afi. He deserved to die.'

Magnus stared at Hallgrímur Gunnarsson's granddaughter for a moment. Then he pushed Ingvar's bloody body aside and resumed pumping Emil's chest.

CHAPTER THIRTY-TWO

IT TOOK A while to sort out the mess. Magnus kept Emil's heart going until reinforcements arrived from Swine Lake with a defibrillator. Emil was then packed into an ambulance for the long drive down to Reykjavík's National Hospital.

Baldur arrested Magnus. And Tóta. Magnus understood, and went quietly. By the time he had got to Stykkishólmur police station, Emil had called Baldur from the ambulance to explain that Sylvía, not Magnus, had murdered Hallgrímur. Magnus himself insisted that one of Edda's people check his hands for gunshot residue; he didn't want a lawyer putting the idea in Tóta's mind that it was Magnus, not she, who had shot their uncle. They found nothing, of course. Then Adam took a full statement. After a call to the Police Commissioner, Baldur had removed himself from the investigation into Hallgrímur's murder, although he stayed in charge of the investigations into Villi and Ingvar's deaths, and Aníta's shooting.

Inspector Thorsteinn from Keflavík was on his way up to Stykkishólmur to take over from Emil.

After Magnus had kicked his heels in the cell for a couple of hours, Adam returned to let him out.

'You can go now, Magnús. But please remain in this area. We'll need to talk to you some more.'

'Of course,' said Magnus. 'How's Emil?'

'He's conscious and proclaiming your innocence,' said Adam. 'He's at the National Hospital. Apparently Aníta is much better as well.'

'Excellent,' said Magnus. He followed Adam along the corridor. He wondered what the hell he should do. He was wearing the sweatshirt and jeans he had put on that morning at Litla-Hraun; the clothes and his coat he had been wearing when he was arrested had been taken away for examination. His wallet and his phone were still at the prison. As for his car, he had no idea where that was now, except he was sure that forensic officers would have crawled all over it.

Presumably the police had let Ollie go and he was somewhere in Stykkishólmur. His brother had some serious questions to answer, but Magnus couldn't face confronting him right then.

Perhaps he should call Sibba. Even though she was no longer his lawyer, she would be willing to help. Poor Sibba.

At least it looked as if her father hadn't actually murdered anyone himself after all.

Magnus contemplated the destruction of Hallgrímur's family. His wife and granddaughter held on suspicion of murder. Three of his four children dead. Plus his son-in-law, Magnus's father. His grandson, Ollie, messed up.

And all of it Hallgrímur's fault. It was extraordinary how much damage one man could cause.

Who was left to clear up the mess? Kolbeinn would find it hard to cope. Aníta, perhaps, when she recovered. Gabrielle? Sibba? And him.

'Hey, Magnús! You look lost without a cell to go to.'

Magnus turned to see Vigdís grinning at him. They both hesitated and then she gave him a hug.

They broke apart. 'You never thought I killed anyone, did you, Vigdís?'

'Of course not,' she said. 'I knew beating up an old man wasn't your thing.'

'Thanks for all your help. I'm lucky to work with someone like you.'

'No problem.' Her voice was casual, but she was smiling. Then the smile went. 'There's, um... There's someone waiting for you. In the lobby.'

Magnus looked through the window of the door in the corridor and saw Ingileif sitting on a chair, staring into space, an unopened book on her lap.

'I've got to go,' Vigdís said. 'The paperwork from this mess is going to take a month.' She turned and strode rapidly down the corridor, away from the lobby.

'Vigdís!' Magnus called after her, but she ignored him.

Magnus pushed through the doors. Ingileif stood up to face him. She was wearing a big red waterproof coat. Her eyes were tired and puffy, and her blonde hair was a greasy mess. Despite that, she looked gorgeous, at least to Magnus.

'You look terrible,' she said.

'Thanks,' said Magnus, grinning.

'Sorry,' said Ingileif.

'For what?'

'You know.' She walked up to him and kissed him softly on the cheek. 'I was stupid. Selfish. But I'm not any more. Can I give you a lift?'

'Sure,' said Magnus. 'But I'm not sure where to.'

'I've booked us two rooms at the Hótel Búdir,' Ingileif said. 'Yours has a view of the Snaefellsjökull. You know Halldór Laxness used to go there to write?'

'As did Benedikt Jóhannesson,' said Magnus.

'Do you want to come?' asked Ingileif. Her grey eyes were unsure. Magnus realized she was nervous.

'Of course,' said Magnus. He smiled. 'But I don't understand why we need two rooms?'

Ingileif's eyes lit up and she reached up to kissed him again, hard this time, on the mouth.

'Hey! There are the northern lights!' Ingileif jumped out of bed and skipped across the room to the window. 'It's beautiful.'

'Yes, it is.'

Their room faced west, towards the glacier. The night sky was clear and moonlight slipped over Ingileif's naked body. Behind her, through the window, Magnus could see a shimmering green curtain hovering above the pale white of the snow-capped volcano, the mountain's lower slopes a deeper black against the dark night sky.

She turned to him. 'Why are you smiling?'

'Why not?' said Magnus. It had been a wonderful evening. Magnus had never been to the Hótel Búdir before; it was too close to Bjarnarhöfn for his father to include it on one of their trips to Iceland. It was in a magnificent location. To the north rose a dramatic wall of mountains and waterfalls that divided the peninsula; to the east stretched a long curved beach; to the south was the sea; and to the west a lava field within which stood a small, isolated wooden church and, beyond that, the glacier. On a clear evening, with the sun slanting low, throwing a soft light on the yellow grass and green and brown moss, it was one of the most beautiful places Magnus had ever seen.

They had gone for a short walk down to the sea through the ruins of an abandoned fishing village, and then had dinner. Although it had only been a week since they had seen each other, it felt much longer. She was different. He was different. *They* were different.

They had made love, a joyful reunion of lust and tenderness.

'Hey, I have a question for you,' said Ingileif, skipping back to bed next to him.

'Yes?'

'Do you fancy coming to Hamburg? I'd like to show you the gallery. And the city.'

'Yeah, OK,' said Magnus. 'What about Kerem? Do I get to meet him too?'

'Hmm. I think I'm going to have to have a conversation with Kerem. He won't like it. So no, I don't think you will get to meet him.'

Magnus pulled her towards him and kissed her. 'I would love to see you in Hamburg.'

She ran her fingers over his chest. 'How are you?' she said.

Magnus felt like asking her 'how am I about what?' but he

knew what she meant. 'I'm glad I finally know what happened to him. To Dad. Who killed him. I've wanted to know for so long.'

'It's good you came here,' Ingileif said. 'The answer was in Iceland all the time.'

'Yes. Although in reality it wasn't Ingvar who killed Dad. It was my grandfather. Ingvar was just his instrument. As was Villi.'

'And now he's been avenged,' Ingileif said. 'Does that feel good?'

'No,' said Magnus. 'You would have thought it would, but it doesn't. It's a tragedy that my father is dead, that he died so young. It turns out that the fact that I know who was behind it, and that that person is dead, doesn't change that tragedy.'

'Hmm.' They lay in silence for a minute, thinking. 'What about your police work?'

'What do you mean?' Magnus asked.

'Ever since I've known you, I've got the feeling that it was the desire to solve your father's murder that drove you on to solve all those others. Now you've done it, will you keep going?'

'I don't know,' said Magnus. Ingileif was right: his father's murder had driven him to become a homicide detective and had given him the determination to wade through the messy tragedies of one investigation after another.

'I think I will. Dad's murder has shaped my life. It changed me. I can't go back now, even if I do know who killed him. And I understand all those other people whose lives have been ruined by murder. I'll still want to help them.'

'One last question?' said Ingileif with small smile.

'Yes?'

'What do you think about having sex three times in one night?'

'I'm all in favour,' said Magnus.

Ingileif giggled, pulled herself up on to her knees and kissed him.

*

Thursday, 22 April 2010
The First Day of Summer

Magnus and Ingileif had an early breakfast at the hotel, and then Ingileif drove them back to Stykkishólmur, the early morning sun glowing yellow and pink off the white cap of the Snaefellsjökull.

When they reached Stykkishólmur, Ingileif let Magnus out at the petrol station on the main road and waited for him in the car. A small group of people huddled in their coats, bags at their feet. One of them stood apart from the others, smoking a cigarette.

'Hi, Ollie,' Magnus said.

Ollie glanced at his brother and then turned away, staring out towards the snow-capped mountains to the south. 'Hi.'

'Couldn't let you go without saying goodbye,' said Magnus. 'Sorry you have to take the bus. I'd give you a lift all the way to the airport, but the police want me to stick around here.'

'I know what that feels like,' said Ollie.

'Is your flight confirmed for this afternoon?' Magnus asked.

'Who knows? They seem to be opening up the airspace over Europe, so they ought to let me back to the States. At least I've got my passport back.' He shivered. It was only a couple of degrees above freezing. 'What's all this crap about the first day of summer?'

'Icelandic joke,' said Magnus. It was exactly a year since he had arrived in Iceland, on the first day of summer 2009. A lot had happened in that time. 'They all get the day off. There will be a parade in Reykjavík.'

'I think I'll skip that,' said Ollie. He took a drag on his cigarette. 'Are they bringing charges against you?'

'Not for murder, no. But they might for interfering with a crime scene. I don't know. We'll see.'

'That won't be good for your career, will it?'

'It would be disastrous. But the Police Commissioner likes me. Or at least, he used to like me.'

'Lucky you,' said Ollie.

Even though Ollie had yet to face him, Magnus could sense the hostility glowing from his brother in the cold. Magnus felt the resentment build inside him. After all he had done for his brother, the risks he had taken, he deserved some thanks, surely.

'You screwed up the crime scene on purpose?' said Ollie, turning to him at last, as if reading Magnus's thoughts.

Magnus nodded.

'I guess you must have thought I really did kill Afi?'

Magnus nodded again.

'You know now I didn't kill him, right?'

'Right,' said Magnus. 'But I know you intended to.'

Ollie shrugged. 'He was an old bastard, you know. He destroyed our family.'

'He did,' said Magnus.

A bus pulled into the petrol station and opened its doors. The driver jumped out, opened up the luggage doors beneath the seats, and began to stow bags as the small group formed a line to get on.

'Ollie?' Magnus asked.

'Yes?'

'You knew about Dad's murder, didn't you? That Ingvar killed him?'

'Actually, I thought it was Villi. I didn't know it was Ingvar.'

'Why didn't you tell me?'

'I was scared,' Ollie said. 'I was always scared of Afi, you know that. I've spent my whole life being scared of him.'

'I would have protected you.'

'I did tell Dad, you know. About that writer Benedikt's murder, Joe's father. When I was a little kid at Bjarnarhöfn I overheard Afi and Uncle Villi talking about it. It must have been the night after it happened. I didn't really understand what they were saying, but they caught me and told me never to breathe a word. I didn't tell anyone for eleven years, and when I did tell Dad, they killed him.'

Magnus knew his brother: he was lying. Or at least he was not telling the whole truth.

'*They* killed him. You didn't?'

'Of course not,' said Ollie. 'I was at the beach with a girl the whole afternoon. A bunch of people saw us. You *know* that.'

That was true. 'But you helped them, didn't you? You helped Afi and Villi and Ingvar?' Those three were all dead now. There was no one to tell what Ollie's role in their father's death really was, apart from Ollie himself.

'Can't you just drop this, man? Haven't you caused enough trouble? Let it go, Magnus, let it go.'

'It was our father, Ollie. How can I let it go?'

Ollie threw his cigarette on to the ground. Anger flared in his eyes. 'Look, Magnus. That bald-headed police guy, he's even called Baldy or something – do you know what he's done?'

'No,' said Magnus.

'He's been in touch with the police in the States. They are going to reopen Dad's murder. They are going to interview me. And according to Baldy, they are going to arrest me and put me in jail.'

'Baldur can't know that,' said Magnus.

'Is he wrong?' said Ollie, his eyes alight with anger and fear. 'Tell me that, cop brother. Is he wrong?'

Magnus didn't answer. It seemed highly likely to him that Ollie was implicated in their father's murder in some way. And he was certainly implicated in the cover-up. While it was true that many of the key suspects were now dead, Ollie could easily end up in jail.

'And when they ask you to testify, what will you say, big brother? You'll tell them everything you can to screw me, won't you?'

'No,' said Magnus. 'I'll tell them the truth.'

'Precisely,' said Ollie. He spat the word out, lacing it with bitterness. 'That's something you never quite understood, did you, Magnus? The truth isn't always good. Sometimes the truth can be bad. Real bad.'

'They won't lock you up, Ollie,' Magnus said. 'I'll find a way to stop them.' But even as he said it, he didn't believe it. Ollie

322

was right. In this case, maybe the truth was bad. It was, after all, what Magnus had always been scared of, what Ollie had done his best to hide from.

The last of the crowd was almost on the bus. Ollie looked away, back towards the mountains in the distance, biting back the frustration. 'I told you to leave this alone all along, but you didn't listen. Joe, you, Afi, Uncle Villi – you all talk about revenge like it's something honourable. Well, believe me, Magnus, if I go to jail for this, you'll know about revenge. And it won't be honourable. I will bring you down with me.'

Magnus saw the hatred in Ollie's eyes. Many times over the years he had seen fear, insecurity, deceit and greed in his brother, but never such pure hatred. It unnerved him.

Ollie turned and climbed onto the bus. The driver shut the doors and the bus pulled away on the long journey back to Reykjavík.

Magnus watched it go. He had hoped that in solving his father's murder he had put the past back in its box.

But now he knew. His father's murder would remain with him. Always.

AUTHOR'S NOTE

Bjarnarhöfn is a real farm on the north coast of Snaefellsnes. Although the Viking inhabitants of the area mentioned in the book – Björn the Easterner, Vermundur the Lean, Styr and the two berserkers – really existed, Hallgrímur's family is entirely fictional. The farm is well worth a visit: it has a fascinating little shark museum, and of course the Berserkjahraun lava field surrounding it.

I am grateful for the help of Deputy Sheriff Dadi Jóhannesson and Chief Superintendent Ólafur Gudmundsson of Stykkishólmur. Also to the governor and the staff of Litla-Hraun prison for allowing me to visit. Audur Möller gave me much useful information about sheep farming in Iceland, and Alda Sigmundsdóttir read over the manuscript for me. Alda's Iceland Weather Report Facebook page is an invaluable and entertaining source of information on all things Icelandic.

Thanks also to Superintendent Karl Steinar Valsson in Reykjavík, my agent Oli Munson at A. M. Heath, and to my editor Sara O'Keeffe and her colleagues at Corvus.

Barbara, Julia, Laura and Nick have been as supportive as always, and shown great patience with my Icelandic enthusiasms. They even joined me on a trip there to research this book. It rained.